# DUSKFALL

Also by Christopher Husberg and coming soon from Titan Books

*Dark Immolation* (June 2017)

# DUSKFALL

## THE CHAOS QUEEN QUINTET

# CHRISTOPHER HUSBERG

**TITAN** BOOKS

Duskfall
Print edition ISBN: 9781783299157
E-book edition ISBN: 9781783299164

Published by Titan Books
A division of Titan Publishing Group Ltd
144 Southwark Street, London SE1 0UP

First edition: June 2016
10 9 8 7 6 5 4 3 2 1

A CIP catalogue record for this title is available from the British Library.

Printed and bound by CPI Group (UK) Ltd, Croydon, CR0 4YY.

FOR RACHEL

## *170th year of the People's Age, The Gulf of Nahl*

BAHC STOOD AT THE bow of his fishing boat, clutching a small oil lamp. Its light pressed against the night, illuminating the large white snowflakes around him. In the distance the flakes were dimmer, floating through black sky and into blacker ocean, disappearing into calm, cold swells.

Bahc breathed in, licking salt from his lips. He loved the taste of the sea after a storm. He removed a glove and patted the rail of *The Swordsmith's Daughter*, feeling the cold grain of the wood. Bahc had designed and built the boat himself, with the help of the other tiellans in Pranna, years ago. When times were different.

Behind him, the deck creaked.

"Just like that, eh?" Gord said.

Bahc looked over his shoulder. Gord also carried a lantern, and his huge frame—massive for a tiellan—cast a long shadow behind him. He wore coarse wool and rugged furs, and his long, thick beard was frosty with ice.

Bahc lifted his wide-brimmed hat up to get a better look at the water. "Aye," he said. "Just like that."

"Least it's in our wake, now."

"We're lost, Gord. We're not in the clear, yet."

Gord leaned against the boat's railing. His breath formed clouds of mist against the cold. "Figured. Now it's just us waitin' for the stars to show themselves again, eh?"

"Aye. We drift, for now, and hope we don't end up somewhere we aren't supposed to be."

Bahc turned. He was about to go below decks to tell the rest of the crew, when something made him stop and turn back. He looked out at the blackness. Dark water, dark sky.

But not all dark.

In the distance, a bright blue light flickered on the water. Bahc's gut clenched.

"Put out your lamp, Gord," he murmured. He was already snuffing out his own.

"D'you think they saw us?" Gord asked, barely above a whisper.

"I don't know," Bahc said, grinding his teeth. "There's some distance between us. Our lights aren't bright. But the night is clearing up."

"The wind's at their backs," Gord said.

It was true. If the vessel emitting the eerie blue light visible off the starboard bow had seen them and wanted to pursue, the wind would bring it straight to *The Swordsmith's Daughter*.

"Then we'd best put it at ours," Bahc said.

"On our way, then?" Gord was already moving to the mainmast.

"Aye. Straight away from them." Bahc walked towards the cabin. "I'll wake the others. We'll need every hand."

"Cap'n," Gord said. Bahc looked over his shoulder. His crew didn't use formalities much on his boat, on his own insistence. But when waters got rough, there was comfort in a chain of command.

"D'you hear that?" Gord's head was cocked to the side.

Bahc heard nothing at first. But then there it was, soft as

the falling snow. A small, rhythmic thud, in time with the water lapping against the boat.

He frowned, walked back to the bow and looked over the side. Something gently brushed against the hull. Bahc squinted in the dark.

It was a body.

Bahc cursed. "Prepare the winch. Try to bring him aboard. I'll get the others."

"You sure?" Gord asked. "Nobody can survive for more'n a few minutes in these waters. He don't look too fresh."

"Get him aboard," Bahc said. "That's an order."

The body fell to the deck with a dull thump. Bahc stared at it, conscious of his crew doing the same. The paleness of the skin, practically blue in the darkness, meant the cold had probably already done its work. But, given the two long, thick arrow shafts jutting from the body, the cold seemed the least of this man's worries.

Bahc saw that his daughter, Winter, was also staring at the corpse. He wished he hadn't brought her. Twenty summers or not, he didn't want her to see the lifeless form.

Not lifeless, Bahc realized. The body—the man—was shivering.

"Shit," Gord muttered. "Is he…"

The man coughed violently, and vomited a stream of water onto the deck.

"Gord, take the helm," Bahc said. "Get us out of here." He turned to the body. *The man*. "Lian, help me get him below into the galley."

"Papa, what are you doing?"

Bahc closed his eyes. Winter. She was involved now, there

was no helping it. Bahc thought once again of the flickering blue light in the distance. He could dump the body and leave; this man was as good as dead, anyway.

Instead he opened his eyes, and reached down for the man's legs. Lian, the youngest crew member, was already lifting the man's arms.

His daughter had seen enough death. Today, at least, she would not see another.

"We're going to save his life," Bahc said.

After a few hours, the man's color began to return. That was good. This wasn't the most extreme case of cold Bahc had seen, but the arrow wounds were serious. Bahc, with Lian's help, had removed the shafts and cleansed the wounds with fire; the acrid smell of burning flesh still lingered. They had warmed the man, removing their own clothing and huddling with him on the floor underneath a half-dozen thick wool blankets, near the furnace in the corner of the galley. Lian had objected at first—said he didn't want to go skin to skin with a human—but it was the only way Bahc knew to warm someone this far gone. Decades of fishing in the Gulf of Nahl had taught Bahc the effects of such cold. Massaging limbs and hot water never worked. You had to warm their blood at the source. Had to warm their heart. Even after all that, Bahc wasn't sure this man would make it.

Or themselves, for that matter. Bahc couldn't stop thinking of what might be chasing them. The blue light in the distance. His crew had gotten them moving quickly, and Gord had checked in twice now to report. There was no sign of pursuit.

But still, Bahc worried. Mostly about Winter.

Bahc put his hand to the man's chest. The man's skin felt warmer than before. He touched his fingers. They were cool, but no longer ice-cold. Bahc pushed off the blankets and stood up.

"Get dressed," he told Lian, reaching for his trousers. "We still have work to do."

Lian nodded. Once they were dressed they lifted the man from the makeshift bed and placed him on the table that stood in the center of the galley.

Behind Bahc, the door opened.

"Think we're clear, Cap'n," Gord said.

Bahc relaxed. "You have a bearing?"

"Aye. We glimpsed the stars just for a moment, but Winter got a good look. Should be moving due south now, and dawn'll confirm that."

Bahc nodded, and looked back down at the man. His skin had gone from almost blue to pale white, which made it easier to see the cuts, bruises, and old scars that covered his body.

Gord remained at the doorway, staring at the man on the table.

"How's he doin', eh?"

"As well as he can be. His color is returning, but that doesn't mean much, given his other injuries." Bahc frowned. Gord still stood halfway in the doorway. "Get out and close the door, Gord. You're letting the cold in."

Bahc turned back to the table. Just as he was about to ask Lian to refill the bucket with more hot water, the man on the table twitched, and then the whole room was a whirlwind of movement.

It took a moment for him to realize what had happened. Bahc found he'd been spun round from the table to face the doorway again, and the jagged end of one of the broken arrow shafts was pressed into the skin of his neck, a strong arm immobilizing him. The man had moved so quickly. The metal pan that held the other shaft and arrowheads clattered to the floor.

No one moved. Bahc blinked. He could just see Lian's shocked face out of the corner of his eye. Gord, still in the doorway, took a slow step forward, hand creeping to the dagger at his belt.

The arrow shaft pressed forcefully against Bahc's throat.

"Don't m-move," the man rasped in a cracked whisper. Bahc felt the man's hot breath in his ear. "Who are you?"

"We're not going to hurt you," Bahc said, trying to keep calm.

The man trembled. "I d-don't... I don't remember..." he rasped.

The door slammed shut behind Gord. There was no one near the door, at least not inside the room. Bahc wondered whether Winter had found her way down, and prayed she had not. Whatever was going on, he didn't want her to have any part in it.

"What in Oblivion..." Gord grunted, looking at the door that had slammed behind him.

A bucket flew across the room, whizzing past Gord's head and crashing into the wall. Bahc would have thought someone had thrown it, but it had come from the corner of the room where neither he nor Lian nor the man were standing.

Bahc felt the man's grasp—and the pressure from the arrow shaft—slacken for the briefest moment. Then the room erupted into chaos.

Tin cups and wooden spoons streaked from wall to wall, propelled by nothing. The pliers Bahc had used to remove the arrow shafts flew upwards, embedding themselves nose-first in the ceiling. A box of fishhooks Bahc had set out earlier to clean shattered; Bahc shut his eyes as the hooks exploded in all directions. The table the man had been lying on shook violently, creaking against the bolts that held it to the floor.

Bahc looked around. Gord had dropped as soon as the bucket flew past. Lian lay on the floor on the other side of the table, not moving.

Bahc felt himself freed from the man's grasp. He turned slowly. The man wobbled, his hands at his sides. He still clutched the arrow tightly in one fist. Bahc took a step away as he saw the man's eyes roll back. Only the whites showed, shining in the lamplight. His face contorted in pain and confusion. Then he fell, his strangled shriek ringing in Bahc's ears, and all movement stopped. Objects flying through midair dropped to the floor.

Bahc stood, breathing heavily. What he had just seen was impossible. Or at least it should be. But he had seen it once before. The day his daughter was born.

The night his wife died.

Gord rose to his feet slowly, muttering something about ghosts. Lian moaned softly. The stranger lay crumpled, chin resting on his chest, eyes closed. Peaceful, as if he'd fallen asleep.

"We tell no one," Bahc whispered, looking around at the mess: utensils everywhere, hooks embedded in walls, containers overturned. "*No one.*"

Gord nodded, slowly. "What about Lian?"

"I'll talk to him." They couldn't let this get out. It was too dangerous. No one—human or tiellan—would understand.

"What're we going to do?" Gord asked, looking around the room nervously.

"Bind the man," Bahc said, retrieving a few long scraps of leather that had been scattered on the floor in the chaos, and handing them to Gord. "And then…"

He trailed off as the stranger groaned.

Bahc sighed. He had made up his mind. "Then," he said, "we take him back to Pranna."

# PART I

SHADOWS

# 1

*One year later, Pranna, northern Khale*

AFTER SHE HAD BATHED and dressed, Winter slipped quietly out of the house into the bleak morning light. She wasn't sure if her father was up yet, but Cantic tradition dictated that the bride should not have any contact with the men in her family, or the groom, until the ceremony.

"The bride," Winter whispered to herself. Sometimes she just had to hear herself say a thing to believe it.

She tried again. "I'm getting married." She had thought the idea might finally sink in on the day it happened, but apparently not. Marriage still seemed as foreign to her as air to a fish.

Winter looked back at her family's small cottage, wondering if she shouldn't find her father, anyway. They didn't put much stock in religion, not anymore. But seeing him would be awkward, and provoke a conversation that she wasn't sure she could face quite yet. She didn't know how to tell him what was in her heart. She wasn't sure she understood it herself.

Deep, slow breaths were the key. They always were.

She shivered in the crisp air and kept walking. It was cold, but not as cold as Pranna could be in the middle of the long winter. The sun hid behind a wall of gray clouds; the threat of snow loomed on the horizon.

Cantic tradition also stated that, the morning of the wedding, the bride was to have a Doting—to be given gifts by those closest to her. Since most tiellans had already left Pranna, that left precious few. One old king's abdication and act of emancipation one hundred and seventy-one years ago had still not erased a millennium of slavery. Old prejudices ran deep. Tiellans were shorter than humans, with slender, pointed ears, larger eyes, and rarely grew hair on their bodies, except for the tops of their heads. Of course, after centuries of interbreeding there were exceptions, Gord being one of them with his unusually tall build and full beard.

Winter still did not understand how such minor differences caused such great conflict. But the results were clear enough: Gord and his brother Dent, Lian and his family, and Darrin and Eranda and their children were the only tiellans who remained in Pranna besides Winter and her father. The fact that so many had left weighed on Winter's heart; tiellans were always reluctant to leave their homes.

"Not always," Winter whispered to herself, glancing at the sea in the distance.

Her Doting was supposed to be at Darrin and Eranda's home, but Winter stopped at the small intersection in the road ahead. To her right, not far down the dirt road, was Darrin and Eranda's hut and the few friends she had in the world. To her left, the Big Hill ran down to the Gulf of Nahl. She saw the dock, and her father's boat, far below. One path offered duty and those who loved her; the other offered freedom and the beautiful terror of uncertainty.

Winter paused, even though she already knew her choice. She allowed herself to imagine, briefly, leaving everything behind. She had never felt at home in Pranna. She didn't know why. Even with her friends, sometimes even with her father, she never felt whole. A piece of her had always been missing, and she had never known what it was, or how to get it back.

She imagined herself at the helm of her own ship. A small crew to call her own. Perhaps a lover. Perhaps not.

And she imagined that life crashing down all around her. There wasn't much room in the Sfaera for the tiellan race anymore, and even less room for a tiellan woman.

*What makes you think you'd fit in any better on a ship, away from Pranna, than you do here?* Winter shook her head. It was a useless daydream.

With a sigh that she could see in the cold air, Winter pulled her cloak more tightly around her and took the right-hand fork.

"Ready to give your life away to a human?" Lian asked her, when they finally found a moment alone during the Doting. Lian spoke with a leisurely, lilting drawl, like most tiellans. Winter did not, because of her father. "The language of captivity," he called it.

Lian's parents and Darrin and Eranda were momentarily distracted with talk of more tiellan persecution in the nearby city of Cineste when Lian had sat beside her, near the fire. Winter had been listening to the others talk. She loved these people, but did not know how to show it. More often than not, she found herself simply observing, as she did now. Even at her own Doting.

Turning to Lian, Winter couldn't tell if he was being sarcastic or genuine. Probably both; he was smiling, but the expression didn't reach his eyes.

"Knot is a good man," Winter said, though the words felt worn from frequent use. "Humans aren't all bad, you know."

"Right. It's just that you're marrying one, is all."

"I don't trust humans, but that doesn't mean I hate them. You're much better at that than I am."

Lian's eyebrows rose. "But this one you trust?"

Winter didn't say anything. Trust had always been a rare commodity for her. She suspected it was the same for every tiellan. Humans cheated you, betrayed you, and would take everything you owned if you let them. Some tiellans would do the same. If she was honest, Winter only trusted a few people: herself, and her father, certainly. Gord, Darrin and Eranda, and Lian, too. Knot… Knot was not yet close enough to count.

They sat in silence for a moment. The others' chatter seemed distant in the background.

Winter knew what was coming. "Please don't ask me again," she pleaded. She wasn't sure she could take it. Not today.

"Still haven't given me a straight answer," Lian said. "I'll keep askin' 'til you do."

"The advantages are clear. Any tiellan who marries a human is better off, no matter who that human is."

"Even if that particular human has no idea who he is or where he came from?"

Winter frowned. She hated this conversation for a reason. Part of her agreed with Lian; what she was doing was difficult to justify. And yet, if Knot could take her away from Pranna, Winter might have a chance to really *live*—not just waste away in a dying town. Even if Knot wasn't the man she imagined, she could cope if it meant getting away. She was a tiellan, after all. She could endure, if she had to.

And, perhaps, if she left, she might find somewhere she belonged.

"D'you remember that time you nearly drowned?" Lian must have grown weary of her silence. "That summer, when we were young."

Winter blinked at the question, but couldn't stop her lips

twitching into a grin, however slight. "Which one?" she asked.

Lian smirked. "I suppose nearly drowning was pretty common for us back then." He looked into her eyes. "You know the time I mean."

Winter did know. She had only been eight or nine, playing on the dock with an earring of her mother's, taken from her father's room without his knowledge. The earring had slipped through Winter's fingers, between the boards of the dock, and into the water below.

Winter remembered not thinking about what she did next. She just did it. She jumped into the water and started searching for the earring. She remembered diving in, coming up for air, diving down again. There hadn't been much daylight left, the water was murky, and Winter had hardly been able to see anything. Each time she went down her hands dug into the mud at the bottom, but came up with nothing. She didn't know how long she surfaced and dived again, but she remembered the panicked constriction in her chest, and the tears mixing with seawater on her face.

The sun set, the water grew colder, but still she continued, even when her muscles began to cramp. Looking back, Winter couldn't say what had come over her. In that moment, all she knew was the *need* to find the earring. There had been nothing else.

Lian finally found her, shivering and spluttering, about to dive once more. To this day, Lian swore it would have been her last dive. He jumped in just as she went down. He took hold of her, and pulled her to the surface.

Clutched in her hand had been her mother's earring.

She looked at Lian. "Are you angling for another thank you?"

He laughed. "No. Just wanted you to remember. Sometimes you think you need a thing, you fixate on it, and you don't know when to give up. But that's the best thing you can do, sometimes—let a thing go. Just wish you knew when to do it."

"Me too," Winter whispered.

Then suddenly Lian reached out, brushing a strand of hair from her face.

Her hand snapped up, gripping his.

"Don't." Winter lowered their hands, his in hers, gently. Friendly affection was one thing, but this was her Doting, for Canta's sake. And the touch reminded her of a time she wasn't interested in revisiting.

"Sorry," he mumbled, and seemed to mean it.

"So am I," she said, but knew she didn't.

The Doting went as well as Winter could have expected. The small cottage smelled of fresh bread and cinnamon, smells that reminded her of her mother. Silly, that anything should remind her of a woman she had never known, but it was true all the same.

The gifts Winter received were plain, but meaningful. A traditional tiellan *siara* of beautiful white wool, a small woodcarving of a man and woman standing close together, a black-stone necklace to bring out her dark eyes, and a swaddling cloth that made her cringe at the thought of having a child.

Then, too soon, a knock came at the door. Three Cantic disciples in red and white robes stood outside. The women—humans, all three—made Winter nervous. Humans always did, though she tried to hide it. Winter looked down at her dress, coarse brown wool that covered her from to wrists to ankles, and the grey *siara* she wore, a long loop of fabric wrapped in folds around her neck and shoulders. A stark contrast to the sleeker, form-fitting dresses and exposed necklines of the human women before her.

Winter felt a stab of disappointment that there were only three. Cantic tradition called for nine disciples of the Denomination to escort new brides to their Washing; nine to represent the original disciples of Canta. Winter wasn't sure if there were only three because the town population had decreased so dramatically, or because she was tiellan and the disciples didn't think she merited a full escort. Her disappointment surprised Winter. It was a detail she had never thought would mean much to her.

She felt a sudden surge of panic, a great weight locked away within her chest threatening to break free. This wasn't what she wanted.

Then the feeling passed. She would do what was required.

Winter said her goodbyes to her friends, the last time she would see them as Danica Winter Cordier, daughter of Bahc the fisherman. Whether she wanted it or not, change was coming.

"Can it be? My little girl is really getting married?"

Winter smiled as her father walked into the Maiden's Room. Fathers were the only males allowed in the area, and only right before the ceremony. Winter was alone; the three disciples had left to prepare the chapel.

Despite her misgivings, Winter adored how handsome her father looked. He wore his only formal suit: loose, faded gray trousers and dark-blue overcoat in the old fashion. So different than his normal furs and wool—his fisherman's clothing.

"Hi, Papa."

She felt his arms around her, his tanned, smooth cheek against hers.

They separated, and she let him look at her. Her raven-dark hair was tied with a bow behind her head, and the disciples

23

had seen fit to place the black-stone necklace she had received around her neck, matching the deep blackness of her eyes.

Winter had changed into a red dress, the only article of clothing her father had kept of her mother's. It was simple dyed wool, but the fabric was fine and cascaded over Winter's thin frame elegantly. The sleeves reached her wrists and the fabric covered her neck, but this dress actually fit her, hugging her hips and chest tightly. It was technically within tiellan standards, but at the same time whispered subversion. Winter imagined her mother wearing it years ago, and the outrage it must have caused the tiellan elders and matriarchs. The thought made her smile.

She waited for her father to speak, wondering if he would. Her father was never much for words.

"Your eyes are your mother's," he finally managed. "Dark as the sea at midnight."

She smiled, trying to keep the sadness from her face. "So you've told me, once or twice before."

"She would be proud of you, Winter."

*Would she?* From what her father had told her, her mother had always been an independent woman. Winter wasn't sure her mother would approve of her daughter giving up so easily.

"I hope so."

Her father sighed, and waved a hand. "Bah. Enough, Winter. I know you're not happy about this. I know this isn't what you wanted."

Winter stared at her father. "You do?"

"Of course I know. You think I can't tell when my daughter is trying to suffer in silence? You are just like your mother, that way. I know you have concerns. But Knot *is* a good man. He's not the type of human that would… he's a good man, Winter. He'll take care of you. He'll give you a life that I never could."

What he said was true. Even someone like Knot, with so little, could give her so much. If they moved to the city, somewhere they could make a fresh start…

"What if I don't want that life? What if the life I want is exactly the one you *can* give me? Or Lian? What if I want to make my *own* life, Father?"

"Goddess rising, you are so like her it's amazing," her father said.

Winter sat down. Even as she said the words, she knew it wasn't possible. There was no making her own life. Knot was her only chance. She needed him.

"Here's the thing," her father said, taking her hands in his. "You're marrying this man. There's no stopping that. But you haven't signed your life away. It is what you make of it. Knot may surprise us all and turn out a tyrant; if that's the case, you have my permission to murder him in the night and escape to make a life of your own."

Winter smiled, although the joke was uncomfortably close to a few situations she had heard of in the city.

"But I don't think that will be the case," her father continued. "I think he'll want you to be happy, and I think he'll want to help you do whatever you need to find that happiness. Don't underestimate that bond, my dear. Marriage, done right, can be much more freeing than we give it credit for. I think the two of you need each other."

Winter was about to ask what her father meant by that when a knock sounded on the door. "Holy Canta calls her maidservant," a woman's voice said. "Will she answer?"

The priestess was ready.

Winter glanced at her reflection in the small looking glass opposite her. The girl who gazed back at her was confident, calm. That girl could almost be happy. Could almost believe what her father was telling her.

"Winter," Bahc said, "today is your day. Accept your own happiness."

Winter cleared her throat. "She will answer," she called, in response to the priestess's summons. She turned and walked towards the door, pausing to kiss her father on the cheek.

"I love you, Papa," she said. Then she opened the door, and walked into the chapel.

She did not flinch as the small dagger slit her palm.

"And do you, Danica Winter Cordier, covenant through blood and in the presence of Holy Canta that you will give yourself to Knot now and forever, through frost and fire, storm and calm, light and dark, dusk and dawn and throughout the turning of time?"

"I so covenant, by my blood," Winter said. The priestess, a rotund woman in her middle years, looked approvingly down at her from a large square pedestal. She took Winter's hand and placed it in Knot's. He had received a similar wound moments before.

Winter looked at Knot. He wasn't smiling, but Winter knew him well enough to know that he wouldn't. But he was content. His eyes were peaceful.

"By the power of the Nine, whom Canta chose," the priestess continued, "whose power flows in me, I bestow these blessings upon you."

The words buzzed in Winter's head, and she found it difficult to concentrate. She was new, now. For better or worse, her life would be forever different.

"That you will love one another," the priestess said.

Winter gazed out at the small chapel. Torches cast a flickering glow up into the rafters of the elongated gable roof, but left the wide wings of the building in shadow. Darrin and Eranda's daughter Sena stood close by her. She was the only tiellan girl close enough to Winter's age to serve as a handmaid, though still not much more than a child.

"That you will serve those around you."

Lian and Darrin sat on the front row of polished, smooth benches, as did Eranda. Gord and Dent sat a few rows back. Winter could not thank everyone enough for coming, but she felt another pang of disappointment that the other pews were empty. It was irrational, she knew. She wasn't even sure she wanted to go through with the ceremony, but she wanted more people there to watch? Yet, had the ceremony happened a few years ago, the chapel would have been packed with tiellans.

"That you will be protected from the Daemons of this world and beyond, and that your souls will never fade into Oblivion."

Then, as if summoned by Winter's thoughts, a group of men entered through the large set of doors at the back of the chapel.

These were not the type of wedding guests Winter had had in mind. It was hard to tell from this distance, but she could only assume that they were human; they all stood as tall or taller than Lian and Gord. Were they Kamites? She swallowed hard.

She counted six of them, each wearing a dark-green robe with a hood that hid his face in shadow. And they were armed. Swords and daggers, shields and spears.

Winter was vaguely aware of the priestess's grip loosening. "What is the meaning of this intrusion?" the woman demanded.

The men stood for a moment, torchlight flickering on their robed frames. They looked back and forth from the priestess to the congregation.

Winter began to fear they truly were Kamites, advocates of the reinstatement of tiellan slavery, and, barring that, the death of all tiellans. They were not a popular group, nor a very public one, but rumors said they had a presence in Pranna.

One of the men, taller than the rest, stepped forward. "We aren't exactly intruding," he said, with a clipped, harsh accent. He sounded Rodenese. Not a Kamite, then. The Kamite order had not spread beyond Khale's borders. Winter sighed, but not in relief. The Rodenese had other ways of dealing with tiellans.

The tall man removed his hood and walked towards the front of the chapel. He was ugly. His blond hair was thinning, his nose hooked and too large. A deep scar ran along one side of his face, from where one ear should have been to his cheek. "We should have been invited, after all," he said. He reached the front of the chapel where Winter, Knot, and the priestess stood. He put his hand on Knot's shoulder. "We're old friends of Lathe, here."

Winter looked at Knot, eyes wide. Was that his real name? Did these men know who Knot was?

Knot tightened his hold on Winter's hand.

Bahc stood. "Knot, son, if you know these men—"

"I don't," Knot said, his voice soft. He kept his eyes on the man with the hand on his shoulder. "Best thing you can do right now, my lord, is turn around and walk out."

The authority in Knot's voice surprised Winter. She had heard him speak like that on the boat, when relaying Bahc's orders, but otherwise he was calm, soft-spoken.

"Is that the best thing I can do right now... Knot?" The man's eyes narrowed. "Suppose you'd know, wouldn't you? Always seemed to know what was best for everyone else. Well, do you know what's best for all of your friends, here, *Knot*? Do you know what's best for your new bride? Give yourself up and no one gets hurt."

Winter looked around nervously. What were these men doing? What was *Knot* doing? She felt frozen, as if watching the moment from far away, engrossed but unable to do anything.

The priestess obviously felt differently. "How dare you storm into a Holy Cantic—"

There was a flash of movement, and for a moment Winter thought the tall man had shoved the priestess. The woman gasped and stepped backwards. Winter looked back at the tall man, one of his arms still on Knot's shoulder. In the other he clutched a dagger, dripping blood.

The priestess crashed to the floor.

"Damn shame," the tall man said, still staring at Knot.

"Oh, Goddess," Winter whispered.

The man looked at her, his face split by a scar and a grin. "Don't think She's here today. Maybe you should check back later." He looked back at his men. "Take them!"

Winter was lost in the sudden chaos that followed. Her father stared at her, pale-faced, shouting for Eranda and Sena to flee. Gord, face red, rose up from his pew. The disciples scurried this way and that, shouting for the Goddessguard.

Knot pulled Winter towards him, his hands strong and sure. Some of the torches must have gone out, and the room was darker, the flickering orange light eerie. The only thing that brought Winter back to focus was Knot's voice as he turned her towards him. His hands held her face, locking her gaze to his. She felt his blood on her cheek, still fresh from the priestess's dagger. There was a glint in his eye she had never seen before, cold and sharp, like a flash of lightning on the water in a dark winter storm.

"I won't let them hurt you," he said.

Winter shivered at the sound of his voice.

Behind Knot, Winter saw a shadow and a glint of steel—one of the robed men charging them with a sword. Before she had time to scream, Knot spun, grabbed the man by the wrist, and somehow used the robed man's momentum to spin full circle and slam him face first into the floor. Knot bent the man's arm back, and Winter heard a horrible snap. Her breath caught in her chest, and she stepped away. The whole thing hadn't taken more than a second. The torchlight flickered; half of Knot's face was drowned in shadow.

Perhaps the light had tricked Winter's vision. And yet, there was the robed man, groaning on the floor. Knot stared at his own hands.

"Knot," she said, "how…?"

He looked up, his eyes wide. He shook his head. "I don't know." His voice was barely a whisper. Then someone screamed and Knot turned away, towards the chaos.

The tall man held one of the disciples in front of Knot, a dagger at her throat. Behind him, another disciple lay on the floor, blood dripping from her mouth or her nose, Winter wasn't sure which. People were shouting, the disciples screaming.

Then Winter heard her father.

Bahc was lying on the floor, groaning and clutching his belly. He looked up at her, but Winter could not see his expression. The room was too dark, and shadows obscured his face. Blood seeped between his fingers. One of the dark-clad men stood above him.

Winter screamed and rushed towards Bahc, but someone grabbed her. A dirty hand covered her mouth and an arm locked around her neck. She felt her own breath trapped in the hand as she screamed, and a wetness against her cheeks. Whether it was Knot's blood or her own tears, she wasn't sure. She struggled vainly, but could barely move. The arm tightened around her neck, and her head felt like it was about to burst, both heavy and light at the same time. Looking around wildly, she saw Knot. Two of the robed men lay on the ground near him. She saw the cold gleam in his eye again. Knot lunged, his palm jutting up into the face of a robed man. The man's head snapped back, and then Knot was moving too quickly for Winter to keep track of him.

Years ago, Winter's father had caught a dragon-eel in a net of deepfish. She remembered him guiding her tentatively to the water-hold where the net had been released. Pointing down into the hold, he told her to watch a real predator in action. "Where is it?" she had asked. There were hundreds of flopping, floundering deepfish, their wide, flat bodies bouncing in the shallow water. Winter couldn't see any dragon-eel. As far as she knew, they weren't even real. Then, faster than she could follow, a slender, sinuous black shape had burst forth from the water, shredding deepfish with razor teeth. The eel was in one corner of the hold, and then the other, then in the middle, then leaping through the air, wreaking chaos among the struggling fish. "It isn't eating them," Winter had said. "Why isn't it eating them?" "Because a dragon-eel doesn't kill for survival," her father had said. "A dragon-eel kills for the pleasure of it." The water had already turned red with blood, and Winter had backed away slowly, never wanting to see a dragon-eel again.

Now, as the man's hold around her neck tightened and blackness threatened the corners of her vision, that image of the dragon-eel was all she could think of as Knot wrought havoc, a blur of brutality in a room of helpless, floundering deepfish.

# 2

KNOT WAS AFRAID.

The fear itself didn't trouble him. No, the dark pull from his throat to his gut was a familiar feeling. What troubled him was that he wasn't afraid of the men who had just attacked his wedding; he was afraid of how easy it'd been to kill them.

The frozen wind from the gulf whipped through Knot's cloak as he made his way to Darrin and Eranda's home. Winter was unconscious in his arms, a curious warmth against the chilly air. Snow had begun to fall, white flakes settling and then disappearing on Winter's face. The snow was peaceful, and that was cruel.

Knot had left nine bodies at the chapel. The robed men were unknown to him, and he had no idea how he he'd dispatched them. Yet he *knew*, as soon as he realized the men were a threat, that he could defeat them. He'd known it in his bones, on some level far deeper than his mind. His body had done the work quickly and easily.

The priestess and two of her disciples were both dead, killed by the robed men. The other disciple had run away in the chaos. Knot had killed four of the intruders, while Lian, Gord, and Dent had taken down another; Dent had lost his life in the process. The tall, scarred man, the one who had first approached Knot, had escaped.

And there was Bahc.

Knot knew he should never have stayed in Pranna. But he'd stayed anyway, and now the guilt carved at him.

He'd stayed because Bahc was kind. And because Bahc's daughter was beautiful. He was ashamed to admit it, but there it was. He'd also stayed because he had nowhere else to go. His memories of whatever life he'd had before waking up in Bahc's house were incomprehensible. A jumble of impossible images, faces he couldn't name, blurry and dark.

But, most of all, he'd stayed because of the life he thought he could make here. These were simple folk, and Knot was drawn to that simplicity, living day by day on what he caught in the freezing gulf. He liked tiellan tradition, conservative and unobtrusive. Whether the rift between humans and tiellans had bothered him in the past, Knot didn't know. But it didn't matter now. He liked the pragmatic way they looked at things. Made the best they could out of the hand life had dealt them.

Which was why Knot hadn't told anyone about the things he *could* remember. And now, because he had stayed, because he had put himself before everyone else, there were nine bodies to account for.

The snow fell heavier, large flakes floating down in the darkness, covering the road and rooftops and fields. Pranna was hardly more than one main street that led north to the Big Hill and the dock, where a number of boats, including Bahc's, were moored in the small harbor. The tiellan quarter lay off to the east, away from both the main street and the dock, connected only by a small footpath. The tiellan homes were hardly more than shacks, with thin driftwood walls and roofs in constant need of repair, in contrast to the sturdier human homes and shops—some even with multiple levels—in the main part of town. The Cantic chapel, the largest building in town, loomed to the west. Knot would have to cross the main street on the way to Darrin's home on the east side.

As Knot neared the town's edge, he heard footsteps crunching towards him, saw a light in the distance. Knot hid instinctively, crouching behind the smithy, cradling Winter close. He let her weight rest on his legs for a moment as he rotated his right arm. His shoulder had never fully recovered from the arrow wound received a year ago. It ached often, and carrying Winter made it hurt all the more.

"You believe the disciple? Seemed a bit off her rocker to me," a man said. Knot could see the two men clearly now in the lamplight, dressed in light armor and carrying spears. Town Watch.

"She said the elf-lover and the other humans did all the killing, attacking the tiellans and the disciples and then going after each other. The elf-lover and one of the foreigners escaped, leaving everyone else to die."

Knot frowned. "Elf-lover" was a term he'd heard more often than he liked in the past year, always in reference to himself. They were blaming *him* for the massacre?

Silence for a moment. Then the second watchman spoke again. "Good riddance to the elves. Should all be gone by now, makes no difference to me if they're dead. What was done to the disciples, and a *priestess* of all people, now that's a real crime."

"Aye. Only reason I'm out here in the snow searching for the bastards. Sure as Oblivion wouldn't be out here for no damned elves."

"Hope we come across the elf-lover first. Been wanting to rough that one up since he arrived."

The other man grunted in agreement, and they walked

past Knot towards the town center. If the Town Watch had been alerted, then the Goddessguard surely had been as well. Knot also knew, though not how, that word would have been sent to Cineste and a brace of the City Watch would arrive within the week. Nine mysterious deaths, including those of three members of the clergy, was too big for Pranna to handle on its own. The Cantic Denomination might even send a Crucible to investigate.

Knot's original surprise at the Watch accusing him was already beginning to fade. The humans in this town had never liked him. Just as bad as the tiellans, it seemed, was a human who fell in with them.

"The other dead humans don't make much sense," the first watchman said. "Chief says they're from Maven Kol, says he's seen robes like that down there."

"Chief has never been down to Maven Kol," the other man scoffed. "He don't know what he's talking about."

"Try telling him that."

Knot twitched. The men were wrong. The robed attackers weren't from Maven Kol; their accents had been Rodenese. He knew Roden by name only; he had no recollection of being there. Nevertheless, something tugged at him, deep within his mind.

The conversation faded. Knot waited until their lamplight was gone, then lifted Winter. If they were blaming him for the deaths, all the better. His plan wouldn't change.

"Knot, you're all right!" Eranda ran towards him, looking down at Winter with fear in her eyes. Knot had trudged through fresh snow that was already nearly a hand deep to the small hut.

"Oh, Goddess," Eranda whispered. She looked up at Knot. "Is she...?"

"Unconscious. But she'll live."

Darrin, Eranda's husband, stepped forward. "Let me take her," he offered. "You've carried her all this way."

"No," Knot said, surprised at how much he wanted to continue holding her. "I... I've got her."

Lian walked in with Darrin and Eranda's youngest boy, Tohn, in his arms. Sena, eyes red, and the younger daughter, Lelanda, followed close behind. Lian glared at Knot, eyes dark.

Knot let out a slow breath. Lian must've come straight here after what happened to make sure Eranda and Sena were alright.

"Knot," Eranda said, her voice strained, "what in Oblivion happened? Lian refuses to speak about it, we don't know—"

"Please," Knot said. "I need to settle her down first. Make sure she's okay."

Darrin looked at Knot, then down at Winter. The man had never been particularly friendly to Knot, but he'd never been hostile, either. Knot had brought Winter here because he was gambling on the man's integrity.

"Very well then," Darrin drawled. He glanced at Eranda. "Let's get the children out of the bedroom. Give these two a moment." He looked back at Knot, his eyes hard. "Then Knot'll tell us what happened."

Knot eased Winter onto the bed, gently covering her with all the blankets he could find. She stirred, her body twitching once in the darkness. Knot froze. Her injuries were not severe; she would wake by morning, weak and groggy and with an aching head, but otherwise all right. He felt a momentary rush of fear at the thought that she might wake now, while he was still here. But she remained still.

Knot remembered telling her once, while they were out on a rare trip alone on her father's boat, how he had always felt a pull to leave Pranna. It was one of the few times he remembered genuinely catching her attention. She had always wanted to leave, too. Tiellan tradition, it seemed, had never sat quite right with Winter.

"Then why *don't* you?" she had asked, looking out at the gray sea. The sky had been cloudy, a light fog misting over the gulf.

"Because I'm afraid," he had told her. "This place keeps me sane. If I left... I fear what I'd become." He had laughed, then. "Which ain't sayin' I don't worry about what I could do if I stay."

She had looked at him strangely. He had come close to telling her, in that moment. Telling her about his nightmares, the faces he saw when he closed his eyes. He had come close, but not near close enough.

"Being around you, around Bahc, and everyone," Knot had said instead, "I feel like I can do this thing. Live a good life. Be a good man, maybe." It hadn't been a lie, exactly. He had felt that way. But he couldn't be around them *all* the time.

He could still remember the waves, cresting gently with small white ridges of foam. How Winter's black eyes seemed to take in the beauty of the world, bright and shining, despite their darkness.

"Being around you," he'd said, "somehow... I want to be better than I am."

In that moment, he remembered thinking that he could love this girl. But he knew she didn't feel that way about him. Then Bahc had approached him with an offer of marriage, and had made it seem so fine a deal for both of them... and Knot had said yes. Put himself first. He had chosen to marry her, despite knowing what she really wanted. He had chosen to marry her because he needed someone to fix him, and she had been the nearest tool at hand.

And now her father was dead. Because of him.

Knot shivered. The thin walls, made of driftwood, did not block out the wind. Kneeling, he rested his head on Winter's sleeping form. He stayed there, feeling her beneath him, and slowly the fear he felt tugging at his gut was replaced by hollowness as he thought of what he would do next.

He stood and touched her face with his fingertips. It was his duty to protect this woman, now. He owed her a debt. And the best way he could do that was to get as far away as possible.

"Bahc's dead," Knot said. "Dent, too." He regretted his bluntness, but time wasn't on his side. He ignored Eranda's gasp and continued. "The priestess and two of her disciples were killed as well. I left Gord unconscious."

"What about Winter?" Lian demanded.

"She'll be fine," Knot said, avoiding his eyes. Tohn was asleep in Lian's arms now, and Lelanda clung to his leg. Lian would make a good father one day. Knot felt another pang of guilt that Bahc had asked him—and he had chosen—to marry Winter. If he hadn't, she and Lian probably would have had a happy life together. And Bahc would not be dead.

*What's done is done*, he told himself.

"She's the reason I came to see you," he said. His gaze moved to Eranda, then to Darrin, and finally rested on Lian. "Take care of her. She won't wake 'til morning, but someone needs to be with her when she does. Someone needs to watch over her." Knot clenched his jaw. He was having trouble finding the words. "One of the robed men escaped. The one who killed the priestess. When I leave, he'll follow."

"You're leaving?" Eranda asked. Her stare was vacant.

"Tonight," Knot said. "I don't belong here. Never did. The

Watch've wanted an excuse to run me out of town since the day I showed up. They blame me for the massacre, and that stays on my shoulders. But I need you all to take care of Winter. You're all she has left, now."

"*You're* her husband." Lian's eyes flashed. The young tiellan hadn't been happy about the marriage, and, now that Knot was abandoning Winter, his distrust would only grow.

Knot didn't have time to make him understand the alternatives.

"She'll be safest here with you. Far as I'm concerned, the ceremony last night never happened." Anger glinted in Lian's eyes, but Knot could tell he agreed when he didn't say a word. It seemed Knot had gambled wisely.

"Will you do this for me?" Knot asked.

"We'll do what we can," Darrin said, "for her."

That was good enough. Knot turned to Lian. The tiellan glared at him a moment longer, but finally nodded.

"Where will you go?" Darrin asked.

"I don't know," Knot lied. No use giving them a reason to follow. "Cineste first, but after that… I don't know. Best you don't, either."

Before anyone could respond, the door rattled on its hinges. "Town Watch!" a voice shouted from outside. Dust shook from the frame.

Knot cursed. "Do as I say, don't argue," he whispered. In one swift movement, he lifted Eranda up from the floor and grabbed a cooking knife from the table, the blade scraping against her throat.

The door burst inwards and three watchmen shuffled in, wearing leather and chainmail, brandishing spears and clubs.

Knot looked at them defiantly, hoping his ruse would work.

One of the watchmen sniggered. "Come to finish the rest of 'em off, have you?" He had a wide, round face made even larger by his thick beard. "Can't say that's a service we wouldn't want, but you were involved with murdering a priestess."

Lian started to speak, but Knot shot him a glare and shoved the knife harder against Eranda's throat, drawing a thin line of blood. He didn't have to see Eranda's eyes to know they showed real fear.

"Move and I'll kill her," he growled at Lian.

The watchmen advanced, trying to surround Knot.

"Why don't you just come with us," the fat-faced man said. "Leave these elf-folk alone."

One of the other men sniggered. "Not like we really care what happens to 'em anyway. You kill her, fine by us, but then you'll have her husband *and* us to deal with. Not in your favor, friend."

Looking around wildly, Knot finally dropped the knife, shoving Eranda towards her husband. "Get me out of here," he mumbled, trying to sound beaten. "These elves stink."

The watchmen rushed in, grabbing his arms. He shot one last look at Lian, who nodded almost imperceptibly as the men dragged Knot away.

Knot waited until they were far enough from the hut to avoid suspicion falling on the tiellan family. It was still dark, dawn was an hour or so away, and snow floated down in large flakes.

He had at least two things in his favor. The first was the snow. If it kept up, it would cover his tracks out of town. The second was the fact that the watchmen hadn't bound him. They dragged him along, one man on each arm, the fat-faced man behind him with a spear point pressed against Knot's back. Their mistake.

Knot planted his feet, and the men stopped.

"What the—"

Knot crashed his heel sharply into the knee of the man who held his right arm. Bone snapped, and the man sank to the snow, screaming. Knot's body seemed to know what to do instinctively. The man to his left still gripped him tightly, so Knot turned and pulled him in front of his body in time to catch a spear-thrust from the fat-faced man behind. He fell limply to the snow. The fat-faced man stared dully at the comrade he'd just impaled.

The man with the shattered leg was still screaming. Knot kicked his face, and he went silent. Wouldn't do to have the entire watch closing in before he'd even left town.

Knot dodged another stab from the fat-faced man's spear. Fat Face must not have been used to the weapon; the swing threw him slightly off balance. Knot weaved in and smashed the palm of his hand into the man's nose, shattering it. Then Knot ducked around him, picking up a club one of the other watchmen had been carrying.

To the fat-faced man's credit, he came at Knot again without hesitation. Knot parried the spear-thrust with a movement of the club, then let his momentum take the club back to connect with the side of the man's fleshy face. The man fell, silent, red seeping from his head into the snow.

Knot picked up the spear. He would leave one man alive, the one he had kicked unconscious, just to corroborate his involvement and steer blame away from the tiellans. The spearhead slid in and out of the other two men's ribs easily. Knot hesitated. He felt a thrill move through him as he killed the two watchmen, the same thrill he had felt in the chapel as he killed the men from Roden. The thrill frightened him, but what frightened him even more was how he craved the feeling again. He wanted to kill this last man, consequences be damned. Knot stood trembling, vaguely aware of the dull ache in his shoulder.

Then he threw the spear into the blood-soaked snow and walked away. Before he had gone a few paces, he bent over and vomited.

# 3

WINTER STARED INTO THE FIRE. Despite the heat of the flames and the heavy wool blanket wrapped around her shoulders, the only thing she felt was cold. Eranda sat beside her, one arm hugging her tightly, but the gesture felt dead and frozen, like a tree limb in winter.

"I'm going to find him," Winter said. She wasn't sure if she had said it already, or had just been repeating it over and over in her mind. She was vaguely aware of Eranda and Darrin looking at each other before Darrin responded.

"Knot saved you last night, no doubting that. Might've saved us all. But he left for a reason, Winter. He's dangerous, or at least has dangerous men on his trail. We've known it all along, whether we said so or not."

"Don't," Winter said. She didn't want to hear it. She had made up her mind.

"Winter," Darrin tried again, "he isn't one of *us*. He's not—"

"I said *don't*," Winter repeated. "He's the only family I have left."

"You feel that way now," Eranda said. "But *we* are here for you. Your own kind. Knot was just a human. He didn't belong in our world."

Winter frowned, feeling some of the coldness fade. Eranda was right.

And Knot… she kept telling herself that he had his reasons for leaving, that he wouldn't have gone if he didn't have to. But a thought nagged at her. What if he hadn't left because he *had* to?

What if he had just left?

He was human, after all. Perhaps Winter never should have trusted him in the first place. She stared into the fire for a long time.

"You're right," she said, eventually. "I do still have friends here." She attempted a smile. "And I need you to help me do something."

"Winter—" Darrin began, but she cut him off before he could continue.

"Not to help me leave," she said. Darrin visibly relaxed. "I need to put my father to rest."

Wind swept Winter's hair across her face as she watched Lian and Darrin walk down the pier, carrying her father's body, wrapped in cloth. Eranda and her three children had arrived a moment before with a torch.

Winter had thought she would be able to help prepare her father's body, but even going near him had been difficult. Touching his face, feeling the coldness of it, had been too much. Winter was grateful the others had been willing to help.

*The Swordsmith's Daughter* rocked gently in the water against the pier behind her, freezing wood against freezing wood. But even in the middle of the long winter, the Gulf of Nahl itself never froze.

In one hand Winter carried the bow her father had given her at the beginning of her thirteenth summer. Fishing had been their profession, but hunting had been her passion. The days she spent in the wilderness with nothing but a bedroll beneath her and a bow at her side, away from humans and away from tiellans and away from everything, were some of the days Winter valued most.

She had sent Lian to ask Gord if he would attend the funeral, but his wounds were too serious. Winter hated to think of Gord, injured and alone. The guilt she felt for what had happened to him, and to all of them, was as constant as a river.

Lian and Darrin both nodded respectfully as they passed, and Winter motioned for them to put her father on a small sailboat that rocked against the dock next to *The Swordsmith's Daughter*. Her father had taught Winter to sail in that boat. Winter had thought briefly about sending him out on his fishing boat, but knew she couldn't. *The Swordsmith's Daughter* meant too much to the community.

Lian and Darrin stepped carefully onto the boat, placing her father's body near the helm. They turned, looking to her.

"Hoist sail." The wind seemed to carry Winter's voice far away.

"Aren't you coming aboard, Winter?" Darrin asked.

Winter shook her head. She hadn't told them her plan, and she wasn't sure if they would approve. At first they had assumed she wanted her father buried in Cantic tradition, beneath the ground near the chapel with a stone statuette of him, to protect him from Oblivion. They would certainly bury Dent there, if the humans allowed it. Winter, still sick whenever she thought of the wretched place, wouldn't go near it. Her mother had received no such treatment; nor, then, would her father. He would want it this way, like the ancient tiellans of the sea.

"Lash the tiller, then disembark," Winter said, nearly having to shout over the wind. While the others had prepared Bahc's body she had soaked the boat with oil.

Darrin obeyed, but Lian stood looking at her. "This is what you want?"

"Do it." She was trying to take charge. "Please."

Lian looked at her a moment longer, his breath rising in the air, and then finally turned to help Darrin with the tiller.

"Cut the lines," Winter said when they had set foot on the pier again.

The two tiellans did as ordered, their daggers slicing through the frozen lines that held the boat. Small icicles fell from each line as it swung back to the hull, shattering into the sea.

The group stood silently, watching the boat slip out into gray waters. The only sound came from the howling wind.

"May Canta guide him home," Eranda whispered.

"Canta is dead," Winter said. Then she raised her bow and touched an arrow with an oil-soaked rag to the torch that Eranda held. The arrow burst into flame. Winter nocked the shaft, taking aim.

She released, and the arrow soared through the air, a blazing orange line against the gray sky. It plunged into the sea a few rods from the boat.

Winter cursed, her eyes stinging. She drew another arrow, lighting it. It fell even further away from the vessel than the last.

Winter lit another and fired. The flames fell into the sea. The wind was carrying the shafts, but that was no excuse. Winter should be able to account for the wind, to find her target despite it. That was what her father had taught her.

The boat would soon sail out of range. Winter fought the panic rising in her chest, the embarrassment coloring her cheeks, and continued firing.

On her sixth or seventh arrow, Winter finally hit the mark.

It struck the bow of the boat, and in seconds the entire vessel was aflame.

Everyone wanted to believe that Canta could save them from Oblivion. Everyone wanted to believe that there was something more to this life, that something of them continued in Canta's Praeclara. But, as Winter watched her father's boat burn, she realized the truth. There was this life, and there was Oblivion. Nothing else.

She would never lie to herself that way again.

Winter flinched as she felt someone's arms wrap around her, and realized that she was sobbing, silently, her body convulsing in the cold. She couldn't take her eyes off the burning boat, alone in the wide, sullen sea.

"You're still going after him, aren't you?" Darrin asked, hours later back in his family's hut.

Winter nodded, fiddling with the straps on the pack she had filled with clothing, food, sleeping gear, and about half of the money she had. Her father's money.

Winter had given the rest of the money, what her father had saved up and hadn't spent on her wedding, to Darrin and Eranda. She left the fishing boat with them as well. She didn't know if Darrin and Lian would be enough to crew the vessel, even when Gord recovered—certainly no humans in Pranna would join up—but it was the least she could do.

"No stopping you, then?" Darrin asked.

"No stopping me." Winter felt a brief pang of regret at leaving this family that had always been so kind to her. But she knew that she couldn't stay. They had been kind to her, but they had never been *her* family. Even if she never found Knot, she still had to leave. There was too much here that would haunt her.

"Why are you doing this, Winter?" Eranda asked, seated near the fire. Tohn slept in her arms.

"He's my husband. We said the vows." She looked up at Eranda. "Tiellans don't break vows."

Eranda raised an eyebrow. "Since when do you care for tiellan tradition?"

Winter frowned. Eranda was right; she had never been much for tradition. But she had always been stubborn. Knot had left her. Maybe to protect her, maybe to just get away from her. It didn't matter. She wasn't about to let him go that easily.

She felt a sense of duty, and she had feelings for Knot— no use denying that—but more than anything, she just needed to *leave*. She wasn't going after Knot so much as leaving what remained of her life behind. Now that her father was gone, she had nothing left to keep her here. She had always wanted to get away from Pranna, to see the world. She had always wanted more than this town could give her.

But she couldn't tell Darrin and Eranda that. They would understand duty before they understood need.

Lian walked in, bundled warmly in wools and fur, a leather pack swung over one shoulder. His wide-brimmed *araif* was tilted at an angle on his head. Winter's gaze lingered briefly on the dagger and short hunting knife thrust through his belt, thinking of her own bow and quiver that she had packed.

"What?" he asked, when he saw her staring at him. "You're not goin' alone. Don't think you can argue with me."

Winter couldn't help but smile. She needed to leave, but she was terrified of traveling to Cineste—where Knot had said he might go first—alone. She had no idea what she was doing; no idea how to find Knot. She had been worried she would freeze up the moment she came in contact with any human.

"I guess I could tolerate the company," she said, trying to hide her relief. And beneath her relief, surprise. Lian loved Pranna, and had always hated the thought of leaving. That reason, among many others, was why their relationship had never worked.

"There's stew in the cauldron, Lian. Help yourself," Eranda said. She was rocking Tohn now, her chair creaking. "We insisted Winter eat. Same goes for you."

"Much thanks," he told her with a smile, "I always got room for a hot meal." Shedding the large sealskin cloak he wore, he dished out some stew and sat down.

Winter glanced at Eranda, who understood her look and nodded. "Darrin, love, would you help me get these children to bed?"

Darrin began to protest, but fell silent when he saw his wife's face. "Of course." He helped Eranda up. "I'm exhausted, anyway." The couple moved quietly into the other room.

Then Winter and Lian were alone.

"Thank you," Winter said, sitting beside him in front of the fire.

"What for?"

"Don't play that game," she said, looking at him seriously. "I mean it. For being there this morning, for helping with my father, for being here now… thank you."

Lian nodded, swallowing. "Don't thank me just yet," he said, returning her gaze. His eyes weren't as dark as hers, more of a grey color, but Winter had always thought them handsome.

She didn't respond, and they sat in silence.

"You know this is crazy, right?" Lian finally asked, looking at her earnestly. Winter punched him in the arm in response. He flinched, spilling stew on himself.

"Yeah," she said. "I know it is."

"Then why're you doin' it?"

"Because it's the only thing left," Winter said, surprised at how good it felt to finally voice her emotions. "I can't stay here anymore."

"Why not?" he asked.

"I just told you, Lian, there's nothing here for me."

"*I'm* here for you," he said. She looked at him. Orange firelight flickered on his face. She shook her head. She had loved Lian once, but she hadn't felt that way about him in years. He was a good man, and a good friend, but he wasn't what she wanted.

"Think of it," he said, setting down the bowl and grabbing her hands. "We could keep up your father's fishing business. Have children, grow old together. We could be *happy*, Winter. We could, I swear it."

"That's one thing you've never understood about me," Winter said. "I've never *wanted* to stay here in Pranna. Not with you, not with Knot, not with anyone. And now that Papa's gone... there's no reason for me to pretend anymore."

She squeezed his hands, but then pulled away. How could she explain to him that she had *never* felt she belonged in Pranna?

There was silence for what seemed a very long time.

Eventually, Winter stood. "We leave early, before they wake," she said, nodding towards the back room. "I don't want a messy goodbye. The children wouldn't understand." *And*, she thought, *I've already shed enough tears in the past two days for ten lifetimes. Don't know if I have any more left.*

When Lian didn't respond, Winter felt a twinge of fear in her chest. Panic rose inside her, but she fought it down.

"Of course," she said, hesitantly, "that's if you still want to come with me. I understand if you don't. If I leave, you could still have a life here."

"I'll go with you, princess," he said, staring into the fire. Winter felt her face flush. Lian had called her that since they were children. "But I'm only goin' for you. Not for him. Find him or not, I don't care."

"I understand," Winter said.

Lian turned to her. She could tell he had expected her to argue.

"What? You're not wrong *all* the time." She attempted a smile.

# 4

*Navone, northern Khale*

Cinzia Oden stood at the doorstep of her family's home for the first time in seven years. A strange sensation had budded in her chest when she left Triah, weeks ago. It had grown steadily as she traveled north, but only this morning, as she entered her hometown of Navone, when the feeling seemed to fill her entire being, did Cinzia recognize it as dread. She never knew that coming home would be so difficult.

Of course, she had never imagined her homecoming taking place because her sister had supposedly begun one of the most dangerous heretical movements since the Parliament had taken power, either.

She removed one of her gloves and touched the carved oak door she remembered from her childhood, now worn and weathered. She felt the wood, smooth and cold beneath her fingers. The carving depicted Canta's first sermon; the listening crowd were faceless except for the nine female figures in the corner, representing the women who would become the Nine Disciples. One of those disciples was Cinzia's namesake. In Khale, firstborn daughters were traditionally named after one of the Nine. Her father had made the disciple's carving to look very much like Cinzia.

She remembered helping her father with his woodworking, and the crisp smell of freshly carved timber. She remembered going to Ocrestia's cathedral with her mother and siblings, her father waving goodbye to them and smiling. She remembered Jane, the sister she had always been closest to, both in age and temperament, crying on the doorstep as Cinzia left for Triah.

Cinzia shivered, pulling her cloak more tightly around her shoulders. She glanced at her Goddessguard, Kovac, standing by her side. "This is my home," she said, if for no other reason than to stall. "I grew up here."

"It is a beautiful residence, Priestess," Kovac said.

"It is, indeed," Cinzia whispered.

*No use delaying.* Then, before she could knock, the door opened swiftly to the sound of someone shouting.

"Do not forget! Return before supper!"

And there, standing in the doorway, was Ader. Her youngest brother, the youngest in the family. He was taller now, of course, and his once bright-blond, almost white hair, had darkened to a sandy color. But he had the same long, bony face, the same wide mouth, so prone to smiling.

"Hello, Ader," Cinzia said, the feeling of dread threatening to burst from her. He looked at her blankly for a moment, his eyes moving from the Trinacrya she wore, to Kovac, to her face, and then back to the Trinacrya again.

Then he grinned.

"Mother," he shouted over his shoulder, "Cinzia's home!"

Inside it was warm; a flurry of faces, hugs, laughs, and tears greeted her. She had grown up as the second oldest in a family of nine, and when her elder brother had died when she was eleven, Cinzia had taken the mantle of eldest child. Their family had been large, but always close.

Cinzia raised her eyebrows as her mother served tea. The

gesture was welcome after her long, cold journey, but growing up, the servants always took care of their needs. Cinzia had not seen any since arriving home. She made a mental note to ask about that later.

Once everyone calmed down, Cinzia and Kovac were invited upstairs to the drawing room. Ignoring the polished wooden chairs and carved, padded benches her younger brothers still elected to sit on the floor. Ader had stayed home instead of going wherever he had been off to when Cinzia arrived. Eward, the oldest of the brothers, stood with arms folded, watching her intently. She noticed that there was one face missing.

"Where's Jane?" Cinzia asked.

Her parents glanced at one another. Their age was showing, much more than Cinzia remembered. Ehram's hair had always been thin, but now it was gone, and his scalp seemed to shine. Even her mother's sun-blond hair looked paler than she remembered.

"Jane had some… business, this evening," her father said carefully, still looking at her mother.

Cinzia looked back and forth between them. *Business?* She did not know what kind of business her sister would need to be worrying about. Jane was in her twenty-first year, two years Cinzia's junior. Old enough to be meeting young men, attending parties, even considering marriage. That was the extent of the "business" Jane might have.

Unless it had something to do with the rumors.

Cinzia was about to inquire further when she heard the front door slam. Quick footsteps padded up the stairs.

"Well," Ehram said with a smile, "it appears she has returned." He looked relieved, of all things. "Jane," he said loudly, just as a woman rushed past the door to the drawing room, long blond hair flowing behind her, "there is someone in here you will want to see."

"In a moment, Father."

Cinzia felt another twinge of nostalgia at her sister's voice, as if a void she had not realized was there was suddenly being filled. The dread she felt waiting outside the door had quickly dispelled in the presence of her family, who neither seemed to have forgotten her nor begrudge her long absence. But she felt the first fingers of it again as she worried what Jane might think of her, after all these years.

Or, perhaps more importantly, what her sister thought of herself. Not just anyone could start a religious uprising that drew the attention of the High Camarilla.

"Hi, Janey," Cinzia heard herself saying. The name tumbled awkwardly from her lips; it was what she had always called her sister, since they were little.

The movement from the hall stopped. There was silence for a moment, during which no one seemed to breathe. Then Jane poked her head into the room.

Her eyes widened as she stared at Cinzia. Then Jane's face broke into a grin, though Cinzia was suddenly not convinced the smile was genuine. Jane laughed her musical laugh and rushed towards Cinzia. Cinzia rose to meet her, and they embraced.

Cinzia inhaled sharply. The tension between herself and Jane was almost tangible. And why would it not be? Cinzia was a Cantic priestess. Jane was a heretic. There was plenty of tension to be had.

Nevertheless, the affection Cinzia felt for Jane was irrepressible.

"I have missed you, sister," Jane whispered in her ear.

"And I you."

They remained together for a moment, Cinzia not wanting to let go. Letting go meant facing reality. But, slowly, they separated, and looked at each other.

Jane was a woman now, no denying that. She had inherited their mother's light-blond hair, the only girl in the family to do so, as well as their mother's pale-blue eyes. Jane had grown nearly a span taller than Cinzia, which was not overly difficult considering Cinzia hardly rose above Ader, now—her parents had always joked that she was the runt of the family.

Jane wore a simple dress, woven wool with no embroidery or decoration. Cinzia suddenly felt very conscious of the crimson-and-ivory folds of her Cantic dress, with Canta's intersecting gold-and-silver triangle and circle embroidered on her chest. The symbol, the Trinacrya, was the universally recognized crest of Canticism, and she had never felt self-conscious of it until now.

The younger siblings gawked at the Trinacrya on her dress, and risked occasional, furtive glances at Kovac in his red-and-white tabard and steel plate armor. His helm rested at his feet, and Cinzia couldn't help but notice Ader taking particular interest in the longsword Kovac had unstrapped from his waist to lean against the wall, within easy reach.

Their family had never lacked money. Ehram had not been born a noble, but Pascia had fallen in love with him despite his low birth, and while his woodworking business was successful, her management of her family's estates in the country had always paid for anything they needed. Nevertheless, Ehram and Pascia had always insisted on a quiet modesty, in appearance as well as demeanor. Cinzia and her Goddessguard's elaborate Cantic dress did not exactly adhere to those standards, and she felt the contrast as she stood by her sister. It was another point of tension between them. Another competition, whether they meant it to be so or not.

And yet, despite their differences, their faces were the same. People had often asked whether they were twins. Looking at her sister now, Cinzia almost felt as if she were facing a looking glass—the same high cheekbones and full lips. Their hair and eyes were different, of course, but otherwise they were nearly identical.

"I have so much to tell you," Jane said, her eyes sparkling the way their mother's always did when she grew excited.

Cinzia sobered, remembering what had brought her to Navone in the first place.

"But first," Jane continued, motioning to Kovac, "introduce me to this handsome young man you have brought along with you. I know that priestesses of the Ministry are not allowed to marry, so either you have some explaining to do, or..."

Cinzia blushed. Jane had always been one to tease, or flatter, or both at once. She saw Kovac shift uncomfortably out of the corner of her eye, his chainmail clinking.

"This is Kovac," Cinzia said. "My Goddessguard."

Kovac had remained silent by her side since they had entered her home, apart from introducing himself quietly when asked. Cinzia noted the slight red tinge to his cheeks. Her sister's comment must have struck a chord; Kovac had passed his fortieth summer. His graying beard was close-cropped, and the beginnings of wrinkles creased around his blue eyes.

"A pleasure to meet you," Jane said, grinning at Kovac. He bowed his head in return.

"I cannot believe our daughter is home," Pascia said. She was still teary-eyed from her first emotional encounter with Cinzia.

"Home at last," her father said. Then he cleared his throat, and Cinzia was surprised again at how easily she fell into the old habits of home. When Ehram cleared his throat like that, it was time to listen. Cinzia faced him, and she felt Jane's fingers entwine around her own. Tension pulsed through the room, and Cinzia wondered if the rest of her family could feel it as well. Nevertheless, she squeezed Jane's hand in return. There was friction between them, but more besides.

"Cinzia, having you back in our home makes us happier than we could have imagined," her father said. "To see that you have done so well, that you are successful, makes us truly proud. But priestesses do not just up and leave their congregations, and as much as we know of your love for us, your arrival here cannot be due to simple affection." He paused before continuing, glancing quickly at Kovac.

Cinzia caught the meaning. "Do not worry, Father," she said. "Kovac is trustworthy."

Ehram nodded. "We assume you have heard something of the happenings here in Navone?"

Cinzia nodded, and she felt Jane's grip tighten around her fingers. "Word has spread. The High Camarilla is taking action, I do not know how soon." She stopped. Breaking this news to her family was more difficult than she had anticipated. She had debated coming here at all; her faith was her faith. She *believed* in Canta, in the Denomination. Hearing rumors of heresy from her hometown had been agonizing.

"I do not know the details of what has been going on here, but rumors say some of you might be involved. I have come here for two reasons. The first is to discover what *really* is going on." She paused, not sure what to say next. Best to be honest. Blunt, even.

"The second reason is to warn you. It appears the High Camarilla have enough information to send a Holy Crucible to Navone. A full company of the Goddessguard and the Sons of Canta escort her."

Some of the younger children gasped. Cinzia's parents, Jane, and Eward remained straight-faced. They did not even nod. Cinzia tried not to think about what that meant. Usually the mere *mention* of a Holy Crucible sent shivers down a person's spine.

Cinzia sighed. Whatever her family's reaction, she was glad to have said what had weighed on her for so long. But saying it did not change much. She looked around at her family. Jane still squeezed her hand tightly.

Finally Ehram spoke. "We knew this day would come," he said. Cinzia felt her cheeks flush, this time from anger. Could it be true? Was her family truly at the center of this?

"We have spoken about what we would do, about our plans when this day came. Now we must put them into motion." Cinzia was aware of her family nodding. Eward's jaw was set. Even the children, eyes wide, watched their father with resolve.

*Goddess*, she thought, *it is true. There really* is *something happening here.* Did she belong to a family of heretics?

Or, if these people were heretics, were they still truly her family?

"Jane," Ehram said, "this is your decision, but I think now would be a good time to let your sister in on what you have been doing for the last few years."

Cinzia, eyes wide, looked at Jane. "The last few *years?*" Familiar dread flooded back into her.

Jane nodded. "Yes, Father. It is time."

"Canta's breath," Ehram exclaimed, "I had completely

forgotten about where you were this evening. Were you successful?"

Jane smiled. "I was. And showing Cinzia what I found tonight is an excellent place to begin."

# 5

*Cineste, northern Khale*

"I CAN'T CHANGE YOUR MIND?" Ildur had asked the same question two or three times already. While the old man had cut a commanding figure on the snow-swept plains between Pranna and Cineste, he looked suddenly very out of place on the streets of the city.

"No," Knot said.

"Too bad. Could use a set of hands like yours. Someone who knows how to handle animals. Good in a fight. A caravan runs into trouble every so often, out on the road."

Knot had joined Ildur's caravan on the way to Cineste. They'd found Knot during a windstorm, the snow and ice whipping fast enough to cut flesh, and offered him shelter. Soon, they'd discovered his usefulness. Leading oxen, loading and unloading supplies, even driving the teams of animals that pulled the three wagons: it all came as naturally to Knot as working Bahc's boat, as naturally as killing the men in the Cantic chapel in Pranna and the two watchmen.

And yet, Knot hadn't fought anyone since Pranna. Ildur's implication surprised him.

"Can't stay, Ildur. Sorry." Knot would've liked to remain with Ildur's caravan, but they were headed south towards Triah. Knot's business took him the opposite direction. The men who attacked at the wedding were from Roden, and Knot

61

felt inexplicably drawn to the place. He hoped he would find answers there. He had left Pranna to protect Winter. He had to find out about his past before he endangered anyone else.

Ildur nodded. "Very well, lad." He pulled a small pouch from his belt, and offered it to Knot. "Recompense. You've paid for more than the shelter and food, with all you've done."

Knot didn't want to take money from Ildur's meager operation, but he accepted it anyway. No use being impractical. He'd left Pranna with almost nothing of value.

"Thank you," he said, hoping Ildur would hear his sincerity.

"It's not charity, lad, it's payment. You deserve it." Ildur extended his left arm. In Khalic tradition, extending one's left arm was a way of showing you meant no harm; that you were a friend. Knot gripped it with his left hand.

"Offer still stands, if you ever need the coin," Ildur called over his shoulder as he walked to the caravan. "We could always use the help."

Knot nodded as he watched the caravan disappear into the crowded street, though Ildur didn't look back.

He sighed heavily. A long journey lay ahead of him, and most, if not all of it, would be on foot. He'd considered commandeering a boat in Pranna to cut across the Gulf of Nahl—such a trip would take him a week at most, instead of a month along his current route—but Roden patrolled its surrounding waters heavily, and they did not take kindly to foreigners. And, being honest, Knot was in no hurry. The time spent traveling—time alone, time to think—might help him prepare for whatever he encountered in Roden.

Knot turned. Two- and three-story buildings rose around him, built mostly of light-colored wood and, in rare cases, stone. Shops and tents and people shouting about the latest silk clothing from Alizia or fine steel from Maven Kol crowded the streets. Knot recalled there was one major market district in the city center, and other shops and merchants' stalls lined the three main roads, leading from the city center to each gate.

The city was uncomfortably familiar to him. He had been here once that he could remember, with Bahc and Winter and Gord, for the Festival of Songs. Even then he had known things about the city that he should not have. The exact heights of the walls and guard towers. Patrol routes of the City Watch. The layout of the main gatehouse. He knew Cineste's population was huge, roughly one hundred thousand people, not quite one-tenth of whom were tiellan.

The knowledge worried him.

The sun had nearly set. He needed to find an inn. As he walked further down the street, he felt the slightest tug on his belt.

His hand moved quickly and caught a small wrist. He looked down into the wide, bright-green eyes of a young girl, eight or nine years old, staring up at him. She wore a cloak with a large hood. Her hand was wrapped around the coin purse at his waist.

A pickpocket.

"Best you can do?" Knot asked, with half a smile. She was trying to rob him, sure, but she was young and looked frail. The life that led her to this didn't bear thinking about. Even less so the life this led her towards.

"Beg your pardon, sir," the girl said, lowering her eyes. "Please, I just..."

With bewildering power, the girl tried to wrench her arm free. Knot held on, barely, surprised at such sudden force. She'd nearly knocked him over.

"Wait," Knot said, but with another gargantuan burst of strength the girl jerked her arm out of his grip and scampered off down the street.

*What in Oblivion?* Knot was half tempted to pursue the girl, just to see who she was.

*Caught me off guard,* he told himself. No other explanation for the fact that she'd nearly pulled him over.

If nothing else, it made Knot realize he needed a weapon of some sort. Next time someone confronted him, it likely wouldn't be a small child.

Eventually Knot found an inn, marked by a large sign with an illegible name carved into the wood. The building was old, made of aging pine, and didn't look particularly fancy. Exactly what Knot wanted. Just a place to rest his head. He'd leave Cineste at first light.

The common room was full, but well lit and clean. He took it in, measuring each variable and potential threat. The process was habit for him, now, ever since waking up in Pranna. There were plenty of people in the room, but only a few who knew how to handle themselves. A group of watchmen, likely off duty, conversed loudly at a corner table. They didn't look overly competent, but the four of them together—and their chainmail, spears, and long daggers—would cause problems in a fight. Word of what had happened in Pranna must've reached the city by now, but he felt strangely confident in his ability to blend in. The watchmen seemed engaged in their own conversation, anyway; they'd pay him no mind.

A man who towered nearly a head over Knot stood stoically near the entrance to the common room. The inn's own security. Despite the fat around the man's belly, Knot guessed he might present more of a problem than all four of the watchmen if things got violent. The man's scarred fists and knuckles and off-center nose were tangible proof. Even the way he stood, relaxed but alert, spoke of violence.

No one else was a threat. Most were either too involved in themselves or unhappily listening to an untalented lute player near the hearth.

"What'll it be?" the innkeeper asked from behind the bar. He looked Knot up and down. Knot lifted the purse and set it on the bar.

"A room," he said. "And some hot water." He could use a bath, and Ildur had been surprisingly generous with his coin.

The innkeeper eyed the purse, then looked again at Knot.

"All right, friend," he said. "One silver for the room. Three coppers extra for the water."

Knot placed the coins on the bar. The innkeeper slipped them into a large pocket in his apron.

"Second floor," he said, pulling a key from another pocket and slapping it down. "End of the hall."

Knot muttered his thanks, and turned towards the stairs.

Knot dreamed of chaos and uncertainty.

He dreamed of watching a woman sleep. Knot sat in a chair beside her. The woman was beautiful, bathed in a soft light. In the distant dark, a man watched them both. He couldn't see the man, but Knot knew he was there, watching.

Knot stood and walked out of the light and into a city covered in snow and ice. Hundreds of flat, squat huts spread out around him. Izet, the capital city of Roden. In the center of the city loomed a large, domed palace. A faint blue light shone at the peak of the dome, and Knot itched to know what the light was. He needed to find out, sure as breathing.

The city was empty. No people, no animals, no wind, no sound. Knot walked towards the great snow-capped dome and the blue light; the light was always further away, no matter how far his feet took him.

In the distance, someone ran quickly across his vision.

Knot rushed after them, but by the time he got to where they had been, the street was empty.

Knot turned. He thought he'd heard someone behind him. For a moment he thought no one was there, but then he saw her. Raven-black hair.

Knot called out. She ran on, as if she hadn't heard him.

To his left, in an alleyway, he saw her again. Running.

To his right, she ran.

Suddenly the city was full of dark-haired women running down the streets, through alleys, between buildings. Knot reached out to touch one of them, but she disappeared as soon as he came close. He reached for another figure, and she too slipped away.

Knot began seeing other faces on the people running. Bahc, Lian, Gord, Dent, the watchmen he had murdered, the tall, ugly man from the chapel, Ildur, and others he didn't recognize at all.

In the middle of them all, standing still, were two men. One was tall, strong, middle-aged, with a shaved head and a large gold ring on his little finger. Knot recognized the man— it was Grysole, the Emperor of Roden. How on earth did he know what a faraway emperor looked like? The other was hooded, surrounded in shadow, and Knot could not place him.

In the distance, the domes of Izet had disappeared. In their place were Canta's Fane, the Citadel, and the House of Aldermen. Knot was in Triah.

Everyone running around him—hundreds of people, faces

he recognized and those he did not—stopped moving. They lined the Radial Road, leading straight to Triah's center. The crowds waited. The bald king and shadow man were gone, and in their place was another man with thick blond hair, facing Knot. The man held a sword up, looking down the blade at him. The man smiled, but his eyes were cold.

Knot realized he wasn't wearing a sword, but before he could react, the pickpocket girl from Cineste was in front of him. Her eyes blazed bright green, blinding him.

"Not yet," she whispered.

Knot awoke, sitting up sharply in the dark. He felt cold sweat on his back. He glanced at the lone window in his room, watching the wool curtains tremble and float in the breeze.

Knot hadn't left the shutters open.

"What d'you want?" Knot asked the darkness, calmly. He didn't care what the intruder wanted, but the question might buy time. Moonlight streamed in and painted a ghostly, silver-white square on the floor, the only source of light in the room.

Knot didn't hear any movement, but a voice came from the corner, from the dark.

"I've heard of you," the voice said. "Strange to think that the great legend is just... a man."

Knot's mind raced. A man's voice, experienced but not old. No more than forty summers. Knot squinted as his eyes adjusted, and finally saw the outline of a shape. The man was tall, his dim frame imposing.

"Don't know what you're talking about," Knot said to the shape in the darkness. "But if you tell me who you are, maybe we can help each other." He reached for the brass candlestick by the bed.

"I'm not a fool," the man said, his voice hardening. "You chose to desert. You had to know we would catch up with you eventually."

Knot's fingers closed around the candlestick, and he threw it as hard as he could at the man. Then he leapt out of bed, whipping the thick wool blanket around and around his left arm. If the man carried a blade, minimal protection was better than none.

Knot knew something was wrong when the candlestick stopped in midair, right in front of the man's face. He suddenly felt too aware of everything. The candlestick floating eerily in the moonlight. The slight breeze fluttering through the curtains. He shivered. A tingling sensation blossomed in his head, directly behind his eyes. A lot was wrong with this scene, but there was something specific, something nagging at him.

Then, faster than he could ever have thrown it, the candlestick flew back towards him.

Knot barely got his arm up in time to deflect, sending it clattering away. Sharp pain shot through his shoulder at the sudden movement, but Knot had learned to ignore the pain. He sprang at the man. Metal scraped against leather and there was a flash in the moonlight. The man whipped a sword towards Knot, and Knot barely dodged the blow. He weaved forward, raising his wool-wrapped arm in time to deflect another slash. He lashed out with his other hand and struck his opponent in the face. The man attacked again, but he was slower this time, and Knot managed an awkward kick at his stomach before moving in, unwrapping the blanket from his arm. Strangely, he felt no fear. From his words, his attacker might be able to tell about his past.

Even if he couldn't, there was still the thrill of the kill.

The man swung again, but Knot danced around the sword, snapping the blanket up and around the blade, catching it in the thick wool. But something wasn't right. Knot kicked the man again, at the same time pulling sharply on the blanket, and the man's sword clattered against the wall.

"Feel free to join in any time you like," the man rasped.

Knot's body registered that there was another person in the room before his mind caught up. He felt the odd, tingling sensation behind his eyes again, and then the blanket was yanked out of his grip. Knot turned and dove for the sword, shining in the square of moonlight from the window.

As if repelled by his hand, the sword slid away from his grasp. At the same time Knot felt the blanket wrapping around his ankles, snaking up his body. In seconds he was bound tightly in a cocoon of wool.

He couldn't move.

"Canta's bones, you could have done that in the beginning," the man said.

The man bent down to grab the sword. Knot flung his bound legs at the man's ankles, tripping him. Knot was about to struggle his way towards the blade again, when he suddenly felt his whole body lift into the air.

"*Enough.*" A woman's voice.

Then Knot was floating, held up by the wool blanket, the sword at his throat. But no one was holding it.

It was just that kind of night.

The blade pressed against his neck; he could feel the edge digging. If he moved at all, it would cut deeper. He held as still as possible, his gaze fixed on the levitating sword.

Slowly, a woman walked into view. She watched Knot warily, glaring at him in the darkness.

"You're sure this is him?" she asked, her eyes not leaving Knot's.

"I'd know his face anywhere," the man said.

Knot strained his eyes towards the man, but didn't recognize him—not from his dreams or his memories, such as they were.

The man swept towards Knot, angrily grabbing the sword from the air. He brought it back around to Knot's throat again.

"Time for some questions, Lathe," the man said.

*Lathe.* The same name the attackers had used for him in Pranna.

"I'm not who you think I am," Knot said.

The man snorted. "Deflection? Really? I'd have expected more from *you*, of all people."

Then, before the man could say anything further, the door to the small room splintered inwards with a crash.

The man shouted. Knot saw a form streak across the room and slam into the woman. Knot fell to the floor, the blanket suddenly as ordinary as it had ever been.

He wriggled free and swung his right arm around, blindly connecting with the man who held the sword. He didn't know what force had come to his aid, but he'd take advantage of it. Knot followed with a sharp jab to the man's face, then pinned his sword arm against the wall and kneed him in the groin.

The sword clattered to the ground. Knot slammed his forehead into the man's nose. From there, it was a matter of reaching around the disoriented man's head and twisting, sharply. The act was simple, and it filled him with satisfaction.

Knot turned back to see the candlestick he'd thrown earlier flash towards him in the moonlight.

\* \* \*

He awoke to more darkness.

Beneath the sound of his own breathing, which he tried to keep even, and his pounding headache, Knot almost missed the faint footsteps on the wood floor. He heard a soft trickle near the washstand, and then the near-silent footsteps came back.

Knot remained still until the footsteps stopped behind him. Then he sprang off the bed, around and behind his assailant, his hands wrapping around their neck.

Knot's arms wrapped around nothing, and he stumbled forward.

"There are some advantages to being short," said a voice in the darkness. "Although being unnaturally quick helps, too."

Knot reached the window and threw it open, allowing moonlight into the room once more. He blinked in the silvery glow, eyes adjusting.

"Sorry, I prefer to work in the dark," the voice said. "If I'd thought you would wake up this soon, I'd have lit a candle."

Knot heard the scrape of flint on steel, and then there was a lit candle in the middle of the room, in the same candlestick that had knocked Knot unconscious. Held by a young girl.

"Who are you?" Knot asked. His throat was dry.

But before the girl answered, he knew. Silvery-blond hair, bright-green eyes. Brighter now, if that was possible. They almost seemed to create their own light.

It was the girl who had tried to pick his pocket on the street earlier that evening.

"I thought you'd recognize me," the girl said with a grin. She motioned towards the bed. "Lie down. I was just cleaning that nasty cut on your forehead when you decided to go crazy on me."

Knot could only stare at her.

"And you should probably close that window," the girl said. "Not many places have a good view into your room, but you don't want to risk anyone seeing the bodies."

Suddenly flashes of the fight that had taken place flooded Knot's mind. He'd snapped a man's neck without a second thought.

And part of him had enjoyed it.

He felt sick. He didn't know these people. Why would he hurt people he didn't know? Why would he hurt anyone?

*Because they were trying to hurt you. That's the way of it. Kill or be killed.*

The thought brought him no pleasure. He felt like an unwitting passenger in his own body.

The man who'd attacked him lay in a corner, his neck bent at an unfortunate angle. The other body, the woman, Knot assumed, was too mangled to recognize.

"What business do you have with Nazaniin high-ups like that, anyway?" The girl nodded at the bodies. "Acumens and telenics aren't easy to come by."

Knot wasn't sure what confused him more. The girl who couldn't have seen more than nine summers with glowing eyes, who talked like she was thirty. The strange words she used— Nazaniin, acumen and telenic?—those *did* resonate in Knot's mind, he was sure of it, although he couldn't put any images with the words. Or that there were two bodies in the corner. People he'd never met before, but who had tried to kill him. They'd called him Lathe, just like the attackers at the wedding. Was that his name? His *real* name? It meant nothing to him.

Also, things had been floating. Knot wasn't comfortable with that.

"What in Oblivion is going on?" he mumbled to himself.

The girl bounced onto the bed, facing him. It was difficult to look at anything other than her eyes. They seemed to draw him in.

"You're asking me?" The girl snorted. She motioned, again, for him to come towards her. "Come *on*. We really should get out of here before dawn. Get over here and let me take care of that cut."

Knot frowned. He felt an odd desire to trust the girl, but there was a problem.

He didn't trust anyone.

Slowly, he walked towards her. There was hardly anything she could do that would threaten him. Then he hesitated. The woman hadn't torn *herself* apart. Knot was missing something.

"It's okay," the girl said. "I won't bite."

Then Knot knew. The thought lit up a corner of his mind. *Ventus.*

"You're a vampire," he said. He sat on the bed next to her. *If she is what I think she is,* he realized, *I don't have a chance, whether I run or not.* Some part of him wondered if he wasn't under-reacting. Vampires were thought extinct, if they ever truly existed at all. But, with all Knot had experienced in the past few days—in the past few minutes—he didn't think he was in a position to question the girl's existence. It explained how she'd torn from his grip so easily on the street, how she could see well enough to strike flint on steel in darkness.

The girl—the vampire—gave him an annoyed look as she raised a wet cloth to his forehead.

"Kind of you to notice. I'm flattered."

She didn't sound flattered.

Knot quelled his body's desire to flinch as she dabbed the cloth at the swollen wound on his forehead.

"You're helping me," he said, remembering the blur that had shot into his room when there'd been a sword at his throat.

"Are you always this astute, or am I just special?" The girl raised her eyebrows. The bed creaked as she shifted to her knees, looking closely at his forehead.

"Why?"

"Direct, too," the girl muttered to herself, dabbing again at his wound. "Everything I adore in a man. Canta must have *finally* heard my prayers."

Knot said nothing.

"Okay," she said, springing up. "Good as new. Now let's get out of here. Dawn is in an hour or so, and—"

"Why hasn't anyone come in?" Knot asked. "You broke the bloody door down. Someone had to have heard it."

"Who says they didn't? A vampire has got to eat, you know."

Knot swore. "Why them and not me?"

The girl sighed, her shining green eyes rolling. "Canta's bones, I didn't *eat* anybody. That was me being funny. Nobody *gets* that anymore." She shrugged. "I just… incapacitated some people, that's all. They're still alive, and they're all still human."

Knot narrowed his eyes.

"Don't look at me like that. I may be a daemon, but there are daemons even daemons fear. Pray to your goddess you never encounter *them*."

Knot frowned. Nothing in the Sfaera said it was safe to trust her. And yet there was something about her, something Knot didn't understand, but…

"You don't want to be here when people start realizing what happened. We need to leave. Now."

The girl extended her hand. Her left hand. "I'm Astrid, by the way."

*A vampire*, Knot thought. He rubbed his shoulder, which still ached from the fight. *Canta's bloody bones*.

Then Knot gripped her hand with his own. No other options.

"Knot," he said.

He didn't ask her why he should trust her. She had saved him, and for now, that was enough.

# 6

*Nazaniin outpost, Cineste*

"BOTH DEAD? YOU SURE?" Nash asked.

"My connection with their acumen is gone," Kali said. *Why can't anyone just obey orders? Why is that so hard?*

"She didn't run out of frost?"

Kali shook her head. "Not unless she has the shortest susceptibility of all time. She only took it five minutes ago." They were in the Nazaniin's Cinestean headquarters, but the local group of operatives—known as a *cotir* within the Nazaniin—was nowhere to be seen. As an acumen Kali could form a mental link with other acumens, and the link she had formed with the acumen in the Cinestean *cotir* had just been severed. Kali felt the resonance of it in her mind, like the vibration of a lute string that had been cut.

Nash sighed, blowing out his cheeks. "Variants," he said.

Kali scoffed, but eyed Nash with a frown. He stood up, closing his eyes. He was stressed; Kali knew the signs.

Kali lounged against a large desk in one corner of the room. Their lacuna, Elsi, stood nearby, staring blankly. Nash was now pacing in front of the door. Kali sighed.

They were in an office of sorts, but they had already scoured the headquarters and taken anything useful. A half-dozen frost crystals, a disappointing amount of money—this particular *cotir* obviously didn't get much work—and a bunch of nightsbane.

The nightsbane surprised Kali; the herb was rare, particularly in the north. How that pair came across such a prize was beyond her comprehension.

The fools hadn't even left a note. *Dear actuals,* Kali imagined them writing. *Gone to get ourselves killed in the vain hope of glory. Don't wait up.* The glaring display of inadequacy was an unfortunate metaphor for the Nazaniin as a whole, lately. An organization of assassins that had once been feared throughout the Sfaera was now hardly more than a spy network, and an inept one at that.

Kali stood, closing her eyes. Her head still rang from the severed link.

"I can't say I'm disappointed," Kali said. "I wasn't particularly looking forward to working with another *cotir*. Especially a pair of variants."

Kali didn't care for variants. They were inferior psimancers, after all. Variants required a terribly dangerous drug to manifest abilities that actuals—people like Kali and Nash—could use innately. Variants were unreliable. And most variants Kali knew used their limited psimantic ability as an excuse for incompetence.

"Why can't everyone be more like me?" Kali said. Joking, of course. For the most part. "I obey orders. I make smart decisions. Why is that so hard?"

Nash snorted. "You're on the other extreme," he said with a smirk. "All business and logic. There's no artistry to your methods."

Kali's frown deepened. "Obedience doesn't require artistry; only competence."

Nash laughed, but Kali wasn't bothered. They'd had this conversation many times before, and both were set in their views. Of course, that was what made them such a good team. As long as they agreed, anyway. Kali wondered what would happen if their differences ever got the better of them.

"We should change our approach," Nash said. "If the Cinestean *cotir* really has been eliminated, we need to be careful. Lathe is too dangerous to underestimate." He said nothing of variants, which didn't surprise Kali. He, too, thought them deficient, but he would never say so out loud. Another difference between them.

"The fools couldn't wait a day or so?" Kali wasn't interested in dropping the subject quite yet. "Hours, really. That's all we needed." Nash was right, of course. They *would* have to be careful. Lathe had always been dangerous, but even more so since he'd become so damn unpredictable.

Nash shrugged. "They didn't know how close we were," he said. "They took a risk. It didn't pay off."

Kali raised an eyebrow. "You're defending them?"

When Nash didn't respond, she felt a sliver of guilt. This was no time to argue. "You're right, we need to change our approach. If Lathe killed them, he's probably already left the city. We'll make a pass at each gate on the off-chance we can catch him."

"What about the tiellan quarter?" Nash asked.

"Good point. He has some connection with the elves. I'll check the gates. You check the elven quarter."

"You have to call them that?"

"Do I have to? Of course not. But I'll do as I damn well please, and a horse is a horse, a fish is a fish, and an elf is an elf."

Nash shrugged, and said nothing more. *Damn right,* Kali thought. Kali was no Kamite, not by any stretch. She had met tiellans who were good, intelligent, capable. But she had other reasons to hate them. Grudges that would not be forgotten.

"*Voke* me if you have any trouble," Kali said, fingering the voidstone in her pocket. "I'll do the same. Otherwise, meet back here at second watch."

Nash nodded, rubbing the bridge of his nose. Kali sighed inwardly, but walked over to him. She placed her hands on his temples, rubbing gently.

"We have our orders," she said.

"I know. That's what bothers me."

"I'm sorry," she said, and she truly was. Almost sorry enough to regret trying to start an argument. "If you like, we can—"

"No," Nash said, too sharply. Kali felt his hands on hers. "No," he said again. "I'll be all right. We have work to do."

"Very well," Kali said, holding his gaze. Then she leaned forward and kissed his forehead.

"Take care of yourself," Nash said as she turned and walked away. He would follow momentarily. Best not to be seen together.

"Always," Kali said.

# 7

*Outside Cineste*

"YOU THINK I'D APPRECIATE the sun," Lian said, "but I don't. Everyone who knows anything about the north knows that clear skies make for colder days than cloudy ones."

It was almost noon, and the sun shone high in a rare blue winter sky. Winter and Lian had finally reached Cineste. The snow had been thick and constant the past few days. White drifts shone on rooftops, balconies, and walls. The city itself sparkled like a jewel.

Shivering, Winter pulled her cloak more tightly around her.

"The cold bites through you on days like this," Lian said, pulling his hat down to cover as much of his ears as possible. "Ignores layers of wool and fur and sinks into your bones."

Winter couldn't disagree. It was freezing. But she didn't say anything. She had hardly spoken since they left Pranna. The more Lian talked—and Lian could talk a lot—the more she was aware of her own silence.

She felt guilty about it, but not enough to break it.

Lian shouldered his pack as they walked down the gentle slope towards the city. "Been a spell since I've been to Cineste. More than a year, maybe two. I think the last time…"

Winter smiled, though her focus was on the city before them. Lian was just speaking for speaking's sake, and while she didn't much care to listen to it, she appreciated what he was doing on principle. Lian blathering on was better than the alternative.

She just couldn't bring herself to say much when there wasn't something that needed saying. She worried what would come out if she did.

"We need to decide what to do next," Winter said, interrupting Lian. "I'm not sure where Knot would be. Maybe an inn, maybe with someone he knows. Or he may have just passed through on his way to Roden."

"To *Roden?*"

"It's the most likely place he'd go. We found him in the Gulf of Nahl. The attackers at... the attackers had Rodenese accents. It makes sense."

Lian looked at her, one eyebrow raised. "We'll address the insanity of two tiellans strolling into Roden later. For now, go back to the part about you not knowing what we're doing next."

Winter shrugged. "Told you I didn't know what I was doing."

"Not sure you ever *did* say that—"

"Lian. Arguing won't help."

"Sorry. It's good to hear your voice. Even if we're arguing."

Winter thought about apologizing. The idea certainly crossed her mind. That was something, wasn't it?

"Won't be much daylight left when we get to the city," she said. "We'll need to work quickly. We should sweep all the inns we can find, first."

"Right," Lian said. "We'll just walk up to every human inn we see and ask after our forgetful human friend, whose name might be Knot, might be Lathe or whatever it was those men called him, might be something else entirely, who could probably kill them in the time it takes to blink. I'm sure they'll appreciate two *elves* asking after a human. Who wouldn't?"

"Don't say that. Please." Winter hated the term. *Elf*. It sounded so dirty. She didn't understand how others could refer to her people that way.

"I'll give it a try," Lian muttered. "But that don't make me wrong," he said, more confidently. "We can't just go up to every inn in the city and start questioning people. We'll only attract attention. The painful kind."

Lian wasn't wrong. The city was, supposedly, slightly more tolerant than the rural areas, but that wasn't saying much. Prejudice against the tiellans had magnified in the past ten years or so, despite the Emancipation. Tiellans had once worshiped alongside humans in Cantic chapels, but new sessions "reserved" specifically for tiellans began to appear, and soon there was complete separation.

"You have any suggestions, then?" If he wasn't going to accept her ideas, he had damn well better be helpful in some other way.

Their feet crunched in the snow as they neared the gates. A small crowd of people waited outside the wall to enter the city.

"Well?" she said, when he didn't say anything.

"Hadn't thought about that, princess," he said with a shrug. "Criticism ain't helpful enough?"

Winter rolled her eyes. "And you wonder why I don't talk much."

Lian punched her lightly on the arm as they descended to the city gate. And Winter laughed.

The rare, spontaneous desire to laugh had long departed after a few hours of scouring inn common rooms.

It was worse than Winter had expected. Not a single inn even let them inside. "No elves," the innkeeper said, gruffly, at each door. They looked down at Lian and Winter as if they were stray dogs, begging for scraps.

That look had both infuriated and terrified Winter. These humans could do whatever they wished to them. A group of humans could beat them, kill them, or worse, and by the looks of things Winter didn't think anyone would care.

Lian was in a rage about being turned away. Lian's anger only increased Winter's anxiety; just by speaking his mind, he could put them in danger.

Winter and Lian had checked the Snow Gate, just in case. The gate was on the west side of the city, opposite the side they had entered, but it was near the tiellan quarter, anyway, and they figured they might as well check. The guard they questioned had given them that same look—pity and disdain mingled in an apathetic glare—and said he hadn't seen any men matching Knot's description. The information was useless, but at least the guard had actually spoken to them.

Now Winter and Lian were in the tiellan quarter. They'd found an inn for themselves, and had just entered the common room. Winter looked around. Tiellans were always easy to spot in crowds, but it was comforting to see a group of her people together. Tiellan tradition dictated a certain way of dressing: floor-length dresses with long sleeves and *siaras* for women; loose trousers, long-sleeved shirts, and wide-brimmed *araifs* for men. Showing as little skin as possible was the goal, though the more form-fitting trousers that many human men wore in the city were still considered inappropriate for tiellans, despite technically covering skin. Winter herself wore a traditional tiellan dress, although she had never much liked it. Tiellan modesty had always felt superfluous to her. And restrictive. Her *siara* was a comforting weight on her shoulders, but the things became horribly impractical when the weather was warm. In the country, or on her father's boat, she could sometimes get away with wearing trousers and shirts as the men did, even if she still wore her *siara*; in the city, such a thing would be far too provocative. She would draw too much attention to herself.

"This place ain't half bad," Lian said, sipping the dregs from a bowl of stew. His mood seemed to have lightened since entering the tiellan quarter. Winter felt better too. "Not half as fancy as the human inns we've been rejected from," Lian continued. "But not bad."

Only a few moments after they sat down, a tiellan man approached them, smiling broadly.

"Welcome, wanderers," he said. His familiar drawl was a welcome sound. "Ain't seen you two around. On your way someplace, or this your destination?"

Winter glanced at Lian. Honestly, she didn't know, but she couldn't tell this man that. "Destination," she said. "We're here visiting from Pranna."

Lian raised an eyebrow. The man, who Winter assumed was the innkeeper, nodded his head. "Very good. Cold it is, up there. We have the freezing winds o' the plain here in Cineste, but you have the freezing winds o' the sea." The innkeeper chuckled. "Either way you're freezing, eh?"

Winter smiled. She wasn't in the mood for small talk, but she didn't know how to make the man go away without being rude.

"Can I get the two of you anythin' more?" the innkeeper asked.

Winter was about to say no, when Lian spoke up. "A mug of ale."

"Aye," the innkeeper said, then looked at Winter.

"Nothing for me, thank you," she whispered, avoiding his

gaze. *Why don't you just look at him?* she asked herself. He wasn't a human. There was no reason to fear him.

The man nodded. He moved as if to turn away, but stopped. He leaned down low, close to their table.

"If you're here for the you-know-what," he whispered, looking over his shoulder, "we're meetin' in the back room at midnight. You're both welcome; we welcome fresh faces."

He turned and left.

Winter peered after him. "What was that about?"

Lian glanced over his shoulder, and then down at the table. "Don't know," he said.

Winter narrowed her eyes. She knew Lian. She knew what he looked like when he was telling the truth, and she knew what he looked like when he was lying. And he was definitely lying.

"You know, don't you? What was he talking about, Lian?"

Lian shrugged, looking around the room. "Look, I... I've been going to these meetings for the past few years, whenever I've come to Cineste."

Winter raised her eyebrows. Anything that would get Lian out of Pranna must be important, indeed.

"They're for tiellans who are sick of the status quo. Who want change, and are willing to do whatever it takes to make it happen."

"Whatever it takes?" Winter repeated. She didn't have to ask for clarification; she knew what it meant.

They were willing to fight.

She shook her head. "Why, Lian? Nothing will come of it. Things have hardly changed in the past century."

"Pointless it may be, but it's *right*," Lian said. "The way we're treated *ain't*, and the Druids—"

Winter scoffed. "The *Druids*? That's what you call yourselves?

85

That's archaic, Lian. From fairy tales and myths. Might as well call yourselves mummers—you'll be taken just as seriously."

Lian frowned, and Winter felt guilty. She wasn't being fair.

"The Druids represent everything good in tiellans," he said. "All the qualities we've lost. And it's not a name from fairy tales; it's from the Age of Marvels."

"Same thing," Winter muttered. The Age of Marvels had come and gone more than three thousand years ago. A time of magic and wizardry, when horrifying monsters and beautiful creatures, now long extinct, had walked the Sfaera. It was a time when the tiellan ruled, and the humans respected and loved them for it.

Supposedly. Many debated whether or not the Age of Marvels had actually occurred.

Winter resisted the urge to roll her eyes. She didn't want to be cruel, but Lian made it so easy.

"The tiellans were once glorious," Lian said, his eyes lighting up. Despite his foolishness, his demeanor caught Winter off guard. She had rarely seen him this passionate. "We were the defenders of nature, the champions of the Sfaera. We lived in harmony with Canta *and* the Elder Gods. We taught humans how to live honorably, how to till and care for the earth."

"You don't really believe that, do you? Next you'll claim the ancient tiellans lived thousand-year lives and spoke with the trees." All things from stories they'd been told, growing up. Every tiellan knew them. But no tiellan truly believed them. Winter certainly didn't. They'd always seemed silly to her.

"They *did*," Lian said. "We can have that glory again. We can become what we once were."

Winter shook her head. "Can't find a glory that never existed."

Lian regarded her for a moment longer, then sighed deeply, sitting back in his chair. "You'll understand, one day," he said. "You'll understand why this is so important."

The two of them sat in silence.

The innkeeper returned with Lian's ale. Lian waited for him to leave, then spoke again. "Don't mean to pour salt on a wound, princess, but we've got to talk about what we're doing here."

"I know," she said.

"We didn't find anything. Not a single clue telling us where Knot could be."

"I know."

"If Knot's left the city, we're already losing ground."

"I *know*," Winter said. She glanced over Lian's shoulder. Despite the inn being in the tiellan quarter, there were still a few humans in the common room. A group of them, young and rowdy, laughed and drank and made lewd comments to any tiellan who happened to pass too close. One other human, an older noble by the looks of him, dressed in a fine, brightly colored waistcoat and dark suit, sat at a table by himself. Everyone else in the room gave him a wide berth. Winter frowned.

"What do you think he's doing here?" she asked, nodding at the man. "Behind you."

Lian casually turned to the side, looking behind him. He shrugged.

"Having a good time, apparently," he said.

The man *was* having a good time. He was smiling, nodding politely to everyone who passed by, human and tiellan alike. The tightness in Winter's chest returned, which made her angry even as fear crept into her. This man looked harmless. Why should she be afraid of a human here, of all places? If she couldn't feel safe in a tiellan inn, where in the Sfaera *could* she feel safe?

And yet, despite her anxiety, Winter wondered. She had never been superstitious—religion and superstition seemed to go hand in hand to her, one as useless as the other—but something tugged at her. Perhaps this man was here for a reason.

"Winter, I hope you're not—"

"I'm going to talk to him," she said. "You never know, right? Aren't you the one that always talks about faith?"

"This ain't what I mean."

Winter was about to argue when she felt a chill. Someone had entered the common room, allowing a gust of cold wind to rush in through the open door. She turned.

Standing in the door was another man. Another *human*.

Some of the tiellans murmured. Winter could understand why. This was their space. They weren't allowed in any of the human inns, but humans were allowed to invade theirs whenever they wished?

The newcomer looked around the room quickly, then took a seat at an empty table. He was short, for a human. About Lian's height. He had dark hair and eyes, and the shadow of a beard.

The humans in the room hadn't seemed to notice this one's arrival. The group in the corner still drank, laughed, while the other human, the finely dressed man, only smiled.

"Winter…" Lian said.

She steeled herself. They needed information—something, anything, to go on. They wouldn't get anywhere if she didn't take risks.

Winter stood and walked towards the finely dressed man's table. She forced a smile but she could hardly breathe, her chest was so tight.

The man smiled back at her. He wasn't as old as Winter had first thought. A portly frame and thinning hair made him seem older, but now she looked at him closely she realized that he'd certainly seen fewer than forty summers. He might even be only five or six years Knot's senior.

"Hello there, miss," the man said, his smile widening. Winter detected the sour stink of ale on him. The smell didn't fit with his smooth, tailored clothing.

"Hello," Winter said, trying to sound confident and friendly at the same time. The combination was difficult, especially while trying to quell the fear roiling within her.

"What's a lady like yourself doing in a tavern rough as this?" The man raised his mug to the room.

*He didn't call me an elf,* Winter thought, with the barest hint of hope. *That's something.* He was the first human in the city who hadn't used the derogatory term.

"I'm looking for a friend of mine," Winter said. "A human. About your age. Average height. Brown hair. Have you seen him?"

"Friend of yours?" The man took a long gulp from the mug of ale in his hand. "What manner of friend is he, if you don't mind me asking?" The man examined her, his eyes roving up and down. "Feel free to sit, my dear. I won't bite; I'm only human, after all."

Winter sat across from the man. She breathed deeply. This man seemed well-mannered enough. Perhaps she had chosen the right person, after all.

"Please," Winter said, looking the man in the eye, "what about my friend? Have you seen anyone like that? His name is Knot."

"You have dark hair," the man muttered. His eyes still

wandered her body. "Not something you see often in tiellans, not in this part of the world. You from around here?"

"Born here," Winter said, a creeping sensation of discomfort beginning in her gut. "About my friend…"

The man gulped more ale. Some of it ran down his chin. "Your friend, of course." The man shrugged. "Afraid I haven't seen him, miss."

The disappointment was sharper than Winter had expected. The feeling must have shown on her face.

"Now, now," the man said, grinning. "Just because I haven't seen him anywhere, don't mean I can't help you out a bit."

Winter moved forward to the edge of her seat. "If you could, I would be grateful."

The man slid around the table, wooden chair scraping against the floor, so he was sitting next to her. "I may not have seen your friend, miss," he said, "but *I* can be your friend, if you like."

Then the man's hand was on her thigh. Winter looked down. The hand was hairy, and heavy on her leg.

"How much for a night?" he asked.

Winter looked up, not comprehending. Then the man's hand rubbed up her thigh, higher. Before Winter knew what she was doing, her hand shot out and slapped the man on the face.

His head snapped away with the blow, and slowly he turned back to her. Winter hadn't meant to hit him that hard. She hadn't meant to hit him at all.

She looked around frantically. The room was suddenly silent. Panic rose within her. She had just hit a human.

"That was unkind, miss," the man said. His jovial tone was gone, replaced by something different. Darker. He stood. He was much larger than Winter had realized, towering over her.

"I would have paid you," he said. "I don't know what you

have against that. The way I see it, a young elf could always use some coin. Now I'll just take what I want for free." He gripped her arm roughly, lifting her out of her chair.

Then Lian was there.

"Let her go," Lian said. He sounded brave, but his eyes were wide as he looked up at the man.

The man didn't say anything. His fist lashed out. Lian crumpled to the floor.

Winter cried out, but Lian didn't respond. The blow must have knocked him out cold.

"Damn elves," the man muttered. Then he began dragging Winter to the doorway.

Winter looked around frantically. The other tiellans in the common room stared at them, but no one stood or said anything. The humans in the corner sniggered.

In that moment, Winter knew she was alone.

Panic raged inside of her, now more than ever, but she pushed it deep down inside her. She looked at the man as he dragged her out into the cold. His eyes were dull.

"Let go of me." She did her best to keep her voice calm.

The man didn't respond.

"Please."

The man said nothing. She tried to yank free. It was like struggling against an iron shackle. The man may have been drunk, but he was strong.

"Why are you doing this?" Winter tried to yank away again, but it was useless. Her breath grew labored, barely misting in the cold.

"Why would I not do this?" the man said, although it didn't feel like he was addressing her. He seemed to be muttering to himself. "You're an elf," he said. As if it explained everything.

Winter looked around for help, but the streets were empty. This man would rape her, leave her for dead. Who knew whether Lian was all right? If a common room full of tiellans wouldn't help her, Winter didn't know who would.

That didn't stop her from screaming. The man struck her.

"Don't do that," he said. He turned into an alleyway, pulling her along. "I would have taken you to a nice room," he said. "I would have treated you well. Too late now. You don't deserve it." He looked down at her. "I suppose you never did."

Then he thrust Winter up against a stone wall, cold against her back even through layers of clothing. Winter struggled to breathe, her chest getting tighter.

"Please——" she begged, but the man leaned in and forced his mouth on hers. She struggled, squirming between the wall and the man's massive frame, but he held her too tightly. His tongue shoved past her lips; she tasted ale and whiskey. She tried to scream, but her voice was muffled. Suddenly, she couldn't breathe at all. She beat the man with her fists, tried to kick him, to knee him in the groin, even as she struggled to breathe. She fought with all her strength, flailing wildly. Her head began to ache, she felt her face getting warm, but she fought.

It didn't matter. The man didn't stop. His tongue invaded her mouth again, but this time Winter bit down hard.

The man growled, and punched her in the stomach. Winter unclenched her jaw and the man pulled away as she doubled over, collapsing in the snow.

"Shouldn't have done that," the man said, spitting blood into the snow. Winter couldn't look up. Her gut hurt too much. She tried to breathe, but could only choke on the pain. She felt him kick her the first time, and felt it less the second. She wasn't sure if he continued after that. He was talking to her, growling, really, but she couldn't focus on what he was saying.

The snow was inviting beneath her, soft and cold.

*I'm going to die here,* she thought. *I'm going to die here, and it's my own fault.* She had dragged Lian to Cineste for nothing. Knot would certainly never know. No one would. In the morning she would be nothing more than another tiellan body. No one would care.

*Perhaps I'll see my father.*

The man was on top of her. Winter felt his weight. She let herself go, hoping she wouldn't be present for whatever came next.

But the man didn't move. He just lay on top of her, the entire weight of him. Winter began to struggle, trying to work her way out from underneath him, but then the man rolled away.

Winter gasped. She cringed, covering her face, expecting the worst.

"Are you all right?"

Winter opened her eyes. She squinted in the darkness. It wasn't the finely dressed man who stood over her.

"Knot?"

"Are you all right?" the figure asked again. "Can you stand?"

Winter looked around. The finely dressed man lay on the ground beside her. Beneath him, the snow was red.

"Knot?" Winter asked again. Then, she felt herself slipping, and collapsed back into the snow.

# 8

*Somewhere between Cineste and Brynne, northern Khale*

"I'D ASK IF YOU were frightened of monsters under the bed, but if you're afraid of anything that small then there's not much I can do for you."

Knot sat up. He and Astrid were in the small camp they'd made, a few days' travel outside Cineste. Astrid sat near the fire, partially illuminated by the flames.

Knot breathed heavily. He had dreamt of creeping through a castle at night, and murdering a lord and his lady. Their young daughter had come into their room just as Knot killed them. An innocent child. In his dream, Knot hadn't hesitated.

Not a dream, Knot knew. Not quite a nightmare, either, but something closer to a memory.

"I was teasing," the girl muttered. Knot couldn't look at her. The girl he had murdered in his dream looked too much like this *thing* that now accompanied him.

"Want to tell me what that was all about?" Astrid asked.

"No," Knot croaked. His throat was dry.

"Have it your way," Astrid said, shrugging.

Knot coughed, reaching for his cloak. Life on the road was cold; the fire and heavy blankets made a difference, but he still felt it. It never quite left him.

"How long before dawn?" he asked.

"Not long." She stirred the embers of the fire with a branch.

"We should move on. Get an early start."

"Whatever you say, boss."

Knot frowned as he gathered his belongings. His pack, his boots, his knife, and a staff he'd pilfered from the inn common room. Meager supplies, but enough. He traveled light. The staff, made of blackbark wood, was a lucky find. Knot felt somewhat guilty for stealing it, but blackbark was strong, almost as strong as steel, and lighter. The staff would make an effective weapon.

Knot looked at the vampire. Whenever he asked why she was accompanying him, she just made a joke. Damn frustrating. But leaving the city, he'd been glad of her. His pursuers tracked a lone man, not a father and daughter.

But now, Knot started to wonder whether the idea had been that good after all.

Astrid stood, donning the large, ragged black cloak that had been folded neatly beside her. Beneath she wore a simple dark green dress and wool stockings. Knot was surprised the girl wasn't freezing to death. Any normal person would be.

It was easier than he liked to think of her as a little girl. She seemed so... normal. Though the way she spoke made him wonder how old she really was. Like a grown woman in a child's body.

*Ain't exactly normal.*

He sighed, tightening his leather boots. "What'd you say the next city was?" he asked. Knot had only told Astrid he was traveling as far as Navone. He hoped to escape the girl's company before he crossed into Roden.

Astrid grunted as she tightened the straps on the small leather pack she carried. "Brynne. Then we turn north, following the Tiellan Road, to Navone. The border city."

"Why can't we cut north-west and go straight to Navone?"

"No roads. And you might fancy trekking over the Sorensan ice fields in the middle of winter, but I don't. They say some of the crevices cut all the way into Oblivion itself."

Knot couldn't say he wasn't tempted, if only to shove Astrid into one of them.

"Have to go through Brynne to get to Navone. Not much leeway this time of year."

Knot nodded. He could picture Navone clearly in his mind. Brynne sounded familiar, but brought nothing specific. *Got to be a pattern, a connection I'm missing.* Sometimes words and locations resonated with him, sometimes they didn't. And sometimes, like Roden, they pulled him ever closer. If Knot didn't know any better, he'd say he had no choice but to make his way there. He needed to figure out why.

The Tiellan Road was well known. During the great purges in Roden decades ago, Roden expelled its remaining tiellan population, forcing them to walk through the Sorensan Pass in the middle of a harsh winter. Navone refused to let such a large group through the Blood Gate, wary of some ploy from Roden. Trapped in the Sorensan Pass, hundreds of tiellans perished. When Navone finally realized the tiellans were harmless, they let the battered, beaten people pass through their gates and onward along the southern road, which then became known as the Tiellan Road.

Knot remembered Khalic history just fine, apparently. His own was still a mystery.

"Ready?" he asked, looking at Astrid. She'd swept a layer of snow over the remaining coals, and was securing her pack.

"I've been ready," she said, grinning. "It's you we're waiting on."

Knot shook his head and trudged towards the road.

* * *

They walked along the Sunset Road as dawn broke around them, heading west. Huge snow drifts, some three rods deep, lay against the rocks that rose either side of them. A few pine groves, lonely in the vast whiteness, dotted the countryside. Knot observed what he thought might be a *rihnemin* rising out of the snow, but he could not be sure. The great stone monuments were some of the only remains of the ancient tiellan kingdoms. Now nothing more than ruins, they were almost indistinguishable from boulders.

"All right, darlin'. You going to tell me why you're still around, or is that too much to hope for this morning?"

Astrid exhaled. Knot noticed her breath didn't mist in the cold, the way his did.

"All right," she said slowly. "I'll tell you."

Knot looked at Astrid in surprise.

Her eyes were downcast. "I don't know exactly how to explain it, but I feel a connection with you."

"A connection?" Knot frowned.

"Something I haven't felt in a long time. As if I already *know* you."

Knot wondered what in Oblivion the girl was talking about. And yet, at the same time, he wondered if there was truth to it. Knot *did* feel something for the girl. Vexation, mostly, but something else, too. A shadow of something forgotten.

Astrid shook her head. "I know it's stupid. I know it's unconventional. But…" she looked up at him, and Knot felt her hand touch his own, "I hope that someday, we can be more."

Knot pulled his hand away. "What in Oblivion…"

Astrid burst out laughing.

*Of course*. Knot didn't respond. Why he'd hoped for a serious answer, he didn't know.

"Canta rising, you need to laugh more," Astrid said, still giggling.

Knot said nothing. He looked back the way they had come, as he did every so often, just to be safe.

"Look, I have my own reasons for staying. You may or may not find them out as we go," she said.

This time Knot did laugh, short and abrupt. "That's it?" he asked. "You expect me to travel in the company of a vampire, and the only explanation you'll give me is that 'you have reasons of your own'?"

"That's it." Astrid smiled. "At least for now. It's not like you can get rid of me."

"That's the problem," Knot muttered. Those with ventus blood were faster and stronger than any normal human, or tiellan for that matter. Vampires supposedly didn't take well to sunlight, but he couldn't be sure that was true. The day looked to be cloudy, the sun peeking through only on occasion. The girl kept her hood drawn over her face, hiding her in shadow. Knot made note of that. Until he found a weakness, he didn't stand much of a chance against her—even with his own mysterious skills.

"At least tell me something about you," Knot said after a pause. "You owe me that much."

"Maybe. What do you want to know?"

"Your eyes glow at night. Right now they're brighter than normal. But in daylight they're dark. Why?"

Astrid shrugged. "I don't know. They change with the light. The brighter it is, the less light they give. Far as the 'why' is concerned, I couldn't tell you. Even immortals don't know everything."

"And... *you're* an immortal?" The idea that this little girl walking beside him could live forever seemed ridiculous.

"I won't die on my own, that's for sure. But if someone tried hard enough..."

"Or you killed yourself," Knot added, half hoping she'd take it as a challenge.

Astrid shook her head. "No. Any harm I do to myself is... negated."

Knot wondered what she meant by that. But, sensing she was being more open than she had been since she joined him, he pressed onward.

"How old are you?"

Astrid touched his hand again, and threw her other arm across her forehead. Her voice dripped melodrama. "That's why our relationship would never work. People would think it's because you're older than me, but we would know the truth. I'm two hundred years your senior; our love is doomed, Knot."

Knot frowned.

"Seriously, who shat in your gruel?" Astrid muttered. "I don't really know how old I am," she said. "I remember the formation of the Parliament and the King Who Gave Up His Crown, and the end of the Thousand Years War. But before that things are difficult to piece together. Nameless faces, meaningless locations. Just shadows, really."

*I know the feeling.* Knot did the calculations in his head. "More than two hundred years my senior is about right." If what she said was true, the girl had seen at least two hundred and fifty summers, probably more.

The road curved in the distance, with snowy hills rising up to either side. They had entered the beginnings of a sparse pine forest, the first major vegetation they'd encountered since leaving Cineste. He appreciated the difference in scenery. Traveling grew mighty dull. Same terrain, same routine, same food day after day could drive a man mad.

Knot tried to make his next question seem a logical progression of the conversation, but he knew his voice sounded strained. "You said someone *else* could kill you. How does that work?"

Astrid giggled; the childlike quality of the sound irked Knot. She truly seemed a little girl. "A bit too early in our relationship to be talking about that, don't you think, love? We haven't even told our parents." She patted his arm. "Maybe one day, Knot. But that's not something I'll tell just any man off the street. Not something I'll tell you right now."

"Thought you said we had a connection."

The girl grinned, her eyes widening, and she laughed.

Knot almost felt himself smile. The girl had an infectious humor, even if it was too much at times. *Most* times.

But the talk of courtship only made Knot think of Winter, and Knot couldn't handle that. Not yet.

"As long as we're getting to know each other," Astrid said after a moment, "what did you do before being a... what was it you said you were? A fisherman?"

Knot clenched his jaw. Maybe there was nothing for it, now. Hiding the fact that he didn't know anything certainly wasn't doing him any favors. So he told her, about his memories—or the lack thereof. Bits and pieces and shades of things. How his body remembered, but his mind did not.

"Is that why you could take on an acumen and a telenic at the same time? Because of what your body remembers?"

Knot shrugged. "Guess so."

"You're a nomad," Astrid said. "Like me. Some pair we

make, eh? The vampire and the nomad. Can't remember who we are. Won't tell each other anything. Don't trust one another. Some pair, indeed."

They walked in silence for a while. After a few minutes Knot turned to check for signs of pursuit. Then he saw them.

He kept walking.

"We're being followed," he said quietly.

The girl nodded. "Four of them. Bandits."

"How long have you known?"

She shrugged. "They watched from the trees for a while, then started following us when we came to the thicker part of the forest."

She had known about them this whole time, and hadn't thought it necessary to tell him. Knot would have to talk to her about that. For now, he looked around casually at the tall, dark-green trees surrounding them.

"You can handle yourself, in the daytime?" he asked her.

"Better than you," she said. "But I'm *always* better in the dark."

If she was as good as she said, there probably wasn't much danger. Unless there were more than he had already counted. And they had bows.

"You might have to handle this one yourself, though," Astrid said.

Knot gaped at her. It didn't seem like a jest.

"Why would I handle it myself," he asked, "when I have a perfectly good vampire?"

"That's exactly why," she said. "Vampires? Not common. If word spreads of a man traveling with a child vampire, I don't think we'll find much hospitality."

"I'd rather be alive and not welcome than dead and... dead."

"Such eloquence. I'll do what I can, nomad. Just don't cry to me when people are burning your dismembered carcass."

Knot paused. Perhaps she was right. Just a bit.

"I'll take the lead," he said. "Same as before. You're my daughter, and we're traveling to... ah... to..."

"Brynne. Canta rising, you *do* have memory problems."

"Whatever, darlin'. We're traveling to Brynne. My cousin set up a job for me there. Cineste was growing too difficult."

"Because of all the yucky elves," she said, making a face.

Knot's glare hardened, but he didn't say anything. It would work with their story. "So," he said, "any suggestions on how to confront them?"

"It's too late for us to decide," Astrid said, as three men stepped out of the trees onto the road ahead of them.

Knot cursed. That made seven, now. "Not sure you'll have the option of sitting this one out," he muttered.

"I can be subtle when I want to be, Father dear."

Knot looked ahead at the three men. The man in the middle was huge, a head taller than Knot. The man on the right was probably just as heavy, but shorter. It was the man on the left, a few fingers shorter than Knot, with a scarred, pockmarked face, who might be a problem. The man's eyes, a deep brown, were cold. Knot had seen this type before. This one wasn't in the thieving business for money. He was in it for blood.

"Hello there," bellowed the tall man in the middle. "We're just humble thieves, looking for coin. What've you got?"

Knot remained silent.

"No one has a sense of deviousness anymore," Astrid muttered. "I miss the days when you bantered with the people about to rob you."

"Don't have much," Knot said. "Few coppers, a silver or

two is all. Ain't worth your time, sirs."

"Coin is coin," the tall man said, "and it's always worth our time. But we welcome weapons, too, and clothing, and nice wool cloaks… like that one you got on there." He nodded towards Knot.

"Heh." The fat man on the right. "This one deserves to be robbed. What kind o' man wears the warm cloak hisself and leaves his daughter in nothing but a ragged one?"

"Unless it ain't his daughter," the tall man said. "Perhaps he's in the trading business, as it were. What d'you think, lads?"

Knot stepped forward. While the thought of Astrid being traded to anyone was enough to make him laugh, Knot thought of her as she appeared to the men. A little girl, not yet ten summers. Like the girl in his dream.

"She *is* my daughter," he said coldly. "And I'd appreciate a kinder tone. She don't like mean folk."

The fat man hooted. "Got ourselves a cheeky one here, boys!"

"Look, friend," the tall man said, "just give us the coin, and your cloak. Any weapons you may have. Then you and your *daughter*," he said with a sneer, "can be on your merry way."

Knot shook his head. He gripped the blackbark staff firmly.

"If it persuades you any, there's four more of us behind you."

Knot glanced over his shoulder, where the four other men stood. "Men" wasn't accurate; one boy hardly seemed older than Astrid.

Knot held his breath. One carried a bow. Stupid of them to bring their bowman out in the open.

"Aye," the tall man continued. "We really don't want trouble." He grinned, his teeth surprisingly straight, albeit a dirty yellow color. "Just your coin."

"Knot," Astrid whispered behind him, "now's the time…"

Knot had already thrown his knife into the fat man's throat.

The tall man roared, brandishing a large club that seemed hardly more sophisticated than a heavy tree branch. But the tall man would have to wait. Knot turned quickly, moving to the man with the bow.

The man, certainly younger than Winter, no more than nineteen summers, looked at Knot with wide eyes. Knot wondered whether the boy had ever seen real combat. Knot's staff whipped across the top of the boy's head with a crack, and he collapsed.

Knot turned, holding his ground, as the other two men in front of him advanced, the tall man in the lead. Knot twirled the staff in his hands. The blackbark whipped around him in a blur, circling from hand to hand, as easy as anything Knot had ever done.

He was showing off. Nothing wrong with that, though, sometimes showing off was the best thing you could do in a fight. The best thing in the beginning, anyway. And in this case, it was working. The men stopped, staring at his twirling staff.

"C'mon, lads," the tall man said, "he's just one man."

"Watch my back," Knot muttered to Astrid. The snow crunched beneath his boots as he shifted his weight. Then he attacked.

The staff blurred straight past the tall man's club and connected with the bandit leader's head with a loud crack. The man stumbled, attempting to swing at Knot, but missed completely. Before the man could recover, Knot's staff cracked twice more against the man's face. His eyes rolled up and he collapsed into the snow.

Knot felt the thrill of it, the rush of blood coursing through him. He'd chosen the staff because the bloodlust he'd felt whenever he'd killed was not something he wanted to cultivate.

It was a lot harder to kill someone with a length of wood. But now, as the thrill rose inside of him, he wished he'd chosen a more effective weapon after all.

Someone grunted behind Knot. Knot looked over his shoulder to see Astrid dodge a grab and then smash her small fist into her attacker's knee. The man screamed as his knee bent backwards beneath him. Astrid leapt on top of him, and the screaming stopped.

The snow crunched behind Knot, and he ducked under the swing of an axe. He lashed out with his staff but only clipped his assailant, who staggered directly into Astrid. The girl leapt into the air, twisting the man's head around with a snap.

Knot rolled to the side to find himself face to face with the pockmarked man, rusty longsword drawn. The bandit swung, and Knot leaned to the side. The man swung again, and Knot leaned in the other direction, thrusting the butt of his staff towards the pockmarked man's belly. The man parried, still smiling.

Before Knot realized what he was doing, or why, he stepped back, jabbing his elbow behind him and into another bandit's nose with a *crunch*. No time to wonder how in Oblivion Knot knew the man was approaching. The bandit crumpled to the ground, and then Astrid was on him with a low growl.

Knot had killed the fat man with his dagger, and he suspected Astrid was killing every bandit she got her hands on. He hoped she hadn't reached the boy. These people were desperate; that didn't mean they deserved to die.

Or so part of him thought. Another part of Knot relished the flowing blood, both through his own veins and from his enemies. A part of Knot reveled in every kill and craved more.

Knot dodged another cut of the pockmarked man's blade, spinning around and swinging his staff. It glanced off the man's shoulder. The man attacked again, swing after swing coming down hard. Knot parried, trying to avoid the blade, but he was getting tired. He wouldn't last much longer, and he wanted to avoid a direct blow to his staff—despite being made from blackbark wood, it wasn't indestructible.

The pockmarked man was fast, but his footwork was off. He stepped forward when he should've stepped left; he stood his ground when he should have stepped back. Knot's momentum flowed from each parry to the next, from each swing to each dodge. The bandit had training but lacked fluidity, discipline.

Knot's staff finally jutted through the man's attack, the blackbark rod ramming into the man's throat. The man choked for a moment, and that was all the time Knot needed to finish. Before his opponent could recover, Knot had drawn his dagger and pierced him three times in the chest.

Knot turned. Standing before him, as if frozen in place by the cold, was the boy. Beside Knot, Astrid stood, someone groaning in the red snow beneath her. Then, the vampire advanced on the boy.

"Wait," Knot said. Astrid stopped, turning.

Looking at the boy, Knot felt a twinge of regret that he had killed in front of this child. Knot wished he could have saved him from that. Such things didn't belong in a head so young.

Nevertheless, there was work to be done.

"Boy," Knot said. The boy remained still, staring. "*Boy*," Knot said again, sharply. The boy flinched, and met Knot's eyes for a moment. Then he looked away.

"Yessir?"

"Who was the leader here?"

The boy pointed, silently, at the pockmarked man.

Knot moved to the man's body. After a quick search—

he took a small dagger the man carried—Knot found a large satchel full of coins.

Gold.

"Where did he get these, boy?"

"F-from another man, sir. A f-foreigner. Ugly, with a big scar all over his f-face."

Knot grew very cold. Could be coincidence, but the description matched. The tall man who had led the attack at his wedding had a scar and a Rodenese accent. Lately, Knot was having a hard time believing in coincidences.

"Very well," Knot said. He slipped a gold coin from the satchel into his own coin pouch—full of coppers and a few silvers, just as he had told the man—and tossed it to the boy. He would have given the boy the satchel, but knew there would be no way for the child to keep that much gold to himself. Not for long.

"Take this and go," he said. "Buy yourself out of this life."

Astrid turned, looking at Knot sharply. "He's seen me," she hissed. "He knows what I am."

Looking at the boy, Knot doubted that was true. Maybe the boy had heard of vampires, but he was in a daze. He wouldn't be able to remember anything clearly, let alone the fact that a child took out half the attackers.

And yet, there was a part of Knot that agreed with Astrid. Not because he thought the boy would present a problem, but because his desire to kill still raged through him. Just as it had after his wedding, after killing the watchmen in Pranna. His hand twitched, fingers clenching.

"Go," Knot said, through clenched teeth.

The boy took off running.

Astrid stared at Knot for a long time. "You let him go," she said.

Knot didn't respond, breathing heavily. The feeling of his blood rushing through him faded, slowly. In its place was only fear.

He had nearly killed the child.

"Canta rising," Astrid murmured. "I thought *I* was a murderer. You *wanted* to kill the boy."

Knot shrugged. "I didn't, though."

Astrid's eyes narrowed. "No, you didn't at that. You showed him kindness, nomad."

Knot shook his head. "A mercy, not a kindness. That money may bring him more trouble than it's worth."

Astrid didn't respond. She walked over to the fat man's corpse, retrieving the dagger from his neck. She cleaned it in the snow and handed it back to Knot. He couldn't tell what she was thinking. Her eyes glowed, faintly.

Finally, she smiled at him. "You all right?" she asked. "You look like this is the first time you've ever killed someone."

"If only," he muttered. He saw Astrid looking at the corpses, and something finally clicked.

She was licking her lips.

Before he could say anything, she spoke. "Look," she said, and for the first time, Knot heard a hint of... what? Sincerity? Embarrassment? "I haven't fed in nearly a month. It's about time I did."

Knot looked at her. It was the first time he had seen her jumbled like this, out of sorts. "Go ahead," he said. "I'll just... take a look around, for a minute. Call if you need anything."

The girl nodded, eyes downcast. "All right," she said softly, "you do the same."

Knot walked into the forest. He needed a moment alone, anyway.

# 9

*Nazaniin outpost, Cineste*

"WHERE'S KNOT?" WINTER ASKED. She had woken up moments ago in a set of bare apartments, a woman's face looking down at her. A human woman. Winter had moved as far away from the human as she could, to the far corner of the bed set against a wall. Kali, as the woman called herself, had managed to calm Winter down. But now, despite how jumbled Winter's head felt, one thing seemed clear. Knot had been there, in the alley. He had found her.

"Knot?" Kali asked. She was older than Winter, perhaps nearing her fortieth summer, but very beautiful. Deep brown hair fell around her face in perfect waves. Her eyes were the color of a warm, summer sky. And she was tall.

"He saved me," Winter said. "In the alley. Where is he?"

Kali frowned. "Nash saved you. You'll meet him in a moment. As for this 'Knot,' I'm afraid I don't know who you're talking about."

"I saw him. I thought…" Winter closed her eyes, trying to control her breathing.

"If there was another man in the alley, we didn't see him," the woman said. "Nash intervened just in time."

Suddenly, the weight of all that had happened came crashing down. The memory of the inn, the man striking Lian and then taking her out into the cold…

Winter couldn't think about that now.

"What about Lian?" Winter asked.

"In the other room," Kali said. "He's all right. He's been asking about you."

"I want to see him."

Kali seemed to consider something, her lips pressing together. Winter pulled the quilt up around her chin self-consciously. She was powerless. This woman could do whatever she wished with her, and no one would care.

Just like last night.

"I'll bring him to you," Kali said. "But you need to rest."

Winter nodded, trying to hide her eagerness. "Thank you."

Kali left, closing the door behind her, and then Winter was alone. She looked around the room, trying to keep her mind from returning to what had happened in the alley. The room was simple, but the polished wood floors, intricately carved dresser in the corner, and large mirror on the wall bespoke wealth. Sunlight streamed in through the glass of a large window. *Glass and mirrors*, Winter found herself thinking. Two things she had never seen in a tiellan home, that was certain. *What company have we fallen in with now?*

Winter blinked in the brightness. She wondered how long she had slept.

She closed her eyes, and wasn't aware of her thoughts until it was too late. She was back in the alley, on the ground, the man's weight on top of her. Horror rushed through her.

She flinched as the door opened again, and Kali walked in. Winter was grateful for the interruption.

Behind her was a man Winter recognized. The other man from the inn, the human who had walked in shortly after she had resolved to speak with the… the finely dressed man. Winter realized, suddenly, that this was the man who had saved her. She could see how she might have mistaken him for Knot. He had similar dull-brown hair, and was roughly the same height. An easy mistake, in the darkness.

Then, walking in after the humans, came Lian.

His left eye was blackened, the cheek below it bruised, but otherwise he looked unhurt. He rushed to her side.

"How are you?" he asked, kneeling beside her bed. "I'm sorry about the inn, I'm sorry I didn't do anything sooner, I..."

"It's all right," Winter said, taking his hand. "I'm fine." What had happened was her fault. Lian had done what he could to stop it, but in the end it had been her fault. All of it. "The man took me out into an alley. He... roughed me up a bit, but fortunately," Winter nodded at Nash, "*he* saved me before things got too bad."

Lian turned to look at Nash, then back to Winter. "Are you really all right?"

Winter smiled, squeezing Lian's hand. "He just hit me a few times, that's it. I'm okay."

Kali looked at her strangely, but Winter didn't care. Lian couldn't know what the man had attempted. He would only blame himself.

"Goddess, it's good to see your face," Lian said.

Winter kept smiling. "It's not so good to see yours," she said. "You're uglier, now."

"Speak for yourself. He did a number on you, too." Lian smiled. That was good. He couldn't know.

Winter took a deep breath, then looked at Kali.

"Where are we?"

"You're in our home. Or, rather, our home away from home." Kali looked at the man beside her. "Nash and I are from

Triah. We traveled north because we heard rumors about a man we've been searching for. Nash was trying to track the man when he overheard your conversation with your attacker. It appears you're looking for someone as well. We thought that perhaps we might help one another. The man we seek is called Lathe, although he goes by other names as well."

Winter's breath caught. That was what the men who attacked at the wedding had called Knot. She exchanged a furtive glance with Lian, but they both remained silent.

"He was once a good friend of ours," Kali said. "Part of our family, you could say. Unfortunately, he disappeared a little more than a year ago. We've been searching for him ever since. We would like to bring him home."

Winter remained silent. She needed time to figure out how to react. Being in the presence of two humans, being completely at their mercy, did not help.

Lian, apparently, felt otherwise.

"We might be looking for the same person," he said.

Winter glared at him, but he ignored her. What was he doing? She couldn't imagine he was doing this just to spite her, not after what they had been through last night.

"The man we're searching for is named Knot, but... we've heard the name Lathe before. We found him in the middle of the Gulf of Nahl, about a year ago. He couldn't remember who he was, or where he'd come from," Lian continued.

Winter caught the first hint of surprise on Kali's face as her eyebrows raised ever so slightly.

"You *found* him?" Kali asked. "In the freezing gulf?"

"Aye," Lian said. "We were fishing, and found him floating out there. Thought he was dead, in water that cold. But when we pulled him aboard, the cap'n revived him." Finally, Lian glanced at Winter, a hint of guilt on his face. "He stayed with us until… something happened, two weeks ago."

"I see," Kali said, folding her long, thin arms in front of her. She exchanged a look with Nash, then her gaze returned to Winter, who suddenly wanted to shiver.

"And you are searching for this man?" Kali asked.

Winter remained silent. She turned to Lian. If she glared at him any harder, she was sure his head would burst. He didn't seem to care.

"We are," Lian said. "We think he might be headed to Roden."

"*Lian,*" Winter whispered, but she knew it was too late. Whatever information they could have kept to themselves was gone. He looked at her, eyes wide, as if only just realizing what he had done.

"Very well," Kali said, exchanging another look with Nash. Winter wished she knew what they were thinking. They were kind to take care of her, but Winter still didn't trust them.

"We must discuss this more," Kali said. "Perhaps our objectives coincide more than we thought. But for now, Winter needs rest." Kali walked towards the door and Nash followed. Then she stopped, turning to Lian.

"Lian, it would be best if Winter rested alone. She needs to sleep."

"You're not splitting us up," Winter said. She knew she sounded defensive. Oblivion, she *was* defensive. Part of her feared that Kali would say no, and there would be nothing Winter could do about it.

Kali met Winter's gaze. "Very well. You are both free to do as you please, of course. We are only here to help." She looked at Lian. "But please do see that she gets some rest. If we are indeed after the same man, he has a head start on us. We need to move as soon as possible."

As soon as the two humans had left, Winter yanked her hand away from Lian's.

"How could you, Lian?"

Lian shook his head. "I don't know what came over me. Before I knew it I was telling them everything, I... I don't know."

Winter glared at him. "I know you don't like Knot. But that doesn't mean you can betray him to people we've just met. Lian, *we don't know these people*. We have no idea who they are, or what they can do."

"That's not why I told them. Honest, princess, one moment I was just as suspicious of them as you and the next... it was like I *knew* I could trust them."

"They're *humans*, Lian. How could you?"

Lian shook his head, his eyes finally showing a hint of anger. "I know," he said, through clenched teeth. "But so is Knot," he added, more quietly.

Winter stared at him for a long time, while neither of them said anything.

"I could forgive you for being a naïve fool, Lian," she finally said. "But not for being an angry one. We're in danger, whether you realize it or not. These people may be working for the same people who attacked us *at my wedding*. The same people that killed my father. You've betrayed us to them."

Lian's eyes widened.

*Good,* Winter thought. *Let him realize what an idiot he's been.* She was speaking out of anger and frustration, but she couldn't help it.

Winter turned over in the bed and faced the wall. She immediately regretted it as pain flared through her ribs.

"Please go," she said. "Kali was right. I need rest. I can't get it with you here."

She was being completely irrational. If anything, they should be sticking together. But she couldn't tolerate him right now.

Winter heard the door close, and knew she was alone.

Something she immediately began to regret. Alone, she only had her thoughts to keep her company. She shut her eyes tightly, trying to think of anything but her wedding, her father, the man in the alley, the sour taste of his tongue.

# 10

Nash followed Kali as she stormed out of the room. She had kept a calm face while speaking with the tiellans, but he could tell she was angry.

"They were remarkably eager to share information," he said. "I don't suppose they had any help?"

"Of course they did," she snapped. "The boy did, anyway. He was easy to break. I could've had him singing the crudest version of 'The Man from Largolan' you'd ever heard in no time. The girl, however… the girl was not as easy."

Nash remained silent as they walked down the hall. The two tiellans were a strange pair. The boy, Lian, spoke with the usual tiellan drawl, but the girl spoke like a human. An *educated* human. They seemed to be in Cineste alone, and apparently had some connection to Lathe. Strange did not even begin to describe them.

"I need to talk to Rune," Kali said, throwing open the door to the room where they'd been keeping their lacuna.

Nash frowned. If Kali contacted anyone from the Triad it was Kosarin—Kali was his star pupil, after all—or Sirana. Those two handled all the logistics of the organization. Rune was the third member of the Triad that governed the Nazaniin, but he was rarely involved in fieldwork.

Nash looked at their lacuna, Elsi. The thing must have been

standing in the corner of the room, in the dark, for hours. Nash shivered. "So we found some tiellans who may, or may not, help us find Lathe. Why does Rune need to know?"

"The fact that we found them isn't the issue," Kali said, closing the curtain and turning to face Nash. "I never thanked you for that. I didn't think your idea to look through the tiellan quarter had merit, but you proved me wrong."

In all honesty, Nash hadn't expected much success. But he had overheard the girl, and something had piqued his interest. Nash wasn't completely surprised; he had learned to trust his instincts.

"That doesn't answer my question," he said.

"We need to talk to Rune," Kali said, "because the girl is a variant."

Nash stared at her.

"That's impossible."

Kali laughed, but the sound was strained. "No need to tell me that. I'm fully aware of its impossibility."

"You're sure?"

"Sure as I can be without testing her," she said. "All the signs are there, in her mind. That's why I couldn't excavate her."

Acumens like Kali could detect psimantic potential, so Nash didn't doubt her. And, as Nash considered it, he began to wonder.

"You think she's the Harbinger?" Less of a question than a statement, though the irony of it wasn't lost on him. Many in the Nazaniin, Kali included, believed the prophecies pointing towards a tiellan Harbinger were misinterpreted; they refused to believe that a being of such power could be a tiellan and not a human.

But, if this girl was a psimancer, she could change everything.

117

Of course, Kali had other reasons for being upset that a tiellan might be the Harbinger. He might feel the same way, had tiellans done that to his family.

"I don't know," Kali said. "She could be the first tiellan psimancer of the People's Age. She could be the first tiellan psimancer in recorded *history*. As much as I hate to admit it, the girl could be the Harbinger. I'll need to test her, of course, but if she is what I think she is…"

She didn't have to finish the sentence. If this girl was the Harbinger, there were dark days ahead.

"The purification of war…" Nash whispered, his mind racing.

"And the stillness of death," Kali finished. It was one of the Nazaniin Prophecies of the Harbinger. The Harbinger, who would bring unity through fire, and peace with the sword.

"How did Rune not see this?" Nash asked. The man was supposed to be the most powerful voyant in the Sfaera.

"That's exactly what I'm going to ask him," Kali said. She pulled out the voidstone and closed her eyes. "Make sure the elves don't interrupt," she said. "They're not ready for this type of psimancy. Not yet."

Nash would keep watch, of course. But he wanted to hear what Rune had to say. For a moment, he wished he was an acumen, so he could see Rune's face. Nash smiled. Watching Rune realize that someone may have found out about the Harbinger before he had would be a beautiful thing.

# 11

*Oden residence, Navone*

CINZIA STARED AT HER sister in disbelief.

"You found them *under a rock?*" Cinzia asked. "You claim to have the Nine Scriptures, the most sought-after treasure of the ages, one of the most coveted relics in Cantic history, and you are telling me you found them under a *rock?*"

They were arguing in Jane's bedroom—the room they had once shared.

Jane's face crumpled into a scowl, but Cinzia did not care. Jane was being unreasonable. Not to mention blasphemous. Little remained of the act they had put on for their family— Cinzia realized that it had indeed been an act. The embrace. The hand-holding. Cinzia felt affection for her sister, but there was more between them. It was complicated, and Cinzia did not see how it could become uncomplicated.

"You cannot expect me to believe this, Jane. It is nonsense. Complete and utter fantasy. I love you, but this is the sort of thing I cannot—and will not—condone. I am of half a mind to let the Crucible have you."

Cinzia immediately regretted that last statement.

"I did not just find them *under a rock*," Jane said. "I did not trip in the woods and find a pile of books." Jane grew somber. "It is so much *more* than that."

They stood in silence for a moment. Cinzia did not know

what to say. It was obvious: in the seven years since she had left, her sister had gone completely mad.

"You will understand in time," Jane said, more quietly.

Jane was maddeningly calm. She had shown brief flashes of irritation, but if Cinzia was honest, *she* was the one losing control. It was odd. Jane, as wonderful and outgoing a girl as she had been when they were little, had had a fierce temper. The Jane that Cinzia remembered would have begun yelling and trying to tear Cinzia's hair out some time ago. But Jane was calm, taking everything in her stride. Mostly everything, anyway.

*I will understand in time? What in the Sfaera is that supposed to mean?*

"I *understand* the situation perfectly," Cinzia said. "My sister is a heretic. That is all there is to it."

"You heard the rumors. Did you think we were doing this for fun? That things weren't exciting enough in old Navone? Or maybe we just wanted you to visit your family, for once?"

Cinzia scowled, but did not meet Jane's eyes. The underlying criticism filled her with guilt. Cinzia *could* have visited in the past seven years. But she had chosen not to.

And she resented Jane for bringing it up. This was not about Cinzia.

"What I mean," Jane continued, "is that I have had a vision of you accepting this. You do not understand it now. How could you? You are a member of the Ministry. But you will, in time. I have seen it. That is Canta's will."

"You are having visions now, too?" Cinzia could not keep the sarcasm from her voice.

"I have been having visions for quite some time."

Cinzia's eyes snapped up. Whatever Jane had said before, about scriptures and the will of Canta, was nothing compared to the blasphemy she had just uttered.

"Wait," Jane said quickly, and Cinzia sensed the worry in her voice. "Before you say anything rash—anything *else* rash—just listen to me."

"I have heard enough," Cinzia said, but she did not leave. Instead she sat down on the bed, resting her head in her hands. She was beginning to feel sick.

"I'm sorry, Cinzia, I began all of this in the wrong place. The scriptures, they are just the latest thing I have been given, the most recent piece of the puzzle. Let me start at the beginning." She sat down next to Cinzia. "Four years ago I was in the chapel, during a sermon, and the priestess quoted from Nazira." Nazira was not one of the original Nine Disciples, but a Cantic scholar whose works had become all but canonical scripture in the Denomination. "'To those lost, and to those who seek wisdom, let them bow before Her; and she will bring light to their minds, and fire to their hearts, and will not turn away, but shall make all things known unto them.' I have believed in Canta and in the Denomination for as long as I could remember. But so much was still a mystery. I thought if Canta were truly out there, she would want *all* of her children to know the truth. Not just the priestesses and disciples, not just the rich or the nobles or even just the humans. And that sermon seemed to be saying the same thing. So… I took Nazira's advice. I prayed."

Cinzia looked up. She had passed the point where she hoped all of this was some elaborate jest. This was real, and her sister was the center of it. Things were worse than she could have imagined. Only a select few of Canta's children enjoyed communication—prayer—with Her: priestesses, matrons, and the other offices in the Denomination. Cantic doctrine was clear: to speak to Canta without one of Her appointed mediums was blasphemy, which could be punishable by death. Cinzia did not like the doctrine, but there it was.

She felt Jane's hand on her arm.

"Please, do not say anything more, not until I have told you all that I am meant to tell you. Then, if you are still angry, so be it. But listen first."

Cinzia looked at her sister, and then nodded. She might as well hear what Jane had to say.

"I prayed," Jane said. "I went to Mount Madise, and prayed." She squeezed Cinzia's arm. "I received an answer, Cinzia."

To Cinzia's surprise, she felt no animosity at this statement. *Perhaps I have heard too much already. I am desensitized to heresy.* But she knew that was not the case. The truth was, she could not have described her response at all. What she felt now was entirely new to her.

"Canta spoke to me," Jane continued. "She *came* to me, in a column of fire and light. And She told me that Her religion—the Cantic Denomination—had gone astray. She told me that many in the clergy were evil, and leading Her children away from Her. She said that it was time for Her true religion to rise again, from the ashes of heresy. Like the phoenix of old."

Cinzia was numb. She wanted to laugh hysterically, but she could not tear her gaze away from Jane, whose eyes were welling up. Before realizing what she was doing Cinzia reached out to grasp Jane's hand, holding it tightly in her own.

"She said that She had chosen me," Jane said. "That I was to be Her prophetess, Her voice to the people. That I was to help lead Her followers through the rising."

Cinzia watched her sister closely. Jane did not seem like a madwoman who had visions and heard voices. Beatific visions were a thing long past. No one in the Ministry had them anymore, not even the Essera herself, the head of the Denomination and Canta's voice on the Sfaera. If no one in the Ministry had them, there was certainly no one else that could.

And yet here Jane was, as serious as Cinzia had ever seen her. It was all too much. Cinzia felt lost at sea, grasping at waves that rose high above her.

"I am sorry, Jane." Cinzia stood. "I... I am sorry." Without a backward glance she walked out of the room, out of the house, and into the night of Navone.

Cinzia found herself, of all places, before the massive bronze doors of Ocrestia's cathedral.

She looked up at the edifice, a silver circle emblazoned on the left door, a golden triangle on the right. The doors were closed, of course, so Cinzia walked around to a side entryway. The minute she entered, her troubles seemed to fade. Her worry and confusion did not disappear, but it all felt less imposing, easier to bear.

Cinzia looked around, taking in the sights of the cathedral with a distant familiarity. It had been seven years since she last set foot inside, but she had come here every week as a youth. Out of instinct more than intent, Cinzia put her fingers to her lips, and then touched the worn foot of a large statue of the Disciple Ocrestia near the entryway. Ocrestia stood tall, her hair long and flowing, wearing a robe over one shoulder. The toes of the statue had long been worn smooth from over a thousand years of reverent contact. Each of the major cathedrals in the Sfaera was named after one of the Nine Disciples; Navone had named their cathedral after Ocrestia, the Third Disciple of the First Three. Other statues and murals along the cavernous hall portrayed scenes demonstrating Ocrestia's attributes: kindness, wisdom, and temperance. Great columns stood tall on either side, and row after row of polished pews lined the center of the cathedral. When all the pews were out, the building could hold nearly twenty thousand people—more than a third of Navone's population. Cinzia had seen the cathedral filled to capacity twice in her memory. But, at the moment, only a tiny fraction of the pews were occupied, despite the evening service having already begun.

Cinzia walked forward quietly, her footsteps echoing on the vast marble floor until she joined the rest of the congregation. A few turned to look at her, but most paid her no mind. Navone housed around a dozen priestesses, and it was not uncommon for one to attend the worship of another, especially a service in the cathedral itself.

The priestess—or perhaps it was a matron, Cinzia couldn't be sure from where she sat—had already begun reciting Cantic history. As the priestess spoke, a choir behind her hummed and sang softly. Cinzia listened as their words resonated in the great hall. She loved this. The peace she felt at hearing the songs, the history recitation. Cinzia's curiosity had been what first drew her to Cantic liturgy. Learning the history of the Denomination, and of Khale itself by proxy, fascinated her. But the more she attended services, the more she found a different meaning in them. Now, they were bastions of peace in a tumultuous world.

The choir's tone became more somber, and the priestess's recitation grew louder. She was reaching the Zenith, the part of the recitation describing Canta's ministry, calling disciples, and then her death.

Cinzia looked up, letting the words and music wash over her, but she did not experience the familiar sense of peace. Instead, gnarled feelings of confusion and frustration reached out from the corner of her mind.

The singing had stopped. Now a group of disciples would walk through the congregation with water and oil, administering to the people. With an effort, Cinzia focused on the ordinance, on connecting with the Goddess she had known her entire life. What would come would come.

After the liturgy, Cinzia remained in the cathedral as the rest of the congregation departed. Cinzia could not bring herself to stand, to leave and face Jane.

Part of her wanted to curse Canta, to shout and scream and demand to know why the Goddess she had worshipped her entire life would put her in a situation such as this. But she could not be so harsh. Cinzia had grown up with the Goddess; she had grown up with the Cantic Denomination. The dimly lit carved wood, the smell of the lightly scented candles, even the hard pew beneath her made her feel at home.

And now Jane threatened to take it all away.

"It is always a pleasure to see another priestess enter this house," a voice said behind her.

Cinzia turned, rising to her feet. The speaker was an old woman, much older than the priestess who had led the ceremony, dressed in faded robes. The Trinacrya shone on her chest, in cloth-of-gold and cloth-of-silver.

"And it's even more of a pleasure to see Cinzia Oden enter this house, after so many years," the woman said with a smile.

Up close, Cinzia recognized the woman. Joyca, the priestess who had served at the cathedral when Cinzia was a child. The woman had been old *then*. Now she seemed truly ancient: her skin wrinkled, greying hair cut in short curls. Even her eyes looked old, a faded blue.

"Priestess," Cinzia whispered. How long had Joyca been

watching her? How much did she know about Jane? Did she know about the Holy Crucible?

"I'm afraid they've made me a matron, now," Joyca said, her voice tired.

Cinzia's face flushed. She should have noticed the woman's office sooner; the gold trimming along the edges of her dress was obvious.

"But please, Sister Cinzia, we're of the same world now, you and I. Call me 'Sister.'"

Cinzia nodded, but said nothing. She kept her eyes downcast, afraid to meet the matron's gaze.

"You're caught in a storm, dear. I was afraid you would come here, when I heard about your family."

"You know?" Cinzia asked.

"Of course," Joyca said. "A good mother always knows her children, even when they're getting themselves into trouble. *Especially* then."

Cinzia felt Joyca's hand on her shoulder, and suddenly she wanted to cry very much. And yet she could not.

"I did not know it was this bad," Cinzia said.

Joyca did not say anything. Instead she put her arms around Cinzia.

Cinzia's eyes widened at the show of affection. She did not remember Joyca being this sentimental. And yet she returned the embrace tightly.

Joyca grunted. "Easy, Sister Cinzia," she said. "I'm not as young as I used to be."

"What am I supposed to do?" Cinzia asked.

Joyca lowered herself to the bench, bending slowly. Cinzia sat next to her, wondering how old the woman really was—she looked as if she had seen nearly eighty summers. Her hair, dark gray with an almost blue tinge, curled around her wrinkled face. The woman's hands were stiff, the fingers bending at a strange angle, like claws.

"I've learned many things, living this long," Joyca said. "The Cantic Denomination is a great thing. It's flawed, as would be any organization run by imperfect people, but we accomplish much good."

Cinzia nodded, wiping her nose on her sleeve. Not the conduct of a proper priestess, but she did not care for protocol at the moment.

"I've learned that, although nations, kings, and parliaments pass away, there is one thing that will not, unless you let it. Family.

"I had a sister, and we were close when we were young. But as we grew, we grew apart. I joined the Ministry; she married a wealthy merchant. I served in a chapel in a small city in the north, and she lived in the great city of Triah. She used to travel to see me often, and we would argue. We argued about our different lifestyles, about politics, about the Denomination. One day, the dispute was so dreadful that we vowed never to see each other again.

"But then, many years later, as I still held tightly to my grudge, my sister came to me in Navone. Her husband had died; she had no children, and was left with enough money to support herself but didn't know what to do with it. So she came here and apologized. She said she was wrong, that she had been stubborn and prideful. The next thing I knew, I found myself apologizing as well. I had told myself for years that, if she ever came to my door, I would send her away. But I didn't. She lived out the rest of her days here in Navone, and we spent a great deal of time together. I couldn't imagine those years without her.

"The point I'm trying to make, my dear, is that you shouldn't make a decision rashly. Not when family is involved."

Joyca cleared her throat. "Don't do something you think you'll regret, unless you know you'll regret it more if you don't."

Joyca stood, slowly. Cinzia imagined she could almost hear the woman's joints creaking.

"But—"

"No buts," the matron said. "You have some things to think about, so I'll leave you to them." She smiled. "Submit to Canta's will," she said. "Don't box our Goddess in with your meager expectations of the world, my dear. Take it from someone who has learned the hard way."

Cinzia smiled as the woman walked off into the dark corridors. A door open and shut quietly, and then she was alone.

She sat back against the hard wooden bench. She looked up at the carved wood above her. Red pine, an homage to the countless red pine forests surrounding Navone.

Had Joyca, who had worked in the Ministry for most of her long life, really just told her to think twice about following Cantic protocol? Had the priestess of Cinzia's youth—a matron, now—just told her that Cantic doctrine did not matter when it came to family?

Cinzia rubbed her eyes. Joyca's presence was comforting, but she was more confused now than ever. She believed in the Cantic Denomination. But she also loved her family and, before today, would have done anything for them.

Perhaps she could still help.

Maybe that was what Canta wanted. It was a test, of sorts. Priestesses and matrons often spoke of Canta sending them difficult trials. Perhaps this was Cinzia's.

She had to save her family. She did not have to abandon them to their heretical beliefs; she could show them the correct path. She could pass Canta's test.

# 12

*Brynne, northern Khale*

"ONE ROOM, FOR ME and my daughter," Knot told the innkeeper.

He and Astrid stood in the common room of The New Parliament, the first inn they'd come across in Brynne.

"Seven coppers," the man grunted. He was a middle-aged man, with a day's growth of dark stubble and a lazy eye. "Meals?"

Knot looked at Astrid. She nodded.

"Aye. We'll come down and eat them here," Knot said, sliding the coppers across the counter.

"As you say," the innkeeper said, handing a key to Knot. "Second room on the left."

"What do you want to eat down there for?" Astrid asked as they made their way up the stairs.

Knot opened the door to their room. "Feels right."

A bed in an inn was more comfortable than a sleeping-mat under the stars, but the places felt tedious to Knot. All the rooms were alike, providing just enough for guests to feel like they had something to pay for. This room was no exception. A bed, a small table and chair. A window opposite the door, wooden shutter closed. No more, no less.

"'Feels right,' huh?" Astrid threw her pack on the bed. "What a privilege to follow someone so inspired."

"You'd think a monster like you would know a thing or two about instincts," Knot said. Maybe Astrid's repeated attempts at banter were rubbing off on him.

"That one burns," the girl said flatly. "And, just to be clear, a killer instinct, I've got."

Knot shook his head, tossing his pack on the chair. "You take the bed. I'll set up on the floor."

"You don't want to share?" Astrid asked innocently. Her eyes widened. "What if I have nightmares?"

When Knot didn't respond, she rolled her eyes. "So much for banter. Do take the bed. I don't sleep; thought you'd noticed."

Knot sighed. He had, of course.

"You still lie down sometimes," he pointed out, but felt like an idiot the moment he said it.

"I'm immortal. I'll get my share of comfort, I'm sure. Take the damn bed."

"We'll figure it out later," Knot muttered. "Let's get something to eat."

They walked downstairs. The common room wasn't particularly large, but it was warm and inviting. The New Parliament was old. Of course, if it had been around when the Parliament actually was new, it would have to be. One hundred and seventy years wasn't a bad run for an inn.

The outer walls were made of stone, which was telling. Not many buildings, let alone inns, could afford stone these days. A fire burned in a large cobbled hearth against one wall. Large round tables dotted the wooden floor, which creaked under Knot's feet.

They sat down at an empty table in the corner where Knot could observe the room. One of the servers approached.

"What can I get you?" he asked. He was young. Knot estimated the lad hadn't seen more than eighteen summers, but he had strong, handsome features, and an air of kindness about him, too. He smiled at Knot, and then Astrid.

"Got hot lamb stew, made fresh. Or there's leftover turkey from lunch, we can bring that out with bread and cheese."

"The stew," Knot said. He hadn't eaten a hot meal since he'd left Pranna.

"And for you, little one?" the server asked, smiling down at Astrid.

"Turkey, please." She was grinning at the server as if she'd just been given a candied cherry.

"Of course. Can I bring you some beer, or perhaps mulled wine?"

"Just water," Knot said. Since he'd awoken in Pranna, he'd felt no liking for drink. He already had memory issues, and he needed muffled senses like he needed a hole in the head.

"I'll bring it right out." The server strode away.

They sat in silence. Knot thought about Darrin and Eranda and their children. About Gord and Lian. And, of course, Winter. She'd surely buried her father by now, although Knot doubted she would've had it done under Cantic authority.

"What *do* you remember?" Astrid asked, interrupting his thoughts.

Knot looked up, breathing deeply. He contemplated brushing her off, but then thought better of it. No use hiding what he knew; if it made no sense to him, it wouldn't make sense to anyone else. And, if he was honest, he *wanted* to say something. He regretted never sharing with Winter exactly what was going on in his head. If he had, perhaps things would be different.

"Not much in the way of specifics," Knot said. "I see faces, sometimes, in my dreams… people who seem to know me, though they never say my name. Sometimes the dreams are just a blur, like I'm wandering in a dark space. Every so often there's a light and I see things that resonate, but it goes dark again before I can remember why or how. Always bits and pieces."

He stopped, realizing he was rambling. He frowned. The only other person he could remember rambling in front of had been Winter.

"I know a bit of what you're talking about," Astrid said, nodding slowly. "On the road today you said that your body remembers things your mind doesn't."

Knot winced. "It's... difficult to explain. Not sure I understand it. First realized it on the fishing boat I worked on. Cap'n tried to teach me how to tie knots, how to use the equipment, how to navigate. But whatever he taught me, I already knew. It came naturally, like I'd done those things my whole life. They started calling me Knot, because I was so good at tying them. Couldn't remember my name, and they had to call me something.

"At first, I thought I must've been a fisherman, before they found me. Would've kept thinking that too, if I hadn't made some... other discoveries."

"Such as?"

Knot hesitated. "A group of tiellans saved me," he said. He glanced at Astrid to see whether she would react to the news.

Astrid snorted, rolling her eyes. "Human, tiellan, I don't care. I've got bigger things to worry about."

Knot nodded. "The humans and tiellans in the town had problems, getting worse by the day, it seemed. Tiellans found me, and I enjoyed being around them, so I stayed."

"So the humans didn't like you very much."

Knot waved a hand. "I didn't care about that. Ignored them. But then, walking home from a late night at the dock, I came across a group of men. They were drunk, and they recognized me. I tried to walk away, ignore them, but they didn't let me leave. One took a swing."

Knot paused again, taking a deep breath.

"What happened when he hit you?"

"He didn't," Knot said quietly. "One moment, I was scared for my life. Next thing I remember, it was only me left standing. The others, four of them, were all on the ground, some unconscious. I hadn't even broken a sweat."

"What had happened to them?"

Knot took a deep breath. "Didn't fully remember until later, but when I did… I beat them. Brutally. Broke arms, jaws, ribs. The humans in the town looked at me different after that."

"So what were you, before?" Astrid asked.

"Don't know. Still don't. I can hazard a guess, especially if my dreams mean anything." Knot's mouth tasted bitter. Remembering some of his dreams, he could hazard a fairly accurate guess, indeed. In all his dreams, someone ended up dead. Sometimes it was himself. Most of the time, it was someone else by his hand.

He looked down at the table, staring intently at the grain of the wood. "Don't ask me what I dream about," he said. "That ain't something I'm ready for."

They were silent. Knot heard other guests laughing, the crackling of the large fire. The server brought them their food and water. Knot didn't touch his.

"So… you remember how to fight?" Astrid asked, her voice barely above a whisper. Again, Knot was surprised at how childlike she sounded. He thought once more of the girl in his dream from a few nights before. The girl he'd killed.

"I remember how to fight," he said. "And a lot more. Things I can't even begin to explain."

He nodded to a group of men around a table in the opposite corner of the room. "Those men work for the Town Watch, though they're all off duty." He nodded towards the bar. "The innkeeper has seen his share of violence, probably as a soldier, and keeps an old weapon hidden somewhere in this room, under the bar or near the door to the kitchen. Our server has been flirting with the woman by the fire, hoping she'll spend the night with him. She's married, though she's been trying to hide it, and can't decide what to do."

Astrid shrugged, glancing around at each person he referred to. "So you're good at observing people. Big deal."

Knot's eyes burned.

"I know that I can kill a man with anything you can think of. Give me a sword or give me a spoon, and I'll give you a dead man."

Astrid met his gaze, her mesmerizing green eyes looking through him. *You know you're evil when a daemon herself is wondering whether it's a good idea to stick around.*

The girl stared for a moment longer, and just as Knot thought she would get up and leave, she looked down at her plate and grabbed her food.

"Better eat your stew," she said, her mouth already full. "It's getting cold."

An hour later Knot sat at the bar in the common room, alone, an untouched mug of beer in front of him. He'd sent Astrid up to their room after they'd finished eating, knowing that if he was looking for conversation he'd be much more successful on his own.

He stared at the large map hanging on the wall behind the bar amidst shelves of whiskey and wine bottles. It depicted the

Wyndrian continent, most of which was shaped like a rough figure-eight. Khale dominated almost three-quarters of the land mass. Maven Kol and Alizia, the two southern countries, occupied small patches of the lower half. The great city of Triah, marked by a gold and silver Trinacrya, was in the center of the figure-eight, where the Great Western Gulf curved inwards in the middle of the continent and almost met the Kolean Sea on the other side.

The map was another strange characteristic of the inn. Only noblemen, traveling merchants, and military leaders owned maps. Hanging one in the common room was no small thing.

Knot mentally traced the ground he'd covered on the map. Pranna was not marked, but Knot knew where it was, almost in the exact center of Khale's northern coast. A black square marked Cineste to the southwest of Pranna. Almost directly west of Cineste was a black star that must have indicated Brynne. And, above Brynne, marked by another black square, was the city of Navone. The border city.

Navone was just south of a narrow neck of land that separated Khale from Roden. While Khale was a massive figure-eight, Roden looked like a misshapen bull's head, jutting out from the northwest corner of Khale with two long, thin peninsulas reaching northeast into the Frozen Sea. The Sorensan Mountains ran the horizontal length of the neck of land between the two countries, making passage back and forth that much more difficult. Knot would have to pass through those mountains. It was the only way to get to Roden.

Knot sighed, and turned his attention to eavesdropping on the conversations going on around him. He dismissed discussions about rebellious children and the state of Cineste's army. Then, one between two men nearby piqued his interest.

He angled himself to get a better view of the speakers.

"My cousin's from Navone," one of the men said. He was small, with sharp, beady eyes and a confident air.

"Best tell him to get out for a spell," said the other, older man. His hair was gray and long, and he wore a short-cropped beard. Knot rubbed his own chin. He hadn't shaved since leaving Pranna, and was growing a beard of his own. Had a mind to keep it, if only to make him look older and help with the father–daughter ruse he and Astrid were attempting.

"Why's that?" asked the beady-eyed man. "What've you heard?"

"Just that there's a new bloody religion in those parts. And you know how the High Camarilla feels about 'new religions' these days."

"Aye," the first man said. He looked up. "You think they're sending the Sons?"

"At least. Mayhap the Goddessguard, and a Holy Crucible to boot."

The beady-eyed man cursed. "Need to get word to my cousin," he said. "A little vacation'd do him good. Although he'd never get caught up in any of that. He's true Cantic, through and through. Better Cantic than me, that's damn sure."

"Don't matter. Holy Crucibles can look inside you. See your guts and your soul. They'll know whether he's a heretic or not, but they'll also find out if he's a thief, adulterer, smuggler, or murderer, too."

"Unnatural, is what they are," the beady-eyed man said, barely above a whisper.

Knot nodded at the two men. "I'm heading up to Roden," he said. "I take it you folks suggest I hold off?"

The two men turned towards him. They looked him up and

down, but didn't seem to think much of him.

"Roden," the beady-eyed man muttered, staring at Knot. "What business you got in Roden?"

Knot shrugged. "Ain't my choice to head all the way up there. I'm the lowest man in the Thredash Merchant Guild. I just do what they tell me." The name came to Knot's mind easily; it was a mid-sized guild in the area.

"You'll stay away from Navone, if you know what's good for you," the old man said. "For at least a month or so. A Holy Crucible's work can take time, from what I heard."

Knot frowned. He couldn't wait a month. "What about skirting around the city?" he asked.

Beady Eyes shook his head. "The Sons'll patrol the surrounding countryside, looking for people doing just that. You'll just bring a world of trouble down on you and yours. Best to wait it out, friend."

"Ain't another way to get to Roden?" Knot asked. Maybe Astrid would know of one, if these two didn't. She seemed familiar enough with the area.

The old man laughed. "Ain't from around here, are ya?" he spat. "Only one way getting in and out of Roden, and that's through Navone's Blood Gate. One way and one way only."

Knot forced a smile. "Business in Roden might have to wait. Can't say I'm overly angry about it. Roden ain't the most appealing of destinations, if you catch my meaning."

Beady eyes nodded in agreement, and the older man, who had been staring at Knot suspiciously, finally nodded as the glimmer of distrust faded.

"Aye." The old man motioned towards the innkeeper. "Can we get you a drink, stranger?"

Knot shook his head, raising his own mug. "No need," he

replied. "This is my last. Meeting a new partner tomorrow, best to be mostly clear-headed when I do."

The two men nodded, then went back to their conversation. After a moment Knot stood, handing his full mug to the first patron he saw.

"On the house," he muttered, and headed up to the room.

He was about to open the door when he stopped.

Inside, someone was talking.

Did the vampire talk to herself? Knot could not remember her doing such a thing. He strained, trying to hear the conversation.

"I don't know if he'll let me… for much longer, not… a reason." It was Astrid, that much was certain, but he couldn't make out much of what she was saying.

There was silence for a moment.

"Don't know *what* he suspects." Astrid again. "Smart, even if he doesn't remember…"

A pause.

Knot felt a stab of disappointment. He'd begun to form a strange affection for the girl. He'd wondered, once or twice, if he and Winter'd had a daughter, whether she would've turned out something like Astrid.

*Right. She'd turn out just like a daemonic monster.* Knot swallowed. He'd let his guard down, even knowing what she was.

He couldn't let that happen anymore. He couldn't really stop her from tagging along, but he would have to be on his guard. The girl was planning something. Whatever it was, he needed to be ready.

"…keep you informed… need to go." Astrid's voice again.

Knot opened the door, hoping to catch a glimpse of whoever the girl had been talking to. The room was dark. He could barely make out Astrid's small form curled up in the corner, on the floor.

Had she been that way the whole time, or had she moved that quickly? He shut the door behind him, and was about to make a comment about how he knew she wasn't sleeping, when she beat him to it.

"Just take the bed," she muttered. "Or I'll eat your face."

Knot almost responded, but kept it in. Despite what he'd just heard, the girl could still make him want to smile.

*You've got issues,* he told himself.

He settled down on the bed, looking up at the wooden ceiling as his eyes adjusted to the dark. The girl was a problem, but she wasn't his only one.

# 13

*Outskirts of Cineste*

WINTER FELT A STRANGE sense of loss as she watched the city of Cineste fade behind her. She had always felt comfortable in the wilderness around Pranna, but this was different. She was leaving all she had ever known.

She looked up at Kali, riding beside her. To Winter's surprise, the trio—Kali, Nash, and their silent servant, Elsi—had provided her and Lian with horses. Winter rode Nynessa, a small, nimble mare. She patted the animal beneath her. Winter had always wanted a horse of her own; she had loved the animals since she was a little girl, had watched longingly as human children rode horses of their own. But her father had never had the money or the need to purchase one. Now, these people had given her a horse for almost nothing. For information, and she barely had any of that.

Winter still didn't trust them. But it hadn't taken her and Lian very long to decide that their best hope to find Knot was with these people, dangerous though they might be. Both Kali and Nash wore curved swords at their hips, and Nash carried a set of strange, circular blades at his belt. Either way, there was nothing she and Lian could do to escape them at the moment.

A part of her hoped that these people might actually *help*. Her and Lian's efforts had been pitiful. That they had ever expected to find Knot on their own seemed foolish. But with

Kali and Nash's help, perhaps it was possible. Nash was friendly and kind, for the most part. He didn't look at her as if she were an object. Or an elf. He didn't look at her often, admittedly, but when he did, it was just as another person. Tiellan or human, it didn't seem to matter to him.

Kali, on the other hand, was all business, which Winter appreciated, but there was something underneath that Winter didn't trust. Who these people really were, and what they wanted with Knot, would hopefully be revealed in time. She assumed it had something to do with what Knot had done at their wedding. Lightning across dark water. The memory of him frightened her, but at the same time gave her hope. She didn't know what Kali and Nash had planned for Knot, but she did not care to find out. If Winter could get to him first, before Kali and Nash, perhaps they could escape. Or at least face these people together.

"You seem lost in thought."

Winter looked up at Kali. Even though their horses were about the same size, the woman towered over her. Winter was short for a tiellan, and that made her significantly shorter than the average human. And Kali's height wasn't average.

"There's a lot on my mind," Winter said, staring at Kali. She couldn't help it. The woman's height wasn't the only strange thing about her. Her clothing was strange—tight-fitting black trousers, a black shirt, and a black leather jerkin were men's attire—and yet Winter felt silly riding alongside her in her loose tiellan dress. She wondered what it would be like to wear such clothing. Any tiellan who saw Winter wearing such things would be ashamed to call her one of their own.

"I don't doubt it," Kali said. "Your life is changing."

Winter nodded, but didn't say anything. She turned her

gaze to the road ahead. What would she say to that, anyway?

"I've been meaning to discuss something with you," Kali said, after a moment. "What do you know of magic?"

Winter raised an eyebrow. There hadn't been any magic for centuries. "Nothing," she said, honestly. "Magic is as meaningless to me as the Denomination. They're both stories people tell to make themselves feel better."

"I'll be more specific, then," Kali said. Winter was aware of Lian pushing his horse closer to them, listening in on the conversation. Nash and Elsi led the way a few paces ahead.

"What do you know of psimancy?" Kali asked.

Winter shrugged. "Never heard of it." Kali seemed a sensible woman. Why would she care about myths and stories?

"Not surprising," Kali said. "Psimancers are rare. They use their minds to enhance certain abilities, and make connections with the world around them." Winter rolled her eyes. Kali smiled. "You think I'm lying. I'm not. But, for now, let's have ourselves a little lecture. You can listen too, Lian, it's all right. I'd like you both to hear this."

"Is she crazy?" Lian whispered.

Winter shrugged. The woman very well could be. What she was talking about sounded like it belonged in the Age of Marvels instead of the People's Age.

If Kali heard Lian, she gave no indication. "There are, essentially, three types of psimancy," she said. "But I don't want to overwhelm you, so let's just talk about two of them, for now. Telesis is the first. We call people who wield this power 'telenics.' They have the ability to move and control external objects with tendrils of power from their minds."

Winter snorted. "You're saying there are people who can use magic to move things with their heads?" She also couldn't help but wonder who the "we" Kali mentioned were.

"Not magic," Kali said, shaking her head. "Perhaps that was a bad way to start this conversation. You're a skeptic, and that actually might work to your benefit. But yes, there are people who can, as you so eloquently put it, 'move things with their heads.' Nash?"

Ahead of them, Nash stopped. He turned his horse around to face them.

Suddenly, Winter's black-stone necklace—the one she had received at her wedding—ripped from her neck and flew into Nash's outstretched hand.

Winter's breath caught. She looked at Lian, then Kali, then back at Nash. It had happened so quickly… it had to have been a trick.

"Give that back," Winter said. She didn't know how they had done it, but they had probably broken it, tearing it off her neck like that.

"As you wish," Kali said. "Nash?"

Slowly the necklace slid off of Nash's fingers, and floated towards Winter. She stared at it, mesmerized. Lian muttered a curse beside her. The necklace stopped directly in front of her, within arm's reach. It floated there, nothing holding it up. Winter reached around the necklace, looking for any hidden strings or wires.

This was impossible.

Before she could snatch the necklace out of the air, it moved towards her again, wrapping gently around her neck. There was a click, and then it was resting on her once again. She reached around, and felt the clasp. It was fastened, as if what she had just witnessed had never happened.

"How…" Winter looked up at Kali.

"Nash is a telenic," Kali replied. "One of the most skilled in the Sfaera."

Winter slumped in her saddle. She was trembling. What she had just seen *was* impossible.

But she had seen it, hadn't she?

"Nash," Kali continued, spurring her horse forward after him, "is what we call an actual. He possesses the innate ability to use his mind to manipulate objects. Born with it, you could say. Another class of psimancers exists, but... they are a bit more manufactured."

"Winter, come on," Lian said. Winter realized she had been sitting there, Nynessa fidgeting in the middle of the road, while everyone else had continued onward. She spurred the horse forward.

"Before I tell you about the other two specialties of psimancy," Kali continued, "I should point out another distinction between actuals and variants. Actuals, like Nash, have the ability within themselves. But variants require something external to bring out their talents."

Kali paused, perhaps waiting for one of them to ask what this "something" was. Winter said nothing. She was still reeling from what she had seen Nash do.

"It's a narcotic of sorts. A substance not unlike what you know as grit, or devil's dust."

"So people can just take this... drug, and they can use magic?" Lian asked.

"It's really more of a science," Kali said, frowning. "Not just anyone can take the drug and discover these abilities within themselves. A very small percentage possesses this proficiency. But yes, when they take the narcotic, their ability is temporarily accessible."

"So why don't they take the drug all the time?" Lian asked.

Winter's mind felt like it was moving at a fraction of its normal speed, refusing to process what she had just seen. This—all of it—was impossible.

"The drug—*faltira*, technically, although most who use it refer to it as frost—can be addictive."

"*Faltira*," Winter repeated.

"It means 'frostfire' in Old Khalic," Kali said.

"What about the other forms of psimancy?" Winter interjected. She felt curious now, even if she still could hardly believe what she'd seen.

"Acumency," Kali said. "While not as outwardly apparent as telesis, it can be just as powerful. Acumens delve into the minds of others, discerning thoughts. You can think of telesis as the external form of psimancy, and acumency as the internal. While the distinction isn't technical, it can be helpful when learning."

Winter frowned. As much as the idea of people controlling objects with their minds alarmed her, the idea of someone digging around in her brain was even worse.

"As I said, there is a third form of psimancy, but it is less clear-cut than either telesis or acumency. And less reliable. Best to leave that discussion for another day."

Part of Winter was suspicious of Kali keeping the third form from them, but another part was grateful. She felt a strange longing to see Nash use the power again; she was already doubting whether she had seen it in the first place. Moving objects? Reading minds? It was outrageous.

And yet she *had* seen it. Something had taken her necklace, and put it back on again. She didn't know how they could have faked that.

"Why haven't I heard about these abilities before?" Winter asked.

Kali smiled wearily. "Because of your own government and the Cantic religion. But, these abilities only started manifesting themselves a few decades ago. The few psimancers who do emerge are voraciously sought by the nobility, the government, and the Denomination. None of them want such knowledge in the hands of the public. Instead they spread rumors of 'magic' and 'sorcery.' In reality, no such things exist."

"Not anymore," Lian said.

Both Kali and Winter turned to look at him.

"What was that?" Kali asked.

"Not anymore," Lian repeated. "Magic and sorcery don't exist *anymore*. But they did, once, during the Age of Marvels."

"The Age of Marvels is a topic of much debate," Kali said.

Winter had no interest in the Age of Marvels. "If this is supposed to be a secret, why are you telling us?"

"Because we're going to test you," Kali said. "We want to find out whether either of you can access the abilities. They are… uncommon, in the tiellan race. Far less common than in humans. But I have a nose for these sorts of things, and I've sensed something about the two of you. Nash and I want to discover if my instincts are correct."

"You're an acumen?" Winter asked.

Kali smiled, genuinely this time. "I am."

The woman looked at Nash. Winter followed her gaze, squinting in the sun. She was surprised to see it was past noon already.

"Nash," Kali called, "how long until we set up camp?"

"Another few hours," Nash called over his shoulder. "Five at most."

"Be sure we have some daylight left when we do," Kali said. She looked at Winter, then at Lian. "We're going to test them tonight."

# 14

*Between Brynne and Navone*

JUST BEFORE SUNSET, THE girl ambushed him.

They'd been discussing when to choose a campsite. Astrid wanted to stop soon, while Knot wanted to continue on for a spell. Knot hadn't even turned his back on the girl—he'd been careful *not* to, especially since the conversation he'd overheard a few nights earlier. But when he looked up, she was gone.

Then she'd slammed into him from his left, and now Knot was fighting for his life.

He narrowly dodged as she swiped at him. Knot wasn't keen on finding out how claw-like her fingers could really be. He wove to the side, gripping his staff loosely. Anger filled him. He should have known. Should have confronted her about what he'd overheard, should have tried to escape instead of waiting for the right moment.

Knot swung at the girl, but it cut cleanly through nothing. Astrid snarled, darting around him, and before Knot could move he felt a thumping pain on his back as the girl slammed into him. He stumbled, the air rushing out of his lungs. She was *strong*. He gasped for air, and felt the girl leap onto his back. His blood boiled at the thought that he'd actually begun to *trust* her.

Astrid wrapped her arms around his neck, squeezing. Knot's head grew heavy. He fell to his knees, turning his head sideways to get as much air as possible, his hands pulling against hers. They were a disturbingly even match.

He dropped to the ground, twisting in the air as he did so, and slammed her against the packed snow. Knot cried out; he'd hit her with his bad shoulder. Astrid grunted underneath him, and her grip loosened for a fraction of a second. Knot felt it and jabbed his elbow into her ribs. He rolled away, sucking in air.

One instinct told him to back away, but another—the one he'd learned to trust, and to fear—told him to press the attack. He pounced, dagger drawn. She caught it with both hands, but even her strength couldn't stop the downward motion of the dagger as it pierced her neck.

The girl laughed, the sound eerie and morbid, gurgling through her punctured throat.

"Won't kill me," she whispered.

Knot withdrew the dagger and attempted to press the blade flat against her neck. If stabbing her wouldn't do it, perhaps cutting her Goddess-damned head off would.

Astrid was too fast. She deflected him before he could press the blade against her, and before Knot knew what was happening, they were rolling. His shoulder slammed against a tree. Snow showered down on them. Somehow Astrid had reversed their positions.

The girl knelt above him, holding his own dagger at his throat.

She smiled at him, her hair and face covered in snow and her own blood.

"Not bad," she said, shaking the snow from her head. Knot wanted to whisper something along the lines of "go ahead" or "finish it." *Might be nice to go out with bold words.* But, honestly, he wanted to *live*, even if his life had gone to Oblivion.

Astrid stood, tossing the dagger aside. "Not bad at all,"

she said, hefting her pack and moving off away from the road. "This means we're setting up camp now, by the way. I won, fair and square."

Knot stared at the girl. She had just tried to kill him. Hadn't she?

Astrid rolled her eyes. "Please. Don't tell me you were scared for your life just now."

Knot stared at her.

"Oh, Goddess," the girl murmured. "You *were* scared for your life." She grinned. "That's adorable!"

Knot stood. He couldn't take her craziness. Not after what she just did.

"You need to level with me," he said, walking towards her. Vampire or not, he needed to know. "The other night, in Brynne. I heard you talking with someone, right before I came into our room. You were talking about *me*. Who were you talking to?"

The girl looked at him, the humor gone from her face.

"Look, I'm sorry if I caught you off guard. I just wanted to see what these fighting skills you're always talking about were like firsthand. No need to get in a knot about it." Her grin returned. "Ha! Get it? Your—"

He grabbed her collar, lifting the girl up to eye-level. Pain seared through his shoulder, but he ignored it. She was strong, but still light. He lifted her easily.

"*Who were you talking to?*" he asked again.

"Get *off* me." She broke his grip and he dropped her to the ground. She pushed him, *hard*, and Knot stumbled back a few paces.

"I don't know what you're talking about," Astrid said, glaring at him. She dusted herself off, although the gesture seemed ridiculous. "In Brynne? I wasn't talking with *anyone*. It was just the two of us. You saw when you came in, I was the only one in the room."

"I… I heard you," Knot said. He realized he was sitting in the snow. When had he sat down? "Talking with someone. You were talking with someone about me."

The girl smiled tentatively. "Sorry to burst your bubble, nomad, but you're not much to talk about. Not sure why I would tell anyone about you in the first place." Her smile faded. "And, honestly, I don't have anyone to tell."

Knot didn't know what to say to that. Was she lying? She had to be.

But, just like that, Knot began to doubt.

Had there been a second voice? Suddenly, Knot wasn't sure. He'd heard Astrid speaking, but had there really been anyone else? Or had he, Knot, the man who had severe memory issues to begin with, imagined the whole thing?

Knot pushed himself up and spat into the snow. How could he trust this girl—or anyone, for that matter—when he couldn't trust himself?

Astrid had made it clear she was accompanying him; not much he could do about that. And the girl had her uses. Perhaps he was better off dropping the whole thing. Wasn't much of a choice anyway. He could try to escape her, and fail. Or he could let her accompany him, and risk her betraying him. The girl's motives would reveal themselves eventually. If she had any.

Knot walked over to his pack and took out their blankets. There were enough trees nearby that they could probably have a fire tonight. Fuel, and relative cover for the flames. It would be good to feel warm again.

When he had set up his sleeping area, he looked back at Astrid.

"If that's what you're like before the sun has set," he said, "don't *ever* blindside me after twilight."

"Try not to piss me off, and I'll see what I can do," she said with a grin. She had recovered surprisingly well. The wound at her throat was almost fully healed, although a smear of blood remained. She lounged in the snow, her back against a rock, reading a small, leather-bound book.

"In fact," Knot said, "let's just settle for not doing that again at all."

"Why not?"

"I don't fight for entertainment." The truth was, he hated every minute of a fight. Every reflex, every movement, only reminded him how much he craved it.

"Could have fooled me," she said, raising her eyebrows. "A man who can nearly best a vampire has to take fighting seriously."

Knot shrugged. "It just ain't who I was, anymore. Ain't that person."

"Ain't ain't a word."

Knot barely resisted a smile. "Ain't my business what is a word and what isn't. Or what ain't."

"You know better. You're educated. Why do you say it? You even *sound* like a nomad, from the east plains."

"You mean I sound like a tiellan?" Nomads were infamous for taking on the lilting drawl of the tiellans—they thought it made them sound tougher.

Knot supposed it had something to do with being raised, essentially, by tiellans for the past year. He'd picked up the accent after waking in Pranna. "I just say what feels right," he said. "'Ain't,' for me, happens to be right sometimes."

Astrid shrugged, and went back to her book. Knot finally

thought he had a moment to himself when she looked up at him again.

"You said you're not that person anymore. Isn't that who we're looking for in Roden? Why are we looking for someone you don't want to be?"

Knot didn't answer. Having heard what he heard—or might have heard—in Brynne, he wasn't sure he wanted to go to Roden at all.

Anger crawled beneath Knot's skin, threatening to burst. He could blame it on Astrid's attack, on the fact that he had no way of knowing whether she was being honest with him. He could blame it on his frustration with his memory, his doubts. He could blame it on a lot of things, but the truth was he'd never felt this angry in Pranna. He'd never felt so fragile.

Had leaving been the right decision?

"We aren't looking for *him*," he said. "We're just trying to find out why I am this way. If I do that... maybe I can find some peace."

Astrid shrugged. "Whatever you say. But if you ask me, that's who you are whether you like it or not. Might as well embrace it."

Knot shook his head. "I don't want to do the things he did. The nightmares are enough to last me an eternity."

"You don't have to do exactly what he did," she said. Her tone was serious, a rare occurrence. "But you can use what he knows to change yourself. You can help people, protect them. You don't have to do whatever it was you did before. Or whatever it was you *think* you did." She looked down again at her book. "And don't whine to me about eternity." Knot thought he saw her expression change from its normal, amused look to something darker. Haunted. "When your thoughts have been tormenting you for three hundred years, then, maybe, we can talk." She stood, setting her book aside, and walked into the surrounding forest.

Knot looked away. Maybe she was right. He didn't want to know the thoughts she might have in her head. He didn't think a vampire would care much about that, but Astrid seemed to.

He busied himself by gathering stones for a fire pit, to hide as much of the light as possible.

Long after the fire had been lit, Astrid returned. She set a pile of broken branches near him. They had found—stolen, really—a good wood axe in Cineste, but she obviously hadn't needed it.

"We're going straight through Navone?" she asked. Her expression was back to one of perpetual amusement. Her green eyes, glowing with their own light in the darkness, chilled Knot. He nodded.

"Even after what you heard the men talking about in Brynne?"

"Just a rumor," he said, placing some of the branches on the merrily growing fire. He was beginning to wonder whether he could use the situation in Navone to his advantage. Whether he could use the Holy Crucible as a tool. Navone might be the key to escaping this monster.

"You seemed worried about it when we left Brynne."

He shook his head. "I've thought it through. Even if there is a Holy Crucible coming to Navone, we may miss her. And if we don't, what danger does she pose us, anyway? The Denomination has nothing against us." *Except involvement with the murder of a priestess and her disciples*, he thought.

"Except being cursed by their goddess," Astrid said, in a strange echo of his thoughts.

And there it was. That was exactly what he was betting on, if they did run into the Crucible. But he would have to be sure. He couldn't chance the girl's escaping and following him.

He still wanted to trust Astrid. He would have to remedy that. She wasn't a girl, after all. She wasn't what she appeared.

"Our story has worked this far," he said. "As long as we don't do anything reckless, I think we'll be fine."

"Whatever you say, nomad," Astrid said. She was smiling.

Knot stared into the fire. It was a risk, trying to get into Roden, especially now. Relations between Khale and Roden had always been strained, but lately things had been building to a head. A storm was about to break.

But that didn't matter. Not yet. One step at a time, and Navone was the first. He would reach his destination one way or another. He *would* find what he was looking for. He had to believe that.

And, just maybe, Winter would be waiting for him when he returned.

# 15

WINTER SAT NEAR THE fire. The sun was just setting, and they had made camp off the road near a large boulder—something Winter recognized as a *rihnemin*, an ancient remnant of her race—and a grove of pines. Nearby, tied to a large tree, the horses snorted and whinnied softly, their breath steaming in the cold air.

The *rihnemin*, caked with snow, was almost the size of her father's fishing boat. Boulders and rock outcrops were more and more common the further west they traveled—it was an odd feature that Winter had not seen east of Cineste—but she was certain this was no boulder. Winter did not know what the massive thing had once been, what it might have represented; any specific markings or writing on its surface had long since eroded. But Winter felt drawn to it.

So did Lian, apparently. When they first set up camp, Lian had walked up to the *rihnemin* reverently, placing one palm flat on its smooth stone surface.

"Your turn," Kali said. She was walking towards Winter. In the distance, Winter saw Nash walking with Lian into the pine grove.

"What about him?" Winter asked.

"No reaction," Kali said. "Disappointing, but not surprising."

In the twilight, Lian shot an anxious glance towards Winter. He looked worried.

She didn't like Lian worrying about her. It was all anyone seemed to do, lately. Perhaps, if she was one of these psimancers, she could protect *him*. But Lian had failed the test. Why should she fare any better?

"Winter," Kali said, looking down at her. "Are you all right?"

"Yes." Winter shook herself. "Sorry."

Kali sat on a log, facing Winter. The woman's frost-blue eyes shone in the firelight. Winter still felt a coldness from Kali. She did not seem to think much of tiellans. She tried to hide it, but Winter could tell by the way the woman looked at her and at Lian. It was the same way Bahc had looked at a net of fish.

"What do I need to do?" Winter asked.

"I have a small supply of *faltira*," Kali said. "I already told you the drug's name means 'frostfire' in the old tongue, and that's how you'll know if you're compatible. If you begin to feel elation or euphoria, and those sensations are accompanied by a freezing or burning feeling, then the drug is reacting to the latent ability within you. If that happens, we will test you further to see what ability you possess. If you only feel the elation, or even a sense of depression or pain, then there is nothing for the drug to react with. The answer will be clear, either way. It should only take a few minutes."

Winter was hesitant, but she also felt a sense of anticipation building inside her. "Can anything bad happen, if the drug doesn't work?" she asked.

Kali shook her head. "Unlikely. In rare cases, people have been known to react against *faltira*, and their bodies have... shut down. But that percentage is very small. Lian had no problems."

Winter nodded. "Give it to me," she said.

Kali reached into her satchel. "Very well." Then she hesitated, gazing into Winter's eyes. "I wasn't exaggerating when

I said that *faltira* can be addictive. I will give you a very small dose tonight. If you *do* react, I will not give you another dose for at least a day, perhaps two. Rationing the doses consistently is essential. Otherwise, the addiction grows unmanageable. The ability becomes useless in such bondage. Do you understand?"

Winter hesitated. She had heard of people addicted to hero, devil's dust, or even wine and whiskey. She remembered a trip with her father to Cineste when she was young. They had had to go through a poor area of the city to get to a tiellan inn, and Winter recalled the gaunt, rotting faces that lined the streets, the people moaning, nearly naked despite the cold, begging for money for their drug of choice.

Was Winter willing to risk becoming one of those people—a husk of who she really was?

The answer came quickly. She was a shadow of her former self already. She had nothing to lose, and, according to Kali, everything to gain.

"I understand," Winter said.

Kali handed Winter a small crystal and a waterskin. "Eat the frost, but take it with some water to help dilute the dose."

Winter's hand shook. The crystal was oblong with numerous facets, each one smooth and flat but a different size and shape than the other. It felt surprisingly light, like a piece of dried bark.

"I just... eat it?"

Kali nodded, watching her carefully.

Winter put the crystal in her mouth. It melted almost immediately, liquefying on her tongue. The taste was sickeningly sweet. She raised the waterskin to her mouth and took a long drink.

Then, she waited.

"Reaction times vary, so be patient," Kali said. The woman continued staring at her. It made Winter uncomfortable; she felt like an object, something to be studied.

"Where is Elsi?" she asked. She didn't know if she could bear the wait in silence, and she hadn't seen the girl since they made camp.

"Elsi is… very shy," Kali said. "She prefers her own company."

Winter nodded, though it seemed odd. Why have a servant who didn't like being around you?

"You still feel nothing?" Kali asked, after a few minutes.

Winter shook her head, a bitter disappointment filling her. "Same as always."

Kali frowned. "Are you sure? You don't feel any sense of excitement, elation? Does your skin feel cold, or your blood burn? Nothing?"

Winter shrugged. Why did Kali care so much whether Winter was a variant or not? Winter obviously wasn't going to react. She suddenly felt foolish to have even hoped. She couldn't be a psimancer, like these people. She wasn't bold like they were, she wasn't strong. She wasn't human.

Then *something*—a feeling, it was the only way Winter could think of it—slammed into her so hard she nearly fell sideways into the snow. Kali was saying something, but Winter couldn't make out the words.

All Winter knew was that, in that moment, she felt *alive*.

Nothing about her surroundings changed. Colors were the same, the cold at her back and the heat of the fire in front were the same, the last rays of sun breaking through the clouds on the horizon were the same. She shivered; her skin felt cold, as if she'd suddenly been struck by a stiff northerly wind.

But inside, she was on fire. Her blood seemed to boil, but instead of excruciating pain, she was in ecstasy.

Winter felt, for the first time in her life, truly powerful.

"Canta rising," she heard Kali whisper. "It's working."

Dark rings started forming at the edge of Winter's vision. Blackness closed in. She realized she hadn't breathed since the sensation had taken over. She gulped in a breath of air, and it filled her lungs like a blissful fire. It was beautiful. She felt connected—with *everything*. "What... now...?" Winter managed. She was smiling, grinning like an idiot, but she couldn't help it. She felt like she could do anything.

"The drug works in three phases," Kali said. Her voice was quick with excitement. "You should feel both a burning and freezing sensation at first. The cold will fade, and soon you'll feel only fire. Once the fire fades, you'll grow cold once more; that's how you know the drug is wearing off."

What Kali said was true. Whatever coldness Winter had felt was fading, and searing heat replaced it, coursing through every part of her.

"We have to decide which path is yours," Kali said. "First, forget about your surroundings. Forget about me. Concentrate on yourself, your feelings. Your own mind."

It was difficult to concentrate on any one thing. Winter was a rock in the middle of a raging river, her thoughts rushing past her too quickly to grasp.

"Concentrate, Winter," she heard Kali say from far away. "Get a hold of yourself and *think*."

Winter tried focusing on something, anything, but she felt utterly lost. The water surged around her. She was being uprooted, unearthed. Soon she'd be washed away.

Winter heard Kali's voice in the distance, more insistent now, but Winter was too far into her own self. Thoughts and memories enveloped her. She still felt the incredible elation, but a nagging fear accompanied it, a dark foreboding that she couldn't identify.

And then Winter's father was taking her hunting in the Alder Forest. Everywhere was white with snow. Winter accidentally broke her bow and Bahc made her craft a new one from a tree limb.

It was years before that, and her father was teaching her to use her bow for the first time. Winter was young. So young, and she could feel the grain of the wood in her hand, could see the straw target ahead of her, painted blue and white.

Then Knot was looking at her—it was just a moment of so many in which he had caught her eye—and he smiled. They were on the deck of Bahc's boat, it was summer, and the wind blew across the sea. Winter smiled back at him.

She was playing on the dock with Lian, they were both children, and the sun glinted off the water. Her father and Gord laughed in the distance.

She was in the murky water below the dock, diving for her mother's earring. The water was dark, and the dark closed in around her. She was cold and tired, and her limbs failed her.

Winter was married to Knot. They were living in her old house in Pranna, and she woke up in the middle of the night with her head on his chest. They had made love, and then fallen asleep together. Starlight winked in through the window, and a full moon illuminated a crib in the corner. Slowly, not wanting to disturb Knot, Winter stood. She walked to the crib, and looked down at her daughter.

And somewhere, deep down, Winter knew that was different than her other memories. She did not have a daughter; she and Knot had never made love. It wasn't a memory at all, it was a fantasy, and it threatened to tear her from her place in the river and sweep her along into Oblivion.

Winter wanted to hold her daughter and never let go, to keep Knot's warmth and the full moon close, but instead she felt herself let the thought flow on, felt it rush away from her in the current. She thought of the time she *had* spent with Knot. She thought of her father, teaching her how to fish. She thought of her mother's earring. She thought of Lian and Eranda and Gord. If an experience came to her mind that she knew she hadn't shared with any of these people, she let it go. Everything else she gathered to herself. She kept her memories close, and let everything else slip away. Soon, she was solid again in her place in the river, and another rock had formed near her. Winter smiled.

Then, she was back by the campfire. Kali was shaking her, calling her name.

"I'm alright," Winter said. *Faltira* still raged inside her. She burned with pleasure, and she felt *powerful*.

"Winter." Kali's voice was cautious. Warning.

Nash and Lian had returned, Winter realized, and they were staring at her. They looked back and forth between her and the massive boulder, the *rihnemin*.

The *rihnemin* that was currently floating off the ground. Higher than Winter could reach if she stood on her toes.

Winter smiled. She felt a connection to the boulder. She didn't know what it was, but she felt it there, just below the surface of her mind.

Then, with a loud *thump* that shook the earth, the boulder dropped to the ground. Snow burst upward, and the fire went out.

Winter slumped back, exhausted, as the euphoria slowly faded.

* * *

"You all right?" Lian asked her.

Winter looked up at him. He'd been terrified not moments before. He'd been worried for her. Of course he would be.

*He doesn't have to worry about me,* she thought. *No one has to worry about me anymore.*

The frost was barely present in her veins, but she could feel it, echoes of the raging flood. Just as Kali said, Winter was beginning to feel cold. *She said this was just a small dose,* she thought excitedly, *diluted with water.* She dared to imagine what she might do with more.

"Winter," Lian said again, touching her shoulder. "Are you all right?" She realized that she still hadn't answered him.

"Yes." She smiled. Or perhaps she had already been smiling. She wasn't sure. "I'm wonderful, actually."

"You don't *look* it," he muttered, sitting beside her. "Wasn't for that stupid grin on your face, I'd say you'd contracted the red plague. You look awful."

"Thanks," Winter mumbled, "just what every girl wants to hear." She wasn't sure if he understood her, if she was even speaking coherently. But she didn't care. Let him talk. Let her look awful.

Things were different now.

Slowly, Winter laid herself back down so she could look up at the sky. Nash and Kali were whispering excitedly on the other side of the fire. Winter wondered, briefly, what they were saying, but dismissed the thought. It didn't matter.

"Listen," Lian whispered. "Be careful, Winter. We don't know anything about what they're giving us. Don't even know if they're telling the truth about all this."

Winter let him talk. She stared at the stars. They were so beautiful, perfect diamonds in a sea of darkness. How long had it been since she had just looked up at the stars?

"I don't think you should take any more of it," Lian said. "Neither of us should."

Winter let out a giggle. She couldn't help it.

"We don't know anything about them," Lian continued. Was he repeating himself? Winter wasn't sure. It was difficult to concentrate on anything but the memory of the *faltira*.

"Oh, Lian," she said, looking up at him. She reached up and ran a hand across his face. She felt clumsy; her hand barely brushed his skin, but that just made her giggle more. "Everything will be fine. You don't have to worry about me anymore."

"I'm worried about you *now*. I don't know what I just saw, but—"

"I *have* it, Lian, it's *inside* me. I can feel it, I can still feel it, just barely… it's wonderful."

Lian didn't reply. Winter let the silence envelop her.

Later, when the frost had completely worn off—it felt like hours, but hearing Nash and Kali still whispering nearby, and seeing Lian still sitting near her, she didn't think it had taken long at all—Winter finally sat up.

"Welcome back," Lian muttered, staring into the fire.

He was being sullen. He was always sullen when he didn't get his way. Ever since he was a child. Winter used to think it was endearing.

Not tonight. Whatever euphoria the frost had given her was gone.

"I need to talk to you about Knot," Lian said. Winter glared at him. The last thing she needed was another lecture about how they shouldn't be out here.

"I need to tell you what happened the night we—"

"I don't want to hear it, Lian. I know you don't like why we're out here, but I don't care. It was your choice to follow me. You didn't have to come."

"It's not about that, it has to do with—"

"No, Lian. I'm sorry."

Lian glared but Winter didn't care. He was being foolish. And stubborn.

"Fine," Lian mumbled. "Still don't think you should take any more of that stuff." He nodded towards Nash and Kali. "We can't trust them."

"It doesn't *matter* whether we can trust them or not," Winter whispered irritably. Now that the bliss was gone, she felt alone, cold, and irritated. "What matters is that they've given us a tool. This can help us, Lian. We can use it to help us find Knot. We can use it against them if we have to."

Lian stared at her. "What have they done to you?"

Winter didn't answer. The question was stupid. *They* hadn't done anything. They had only shown her something that had always been a part of her. But seeing Lian's face, his eyes so vulnerable, made her think again of that night in Cineste, in the alley. She shivered. It was her fault. She had put them in danger.

But now she had the means to stop anything like that from happening ever again.

She looked around at the other two. Nash appeared to be checking the perimeter of the camp. Kali was near her tent.

Winter wanted to demand another *faltira* crystal from them. She wanted to feel the power and elation again. *Don't be a fool,* she told herself. Kali had been very clear about the addictive properties of the drug. She couldn't risk it, not when she was so close.

With an effort, Winter quelled the urge. Things were working out better than she could possibly have hoped. She just had to be patient.

# 16

KALI RAN HER HAND through her hair. She did not like having short hair, or brown hair, for that matter. She glanced at Elsi, sitting alone near the tent, envious of the thing's shining blond hair. And how short the girl was. Kali had thought she would like being tall, but she had been mistaken; it robbed her of subtlety.

On the other side of the fire, Nash was teaching Winter the first elements of telesis. Kali had heard it all before. Once chosen as a candidate for the Nazaniin, she had been taught the details of both telesis and acumency. Clairvoyance remained a mystery to most. Kali suspected it was similar to the other two cognitive arts, considering how similar telesis and acumency were to one another logistically, but that was speculation. Voyants could predict future events, though their accuracy varied greatly; that summarized Kali's knowledge of clairvoyance. The other two forms of psimancy were much more familiar to her.

Nash would begin with the basics. A telenic used *tendra*—an Old Khalic term meaning "arms"—to manipulate objects. A *tendron* was invisible to the naked eye; when a telenic released a *tendron*, no one—psimancer or otherwise—could see it. A telenic could not even visualize their own *tendra*; he or she would be aware of them, but the awareness was tactile rather than visual. *Tendra* functioned as ethereal limbs, allowing a telenic to manipulate an object in whatever way they wished.

But telenics were limited to moving inanimate objects; they could not manipulate living things. In Nazaniin experiments, *tendra* passed through human, tiellan, and animal subjects with no visible effect.

A telenic measured power in three ways, namely by the quantity, strength, and range of their *tendra*. The weakest telenics Kali knew could only release one *tendron* that was no stronger and could reach no further than their own physical arms. Nash, one of the strongest telenics Kali knew, could consistently access nine *tendra* at once, although once or twice he'd tapped into a couple more. Each of Nash's *tendra* could lift objects heavier than Nash himself, and reach thirty or forty rods in any direction—many times Nash's own reach. The further out a *tendron* reached, the weaker it became, but in general the strength was consistent.

Kali sighed. She was deliberately distracting herself. She was trying not to think of what she had just discovered.

Winter was the Harbinger.

Rune had refused to verify it, but he was always loath to admit anything he hadn't foreseen himself. Winter's psimantic ability, especially as a tiellan, all but confirmed her as the Harbinger. She had lifted that boulder like it was a pebble, and with only *one* tendron, according to Nash. Such strength was unheard of among telenics.

Kali's discovery would create ripples within the Nazaniin that could not be called back. Many who studied the prophecies, Kali among them, had long dismissed the idea of a tiellan psimancer. Some feared the idea; if one tiellan could access the Void, then perhaps all tiellans could learn to do so. It was a slippery slope from there to tiellans returning to the power they had possessed during the Age of Marvels. Revenge for centuries of captivity would surely follow.

Kali did not fear a tiellan psimancer. She had believed that such a thing was impossible. Until now.

She thought of the glory she would receive for being the Nazaniin agent to discover and bring in the Harbinger. Many agents devoted their entire lives to the quest, although Kali had never been that devoted. She would take the credit, of course; it just wasn't an honor she'd ever sought. Nevertheless, Kali tried to focus on it, if only to keep her from going mad. She had been excited at Winter's ability at first, until she realized the implications. Twisted irony. If Kali believed in Canta, she would have thought the Goddess more fickle than ever. For the Harbinger to be a tiellan, and for Kali of all people to be the one to find her. A volatile, petty goddess indeed.

Kali placed her hand on her chest, feeling the parchment she kept in the hidden pocket there. She rarely unfolded it anymore, but she was always aware of its presence. She would never forget what happened to her family, and she would never forget the tiellans who had caused it.

Kali looked at Winter. The tiellan psimancer. The girl feigned innocence, but Kali had her suspicions; she might not be as innocent as she appeared. Lian had been uncharacteristically silent since the testing. Lian feigned nothing; he hated humans, and apparently did not care who knew it. Kali knew his type. She had seen the atrocities of which elves like Lian were capable.

And yet, here Kali was, having to pretend they were her equals.

Having to admit that one of them was the Harbinger.

She needed to stick to her orders; emotions would only cloud her judgment. And if her orders required tolerating the company of two tiellans—even befriending them—Kali would do it. It was her duty, and Kali was nothing without that.

"You can't control her," said Lian.

Kali looked up and glared at him. What gave him the right to interrupt her thoughts?

"What are you talking about?"

"Winter," Lian said. "You'll try to control her, her new powers. But you don't know her. Winter could never be controlled."

"You're mistaken." Kali wanted to say a lot worse—how dare he challenge her?—but she kept calm. Pettiness did not become her.

"How do you know? You reading my mind?"

Kali shook her head. The boy's understanding was pathetic. "You're not worth the effort. And you aren't difficult to read, with or without psimancy. Best stop talking before you get yourself into real trouble."

Nash glanced at her, across the flames. He was still talking with Winter, but he knew. Perhaps he had overheard, perhaps he sensed her mood, but he knew.

Kali sighed. She risked a lot being so rude to the boy. And yet she couldn't help herself. The familiar rage was rising.

Kali stood.

"Where are you going?" Lian asked.

Kali didn't respond. She needed to get away from him, from them all, before she did something she would regret.

# PART II

EVERYTHING
THAT RISES

# 17

*Navone*

CINZIA REACHED FOR A towel, shaking water from her hands. She and Kovac were washing dishes after eating dinner with her family, an image that Cinzia found both amusing and strange. For one, her family had always had servants for such tasks. Cinzia had never washed a dish in her life until she left for the Ministry, where she quickly learned that Canta's disciples did not live in quite as much comfort as a noble family—at least not until they were ordained priestesses, anyway.

Secondly, Cinzia was washing the dishes with Kovac. The act felt oddly intimate. He scrubbed with water and soap, his shirtsleeves rolled up, revealing his scarred, sinewy arms. Cinzia dried with a threadbare towel. She felt good accomplishing something with visible, immediate results.

"You are unique, my lady," Kovac said after a while. "You are not like other priestesses I have known."

"I do not see how I am so different," Cinzia said. "I do what every priestess does."

Kovac shook his head. "When it comes to Cantic duties, yes. That is as it should be. But who you are away from the chapel is different." Kovac smiled. "Most priestesses would not condescend to wash dishes at all, let alone with their Goddessguard."

Cinzia frowned. She had noted the aloof relationship most women in the Ministry had with their Goddessguards.

It seemed a waste of a good relationship. She hadn't found it practical either. What use was a Goddessguard if he did not care enough about you to protect you when it mattered?

"There is no reason for me not to help," Cinzia said. "This is my family. As our guest, you are the one out of place, if either of us is."

Kovac smiled. "I am only doing my duty, my lady."

Cinzia listened to the soft swish of water in the basin as she dried another plate. Her thoughts turned to what seemed inescapable: Jane's vision. *Visions*, Cinzia corrected herself. Plural. Jane claimed to have experienced more than one, each accompanied by a messenger, and each messenger with its own name, story, and personality. Which was outrageous. Anything from the Praeclara was of the same mind and will as Canta Herself. *Children* knew that... and still Cinzia felt drawn to the story. Despite all that she had learned, all she *knew*, a part of her wanted to believe Jane's ludicrous claims. But Cinzia's faith in the Cantic Denomination—her faith in *Canta*—had not developed overnight. She had cultivated it for years. Considering leaving something like that behind, let alone thinking it might be false, incited a plethora of emotions that she could not handle.

And even if the visions were somehow true, if the impossible was possible and Canta had chosen to manifest Herself... why would She appear to *Jane*, of all people? The girl who had put mud in the family stew as a joke, who dressed in a tattered sheet and leapt out at her siblings to scare them. And beneath that question lurked another.

Why not Cinzia?

Cinzia had devoted her life to the Goddess, done everything She had asked of her and more, and Canta chose to send visions to *her sister*? Was it a cruel jest? Cinzia had always thought of

Canta as merciful and loving. Now she wasn't so sure.

She wiped the last plate clean, and sighed deeply.

"Everything all right, my lady?" Kovac asked, drying his hands on a towel.

Cinzia looked over her shoulder. Her family had retired to the drawing room. "I do not know how to help them, Kovac," she said. She was convinced this was a test, an opportunity to prove her worth. But, if so, it was a test she was failing. "They will not see reason. They—"

A large crash echoed from downstairs, in the woodshop.

Kovac glanced at her. "Wait here," he said.

Eward was already standing in the doorway to the woodshop as Cinzia followed Kovac down the stairs.

"It's all right," Eward said. "Whoever it was has gone."

She felt a rush of affection; Eward had run towards danger, not away. Kovac glared at her but Cinzia shrugged; he could not have expected her to wait upstairs. They walked into the shop, her father behind them. She was about to ask what had happened when she saw the large glass window of the shop, or what was left of it. A few shards of glass still protruded from the frame.

A large stone lay on the floor, surrounded by shattered glass. Someone had painted a Trinacrya on its surface.

"What happened?" Pascia rushed into the room, Jane behind her. "Is everyone all right? Is anyone hurt?"

"Everyone is fine," Ehram said, picking up the stone. "It was just a warning."

Cinzia saw Kovac raise an eyebrow. She looked at her father. "Just a warning, Father? As opposed to what?"

Ehram sighed, and a look passed between him and her mother. Pascia stepped forward, taking Cinzia's hand.

"Cinzia, sweetheart… as word of Jane's visions has spread,

the people of Navone have not been as kind to us as they once were."

"What do you mean?" Cinzia asked. She wished she could sit down. She had assumed—hoped—that no one in the city knew what her family was doing.

"Someone please answer me," Cinzia said. *How can they expect me to help them when they don't tell me anything?*

"It started with my woodworking," Ehram finally said. "At first we didn't understand why customers that had come to us for years were suddenly avoiding the shop. Then one of them let slip that rumors were spreading. Rumors of Jane, and visions, and daemons."

"Ehram," Cinzia's mother said cautiously, but her father kept going.

"They told us it was not good to be seen doing business with anyone of questionable beliefs."

"As if we had not shown them our devotion through the decades," her mother added with more than a hint of bitterness.

"Things got worse," Ehram continued. "The children rarely go out now, as I'm sure you've noticed. There have been a few incidents..."

"Sammel's face?" Cinzia asked, suddenly understanding. She had noticed bruises. Faded, probably weeks old, but there nonetheless. He was just a *boy*, for Canta's sake.

Ehram glanced at Kovac. "This isn't the first warning we've received. People aren't just ignoring us anymore. Since word of the Crucible, they've become more aggressive."

Cinzia gripped the grainy wood of the workbench closest to her. Her gaze shifted to Jane, standing there, calm as ever.

The heavy feeling within Cinzia ignited, became a passionate fire.

"How could you," she whispered, staring at Jane. "How could you bring this down on our family?" Her voice was rising, but Cinzia did not care. "How could you do this to them?"

Ehram began to speak, but Jane interrupted him.

"I can speak for myself, Father. Cinzia needs to hear it from me." Jane returned Cinzia's gaze, her eyes peaceful. "You know so much about Canta and Her doctrine. You know about faith, and trust, and sacrifice. You know that Her plan is greater than we can fathom."

Of course Cinzia knew. But what did it matter if Jane led their family down a path that could only end in tragedy?

"Believe all of that, Cinzia. It is as true now as it has ever been. Our family... they believe it, too. They know that the work I—we—have been chosen for is important, and it is real. Bigger than any one of us, even our entire family."

Cinzia's rage boiled over. "How can you dilute Canta's doctrine like that and still call yourself Her servant? And to endanger our *family*?"

"Silence." Her father's voice cut into Cinzia like it had when she was a little girl. "I know you are confused, Cinzia. But Jane is right. We understand the scope of what is happening. That makes us fanatics, zealots, even heretics, but it is true. And now, we must do what is best for our family, and for the work." He looked at Jane.

"No, Father," Jane said. "Not yet. I know we have made plans, I know the lengths we have gone to ensure our family would be safe... but they do not matter now."

Ehram paled. "They do not matter? Why? For Canta's sake, what's happened? Is the Crucible here already?"

"No. In two days, maybe three, with a full company of the Sons of Canta and her own Goddessguard. But not yet."

Cinzia wondered how in the Sfaera Jane could know that, but she was too dumbstruck, too awed at the ridiculousness and tragedy of what was happening to voice the question.

"What is it, Jane?" her mother asked. "Why can we not go through with our plans?"

Jane straightened. "Canta wills us to stay. I have had another vision." She glanced at Cinzia, but quickly looked away. "Canta Herself spoke to me and…" She stopped, looking up at the ceiling, as if imploring for help. "We have to stay in Navone, and await the Crucible. That is Canta's will. That is what She would have us do."

Cinzia saw it in their eyes. Fear was blatant on her mother's face, Ehram was ghost-like, Eward frowned; but Cinzia saw something more in their eyes.

They would do as Jane said. They would stay. And there was nothing Cinzia could do to change their minds.

# 18

*Brynne*

Winter hardly recognized herself as she looked into the mirror Kali had given her—a mirror worth more than all the wealth she could ever possess in Pranna. They had stopped for the night in a town called Brynne; Kali had rented the room at an inn called Canta's Jewel. The sun had already set outside, and candles illuminated the chamber.

The bed Winter sat on was one of the most ornate and expensive things she had ever seen in her life. The quilt was thick and downy, the sheets rose-petal soft, of a material Winter had never seen before. Four ornate carved posts jutted up from each corner. Sheer curtains hung around the bed, parted and tied to the posts. Kali obviously enjoyed a certain level of comfort, and Winter couldn't say she objected. Persecution had all but disappeared since joining Kali and Nash, now replaced with indifference.

The speed with which Winter grew accustomed to such things frightened her. Kali's silvery mirror no longer filled her with awe. It was just a tool, now. Wide black eyes stared back at her from the mirror. Eyes more tired than she remembered, dark lines forming underneath. Her hair was the same, long and black and straight. Skin pale as ever.

Of course, her new clothes made a difference. Winter had asked whether the odd clothing Kali wore caused her problems, and Kali had only laughed. Kali must have deduced that Winter's interest in her apparel was more than passing—or simply read her mind; Winter still wasn't sure of the extent of Kali's abilities—because the next morning Winter had found on her bed a new black leather outfit almost identical to Kali's. Winter had only just now worked up the courage to try the clothes on. She raised one hand tentatively to her neck, letting her fingers brush lightly against the bare skin. The shirt she wore had a tiny collar, but a deep neckline left little to the imagination. She still wore her mother's necklace. It did not seem right to go without it—she needed something from her home.

A part of her felt guilt for wearing such clothing, but another part reveled in it. *If Gord could see me now*, Winter thought. *Or Lian's parents.* Which would be worse? Or more entertaining, for that matter. Tiellans had always been a bit too priggish in her opinion.

But, as Winter gazed at herself in the mirror, she knew it was more than the clothing. She felt as if she were looking at another person entirely.

"You look different."

Winter looked up, setting the mirror down on the bed. Lian stood in the doorway. Quickly, she looped her *siara* around her neck and shoulders, covering up the necklace and her bare skin. She wondered how curious she must look, how the *siara* must contrast with the fitted leather.

"Used to smile a lot more, that's for sure."

Winter felt her cheeks flush. To have someone see her like this, to have *Lian* see her like this, of all people... *No. If Kali can wear it and not care what people think, I can, too.* She sat up straight.

"Used to talk a lot more, too," Lian said.

"Sorry," Winter said. She smiled, though her hands fidgeted

on her lap. She picked up the mirror just to still them.

"I'm sorry, too," Lian said. His frame nearly filled the doorway. He'd gained muscle in the past few years working on her father's boat. "Can I come in?"

Winter nodded. She and Lian had hardly found time to talk alone. Travel with Nash, Kali, and Elsi was quick and efficient, and free time scarce.

Lian closed the door quietly behind him and moved to a carved chair across from where Winter sat on the bed. Lian was staying in a room with Nash, while Kali and Elsi shared another. Winter had argued that she didn't need a room of her own, but Kali had insisted. It wasn't proper for a young woman—even a tiellan, Kali had said, which had made Winter frown—to share her room with anyone.

She and Lian sat in silence for a moment. Winter clenched the mirror, watching Lian watch her. Anxiety spun within her.

"How're you doing?" Lian finally asked.

Winter maintained her smile. Lian was right; smiling didn't come as easily to her as it once had. "Well enough," she said. "We're covering a lot of ground. Kali says that at this rate we'll arrive in Roden in less than a month. We might catch up to Knot before that."

"I know all that," Lian said, waving his hand. "Don't mess around. How are *you* doing?"

"I'm fine," she said. "Overwhelmed, but I'll be all right."

"What do you expect to come of all this?" Lian lowered his voice. "If we find Knot, how're you going to deal with them?" He nodded towards the room Kali and Elsi shared next door. "They want Knot, or Lathe, whoever he is, just as bad as you. Probably more. Don't know if there's much we can do about it."

Winter shrugged. "We'll do what we have to." She tried to

sound like she meant it, but the truth was, she had run the same question over and over through her own mind.

"For Canta's sake, is that really your plan? 'We'll do what we have to?'"

"Don't say that name around me."

Lian just stared at her. Winter didn't care. What did Lian expect from her? This was her path. She had chosen it. She wished he could accept that.

Lian sighed, and then came over and sat down on the edge of the bed. She was suddenly very conscious of his proximity.

"Winter," Lian said, then he hesitated. Winter shifted uncomfortably. It was odd. He wasn't touching her. But she felt... she was beginning to feel the way she had felt in the alley, in Cineste. The cold stone behind her. The man's warm, stinking body pressing against her.

Winter shut her eyes. She had to stop thinking about that night. The images kept creeping into her head, and every time they did, she felt worse. She tried to think of something else, anything. Her father. Knot.

*Faltira*.

She had taken frost three times since her testing. Each day Nash had worked with her. Each time had been more incredible. The way it made her feel was like nothing Winter had ever imagined. It made her feel like the person she had always wanted to be.

"Winter," Lian began again, "you know I've loved you since we were little. I've loved you... I've loved you in more ways than one, I guess." He was blushing.

"You're changing," he said. "This drug, what it's doing to you... you're different. *We're* different."

"I'm married now. Ever think that might be why you're

feeling different?" Winter blinked. She didn't know where that gibe had come from.

If Lian was offended, he didn't show it. "These clothes, this life, *faltira*—this ain't who you are."

"What do you know about who I am?" Winter asked. Why was she being so rude? She felt angry with him, vindictive, and she didn't know why.

Lian only watched her, patiently.

"I'm sorry," Winter said, and she meant it. "You're my best friend, but you have to understand that what I'm doing, I'm doing for all of us. If I can become like Nash, if I can hone this skill…" She met his eyes, now, despite every desire telling her to look away. "I won't be helpless anymore. You won't have to worry about me, try to protect me. You won't have to put yourself at risk. Nor will Knot."

Winter did not tell him the other reason she felt drawn to *faltira*. How could she tell Lian that she had never truly felt connected with him? Or with anyone in Pranna, for that matter— besides her father. How could Lian possibly understand that?

"That's never *mattered*. People worry about you because they love you, Winter. That's why I'm here. That's what friends do, we protect each other."

"And it's my turn," she said. She could tell he didn't understand, but it didn't matter.

"They said it's addictive. Who knows what they *ain't* saying."

"I'm doing fine. Nash says my training is going well. He says I have *potential*." Truth was, she did worry about frost's addictiveness. She seemed to crave the drug more and more each day. Winter was scared. But she couldn't tell Lian that.

"Course that's what Nash tells you," Lian said. "Just don't know why you accept it so easily."

Deep down, she knew he was right. Less than a week ago she'd been unwilling to trust Kali or Nash. But, since discovering *faltira*, things had changed. The old Winter never would have trusted someone this easily.

*And the old me was weak*, she thought.

"All I'm saying," Lian continued, "is that this stuff is changing you. You ain't the same girl you were in Pranna."

"I don't want to be that girl."

"Then maybe she's already gone."

Winter's jaw clenched. "Just because you're jealous doesn't mean you can lecture me on how to live my life."

Lian spluttered a protest, but Winter could tell: he *was* jealous. She didn't know why she hadn't seen it before. Why wouldn't he be?

"You've always been the stronger one," she said. "The protector. Now you're about to lose that, and you're taking it out on me."

"You're crazy," Lian said, standing up.

Winter shrugged, but she knew she'd gotten to him. Lian walked to the door, but before he opened it, he turned. "I'm the only ally you have, Winter," he said. "Don't push me away." Then he opened the door, and nearly ran into Nash waiting outside.

"Everything all right?" Nash asked. Lian pushed past him and stormed down the hall. Nash looked at Winter. She didn't say anything. Nash shrugged. "Ready for your training?"

She eyed the pouch at his belt. In it, she knew, was more *faltira*. She nodded.

"Very well." He walked in and shut the door behind him.

"Something happen between the two of you?" Nash asked. His concern surprised her. She didn't know whether the question was genuine or not, but he at least pretended to be. Kali didn't even bother pretending.

"Everything's fine," Winter said. Strange. She couldn't keep her eyes off the pouch. "He's still getting used to the idea of me as a telenic."

Nash nodded. He stood opposite her, straight and tall. Winter wondered whether he had been a soldier.

"Psimancy is a great power," Nash said, "but it is a power many do not understand. And what people do not understand, they fear." He took a step towards her, finally reaching into the pouch at his belt. Winter could hardly contain herself. She yearned for the feeling in her veins. "Shall we begin?" Nash said, the frost glinting in his palm.

Winter moved to the edge of the bed, trying not to appear too eager. She took the crystal, swallowed it, and in moments the drug took full effect. Winter felt the burning heat, the chill over her skin. She felt alive again.

"It's amazing how quickly frost affects you now," Nash muttered, but Winter could barely hear him. He sounded far away.

Winter's ability to hone in on reality was improving, though. Concentrating on anything other than her own feelings during her first two attempts with frost was all but impossible. The third time she had managed to acknowledge her surroundings, and now it seemed even easier to focus on what Nash was saying. *Faltira* didn't seem to enhance her senses per se, but she did feel more *connected*. It was a feeling Winter had longed for her entire life.

"How long does it usually take?" Winter asked, trying to keep the inevitable smile from spreading across her face. She seemed to be constantly grinning whenever she took frost. She probably looked like a maniac.

"A quarter of an hour," he said. "Sometimes longer. But with you the transition seems shorter and shorter each time. We always knew that some had more affinity to frost than others, but this is very impressive. Although the tell hardly works for you." Nash bent down, peering into her eyes. "Your eyes are already black as night. Normally it's quite a sight, to see someone's eyes go completely dark. But with you there's no change at all." Nash straightened. "Now, what did we discuss last time?"

"The Void," Winter said quickly. She wanted to appear in control of herself. "The source of a psimancer's power."

Nash nodded. "Tell me about it."

Winter took a deep breath, letting frost's myriad of sensations wash over her. "The Void," she repeated, desperately trying to concentrate, "is the source of a psimancer's power."

Nash frowned. "You already said that," he said. "A psimancer needs to multitask. You need to speak, to move, to fight, *while* using your powers." Nash nodded towards the desk near the large mirror. "Reach out with a *tendron*," he said. "That goblet of water on the table—bring it to me."

Concentrating, Winter reached. With ease, she grasped the goblet with a *tendron*. One moment, the silver goblet was resting on the table. The next, it rose sharply into the air. It wobbled slightly, a small stream of water cascading over the lip. She knew where her own *tendra* were at all times, what they were doing, she was *aware* of them, but when she looked at the space she knew they occupied, she saw nothing.

"Don't stop talking," Nash said. "Tell me more about the Void."

Winter frowned. She concentrated, moving the goblet slowly through the air towards Nash. "The Void exists beyond our understanding," she muttered. "It exists beyond us, but...

but touches…" The goblet trembled slightly. "It touches every part of our world nonetheless," she said.

"Not too quickly," he said. "Control first. Speed will come."

Winter nodded, trying to dull her impatience. What she had done that first night, with the boulder, filled her mind. She had *strength*, and she wanted to use it. Moving a goblet around seemed stupid.

"Actuals have inherent, unlimited access to the Void," Winter recited. "Variants, like me, have limited access. We can only access the Void, and thus our powers, through *faltira*."

Suddenly, the goblet was torn from her grasp. She gasped as it fell to the floor, bouncing off the stone and splashing water onto a woven rug.

Nash hadn't moved from where he stood, his legs slightly apart, his arms clasped behind his back, looking right at her.

"How did you do that?" she asked.

"You were barely grasping it," Nash said disapprovingly. "You must be in complete control of whatever you grip with your *tendra*. Nothing should be able to intervene with your control. Complete and total mastery."

"How am I supposed to know when someone is trying to interfere?" she asked. "I can't sense someone else's *tendra*."

Nash raised an eyebrow. "You're sure about that?"

Winter hesitated. She assumed, of course, that she couldn't. She certainly couldn't sense anything from Nash whenever he released *tendra*.

"I don't think so," Winter said.

The goblet lifted into the air again. Nash was lifting it with a *tendron* of his own.

"Focus," he said. "Not on the goblet, but on the space around it. The goblet is only an object."

Winter concentrated, but there was nothing. "I don't see any..." Her voice trailed off. She *could* sense something there. She couldn't see it, but... the sensation was the same she got when she knew someone was behind her, or the prickling feeling when something or someone was just about to touch her, but had not yet done so.

"Canta rising," Nash muttered. "You sense it, don't you?"

Winter nodded, her eyes wide.

"Took me weeks to sense someone else's *tendra*," Nash said. He shook his head, and the goblet moved back to the table where it had been in the first place. "We'll discuss sensing later," he said. "Let's stick with the basics. But first, you got something wrong, earlier."

Winter cocked her head. "What?"

"Actuals do not have unlimited access to the Void. They have innate access, true, but their access is limited as much as a voyant's. I can only draw so much from the Void before my body begins to betray itself. My senses shut down, one by one. That's how I know I need to stop. Some psimancers don't heed those warnings, and they face... consequences."

"Such as?"

"We don't need to get into it now. But remember, no psimancer has unlimited power—no matter how great an actual's strength, or how much frost a variant consumes. We aren't invincible, Winter." Winter nodded. "Very well. Now, try again."

Winter reached towards the goblet. She lifted it gently off the table and moved it towards Nash. It floated in front of him, and Winter braced herself, anticipating another attempt to knock it away.

Instead, Nash raised his eyebrow. "I don't want an empty cup," he said. "Fill it with water, please."

Winter nodded, and began moving the goblet back to rest on the table. She could feel sweat beading on her brow.

"No," Nash said, and the goblet stopped in midair. "Leave it there, in front of me."

"How?" He was asking too much. She couldn't do this, not yet. A bead of sweat dripped down her nose.

"You know how," he said. "You're holding the goblet with one *tendron*. You have others. The jug is there, on the table."

Winter had only ever used one *tendron* before, as far as she was aware. She wasn't sure how—

And then, as she held the goblet in front of Nash, the silver jug rose slowly off the dresser. She was aware of another *tendron,* her own, guiding it slowly.

"So simple," she said with wonder. Picking up the jug was much easier than the first time she had consciously used a *tendron*.

"Once you find your first *tendron*, the others are progressively easier to access," Nash said.

Winter concentrated, trying to sense another *tendron*. *There*. She reached for a silver plate, resting on the table, and lifted it into the air.

"Don't," Nash said sharply. Winter dropped the third *tendron*, looking at him. "Only two for now," he said. "*Control*, Winter." He nodded at the goblet in front of him, now overflowing with water from the still-pouring jug.

Winter frowned. How was she supposed to focus on so many things at once? "Sorry," she mumbled, moving the jug back to the table. She left the goblet in front of him, waiting for him to take it.

Winter moved her tongue around in her mouth. Had she bitten it? She thought, for a brief moment, she had tasted blood.

Then, seemingly out of nowhere, a huge force slammed

into Winter's *tendron* holding the goblet. The attack caught her off guard, but she was surprised to see the goblet still there. Not a drop of water had fallen.

"Very good. I put a lot of power into that attempt, but you kept control. Very good, indeed."

"I… I think I *felt* it, before it happened. I tasted blood in my mouth. Did something go wrong?"

Nash shook his head, smiling at her. "That's your tell. The way you can recognize whether psimancy is being used around you. The taste of blood is a common manifestation."

Winter nodded in relief.

"You attacked my *tendron*, not my grip on the cup itself," Winter said, her mind racing.

Nash's smile grew wider. "That's your first lesson in breaking. If you want to break someone's control over an object, attack their *tendron* directly, not the object with which it interacts. Go for the link. Exerting force on the object itself is all but useless."

Winter nodded. It seemed to make sense. If an object were knocked from her grasp, she could still recover it if she was quick enough. But if her *tendron* were severed, she would completely lose control.

"Now," he said, "the frost should be wearing off, if the past few days have been anything to go by. How do you feel?"

"Fine," Winter said, but he was right. The fire was fading, and her sense of power and capability with it.

Nash looked her up and down with his storm-gray eyes. "Be honest with me, Winter. The first months of a variant's instruction are extremely important. I can help you overcome the worst of the addiction, with careful rationing and counsel, but if not, the addiction could destroy you."

Winter shrugged. "What do you want me to say? That I don't feel the pleasure and joy after it fades? I don't. That I feel let down and disappointed and inadequate when I'm not on frost? I do. That is how I feel."

Nash frowned. "Very well," he said, after a moment. "You're being honest, and that's important. Those feelings are normal. But if you start feeling a *need* to take frost, let me know immediately, if you can."

Winter shivered; the heat was gone, and she was left with only cold. She was her normal, useless self.

"What do you mean, 'if I can'?"

He looked at her, eyes hard as iron. "If you *do* start feeling an unreasonable need to take frost, it's probably too late. You won't recognize the need as unreasonable, at that point. Then, it will consume you."

"It can be that powerful?" She remembered walking the streets of Cineste with her father when she was young. The hollow faces, the torn, soiled clothing that had once been so expensive.

Nash nodded. "I've seen *very* powerful psimancers fall to frost addiction." Winter thought, but wasn't sure, that she detected a hint of sadness in his voice. "No variant is immune. You must take extreme caution."

Winter nodded, feeling a bit nervous. What *had* she gotten herself into? Perhaps Lian was right. This was too much, too early. Too dangerous.

Then, reaching into the pouch at his belt, Nash handed her a small stone. Winter looked up in surprise. She had been hoping he would give her a frost crystal; he had said nothing of stones. The thing, matte black, was no larger than the end of her thumb, oblong in shape. It was perfectly smooth, and had no markings or imperfections that she could see.

"What is this?" she asked.

"A voidstone. A basic tool for any psimancer. They have many uses, which we will discuss—the first of which is communication. Once you are ready, we will be able to communicate instantaneously, no matter where you are in the Sfaera. But first we must attune you to one."

Winter stared at the small stone. She could hardly believe such a thing was possible—instantaneous communication?—but she had seen so many things that seemed impossible in the last few days, she had a hard time finding a reason to doubt.

"Carry that with you," Nash said. "Keep it close, press it against your skin. You need to bond with it, in a way, before we really teach you how to use it."

The thing didn't look like much. Then Nash dropped something else in Winter's palm.

A single frost crystal.

"For *emergencies*," he said. "Only take it if there is no other choice. I'll check with you, to make sure you still have it, every morning and every night. Otherwise, you are to only eat frost given to you by me or Kali."

Winter nodded. The difference between the stone and the frost crystal was tangible; one was heavy, dull, seemingly useless. The other was light, jagged, and contained more power than Winter had ever thought possible.

"Keep the frost somewhere safe," Nash said. "Not easily accessible, otherwise it might be too tempting. But not completely out of the way, either. If you need to take it but cannot reach it in time, it is worthless."

"Yes," Winter whispered, keeping her eyes on him, with an effort. The weight of the *faltira* in her hand seemed to burn a hole through it.

"Very well. Our lesson is over, then. Get some rest. We have another long day of traveling tomorrow."

Nash left the room, and Winter was alone.

Alone, with the *faltira*.

# 19

## *Navone*

NAVONE STOOD IN THE foothills of the Sorensan Mountains—the same mountains that marked the narrow border between Khale and Roden. The city was roughly square-shaped, each corner facing a cardinal direction. Only two gates allowed access to the city; Knot and Astrid had entered the main gate on the southwest side that afternoon. The second was along the northeast wall, directly opposite from where they'd entered, and led to the border crossing into Roden.

Knot could picture the Roden Gate, as it was called, clearly in his mind, though he and Astrid were still far from the border crossing. Like the main gate, the Roden Gate was built into the thick wall of the city and flanked by large circular towers on each side. But what lay beyond the gate demonstrated the strategic advantage of Navone's geography. The north and east corners of the city ran directly into the high granite cliffs, forming the very mountains into extensions of the walls and creating a small field between the Roden Gate and the Blood Gate.

As one of the only traversable passes across the Sorensan Mountains, the Blood Gate consisted of two massive, circular towers built into the rock cliffs on either side of the pass, towering over Navone and the large gate they protected. The gate itself was more of a tunnel, fashioned from stone and protected on either end by a portcullis and massive oak and iron-reinforced doors. Simple in design, complex because of its sheer size, but effective in purpose. The Blood Gate stood impregnable for centuries. But then Roden invested in a powerful navy, circumventing the Blood Gate, and the game had changed.

The Blood Gate was a worry for another time. For now, Knot needed to find out about the Holy Crucible.

"What do you think?" Astrid asked him as they moved quietly through the merchants' line of the city. The sun sank in the distance; only a couple more hours of light remained.

Market tents lined the cobbled street, and people hurried back and forth. Merchants shouted above the crowd, advertising their wares. A few Borderguards patrolled the streets, spears high. No sign of Sons of Canta or Goddessguards, but there was a sense of unease in the bustling throng. There were few greetings but many distrustful glares.

"Not sure," Knot said. "Sons would be patrolling if the Crucible had arrived already, but the Borderguard barely had a presence on the walls to begin with." Only a few had stood on the walls, with two manning the gate when they'd entered.

"Perhaps the Sons are too sneaky for you," Astrid said.

"Doubtful. Doubt the Goddessguard would be, either." It took Knot a moment to realize she had said it in jest.

"Who *is* too sneaky for you, hot shot?"

Knot sensed the sarcasm, but he shrugged. "Don't know." He looked down at her. For some reason he thought her extra strength might make her more awkward, but she was less noticeable than a shadow in darkness, even in daylight. Or she could be, anyway, when she wanted to be. Not a comforting thought.

"All the same," he said, "it seems the Crucible ain't arrived. Might as well take our chances for the night."

Part of him had hoped to find the Crucible already in the city. Running into the Crucible might be his only chance to get rid of the girl. *The vampire,* he corrected himself. Since their last fight, he and Astrid hadn't spoken about what he'd heard, or thought he'd heard, in Brynne, and Astrid still refused to tell him why she was following him.

If she would just *tell* him, he might be able to understand. Despite everything, Knot liked the girl. But he couldn't trust her.

"What if the Crucible *has* arrived? And we've just underestimated her?"

"Or overestimated," Knot mumbled. "If that's the case, we'll make do. But I'm not keen on traveling through the Sorensan Pass during the night." Hopefully the Crucible would arrive that evening. Knot looked down at the girl. He didn't know what the Crucible would do to a vampire. Nothing pleasant, that was sure. But Astrid was a risk he couldn't take.

"Humans," she sniffed. "You need so much maintenance, it's pitiful."

Knot led the way through the merchants' line towards the Circle Square at the city's center. "People are on edge," he said. "Scared of what's coming."

"Never trust a religion with secrets, that's what I always say," Astrid said.

Knot raised an eyebrow. "So there are religions you *would* trust? Strange words from someone religion makes it a point to condemn."

"Their loss," she said, though she avoided his eyes. "I think they're jealous."

Knot conceded a half-smile.

"So, which inn is it tonight?" Astrid asked. "The Horse's Testicles? Or perhaps we could find one called The King Who

Gave Up His Crown; I heard the longer an inn's name, the more comfortable it is, yes? Or, if we're lucky, we might find an inn called Canta's Daemons. Perfect for the two of us, wouldn't you say?"

Knot ignored her.

"Really," Astrid continued, "one of the most ridiculous things I've noticed in my centuries on this miserable Sfaera is how you humans try so outrageously hard with your names. Especially the inns. Just once, I'd like to find an inn that was called Fin's Place, or The Sleep Easy Lodge."

Rounding a corner, they entered the plaza that stood at the city's center. Five different roads converged on a wide, open circle. Three steps led down into a square within the circle, the top step of each corner of the square just touching the outer rim of the circle, giving the place its name: the Circle Square. A massive stone fountain depicting a stylized version of the Sfaera stood in the middle of the space. The globe rose nearly as tall as the two- and three-story buildings around it. Water poured from the top, trickling down into a pool below. Knot wondered how the thing functioned in the cold.

Around the fountain, a group of children bundled in furs played a game of stone-hop. Eight or nine of them, each about Astrid's age.

The girl watched them, her face expressionless. Whatever good humor she'd been in a few minutes earlier seemed gone.

"I'll be back," she said. Then she walked towards the children.

Knot sat down on a stone bench. They hadn't rested at all that morning, to assure their arrival in Navone before nightfall. His feet and the backs of his legs still ached, and sitting down felt good.

A woman sat beside him, but Knot ignored her. She

was no threat, and the last thing he wanted was a mundane conversation. When Knot looked up, he was surprised to see Astrid playing with the children. She was laughing and jumping, occasionally tossing something into the fountain with a splash.

Knot experienced a moment of unease in which he wondered whether this wasn't some form of hunt for her. He'd only seen her feed once, on bodies already dead. She'd mentioned she only truly had to feed a couple times each month.

He kept one eye on her anyway.

As he observed Astrid and surveyed the city circle, looking out for any other, less expected threats, his thoughts wandered.

He remembered a dream from the night before. He seemed to be having dreams every night, now. In most of them he crept about in shadow, but last night's dream had taken place on a massive open battlefield. It was nighttime, or so it seemed, the entire sky dark except for a tiny, bright blue light above. Knot had attacked with his squad, slaughtering a faceless enemy. But Knot had stabbed one of the men he'd fought alongside. One of his brothers. Just like every dream before, this one ended in death.

He chewed on his cheek, lost in thought, watching the children at the fountain. Knot could tell that some of them were wary of Astrid. Whether that was because Astrid was a stranger, or because they sensed something deeper, Knot couldn't tell.

"Hello," the woman beside him said.

Knot was suddenly alert. He'd forgotten she was there. As he looked at her, he knew, suddenly, that his first impression of her had been wrong. She wasn't a threat necessarily, but something wasn't right with this woman. He wasn't sure what. That was the problem with inhumanly honed senses that he didn't understand.

"Hello," Knot said, hoping she would leave the conversation at that. Now that he got a good look at her, he realized she was quite young. Winter's age, perhaps twenty-one summers at the most.

"Welcome to Navone," the woman said.

"Thank you."

"Is that your daughter?" the woman asked. "She is a beautiful little girl."

"Thank you," Knot said again. The woman wasn't just being conversational, Knot realized. The way she fidgeted made him wary.

"Do I know you?" he asked. It was a long shot, but perhaps he had known her... before.

"No," the woman said. "My name is Jane. I live here, in Navone." She had long, blond hair, and striking blue eyes. A beautiful woman, Knot admitted. Despite her simple, well-fitting dress, he could tell she was noble. The way she bore herself, the straightness of her back. A modest noble, perhaps, but a noble nonetheless.

Knot glanced back at Astrid. The children had formed some kind of crowd. Knot could no longer see Astrid. They'd apparently found something to gawk at.

"And you," the woman, Jane, continued, "are just passing through Navone, are you not? You and your... she *is* your daughter, yes?"

Knot frowned. That was the cover they had been using, but there was something off in the way this Jane said it, as if she *knew* something, a joke she wasn't sharing. And Knot couldn't help but wonder why she'd be so friendly when the entire city seemed on a knife's edge.

"She is," Knot said cautiously. He checked his surroundings. If the woman's goal was to distract him, he wanted to be ready for the why. But he could see no one lurking at the edge of the city circle, or observing him and this woman.

"My name is Benir," he said, hoping some information, albeit false, would satisfy the stranger. "My daughter is Lucia. We were just looking for an inn. We're staying the night, and then we must be on our way early tomorrow."

"I see." Jane glanced at the crowd of children, and frowned. "Oh, Goddess…"

Knot followed her gaze. Some of the boys, who he saw must be at least eleven or twelve years old, were pushing someone between them.

Astrid.

Knot stood. He recognized the body language. He'd seen this sort of thing all too often in Pranna. When just a few of the wrong humans got a tiellan alone.

The boys laughed as Knot walked towards them. He was aware of Jane following him. A tight ball of apprehension formed in his stomach. For the boys or Astrid? He wasn't sure.

"So you're an outsider *and* you don't have a mother?" one of the boys asked. The others laughed, though the older boys seemed to be the bullies, the ringleaders. The other children's laughter was strained.

"I didn't *say* I don't have a mother," Astrid said. Her defensiveness surprised Knot. "I just said she isn't *here*."

One of the boys sneered. "She probably left you."

*Canta rising,* Knot thought. *Are children always so cruel?*

"She didn't *leave* me," Astrid said. Her voice was taut with emotion. Astrid took most things in her stride; was this just an act, as well?

"Lucia," Knot said, trying to sound firm. The children turned and Astrid rushed to him, wrapping her arms around his waist. Knot looked down in shock. He still had no idea how to read her, but something welled up within him. He put an arm around the girl. He knew it was fake, the moment he did it. He was going to turn this girl—this daemon—over to the Crucible the first chance he got.

But comforting her still felt like the right thing to do.

"Your daddy came to save you?" one of the boys sneered. Knot glared at him, but before he could respond, another voice cut in.

"Jakob, didn't I see you sneaking into Garen's shop? Perhaps your mother would like to hear about that." It was Jane.

The boy who had spoken looked down and muttered something incomprehensible.

"Sorry?" Jane asked, stern as iron.

"Nothing, Miss Oden," the boy said.

"Very well. Off you go, all of you. You've caused enough trouble."

The children dispersed. Knot heard a few of them mutter something about not having to listen to "that woman." He didn't know what to make of it. Instead, he looked down at Astrid.

"You all right?" he asked.

"I'm fine," she said, finally letting go of him. Knot was about to make a comment about how the mighty vampire couldn't take the peer pressure, but Jane's presence stopped him. There'd be time for sarcasm later. Perhaps Astrid would tell him what in Oblivion was behind the whole incident.

"I'm sorry about that," Jane said. Knot turned to look at her.

"It's fine," he said, his arm still around Astrid. *Best to keep up appearances.* "I appreciate your help. I'm not the best at… that."

Jane smiled. "You mustn't take it personally. Everyone here has been under a great deal of pressure lately." She knelt down in front of Astrid.

"They didn't mean it, angel," she said.

Knot resisted the urge to scoff.

"Whatever they were saying, they didn't mean it," Jane continued. "You know that, don't you?"

Astrid nodded and Jane stood. "Normally I would be pleased to offer my family's hospitality," she said, "but I'm afraid we aren't in the best position to offer sanctuary at the moment. That said, I can show you to an inn or two that might suit your needs, if you like."

She began walking, heading for one of the main streets leading off the Circle. Knot looked down at Astrid. The girl didn't return his gaze. He shrugged, and followed Jane, Astrid trailing behind them.

Knot kept a wary eye on their surroundings, still vaguely suspicious of a trap. But the woman seemed innocent enough. There was something odd about her, to be sure, but he couldn't put his finger on what.

"If you don't mind me asking, miss," he said, "why're you being so kind? The entire city seems uneasy."

Jane smiled. "Nothing wrong with a bit of kindness, even when circumstances dictate otherwise."

Knot frowned. He wondered what Jane knew about such "circumstances." "Word has it trouble's coming to Navone."

Jane was silent for a few moments. Knot was beginning to think she hadn't heard him when she finally spoke. "Trouble, yes, I'm afraid so. A Holy Crucible is a serious thing."

The response was cryptic at best, though Jane's ears were turning red, Knot noticed. *Strange*. "Just hope they can find the ones responsible," he said. "That's all us Goddess-fearing folk can do."

Knot gave Jane credit for the way she retained her composure, but his trained eye caught the signs. Her pupils were dilated, eyes wide. Her breaths came too quickly. She was nervous, but this was more than the typical nerves people displayed at the mention of a Holy Crucible. Jane was *scared*.

And she was lying.

"I pray our city can find peace," was all she said. Knot didn't have to inquire further. This woman probably knew someone involved. She was trying to act normally, but Knot could see past the act.

"Here we are," she said, smiling, as they approached an inn. "Canta's Grace."

*Not quite Canta's Daemons but I suppose it'll do.* Knot looked down at Astrid. Still she avoided his gaze.

"Well… thank you." Knot was still oddly off-guard from Jane's behavior. He wasn't used to simple politeness.

"Anytime." Jane's eyes were gleaming. "I have a feeling we shall meet again."

*Goddess, I hope not,* Knot thought. *Last thing I need is to get caught up in whatever is happening in this backward city.*

Jane looked down at Astrid. "And you as well, Lucia. Keep yourselves safe, until then. Travel in the hands of the Goddess."

"Thank you," Astrid muttered, as Jane walked off into the evening.

"That was… odd," Knot said. "Do you think we can trust her?"

Astrid shrugged, and said nothing.

\* \* \*

In the common room of Canta's Grace, Knot sat with an untouched cup of mint tea. Despite what he thought he'd heard in Brynne, he was having second thoughts about turning Astrid over to the Holy Crucible.

*She was putting on an act in the Circle Square,* he told himself. *She's already proven her ability to put on a show. A mummer fit for a king.*

The girl had only shown real emotion a few times in his presence. Anger, certainly, when he accused her of keeping secrets from him after Brynne. When she was feeding, after the bandits attacked them on the road, he'd seen something like shame.

And today, he could have sworn he saw sorrow in her eyes.

*Which she could easily have faked.*

He heard footsteps and Knot's hand strayed to the dagger at his waist. He was seated at the bar, near the corner of the room, but there was still space enough for someone to sneak up on him. Behind him a man coughed, and Knot turned. His hand relaxed on the dagger. The innkeeper, a tall portly man with watery eyes.

"Sir," the innkeeper said, nodding respectfully.

Knot eyed him warily. As far as the innkeeper knew, Knot was only a common traveler. The innkeeper reached into his apron and pulled out a sealed letter. He handed it to Knot.

"This arrived for you."

Knot shook his head. "You must be mistaken."

"No, sir. It was just delivered moments ago. The man pointed you out specifically."

Knot's eyes narrowed. "Who brought it? Did you recognize him?"

Sweat beaded on the man's brow. "No, sir. He wore a Borderguard uniform, but I've never seen the man in my life."

*A Borderguard.* Knot frowned. *What would a Borderguard want with me?*

Knot took the letter. The innkeeper nodded, practically bowing in relief, and backed away.

Knot turned back to the bar. He didn't recognize the seal imprinted on the wax; it looked like a set of extended eagle talons.

Knot broke the seal and opened the letter. His hand trembled. For the first time, Knot realized, he might learn something about his past. About himself.

It was addressed, in a flourishing, slanted script, to someone named Madzin. The name meant nothing to Knot. But, then again, nor did Lathe, the name the scarred man at the wedding had used.

Madzin,

I confess to wondering why you did not contact me as you usually do. Am I not the first person you seek whenever you arrive in Navone? If I have done anything to offend you, I sincerely apologize and hope to make amends. The last thing I want is to anger you, or your... friends, shall we call them?

It has been some time since we last saw or heard from one another. Almost two years, by my count. Perhaps you wonder if I am even around. Well, old friend, I am, just so you know. This letter is to assure you of that, should you ever need anything from me. My services are at your disposal, as always. The last time I helped you into Roden, I didn't see you on your way back, but now here you are, at the border once more. I am sure you have your own ways and means.

I'll not bother you further, friend. I hope all is well with you, and that your dealings in Navone, and wherever you go from here, are successful.

Sincerely yours,
Captain Jey Rudak, Fifth Borderguard

Knot read through the letter once more, just to be sure he read it correctly.

Knot had passed through Navone into Roden less than two years ago. A spike of hope jutted through him. Roden *was* where he needed to go; this letter all but confirmed that theory. Knot would have to seek out this Captain Rudak. The man might even be able to help him get across the border. The letter seemed an astounding stroke of luck. Knot's instinct was to distrust such a boon, but he had to pursue the lead. He had to know.

Knot left his tea untouched and stood. He briefly considered leaving the city that very moment. He could just go, and Astrid might not find out for hours.

She would catch him, though. She knew where he was traveling, and she would have no trouble finding him again. Or he could leave now and take her with him. And perhaps run into the Crucible just as the Goddessguard was securing the city. Or perish in the Sorensan Pass.

Whatever road he took, there were risks.

Knot walked quietly up the stairs. He stopped, right outside the door of their room, and listened. His ears strained, but he heard nothing. No secret conversations. No hushed whispers.

The room was dark, the window and shutters closed. Knot could barely make out Astrid's form in the corner, lying on the floor. Silent. No wise cracks, no jests.

Knot walked towards her. Risks were a part of life. He had seen so much death—caused it, in his dreams, and otherwise. He didn't want to cause any more. Gently, he picked the girl up, and laid her on the bed. She was still awake, he could tell. He thought she might say something, but she didn't. Instead, she drew into him, held him tightly.

Turning Astrid over to the Crucible was the prudent thing to do. He knew that. *Canta's bones, she might be manipulating me right now.* But, in that moment as he held her, Knot realized he could not do it. He would not.

He laid her down, drawing the quilt up around her face. He stood watching her, and then moved to the chair next to the bed, to wait and see what the morning would bring.

# 20

*Somewhere between Brynne and Navone*

THE ATTACK CAME EARLY, as they were breaking camp. Winter was crouching to roll her blankets when she heard a hiss above her. Winter could recognize the sound of an arrow anywhere.

Her head snapped around, looking for the source. They had camped near a group of boulders on a small hill with good visibility of the surrounding countryside, but she could see no one. At the same time her horse, Nynessa, directly in front of her, screamed.

Then, everything erupted in violence.

People yelled, more horses screeched, Lian shouted her name somewhere. The snapping hiss of more arrows.

Winter looked around. She heard another shout, and turned in time to see Nash barreling towards her.

He knocked her to the ground, forcing the air out of Winter's lungs. She gasped, trying to suck in a breath. She saw Nynessa, lying still, the snow stained dark red around her. The smell of blood and shit hung heavy in the air.

Winter sat up in time to see Nash leap over the boulders and rush towards a group of figures that had appeared in the distance. She wasn't sure how many there were; eight or nine, maybe. But they were wearing dark-green robes. Just like the men who had attacked her wedding.

A scattering of small black lines rose in the air towards

Nash. Arrows. They would cut him down before he reached the robed men. But before Winter could warn him, the shafts scattered in the sky, falling harmlessly in different directions. Nash pressed forward, drawing his sword. At first Winter couldn't imagine how the arrows had scattered in such a way. Then she remembered.

Her hand shot into the pouch at her waist. The *faltira* crystal had weighed her down like an anchor dragging along the ocean floor since Nash had given it to her. Winter had sensed it, yearned for it, but now that she needed it, she'd *forgotten*. She slipped the frost into her mouth as she turned to see Lian, Elsi, and Kali crouching behind the boulders. Both Elsi and Lian fired arrows towards the group of men. Kali only stood there, staring into the distance. Her face was strained with concentration, her body still.

Lian shouted in alarm, and Winter looked to her right to see two green-robed men leap over another rock outcrop. Winter reached for the dagger at her waist just as Kali turned to face the two men, drawing her long, curved sword from its sheath.

"He isn't here," one of the robed men growled.

*Knot,* Winter thought suddenly. *They're still looking for Knot. They thought he would be with me.*

The man looked at Winter and smiled. "You'll have to do."

Before Winter could wonder what they meant, Kali leapt forward and attacked.

Winter knew that Nash was skilled in combat, and for some reason she'd assumed he did all the fighting. Winter had been wrong. The men advanced wielding longswords. One of them lunged, but Kali parried easily and spun between the two men. She dodged the other man's swing, kicking behind her at the first man, knocking him off balance. Kali turned in time to deflect another slash from the second one. Winter blinked, surprised at how fast Kali ducked through the man's attack and stepped into him, burying her sword in his belly. Winter felt a chill. Could she be like that, one day? Could she become such a warrior?

Winter's eyes widened as a third man crested the rocks. "Kali!" she shouted. Then she tasted blood.

Kali turned, but remained still. The man she'd kicked stumbled to his feet, but instead of advancing on Kali, he turned towards the third robed man, sword raised, and attacked. It was only a matter of a few blows before one of the men slashed the other across the chest. Blood sprayed bright on the snow. Then Kali stepped behind the remaining robed man and stabbed him in the back.

Winter blinked. What had just happened?

*Acumency*. Was it possible Kali could do more than delve into another's thoughts? That she could make a man want to fight his ally?

The sound of combat drew away Winter's gaze, and she looked back at Nash fighting in a clearing of snow spattered with red.

Four men surrounded him, but they were obviously hesitant. Steel whirred around him, and Winter suddenly realized the utility of the small, circular blades he carried at his belt. They cut savagely at any of the robed men that moved too close. Then Nash created a second blur of steel with his sword, smaller than the spinning blades but just as deadly. She saw now what he meant about multitasking, controlling the small blades with his mind and the sword with his body.

His sudden, incredibly fast movements were familiar. Winter had seen them once before. The entire scene seemed familiar. Attackers, hooded and robed, all in green, surrounding a man who seemed more than a man.

Winter had been helpless then, as she watched Knot battle the strange men from Roden. Now, as Nash fought, she had a realization: she wasn't helpless anymore.

And then the frost hit her.

The dose was *massive*, consuming her whole body in joyous fire and shivers of pleasure. Much more powerful than the doses Nash had been giving her. Winter's spine vibrated, charged with energy. She couldn't contain the power if she wanted to. It rushed through her like a great river, immersing her. No one could stand against her. Not when she felt like this.

But their attackers were already dead. Nash stood over four bodies. Dull disappointment burned in Winter's gut.

No. There, in the distance: two men fleeing on horses. Winter could stop them.

With one of her *tendra*, Winter reached into the ground below one of the boulders. Then she *lifted*. The boulder, roughly the size of a horse, rose into the sky. Winter concentrated, putting all her energy into forming two more *tendra*, reaching out to either side of the rock to keep it steady. Winter tried to breathe evenly. She took aim, instinctively more than anything. Then she reached back, and threw.

The boulder flew through the air. She tried to follow it with her *tendra*, stretching them out to keep it from wavering. For a moment she thought she had overshot, thought the boulder would sail past the escaping men. Then the massive rock smashed into one of the riders, crushing both him and the horse into the ground. The other rider's horse stumbled, frightened, but recovered quickly and continued to gallop into the distance.

Winter cursed. The two men had been riding close enough

that she could have stopped them both. Now one was going to escape. Winter did not think she could throw that far a second time. She was about to lift another boulder and try anyway when someone shook her. She saw Kali, standing right in front of her.

"With me!" the woman shouted, thrusting a set of reins towards her. "We find him," she nodded towards the rider, "and we find out what they wanted."

Winter looked longingly at another boulder,. Then, she took a deep breath, and took the reins. Kali was right. They needed to catch the man and question him.

Winter mounted the horse, following Kali as she galloped after the escaping man. They passed Nash, still standing by the four bodies.

"Stay with the others," Kali yelled to him as they passed. "We'll bring the bastard back."

The *faltira* faded far too quickly as they rode. Coming off such a high was difficult; no wonder frost addiction was a problem. But she was still in control. Frustrated, but at least she wasn't craving another hit already. Not that it wouldn't be nice. Winter glanced at Kali's belt, wondering whether the woman carried a pouch similar to Nash, filled with frost. Best not to think about it.

Soon the robed man steered his horse off the road and onto the snow-covered plains. Horse tracks were easy to follow in the snow, and Kali slowed their pace. Winter hoped it was just a matter of time until they caught up with him. The plain sloped into a low valley ahead of them where patches of trees provided cover. She couldn't see the man anywhere.

"You've yet to wear the clothing I gave you," Kali said, after they'd been riding in silence for several hours.

Winter shrugged, looking down. She had tried the clothes

on a few times, but had not yet found the courage to wear them outside. Her *siara* was wrapped warmly around her neck, and she still wore the same dress she'd brought from Pranna. Ugly and impractical, but familiar.

"That's all right," Kali said. "It took me a while to get used to them. I assumed it would take even longer for an…"

Kali didn't have to finish. Winter knew what she was about to say. *But at least she didn't say it this time.*

"Why did you tell Nash to stay behind?" Winter asked, trying to change the subject.

Kali stared straight ahead. "Someone needed to remain with the others."

"Why take me?"

"Best not to tail a man like this alone. Nash and the others can get moving. With any luck, we'll catch this bastard and meet them on the road."

Winter frowned. That hadn't really answered her question, but she let it go. She thought back to the man who Kali had seemingly forced to kill his ally. "I've learned a lot about telesis," she said. "But you've told me almost nothing about acumency."

Kali sighed. "Best not to overwhelm you. Learning your own craft is difficult enough."

Winter tried to suppress her frustration. Why wouldn't Kali just tell her? What was so different about acumency?

"Nash says I'm picking telesis up quickly. I'm ready for more."

"I suppose telling you a few basics won't hurt," Kali conceded. "Logistically, the two arts are very similar. I have my own *tendra*, but mine act differently than yours. I assume by now you've discovered some of telesis's limitations?"

Winter nodded. "The farther the distance, the less strength a *tendron* has. And *tendra* cannot affect living things.

They can only interact with inanimate objects."

"Very good. Acumenic *tendra* are, in some ways, the opposite. They only interact with living things. My *tendra* interact with the minds of others, and nothing else. I can perceive thoughts and intentions."

"What did you do to that man this morning?"

"That was a more aggressive form of acumency. Once I decipher a person's sift, I can rearrange certain things. This morning, I altered the man's loyalty. Turned the two against each other. I could freeze a man in place just as easily, send a psionic burst into his mind, stunning him, or…" Kali hesitated.

"Or what?" Winter asked.

"Or stop a man's heart."

Winter nodded. Telenics killed just as easily; at least Kali wasn't holding back.

"What's a sift?" Winter had never heard the word before.

Kali's lips pressed together. "Something very complicated," she said. "A distilled soul, essentially. Someone's essence, everything they are, condensed. *Sift* is the term we have for this; *lacuna* is the term for what is left behind."

"Left behind?"

Kali laughed softly. "So curious. There is much to tell you, but that will have to do for now. We can talk more about acumency later."

They rode down the side of the valley. Winter was gaining a newfound respect for the woman. Despite the obvious dislike Kali had shown towards Winter and Lian in the beginning, she seemed to be coming around. While Kali was terse, even unkind at times, she could handle herself in a fight, and she could protect those she cared about from just about anything. Maybe Kali wasn't tiellan, but she was a woman, and she certainly wasn't weak.

Not for the first time, Winter wondered whether she might find a home of some kind with Nash and Kali. With psimancers. She did not know how to reconcile that with their pursuit of Knot, but perhaps an agreement could be reached. Perhaps Winter could finally find a place she belonged.

"I'm sorry about this morning," Winter said, surprising herself.

Kali turned to look at her. "What are you talking about?"

"I… when those men attacked, I froze. I didn't do anything to help. I just stood there."

Kali shook her head. "You managed to take out one of the riders. That throw with the boulder was accurate. You may have been useless otherwise, but so is everyone in their first battle."

"But I basically wasted a frost crystal," Winter said. "I hardly did anything."

Kali turned her horse so she faced Winter directly. Winter stopped in surprise.

"You need to stop this," Kali said. "If you're going to survive in this world—as a woman, as a *tiellan*—then you need to be stronger. Dwelling on your inadequacies will get you nowhere. Taking upon yourself blame you do not deserve…" Kali closed her eyes, reaching beneath her cloak. For a moment Winter thought Kali might show her something, but her hand was empty when it reemerged.

Kali opened her eyes. "I know you blame yourself for what happened in the alleyway."

Winter blinked. She did not know why—Nash was the one who had saved her in the alley, after all—but it surprised her that Kali knew. Or, perhaps, it surprised her that Kali seemed to care.

"I've seen how your eyes empty when you think no one

watches you. I know that look because I've had it myself.

"What happened in the alleyway was not your fault. It doesn't matter if you're a tiellan, if you're a human, or what you did or did not wear or do. He treated you like an object. He thought you were something he could use and discard. That was *his* error. He chose to act like a narcissist, an egoist, and a bastard, and you don't deserve any of that blame. So bloody stop shoveling it onto yourself."

"If you're right," Winter said quietly, "why do I feel so guilty?"

For the briefest moment, Winter thought she saw Kali's eyes soften.

"You might think you could have said something to prevent it. You might think you could have fought harder to stop him." Slowly, the softness left Kali's face, and she looked out into the distance. "There could be any number of reasons, but they don't matter. What matters is that he chose to attack you, and you didn't want him to. The fault doesn't lie with you. End of story."

Winter swallowed. She couldn't tell if Kali was angry, or just being stern. But what Kali said… could it be true? Winter *had* gone over the incident over and over in her mind, wishing she would have defended herself more aggressively, or just realized what was happening sooner. There was so much she could have done differently.

But none of that caused what had happened to her. None of that excused what the man had done.

"All right," Winter said. She didn't feel better. The truth was, she still felt guilt. But, now, she could acknowledge that she *shouldn't*. And that was a beginning.

"You have strength within you. *Use* it, Winter." Then Kali turned her horse, and continued down into the valley.

After a few moments, Kali held up her hand indicating they stop again.

"There's a stream down here," Kali said. "Might even be running, with the warmer weather we've had recently." She was right. As they approached, Winter saw the glint of running water, heard a faint trickling.

Kali placed a finger to her lips. Winter nodded. Kali reached a hand out to her. She held another frost crystal. Winter looked at it, resisting the urge to snatch and consume it immediately. Instead, she reached out slowly, and put the frost in her satchel. Odd that she was sweating. The wind had picked up, and Winter shivered despite the trickle that ran down her temple.

They reached the stream, which was indeed partially thawed. Mud churned in a few places on the banks, while remnants of ice jutted out into others. The tracks stopped at the water directly in front of them. Winter was about to suggest the man had ridden his horse down the stream to throw them off when she saw, to her surprise, that the tracks continued away from the stream, at an angle, a few rods downstream.

Kali had noticed as well. She led the way to the tracks, urging her horse into the water.

"Kali, wait," Winter whispered. Kali stopped and turned. Something wasn't right. The way the tracks led away from the water, the way they looked…

"He didn't go that way," Winter said. The tracks were too light, the cadence of the horse's steps too irregular. The horse had been riderless.

Winter nodded downstream. "He left the horse and continued on foot in the stream."

Winter was worried the woman would argue, but Kali nodded.

"Stupid of him," Kali said. "His feet will freeze if he doesn't get them dry and warm."

Winter nodded. It *was* stupid, but it was a trade-off of sorts. Leaving his horse had been a good move.

They moved downstream, quietly. The stream cut into the valley floor, creating two high earthen banks. In the summer it was probably more like a river, rather than just an icy, ankle-deep trickle.

"There," Winter whispered. Ahead of them, a set of footprints, barely visible in the frozen mud, led away from the water. She slid down from her horse.

"Goddess," Kali muttered. "Good thing I brought you along."

Winter tried to ignore the pride filling her chest. She bent down, looking closely at the prints. "Kick debris," Winter said, pointing at the barely noticeable cone of mud, snow, and water in front of each footprint. It had taken Winter a long time to recognize kick debris while she was growing up, but her father had been a good teacher. "We know he isn't backtracking, at least. Definitely went this way."

Then she froze.

"What is it?" Kali whispered.

Winter waved behind her, quieting Kali.

There, overstepping one of the man's footprints, was something much larger. The print, from heel to toe, was at least as long as Winter's forearm. In front of each toe, long claw marks pressed into the mud.

Winter turned to Kali. *Snowbear,* she mouthed.

In northern Khale, most bears hibernated during the winter. The snowbear, on the other hand, had no such need. It hunted through the winter, taking whatever prey it could find, often stalking heavily trafficked areas by roads or water sources. Snowbears would usually leave humans and tiellans alone in the summer, but in the winter, food was food.

Winter stopped. Had she just heard something? Heavy breathing, perhaps. A soft rumble.

She looked back at Kali, who slowly unsheathed her sword.

Then Kali's eyes went wide.

Instinctively, Winter ducked and rolled to the side, just as something huge lumbered behind her.

She had been right. The massive beast stood on its hind legs, roaring. Snowbears were the largest type of bear Winter knew of; this one towered over Kali on her horse.

Kali shouted, spurring her horse towards the animal, but the bear was already charging. Winter didn't have time to reach for the frost. She had to do something *now*. So she did the only thing that came to mind. She rushed towards the animal, drawing a long, thin dagger from her belt. Just as the bear was about to come down from its hind legs, Winter dropped beneath it, sliding over the ice. She passed between the beast's massive legs, thrusting the dagger up as she did so.

Stabbing the animal stopped her sliding short, but now she was directly underneath the bear. Winter froze, fighting panic. The bear could crush her easily. She pulled the dagger out of the bear's thigh and hot blood splashed down on her as she tried to shimmy out from underneath the beast. The bear, roaring in pain, came back down on all fours just as Winter slid away. Ice shattered. Winter felt the freezing water of the stream gurgle up and around her.

Winter bared her teeth, gripping the small dagger as the bear turned to face her. She was suddenly aware of how ridiculous she must look—how foolish. A small tiellan, holding a little knife and growling in the face of a massive snowbear. What chance did she have?

Then Kali barreled into the animal, slashing downward with her sword.

The bear screamed this time—a very different sound from a growl—and turned angrily to face its new attacker. But the damage was done. The bear swiped at Kali, but her horse moved nimbly aside, sidestepping into the stream. Kali stabbed down again, this time burying her blade in the animal's neck. The bear moaned, then collapsed to the ground with a thud.

"Canta's bones," Kali gasped, "that was the most insane thing I've ever seen. You charged a *snowbear*, Winter."

Winter looked at her, shivering.

Then Kali smiled. "I told you," she said. "Second battle. You didn't freeze up. You did something incredibly *stupid*, but you didn't freeze up. And you didn't have frost to help you. I'm almost impressed."

Winter looked down at herself, covered in blood and ice. Her hands were shaking. And yet… and yet she felt good. *Alive*. She almost felt the way she did when she took frost, although the feeling wasn't nearly as strong. Perhaps Kali was right. Perhaps she *did* have strength within her.

Winter couldn't help but smile.

The man they had been tracking had also encountered the snowbear, but hadn't been as lucky. Winter and Kali found his remains in the bear's cave, around the bend in the stream.

"We tracked him this far for nothing?" Winter said, suddenly feeling sick as she looked at the mess of blood and entrails.

"Not quite," Kali said. "We found out how bloody good at tracking you are, for one. We found out, too, that you have no sense of self-preservation." Kali glared at her, and Winter blushed, but there was a glint in Kali's eye that made pride well up in Winter's breast.

"The man can't inform anyone else of us or our position anymore, so that's something," Kali continued. "Now we can catch up with the others on the road, hardly having lost any time. All in all, I'd call it a win."

Winter nodded, looking from the man's remains down to her shivering body, both covered in blood. A win, indeed.

# 21

*Canta's Grace, Navone*

"I'm sorry, sir," the innkeeper said. "Holy Crucible's orders. No one leaves the city, and any travelers must remain in their lodgings until they've been checked."

Knot swore.

"So much for avoiding trouble," Astrid muttered behind him.

"Look," Knot said to the innkeeper, spreading his arms wide, "I'm just a merchant, trying to ply my trade. Got no business with the Denomination, I'd just waste their time."

The innkeeper's eyes narrowed. "You and everyone else in Navone. Stay in the common room, or your own room if you want. Sons're already out and about." The innkeeper didn't have to point out the group of armored men seated at one of the tables in the common room; they'd been the first thing Knot noticed on his way down the stairs. The Sons were different from watch or guardsmen. Their reputations preceded them, of course, but Knot could *see* their experience in the way they carried themselves. Each had a sense of stiff organization and obedience, even in the common room.

"They say the Goddessguard're among us as well," the innkeeper said, whispering now. "Some of them are patrolling from house to house, questioning everyone inside. Weeding out the heretics. Others're just sneaking around. Spying, seeing if there's any among us who support the heretics, making sure we're following the rules. Anybody who don't live here could be one of them, any traveler, any... er..."

The man's voice trailed off as he refocused on Knot. He coughed and didn't meet Knot's eyes. "Anyway," he said stiffly, "I just hope they're able to quell this business quickly. Heretics are giving our city a bad name. Long live Canta's Holy Denomination, and all that." The man went through the motion of trining himself, tapping his thumb and first two fingers on top of his forehead, then below each eye.

Astrid sniggered as they turned away. "You, a *Goddessguard*. People've lost all sense in this city. What did he think I was, the Crucible in disguise?"

Knot ignored her as they walked away from the bar, towards a window that looked over the small alleyway outside the inn. If he pressed his face close to the glass he could glimpse one of the main streets they'd traversed the night before. Seemed empty, for the most part. That didn't bode well for anyone planning an escape. Anyone but Sons of Canta on the streets would stick out like a broken nose.

That was far from the worst of their problems. The sun had risen bright and clear that morning, in a near cloudless blue sky. Snow glistened on rooftops as the icicles hanging in front of the window slowly melted.

Being caught by a squad of Sons was one thing. Being questioned by them, risking them ordering Astrid to remove her cloak in broad daylight, was quite another. The girl could be out during the daytime as long as she was covered, by clouds or a cloak or a rooftop or otherwise, but if she was exposed to any direct sunlight there'd be problems. Those were her words, anyway, and Knot didn't feel inclined to test them. He wondered for a moment what it would be like, to know that the sunlight would never touch his skin again.

Knot still hadn't decided what to do with the girl. But one thing was sure: he didn't want anything to do with the Holy Crucible.

"We could take side roads. Sneak through the city," he said, knowing the suggestion was folly even as he said it. "Might be able to make it."

"What then?" Astrid asked. "We get to the city wall, leap over it and onward to freedom? Things are never that easy."

Sons would be patrolling the wall, of course, and likely the surrounding countryside. But the letter Knot had received the night before… if he could find this Captain Rudak, they might stand a chance.

"Don't know," Knot said after a moment. "I'm making this up as I go along. Might be we could fight our way out, all things considered."

Astrid laughed. "I'm all for spontaneity, nomad, but we aren't invincible. Can't fight our way out of everything."

He raised his eyebrows. "Since when did you get all peaceable?"

"Since when did you get so warlike? Thought you wanted to harm as few people as possible. Are you finally willing to face your true nature?" She was grinning.

He didn't answer, and turned back to the window. Truth be told, Knot *didn't* want to face his true nature, whatever that was. Dreams were bad enough; what he had seen himself do in reality was even worse. And the fact that he enjoyed it didn't bear thinking about.

"Why don't we wait until nightfall?" Astrid asked. "More cover for us, and if it does come to a fight, I'll be much more effective."

"Don't know if we can wait that long," he said. "The Goddessguard, the Crucible herself, are scouring the city. Might be they reach our inn before then." He thought about it for a moment. "Ain't no immediate danger if they question us inside, though. Wouldn't need to worry about your cloak, at least. Our story just might hold."

"What if it's the Crucible herself?" Astrid asked.

"What if it is?"

"A Holy Crucible *knows* things. She sees into people. She'll see into me. Oblivion, she'll probably see into you, too. It's not like your past is all perfume and flowers."

Knot turned back to the window, looking out into the alley. "You really believe that?"

The girl didn't respond. It didn't matter. All that did was getting out of here, and they'd do whatever it took to make that happen.

"We wait 'til nightfall, then."

Astrid nodded. "Nightfall."

In the end, Knot and Astrid didn't have to wait long. After they'd played a few games of warsquares down in the common room, the doors to the inn burst open.

A fully armored Goddessguard, his tabard a bright scarlet bordered with white, strutted into the room. Goddessguards typically wore full plate armor, polished and etched with gold. This man was no exception. The Sons who'd been there since that morning stood at attention while more of the soldiers walked in. They wore barbute helmets and chain mail. Eleven in all, including the Goddessguard.

"Good day," the Goddessguard said in a gruff, gravelly voice that seemed to imply anything but. He removed his helm, placing it under one arm, and raised his other hand high. The room fell silent. "No need to fear us," he said. "We have been called here for a specific purpose. We are doing Canta's work, and require your assistance. We'd like to speak to all of you, one group at a time. The Sons will direct a queue, and you'll all have the opportunity to speak with me shortly. Cooperate, and this will all pass quickly."

The Goddessguard nodded, and the Sons moved ahead of him, shouting orders. Slowly, people began rising up from their seats, unsure of what to do. Something between a mass and a line formed by the Sons, near the bar, as people milled about and whispered under their breath. Being examined by a Goddessguard under the direction of a Holy Crucible was certainly not something that happened every day; many even looked excited. Why not? They had nothing to fear, after all. Most people probably didn't. Only the daemons in the room had to worry their heads.

Knot stood slowly. *At least it isn't the Crucible herself,* he thought, though why that really mattered he couldn't say. He didn't believe what Astrid had said earlier—nobody could see into another's soul. But the fact that just a Goddessguard was doing the interviewing made him feel better.

Knot put his hand on Astrid's shoulder. "Might as well get it over with. Then we can make our move tonight."

The girl looked up at him, and Knot thought he saw a brief flicker of fear. He wasn't sure, but as quickly as it came, it went again. She nodded.

They approached the other customers near the bar. Some were obviously scared. Perhaps they were thieves or adulterers. He couldn't imagine the Crucible wasting time on such things. Seemed the Denomination already knew who these "heretics" were, anyway—as did the whole damn city, for that matter. The rest of the crowd looked bored, impatient, even excited, but everyone was compliant. There were twenty-seven in all, not counting the Sons and the Goddessguard, who sat at a table questioning each person in turn.

It took them the better part of an hour to get near the front of the queue. The Goddessguard was thorough. If they intended to question the entire city this way, the Crucible would be here for weeks.

They were only a few places from the front of the queue when there was a sudden crash, and several Sons hauled a whimpering middle-aged woman towards the door. Then she screamed and all eyes were on her.

"You can't do this!" she shouted, her eyes wild and frantic. "I'm a faithful Cantic. I go to chapel, I've taught children Cantic doctrine. I haven't done anything wrong!"

The Goddessguard stood. "Canta's will has been revealed," he said, his voice hard. "The Crucible will determine your rightness before our Goddess."

The screams continued as the Sons dragged the woman out, the door closing behind them with a slam. The sound rang in the room for a moment, its resonance fading into silence.

Then the whispering began. Quiet at first, then frantic, demanding an explanation for what had just happened. The Goddessguard ignored the whispers and continued the interviews. The Sons stared with hard eyes, fingering swords and halberds.

People were feeding on each other's fears, Knot could feel it. The whispering grew louder. Then someone shouted, demanding to know what was going on. Knot kept his eye on the Goddessguard, who looked up. The man stood, his voice ringing out above the cacophony.

"Silence!" he shouted. "There will be peace in this hall, in Canta's name. There *will* be peace!"

It was too late, Knot could see that. The Goddessguard had reacted too late. The crowd had worked itself into a frenzy.

*Perhaps this is our chance,* he thought. *Now is the time to escape.*

And then, out of the corner of his eye, he saw a flash of movement. A young couple, a man and a woman, pushed between him and Astrid, knocking Astrid to the ground and shoving their way towards the door guarded by a pair of Sons.

They never made it.

The Sons guarding the door moved fast, for grunt-level men. They were well trained. The first guard drew his sword smoothly and in one motion cut off the woman's arm as she reached towards the door. He then brought the sword around to plunge through her chest. The other guard, who'd been leaning on a long halberd, swung the butt of his weapon into the man's feet, knocking him to the ground. He lifted his weapon high and slammed the blade into the man's throat. It didn't sever the head, only slicing through about half of the flesh, but the man was dead in an instant. Blood leaked across the floorboards.

There was a scream and Knot looked down at Astrid, but she wasn't beside him. He tensed. Then he realized that the crowd was not looking at the bodies, despite the slaughter that had just taken place. They were looking at the floor, in the patch of sunlight near where Knot stood.

Between the square of sunlight from the window and the wall, a small form cowered. Tendrils of smoke rose from her body as she scrambled into the shadows.

*Astrid.*

"Shit," Knot said.

"Vampire!" roared the Goddessguard.

Knot rushed towards the girl. He hadn't brought his staff, but a small dagger was concealed beneath his clothing. It would have to do until he could find something more suitable. The room was filled with the shouts of terror from the crowd and the barked orders from the Goddessguard to the Sons.

Knot swore again, under his breath.

"You all right?" he asked, reaching Astrid's crouched form. She didn't look severely wounded, but the skin of the hand she reached out to him was grayish and discolored, still smoking. Knot sighed in relief. Could have been worse.

Then she turned to look at him, and he gasped. The entire right side of her face was a mass of blackened, boiling skin. Flesh hung by thin strips, pink and gray and sickly. Knot's hand trembled as he helped her up. She looked at him with one eye green and slightly glowing, the other a burned bloody mess, only the hint of a glow in its depths.

"That bitch pushed me into the bloody sunlight," she rasped. "I'm done with this. Let's kill some people."

And then she was off.

Knot turned just in time to see one of the Sons charging him with a halberd. He dodged the man's lunge, drawing his dagger with one hand as he used the man's momentum against him with his other, gripping the halberd shaft and adding his own weight to the strike. The man flipped over his own weapon, and Knot slid his dagger in and out of the man's throat.

So easy. Knot hated how easy it was. He hated it, and he loved it.

He sheathed his dagger in favor of the halberd. It wasn't his staff, but it would do for now. He swung the weapon experimentally, getting a feel for its balance.

"No one gets out!" the Goddessguard shouted. "Man the doors!"

Knot looked around. Most of the crowd had either run

upstairs or were cowering in a corner of the common room. Some still tried to get out, but several Sons blocked their way. Near the bar, the Goddessguard and at least four Sons contended with a screeching blur. By the looks of things, they weren't winning.

Knot would have liked to watch Astrid fight. Even in daylight, everyone around her seemed to move at a snail's pace. But, instead, he swung his halberd into one of the Sons' backs, feeling the blade pierce armor and bury itself deep in the man's spine.

It was a pleasure to kill.

Three soldiers looked back at him. Then only two. Astrid streaked past the other, latching onto his head and snapping it around so it now faced the opposite direction as the man fell.

He moved in on the two Sons, halberd spinning in his hands. He felt a brief sense of elation as the men advanced, stepping slowly apart to flank him.

Knot parried an attack smoothly, simultaneously weaving away from the other soldier. He blocked another blow and then stabbed the butt of his weapon—a long metal spike—backwards, feeling it sink into flesh. He yanked the weapon forward, rolling to the ground as he dodged another strike from the first Son, and then swung the halberd into the man's head. The shaft of the halberd smashed in the front of the man's helmet, and blood gushed down his face. Knot took a step back, taking the halberd at the very edge of the weapon's grip, and swung it like a woodcutter felling a tree. Searing pain lanced through his injured shoulder, but the blade buried itself into the side of the man's head. Red and gray splattered the floor.

Knot yanked the halberd away with a burst of strength, but some of the man's gore caught on the blade and held it. Knot shook the weapon violently, freeing it, and turned to advance towards Astrid, who was now backing towards the window that had first exposed her. The Goddessguard circled around her, while two Sons remained. She dispatched one as Knot watched, her fist crushing the man's face like a hammer.

Then the doors to the common room slammed open, and ten more Sons of Canta filed into the room, led by another Goddessguard.

Knot swore. That didn't help their odds.

Astrid turned to face their new enemies. Knot lunged at the remaining Son near Astrid, stabbing the spike of the halberd into the man's back.

The Goddessguard turned to face Knot. The amount of armor the man wore would slow him down, but the Goddessguard would be used to that. He swung a shining longsword in one hand, and brandished a rectangular curved shield with the Trinacrya emblazoned on its face in the other.

Knot advanced, gripping the halberd loosely. Swinging it ostentatiously around as he had before wouldn't intimidate this man, and it would only be wasted energy. He had a feeling he'd need it.

The Goddessguard attacked first, slicing in with his longsword. Knot parried but the man's shield nearly knocked him off balance. Knot recovered, twisting, muscles screaming as he ducked beneath another sword swing, then leapt up again to slash at the man. The Goddessguard blocked the attack easily.

The halberd was useless in such close quarters. Knot needed a different approach. He spun around again, trying to get behind the Goddessguard. He parried another sword strike and charged in, pushing his opponent against the wall. Knot pressed the halberd's shaft across the man's throat. The sword lashed back towards Knot from one side, and the heavy shield bashed into him from the other. Knot was forced to loosen the chokehold to parry the wild slash, but the shield hit him square in the hip. The Goddessguard lunged away, resetting his feet, shield up.

Knot stepped back and swung the halberd with all of his strength. The weapon clanged against the man's shield. Knot swung again. He began to swing a third time, but at the last moment directed it towards the man's legs. The halberd collided with the shield once more as the man lowered to block.

Knot gasped, his breath ragged. His hands ached. His opponent was fast, despite the armor. But his bloodlust had risen. There was only one way this could end.

Knot grinned. The Goddessguard looked at him blankly, not reacting.

As fast as he could, Knot drew his dagger from his belt and threw it at the man's eye.

The shield rose quickly as Knot launched himself forward. The man saw Knot coming, but it was too late. Knot swept the halberd at the man's feet, tripping him up, and then brought the blade of the halberd down on top of the Goddessguard. The shield blocked it, but the blow was enough to send the man the rest of the way to the ground.

Knot slammed the end of the halberd into the man's chest. The spike pierced armor and flesh and sank into the floor below.

Knot turned just in time to see two swords pointed at his chest.

Two Sons, eyes burning behind their helmets, glared at him. He saw, beyond them, the remaining Sons and Goddessguard.

Astrid lay on the ground beside them.

Knot didn't think she was dead; it seemed a violent beating would not be enough, not by a long shot. But the sons were already fixing chains to the girl's body.

"Don't worry, the daemon is still alive," the remaining Goddessguard said. His voice was a stark contrast to the man Knot had just killed, high and condescending, with an accent that sounded vaguely familiar. The man was noble-born.

"No reason to lose sleep over her, she's in our custody now. Although I've heard sleep is difficult when you're dead." The man nodded at the Sons guarding Knot. "Do it quickly." The Goddessguard glanced at Astrid as a group of soldiers wrapped her in chains and a heavy, dark cloak. "Her Grace will be quite interested in our discovery."

He left the common room, three Sons dragging the chained bundle behind them. Knot looked at the two men whose sword-points grazed his chest. His dagger was gone, as was the halberd. He had nothing that could parry one sword, let alone two.

And then, behind the Sons, a shape moved. With a crash, one of the soldiers collapsed to the floor, broken pieces of wood flying through the air.

The other soldier looked at his companion, eyes wide, and Knot took the moment to weave around the sword point and hammer his palm into the Son's nose. Knot gripped the man's sword hand and slammed his other arm into his elbow, breaking it backwards with a sickening crunch. The man screamed just for a second before Knot's hand clamped across his mouth. He reached his other hand behind the Son's helmet, and snapped the man's neck.

Knot stepped back. Behind the dead Sons of Canta stood an older man. He had very little hair, and wore spectacles. He also held the remains of a broken chair in his hands.

"That was my wife they took," the man said, his voice surprisingly deep. "I don't know who that was you were fighting with, and Canta knows, right now I don't care. But you seem capable, so you're going to help me. Understand?"

Knot looked at the man, and nodded. He needed an ally; this man seemed as good as any.

"My name is Olan," the man said, extending his left arm. Knot gripped it. Olan was surprisingly strong, despite his bookish appearance.

"Knot. We need to get out of here, before the Sons return." He indicated the corpses. "They'll know when these two don't come back."

The man nodded, and dropped the splintered chair. He glanced at the crowd still huddled in the corner of the room.

"Nothing we can do about them," Knot said. "I need my pack, then we're getting out of here."

Knot ran up the stairs, hands shaking. He tried not to think about what they would do to Astrid, and he tried not to think about what he had felt while killing those men. There seemed to be a whole lot he was trying not to think about, lately.

Olan was cleaning his spectacles when Knot flew back down the stairs with his and Astrid's packs. He handed one to the man.

"We have a lot of work to do."

"I think I know where we can start," Olan said.

Knot met his eyes, wondering briefly whether he could trust this man. Trust seemed in short supply lately. But Knot had no choice.

# 22

"YOU CANNOT BE SERIOUS," Cinzia said, looking at Jane. She had heard a lot of crazy things in the past few days, but this topped them all.

"This is what I must do. I have seen it."

"It is *suicide*," Cinzia said. Jane had already said goodbye to the rest of their family, and Cinzia now walked with her through an alley behind their home. They both wore hooded cloaks, and Cinzia looked at both ends of the alley every few seconds. Sons of Canta patrolled the streets. Kovac waited inside the door, just in case.

"It is not suicide, it is Canta's will. She directs me, now. And you need to be prepared..."

Jane trailed off. Cinzia could not meet her eyes. She could not believe her sister was even *contemplating* this. Cinzia had thought she would have been able to exercise some influence over her family by now, to convince them how insane all of this was, but things were only spiraling downward, further and further out of her control.

"Prepared for what?" Cinzia asked.

"Canta's plan is bigger than me, bigger than our family. Whatever happens will be for the best. Whatever happens to *me* will be for the best."

"How can you *know* that? How can you stand there and

tell me that because of some *vision*—something you tell me I cannot yet understand—you are turning yourself in? How does that help you or our family? Or Canta Herself, for that matter?"

"I do not know," Jane said. "But I trust that someone else does. That is enough for me."

Cinzia was speechless. She wanted to tell Jane that *she* trusted Canta, too, but that they had seemed to devote themselves to two very different goddesses. But the truth was, Cinzia was tired of arguing, and she knew her sister had made up her mind.

Then Jane hugged her. The sudden contact reminded Cinzia of how they used to be as children, sleeping side by side at night, shoulder to shoulder, hip to hip.

"I love you, Jane," Cinzia finally said.

"I love you, Cinzi," Jane whispered.

"It's not fair," Cinzia said. "Just when I return, you leave."

"Canta will protect me," Jane said, releasing her. "And… Canta's plan extends beyond death. I know that, now. You will know it too, one day. Take care of our family, sister."

Jane stepped away. "They will look to you."

Cinzia stood there, frozen, as her sister kissed her on the cheek.

"Canta guide your path," Jane said. Then she turned, walking towards the main road.

"Yours as well, Jane," Cinzia whispered. She stood there for a long time, staring at the patch of sunlit road where her sister had slipped away.

"Canta," Cinzia whispered, "what do I do now?"

No answer came.

"There have been some developments," Eward told her when she came back inside. "Mother and Father want to speak with you."

Cinzia followed him through the house and down to the cellar. She descended the wooden stairs, each step creaking as she put her weight on it. Eward held a small lantern that produced a globe of yellow light, but otherwise the space was dark. The mustiness of it hit her suddenly, like new wine and mildew.

As soon as Jane had told them about the imminent arrival of the Crucible, and her desire to turn herself in, their family had moved into a hidden complex of underground rooms, accessed through a tunnel in the cellar. It had been used during the days of tiellan slavery as a safehouse for tiellans fleeing the purges in Roden.

Cinzia used to sneak down there with Jane, against their father's wishes. Cinzia had a difficult time believing that those times were so long ago.

"I am not happy about her decision either," Eward said, obviously seeing Cinzia's concern. "Have faith, sister. Canta is at the helm."

Cinzia said nothing. She was not sure she wanted to know what her brother's, or Jane's, idea of "faith" was anymore.

Eward walked towards the wine barrel that served as a cover for the passageway. He reached behind a wall sconce, pulled a lever, and the large barrel rolled to the side, revealing a narrow hallway. The mechanism was impressive. A complex system of pulleys and gears moved the barrel easily, and once they were inside the tunnel, the flip of another lever rolled the thing back into place.

"What is this new development, Eward?" Cinzia asked warily. She almost did not want to know. Almost.

"See for yourself," he said, as they reached the end of the tunnel and he opened a door, revealing the man-made cavern beyond. It was nearly empty: a few chairs, makeshift beds and blankets, food and water, clothing, anything from their house that they could not bear to part with, and nothing else.

In a far corner, the younger Oden children sat in a circle, laughing and playing. They had accepted the transition into the strange space surprisingly well. Cinzia envied them. Even Ader seemed to have a firmer grasp on things than she did.

Her father and mother stood near the center of the room with two men. Cinzia recognized one of them as Olan Cawthon, who had been the Odens' house steward. He and his wife Nara were two of the few servants that had remained in the city after the Odens' reputation had made them dangerous to be associated with, and were also part of the small group who knew about Jane's visions, and supported her. But where was Nara? Cinzia knew the two had planned on getting out of town before the Crucible arrived.

Apparently, they had not been successful.

The other man, Cinzia did not recognize. He was, in almost every way, average. Average height, average build, his hair and eyes unremarkable brown. A short beard covered his angular jaw.

Cinzia had looked into many eyes as a priestess in Canta's Denomination. People were required to confess their sins at least twice a year in the confession hall, during Penetensar and on the Day of Consecration. Cinzia could not possibly count how many confessions she had heard, but she had come to recognize certain traits in the eyes of those who knelt before her. Marga Soln had lost each of her five children, and the pain was evident. When Cinzia oversaw Alek and Seira Hone's wedding ceremony, every day afterward their eyes shone with happiness. Even Cinzia's own matron, who oversaw Cinzia's leadership of her congregation, displayed pride and power in her eyes.

But looking into this man's eyes, Cinzia remembered

another man. It had been after a midnight service of forgiveness during Penetensar. He had been at least partially inebriated, but Cinzia allowed him to confess anyway. If that was the only thing that would get him to do so, who was she to hold it against him? Cinzia did not remember much about the young man, but his eyes… his eyes were a deep, clear green, but they held no joy or passion or pain. They held nothing.

This man had those same eyes. Cinzia shivered. There was nothing behind them. They seemed the eyes of a dead man.

"Cinzia, this is Knot," her father said. "He and Olan had some problems this morning, at an inn."

"Nara was taken," Olan said quietly. "Along with a… a friend of Knot's. We fought our way out, and I led him here so we could organize a party to bring them back."

Cinzia looked at Olan. "I am so sorry," she said. She had known Olan all her life. No one needed to mention what might happen to someone taken by a Crucible. They had all heard rumors, and Cinzia had heard a lot of truth.

Olan looked at her through his spectacles, his round face unusually hard. His father had come from Maven Kol, in the south, and Olan's skin was slightly darker by nature than what was the norm in northern Khale, with almost a golden undertone.

"She is alive," he said. "Or, she will be, until the executions tomorrow."

"*What?*" Cinzia's heart pounded against her chest, as if struggling to escape. Her mind raced. Executions? Jane would surely be among the condemned. Canta, or whomever Jane thought she was communicating with, had told her to submit herself, only to be killed the next day? It did not make sense. Cinzia could taste bile in her throat, like stale vinegar. Why would Canta let this happen? She had once thought this a test;

now Cinzia did not know what it was.

Then, she had an epiphany.

"We must rescue her," Cinzia said.

All eyes turned to her. She continued, more sure of herself. This *had* to be what Jane's visions meant.

"Jane said it was Canta's will that she submit herself to the Crucible. I cannot imagine it was to die. What if we are her means of escape? What if this is a test for *us*?"

Cinzia felt the excitement rising. She could finally take control of this mess. Of course, the idea that Canta would send Jane to brave execution only to have their family save her was preposterous; Cinzia believed none of it. But if she could get her family to believe, perhaps she could convince them to take action.

"We've discussed the possibility of a rescue, Priestess," Kovac said. "But it will be difficult. An entire complement of the Sons of Canta will be guarding them, and at least ten Goddessguards."

"We're rescuing them," Olan said, his voice even and quiet. "I'm rescuing Nara. I won't leave her to be executed. I'll go alone if I have to, but I'm going."

Cinzia nodded. *Good,* she thought. Easier to enlist her family's help if Olan was already committed. There might yet be time for Jane.

Kovac stared at the two newcomers. Cinzia felt a sudden rush of gratitude for her Goddessguard. To say she was relieved that Kovac had chosen to stay with her in Navone was an understatement. But she had always suspected he had become her Goddessguard more out of protectiveness than any ecclesiastical devotion.

"Need to move soon, then," the other man, Knot, said. It was the first time he had spoken. He spoke with a drawl that was almost tiellan, each syllable slow and lazy. Knot's dead gaze fell on Cinzia, and her hand moved involuntarily to the Trinacrya on her necklace.

"Who was this friend of yours that was taken?" she asked.

For the first time Cinzia saw a hint of… something, there, in his eyes. A spark of life.

"Not a friend," he said. "My daughter."

"Canta rising," Cinzia whispered. She knew a Crucible could be harsh, but *this*? "How old?"

Knot coughed before answering. "Ninth summer."

"Why would they take her?" Cinzia wondered aloud. "What need would the Crucible have for a child?"

She saw Olan shift uncomfortably out of the corner of her eye. *They are not telling us something.*

"Don't know," Knot said. "But I'm getting her back."

"We need to keep our numbers small," Kovac said. "Perhaps just the two of us would be sufficient." He indicated himself and Knot.

"I'm going," Olan said.

"I can go, too," Eward said. Cinzia turned in surprise; she had almost forgotten he was there. "It's Jane," he said, looking around at each of them. "It's *Jane*," he repeated.

"You are not going, Eward," Ehram said, stepping towards his son. "We need you here."

Cinzia turned to Kovac, who seemed to be exchanging a glance with Knot. The two seemed to have developed a connection. Despite Cinzia's misgivings about Knot, this comforted her. She might not trust Knot, whoever he was, but she trusted Kovac.

"Too many," Kovac said. "Our attempt would be stopped before it began. Knot and I are the only people with combat experience. It needs to be the two of us."

"*I'm going*," Olan said, "whether you like it or not. It's my *wife*, for Canta's sake."

Kovac and Knot exchanged another glance. Finally, Knot nodded.

"Are we sure this is what we should be doing?" Cinzia's father asked quietly. "Jane said it was Canta's will that she turn herself in. Won't Canta get her out of it? What if we interfere with Her plan, somehow?"

Cinzia shook her head. "If Canta's plan is to deliver Jane, it will be through us."

Her father watched her, torn. He genuinely *did* believe Jane, Cinzia realized. She had known it before, of course, had heard him say it. But she had never fully believed it until this moment. He truly believed this impostor goddess would rescue his daughter.

But Cinzia also knew that he wanted Jane back, safe. Ehram must have been torn to pieces over it all.

"We need to do this, Father," she told him. "We are Canta's best tools. We are Jane's only hope."

"Very well." Ehram turned to Eward. "Kovac is right, son, it will be too many. I already have one child in the hands of a Crucible; I do not want to watch another do the same."

"Two children, actually," Cinzia said. "I am a priestess, and the best hope any of us have of getting close to the prisoners." She looked at Kovac. "You know I'm right."

Kovac nodded.

Eward was not convinced. "Father," he began, but Ehram cut him off.

"No, son," he said. "You stay here with us. We still need looking after, you know."

Eward looked down. "Yes, Father."

"Very well," Kovac said. "Let's get started." Cinzia felt a thrill of excitement at the thought that she was finally doing something. They could do this. They could save Jane, and Nara, and Knot's daughter. And, when Jane was back, Cinzia would get to the bottom of this mess. She would not let her sister be lost to whatever shadow had gotten her into this in the first place.

She listened intently as Kovac presented his plan.

Later that night, Cinzia, Kovac, Knot, and Olan approached the Assembly Hall. The Holy Crucible had temporarily taken over the building—a strange move in Cinzia's opinion. The Cantic Denomination, when possible, retained distance from matters of government. Three members of the High Camarilla holding permanent seats on Khale's minor council made it difficult, but it was a distance the Denomination was supposed to respect. Cinzia had assumed the Crucible would work from Ocrestia's cathedral, or one of Navone's chapels.

"Who goes there?" a voice called out as they approached. A pair of Sons guarded the large doors to the building.

"Sister Alla Shethon, of Triah," Cinzia said. They had decided on false names, in case anyone had already mentioned to the Crucible that Jane had a sister in the Ministry. But if that information had already leaked, their mission might be doomed to begin with. Cinzia dried her palms lightly against her dress.

"I offer prisoners for the Holy Crucible, as well as my services in purging this city."

The Sons regarded her, then Kovac, their eyes finally resting on Knot and Olan, bound behind them.

"Very well, Priestess," one of the men said. "Enter, and report to Laurent."

Cinzia smiled. "Thank you for your service," she said. The Sons opened the large oak doors, and one of them went inside to report their arrival. Once the doors were fully open, Cinzia and her small company entered.

The Assembly Hall was more than just the massive hall in which the city council met to discuss policy. It consisted of meeting rooms, and a dozen or so offices in which the members of the government worked. Cinzia walked quietly down a hallway towards a tall blond man, in full Goddessguard armor, waiting for them. The Son from the doorway waited at his side.

"Priestess Alla, I presume?" the man asked. He was handsome, his features strong and defined.

Cinzia nodded.

"I am Laurent, Her Grace's chief Goddessguard. She will meet with you momentarily." He glanced behind Cinzia, towards Knot and Olan. "Gad and the others will keep your prisoners under close watch. They are in our care now. What is the nature of their crimes, if I may ask?"

Cinzia steeled herself. "I am afraid I must discuss that with the Holy Crucible first," she said, with as much authority as she could muster.

Laurent looked at her, and for a moment Cinzia feared he would refuse. But then he nodded, and indicated the Son, Gad, should step forward. Gad gripped Knot and Olan by their arms.

Cinzia gave Knot and Olan one last meaningful look as they were hauled off down the corridor. Olan returned her gaze, his eyes determined. Knot did not look at her.

"Come with me, Priestess," Laurent said, beckoning her to follow.

"Come, Fernac," she said to Kovac.

"I'm sorry, Priestess, but the Crucible would like to meet with you alone first," Laurent said. "Your Goddessguard may wait here with my men, until you return."

Cinzia looked to Kovac, who nodded.

"Very well. Lead the way," Cinzia said.

She followed the blond man up a set of wooden stairs, then across the hall to the magistrate's quarters. The Goddessguard knocked at the door, and a voice resonated from within the chamber.

"Come in, Laurent. Introduce me to this priestess so willing to help our cause."

Laurent opened the door, motioning for Cinzia to walk in. Standing behind a large desk, awaiting her entrance, was not who Cinzia would have expected.

"Nayome?" Cinzia asked.

The woman smiled. "Sister Cinzia," she said. "Welcome. I've been waiting for you."

Cinzia stared at the woman. Cinzia *knew* her. Nayome Hinek had been two years ahead of Cinzia in the Cantic seminary. They had been... friends, once.

Nayome was very small, shorter even than Cinzia, and her blond hair formed a tight bun high on her head. Nayome's clothing was typical of the upper levels of the Ministry—fine silks and bold colors, deep red and creamy white, and the Trinacrya she wore was made of plates of real gold and silver, woven into the cloth of her dress.

"Goddess rising," Cinzia whispered. "What in Canta's name are you doing here?"

Nayome's smile faltered, but returned quickly. "I appreciate our friendship, Sister Cinzia, but I would appreciate your adherence to traditional honorifics even more, as is appropriate."

Cinzia inhaled sharply. "Of course, Your Grace, I did not mean to—"

Nayome waved a hand. "Think nothing of it. If it were up to me, I wouldn't care for such formalities, but the High Camarilla insists, of course, and all we can do is follow."

Cinzia's mind raced. Nayome knew her, knew her as Cinzia. Of course she would know of Cinzia's connection with Navone, with Jane.

It was over. Their plan would fail. Strange that she did not feel shock, or sadness, or even fear at a moment like this. At a moment when she realized all was lost.

"You are surprised," Nayome said as she walked around the desk, towards Cinzia. "Of course, why wouldn't you be? I am the youngest Holy Crucible appointed in decades."

Cinzia frowned. If she remembered one thing about Nayome, it was her arrogance. Something that, apparently, had not changed.

"But it's more than that, isn't it?" Nayome continued. "You were not expecting someone you knew. You were expecting someone you could fool?"

Despite how short the woman was, Cinzia felt very small in her presence. The mantle of a Holy Crucible had changed Nayome.

"Do not worry, Cinzia, I'm not angry. The false names you gave us, the lies you have told, it's all understandable. Forgivable, even. This is your family, after all. Your own sister. What wouldn't a woman do for her sister?" Nayome's eyes narrowed. "But you are difficult to read, I must say. You and your sister have that in common. Curious."

Cinzia had heard the rumors: even within the Denomination, Holy Crucibles were said to be different, somehow. Endowed with Canta's power of discernment. But the Arm of Inquisition was the most secretive of the three branches of the Denomination, so it was difficult to say what rumors were true and which were not.

"What are you going to do with her?" Cinzia asked. She felt no fear, which disturbed her. Nayome had complete power over her and Jane.

Nayome sighed. "Your sister?" she asked. "She is a heretic, after all. She confessed, and with no encouragement. Prayers, visions, revelations. And as far as I could read, there was honesty in her words."

Cinzia nodded, looking down. "She truly believes what she says. That Canta speaks to her."

"Which means one of two things. She is either completely mad, or there is something much darker at work. Something beyond what even I know how to deal with. And that," Nayome said, stepping towards Cinzia, closing the gap between them, "is where you might just be in luck."

Cinzia looked up. "What do you mean?" Cinzia felt no hope; she was defeated, and she knew it. And yet Nayome's words piqued her curiosity.

"As a fairly new Holy Crucible, I need to demonstrate decisiveness in judgment; hence the executions on the morrow. Navone needs to understand that there are swift consequences to heresy. And yet… there is much we can learn from your sister at the Arm of Inquisition—and in the Denomination as a whole. So I'm afraid I cannot yet order your sister's execution with a clear conscience."

Cinzia narrowed her eyes. "Then what would you do, instead?"

"We cannot simply execute someone in her place,

unfortunately," Nayome said, frowning slightly. "Your sister is far too recognizable."

A brief emotion pierced the hollow feeling that seemed to envelop Cinzia. *Anger.* How could Nayome talk so easily about executing anyone, let alone someone who might be innocent—even if it was in Jane's place?

"So we are left with only one option," Nayome said. "We need to fake your sister's death, and then take her back to Triah with us."

Cinzia shook her head. "I do not understand…"

"You don't need to, child. I'm only telling you this so you will cease interfering. Your sister will not die tomorrow. I'm afraid we have no choice but to execute the woman Laurent found yesterday; she is not worth keeping alive. The same goes for the two prisoners you brought us this evening. But your sister, and the vampire, are to be taken back to Triah with us for extensive questioning."

Cinzia blinked. *The vampire?* She did not know Nayome had found a vampire in Navone. She was not even sure if she believed such a thing was possible.

As she thought of Jane, Cinzia's anger grew. Nara, Olan, and Knot would die. Nayome would save Jane, only to take her back to Triah. A Holy Crucible took captives for one reason: to get information. And a Holy Crucible, as a ranking member of the Arm of Inquisition, would stop at nothing to get it.

"You'll stand with me tomorrow," Nayome said, looking at Cinzia, "and denounce your sister. You needn't worry about her, we have a harness she can wear that will remove the strain of the noose. She will be safe. Then you both will accompany us back to Triah, where you will help with our investigation."

Cinzia bowed her head, hoping to give the impression of

meekness. But the hollow feeling was gone. Now, there was only wrath. This—torture, death, deceit—was not part of her faith. She believed in Canta, she believed in the Denomination, but this had nothing to do with either.

She would stand with Nayome tomorrow, but she would not do as Nayome asked.

Cinzia would make a very different decision indeed.

# 23

KNOT RUBBED HIS WRISTS, looking down at the two unconscious Sons: the man called Gad, and another who had joined them on their way down into the cellars. Incapacitating them had been simple; Kovac had made sure Knot's bonds were barely tied.

Knot glanced at Olan, wondering what the man would think of him. The type of violence Knot used seemed to put people on edge. But Olan, for whatever reason, didn't seem fazed.

*He's worried about his wife*, Knot reminded himself. *He's got more important things on his mind.*

They tied up the Sons and dragged them out of the corridor and into a room, locking the door. Knot dropped the torch he'd taken from Gad onto the floor and stamped the flames out.

"What are you doing?" Olan hissed.

"Our eyes will adjust. Keeping a torch with us would be like taking daisies into a beehive."

The man grunted. "Think the others are being kept down here?" he asked. "We could try to find them, save Kovac the time."

Knot took a slow breath. "Worth a try," he said. "But I doubt they're all down here. We can look around, but we don't leave the cellars. We wait for Kovac." Knot didn't like so much of the plan resting on the priestess and her Goddessguard. They seemed like competent people and the priestess was damn pretty to boot, but that meant little. Competent people did bad

250

things all the time. Beautiful people, too.

"How many doors did we pass?" Olan asked.

"Seven."

The man grunted again. "How'd you see them all? I only counted three."

Truth was, Knot didn't know how. But he knew there were seven doors, and he knew where they were. But he wasn't about to admit that to Olan without a valid explanation.

They made their way back up the corridor the way they had come, moving their hands along the wall as their eyes adjusted to the darkness. They came to the first door, a few paces down the corridor from the room where they'd locked up the Sons of Canta. Knot tapped lightly on it, but no one answered. He tried the keys he'd taken from one of the fallen men, finally finding one that turned the lock. He opened the door cautiously, but inside was only a table and a few bare shelves.

They tried the other doors with the same result. Empty room after empty room. Knot began to wonder what they'd walked into. Something wasn't right; he could feel it. He'd thought they would find prisoners in these rooms; not Astrid, perhaps—she'd probably been confined to a real dungeon. The sun had set about an hour ago, and she'd be at her strongest now. Knot couldn't imagine how they'd contain her. Didn't want to imagine it. But he'd hoped to find Jane and Olan's wife, at least. Jane, the girl he'd met in the Circle. Knot had figured she'd been associated with the heretics; he hadn't thought she'd be the ringleader.

"There should be at least *some* prisoners in these rooms," Olan whispered, voicing Knot's thoughts. "Why else send us down here?"

"We still wait for the end of the hour," Knot said. He couldn't answer Olan's question, and Kovac had told them he'd try to reach them within an hour of their arrival. Checking each of the rooms had taken them half that time. They could wait a little longer. Wasn't the brightest idea to change a plan unless everyone involved was aware. Otherwise, missions ended in disaster. Knot knew that from experience.

Knot shook his head. *Experience?* The idea was ridiculous. He remembered nothing about plans, missions, or changing them, for that matter.

"Very well," Olan said, but Knot could tell by the man's voice that he didn't like it. *I don't like it, either,* Knot thought. *Not much we can do about it.*

They waited in a small room off the corridor, closest to the stairs that led up to the ground floor. Then, abruptly, they heard a sound. They crouched down, peering round the doorframe towards the stairs, where a faint orange glow appeared, then worked its way down accompanied by a set of heavy footsteps. A man in Goddessguard armor appeared at the foot of the stairs, carrying a torch. Knot couldn't help but feel a deep, grinding sensation in the pit of his gut. Something had gone wrong. This Goddessguard wasn't Kovac. It was the blond one, Laurent, who'd escorted Cinzia to the Crucible when they'd first arrived.

Descending the stairs behind him were two more Goddessguards—one of them the man that had taken Astrid earlier that morning—and ten Sons of Canta, each carrying a crossbow. The grinding feeling in Knot's gut intensified. Their mission was over. If Kovac and Cinzia were compromised, he and Olan didn't stand a chance.

"Go ahead and show yourselves, gentlemen." Laurent swung the torch, scanning the corridor. "Your friends aren't down here, as you've probably discovered."

Before Knot could stop him, Olan leapt from their hiding place and charged at the Goddessguard, screaming something incomprehensible. The scream turned to a shout of pain as a crossbow bolt pierced him through the shoulder. Olan fell to the ground as three Sons ran forward to hold him down. He grunted beneath their weight as they bound him tightly.

"That wasn't very intelligent," Laurent muttered. He looked up, and spoke louder. "I know there's one more of you. Best show yourself before you end up like your companion. Or worse. There's always that."

Knot raised his hands above his head and slowly stepped out into the corridor. He didn't know what'd gone wrong, but there was nothing for it, now.

"Ah," Laurent said, "there you are. How pleasant of you to come peacefully."

"I know this one, sir," a familiar voice said. The Goddessguard who had taken Astrid. "He was there this morning when we took the vampire. Killed at least five Sons, and Tyrik as well. Almost as tough as that vampire, sir."

"I see." Laurent regarded Knot. "Well, don't worry, you'll be with that wretch soon enough. Might even execute you together, so there's that to look forward to." He smiled.

Three other Sons rushed towards Knot, roughly taking his hands and binding them securely. He wondered, briefly, whether the priestess had betrayed them. He didn't know what advantage there'd be in such a thing. Didn't matter now. What was done was done. Knot felt whatever hope was left inside of him disappear, like smoke in a strong wind. He'd gone after Astrid for nothing. He'd come here for nothing. He had killed so many people for nothing.

And he had left Winter, for nothing.

# 24

Nash looked up at the sun, sinking towards the horizon. It had been a clear day, but clouds now rolled across the sky. Snow was coming.

They had just arrived in Navone. There was still no sign of Lathe, but the rumors they'd heard on the road looked to be true: a Holy Crucible was in Navone. The Sons of Canta who guarded the gate were evidence of that.

"Nash, take Elsi and Lian and secure the horses. Find an inn. Winter and I will look around."

Nash frowned. Kali had been spending more time with Winter lately. The girl could learn much from Kali, but at the same time Nash was beginning to feel an odd sense of unease. He could not say why.

"Why don't I take Winter to look around?" Nash said, looking at the tiellan. "I've been meaning to explain more about her voidstone." Winter met his eyes, but he couldn't read her expression. The statement was technically true, but there was certainly no need for Nash to go over the basics with Winter at this very moment.

Kali glared at Nash, but he didn't back down. Kali would not enjoy being with Lian; the two did not get along. That Kali even wanted to be with Winter was an odd shift. A few weeks ago, she would have avoided tiellan contact at every opportunity.

But everything had changed. Winter was the Harbinger.

"Very well," Kali muttered. "Meet us in the Circle Square." She gestured at Lian and Elsi, and the three of them led the horses away.

Nash nodded for Winter to follow him. They walked through the streets of Navone in silence for several minutes.

"Why did you ask me to come with you?" Winter asked. She looked pensive, her dark eyes not seeming to focus on the city around her.

Nash clenched his jaw. He didn't owe her an explanation. He couldn't explain his discomfort to himself; how could he explain it to Winter?

"You don't trust her, do you?"

Nash shook his head. "It's not that." But even as he said it, he wondered. Winter was perceptive. Nash speculated whether it was some aspect of being the Harbinger, or if the woman was simply that astute.

"Kali and I… we have a history," Nash said. "We understand one another."

"But now you don't."

Nash sighed. "I think you might be spending too much time with her, that's all. I'm worried."

"About me?"

"Yes. And Kali. And myself, for that matter."

"But there's no reason to—"

"This conversation is done," Nash said, perhaps too curtly. But it was true. He'd already implied more than he should.

Winter shrugged. "Fine."

They walked in silence. Nash couldn't help but watch Winter's hand stray to the pouch on her thin leather belt every few moments. She still wore her tiellan dress under her cloak;

Kali's choice of clothing had not appealed to her, it seemed.

In the pouch was the dose of *faltira* he had given her after they were attacked on the road. Nash was about to ask her about it when Winter broke the silence.

"The frost you gave me," Winter said, "that I took during the attack... it was strong. Far stronger than anything else I've tried."

Nash nodded. "The doses we give you each evening are small compared to what a fully developed variant would use. The frost you took during the attack was much closer to that size."

"What about the frost I have now?"

Nash looked at her. "It's a full dose."

"But this frost crystal isn't any larger than the ones you usually give me," Winter said. "How is it more powerful?"

"More concentrated," Nash said. "*Faltira* recipes require expertise and knowledge. Many amateurs attempt to create it, selling diluted and contaminated versions on the street. But only a real alchemist can manufacture a pure product."

"I didn't realize the process was so complicated."

"Complicated, volatile, and dangerous."

Winter was silent for a moment. She seemed to be processing everything. Nash could understand; it was a lot to take in.

"Where do you get it?" Winter asked after another pause.

Nash thought before answering. He knew this question would come up sooner or later. It was important for any psimancer, variant or actual, to be self-reliant. To know how to sustain himself when on a job. But new variants were fragile. If you gave them too much control over their *faltira* intake, it could destroy them.

He felt a sense of responsibility. He did not know what the other Nazaniin would do to Winter when they eventually arrived in Triah; he was not sure he wanted to know. She was the Harbinger, yes, which implied she had power. But people were always willing to exploit power. The greater the power, the farther they would be willing to go.

Nash thought of Kali, of the time she had been spending with Winter. Kali would do her duty, to be sure. She was not one to exploit others, not of her own accord. But if her duty required it…

And, suddenly, Nash knew. For Kali, Winter was only a mission. She would do whatever was required of her, whatever her orders dictated. No matter the collateral.

Nash could not allow that. The Harbinger was too important. Someone needed to teach her, nurture her. Someone needed to protect her until she could protect herself.

"The purest *faltira* comes from our own facilities," Nash said, resolved. "Where the best alchemists in the world produce it. Although bastardized forms of the drug have become as popular as hero and devil's dust in some cities. Almost any dealer sells frost these days, although it's expensive. And the dealers are cautious."

"Why?"

Nash grunted. "Because we aren't very happy if we catch them selling it. And we don't give warnings."

"But you can just… buy it off the street?"

Nash nodded. "It's dangerous, but if necessary, yes. Street *faltira* can be unstable. It can make you sick, or worse. And the dealers don't sell frost to just anyone. They usually look for a set of key words. If you tell them you are looking for something to make you 'burn,' for instance, or something that will give you 'chills,' they'll usually catch on."

Winter nodded. Again she seemed lost in thought. Curiosity

was good. It was an important aspect in a psimancer; curiosity led to new ways of using psimantic abilities.

Winter's hand moved back to the pouch at her belt.

"So this is a full dose?"

"More or less. Each psimancer is different. A full dose for you may be an overdose for someone else, or vice versa. But what you have now is a pretty standard amount."

"And the stronger the dose, the more powerful the abilities?"

"Not necessarily," Nash said. "Each variant's power is limited, and a maximum dose reaches that limit. Beyond that, it doesn't matter how much frost the variant takes. Although a variant rarely ingests their full amount of frost. That much power tends to… cloud judgment."

"What happens if you take more than the maximum dose?"

"Impaired judgment, certainly. It really depends on the variant, until you get into *extremely* high doses. The power a variant wields does increase slightly beyond their maximum dosage, but the small increase in power is never worth the risks. In a few cases, variants kill themselves by ingesting too much of the stuff."

"Like a hero overdose?"

Nash nodded. Winter seemed to have at least some familiarity with street narcotics. An overdose of hero or devil's dust would shut a person's body down; their heart would cease to beat, their lungs would cease to work.

"Similar," Nash said. "A variant's body essentially numbs itself as the desire for more frost increases. The more you take, the less you feel, and the more you want. Eventually, your body can't handle it anymore."

Beside him, Winter shivered. He remembered wondering why anyone would want to take more than one dose of *faltira*.

But then he saw the recovery ward beneath the Citadel in Triah, and he'd understood. Those people had been willing to do anything—*anything*—for another hit, and as many hits as possible. There was no reasoning with that kind of desperation.

Suddenly, Nash felt the slightest tug on his mind—it was as if someone had grabbed the end of one of his *tendra* and was giving it a good yank.

Kali was voking him.

Nash reached into a pocket of his coat, pulling out his voidstone. The stone glowed, a faint red light emanating from it.

"What is—"

Nash held up a hand as he gripped the voidstone, and sent a *tendron* into the artifact. Immediately, he was connected with Kali.

*What is it?* Nash asked. The question was in his mind; Winter would not hear it. Only Kali, wherever she was, would hear the words.

*You both need to come to the Circle Square. Now.*

*Very well.* Nash knew Kali's tone. It was the tone one didn't question.

"We need to meet the others," Nash said. "Something isn't right. I'll answer your questions in time. I still have much to tell you. But for now, you need to trust me." He looked Winter in the eye. "Do you trust me?"

Winter hesitated, then nodded.

*She's a good liar*, Nash thought to himself.

# 25

WINTER'S EARS PRICKED UP as she picked up a low murmur coming from the north. The sound of a crowd, coming from Navone's city center. She and Nash turned a corner, and the sound grew louder.

At the end of the street Winter saw a wall of people. The anxious buzz of anticipation was thick in the air.

Nash had asked Winter to hold off on her questions, so she did, despite having a great many. Winter liked Nash. He was kind to her. There was something about him that Winter trusted, which was more than she could say for Kali. She didn't mind Kali, but for very different reasons. They both had their use.

Two City Watchmen stood at the edge of the crowd. They didn't seem to care who passed in and out; their attention was on the center, just as everyone else's seemed to be. As they approached, Winter saw a large fountain shaped like a globe looming over the crowd. At the westernmost edge of the circle stood a dais, about as tall as a man, with several people standing on it. All around her, tiny snowflakes began to fall. Clouds covered most of the sky, though the sun shone through a line of blue in the distance. It would make a beautiful sunset, Winter thought, especially with the snowfall.

They found Kali, Elsi, and Lian in the crowd. The others

greeted them silently before turning back to the dais. Around her, Winter saw mostly humans, although towards the back of the crowd a few pockets of *siaras* and *araifs* huddled together in the cold. And, as Winter looked more closely ahead of her, she realized the platform wasn't a dais at all.

It was a gallows.

"An execution?" Winter whispered.

Kali nodded.

Lian cursed under his breath. "I've seen enough death the last few weeks."

"This is to our advantage," Kali said. "It gives us time to understand what's going on. A Crucible and her forces are not something we have time to deal with, right now."

"Why would you care what a Crucible does?" Winter asked. Given the powers Nash and Kali wielded, she did not think they would have to fear anything.

"We don't have a monopoly on psimancy. The Denomination is powerful; they have their own uses for such abilities. Their powers of discernment aren't as Goddess-given as they would like everyone to think."

*Of course*, Winter thought. No wonder people were so afraid of Holy Crucibles.

Four people stood on the gallows, their faces covered by cloth sacks, each standing beneath a noose. To one side of the four was a shifting bundle of heavy burlap. Half a dozen Goddessguards and at least ten Sons stood around the pile of cloth. A group of women dressed in Cantic livery stood on the other side of the platform accompanied by at least half a dozen more Goddessguards in full shining armor, and behind them stood a group of men in rich robes.

"Who are they?" Winter pointed at the men.

Nash peered at the group. "Probably the magistrate and Navone's city council."

"They've already found heretics, after four days." Kali spoke softly, almost to herself.

"Not unheard of," Nash muttered. "Some Crucibles are more effective than others."

"What is that?" Winter asked, glancing at Nash. "Underneath the cloth? It's moving."

"I'm not sure." Nash's eyes did not leave the strange bundle.

Winter turned back to the gallows. She counted at least two dozen more Sons of Canta patrolling the perimeter of the platform.

"No wonder they found the heretics so fast," Winter said. "They brought every soldier in the Denomination to Navone."

"The contingent *is* unusually large," Kali muttered. She, too, stared at the bundle of cloth with narrowed eyes.

Winter felt the rhythm of the crowd around her, heard the whispers and murmurings. A pregnant hush had settled on the massive group. Winter looked more closely at the four hooded figures. Two women, two men, all in dirty, torn clothing.

"Don't seem like the type of people who'd start a religious rebellion," Lian said beside her.

Winter nodded, still looking at one of the captured men, focusing on the rough burlap sack covering his face.

"Get a lot of heretics in Pranna, do you?" Nash grinned. Lian smirked.

Winter was glad to see the two getting along. She worried about Lian. Seeing him even attempt to smile again—even if it was nothing more than a smirk, something she knew wasn't genuine—made her miss him.

*Odd to miss him when he has been traveling beside me for weeks.*

One of the women in Cantic robes stepped forward, addressing the crowd in a loud voice. It was one of the younger women, and she was very short—perhaps as short as Winter herself, even though the woman was human. She wore her pale blond hair in a loose bun over her head, and had a small, heart-shaped face.

"We thank you for cooperating as we purge the evil from this city," the woman said.

"That's the Crucible," Nash whispered behind her. "See the white flame behind her Trinacrya?"

Winter nodded. The bright white flames embroidered on the woman's dress behind the circle and triangle were clear, even from a distance.

"That's the symbol of the Arm of Inquisition. They say that for all the peace that the Trinacrya has brought to the world, the Trinacrya on fire has brought just as much violence."

"She is so young," Winter said. "I thought one of the older women would be the Crucible."

"It is... odd. Not unheard of, but odd."

"Have confidence in knowing," the Crucible continued, "that after today your city will be clean, purged through Canta's fire. You will have nothing to fear, and Canta's light will once again shine down upon you."

The magistrate and the small council behind the woman applauded vigorously, and the rest of the crowd eventually joined in, although they seemed far less enthusiastic. Winter's hands remained at her side. She suspected that, whether a Holy Crucible said Canta's light would shine down on them or not, these people's lives would carry on quite normally.

"You will be relieved to know that we captured an ancient evil lurking in your city," the Crucible said. A ripple of whispers flowed through the crowd. "Among the associates of the heretic and her followers, we found a true daemon. Beneath the cloth," and here the Crucible pointed dramatically towards the bundle to her left, "is a Ventus."

Winter felt nervous energy radiating from the crowd, but she doubted what the Crucible said was true. Vampires had been extinct for hundreds of years. One of the only creatures left over from the Age of Marvels, apart from humans and tiellans, they had eventually been hunted down and exterminated—assuming they ever existed in the first place. What did the Crucible think she could gain by pretending to have found one?

Winter was about to ask Nash when she saw his face. He was pale. The way his eyes widened unnerved her.

Winter looked back at the gallows, an icy claw of fear gripping her insides.

"You will have the privilege, in a few moments, to see such a daemon firsthand. Unfortunately we cannot execute it, as we need to take it back to Canta's Fane for exorcism and study. But you will all stand witness to its daemonic presence."

The Holy Crucible turned to the Sons who stood near the other captives on the gallows.

"Now, one of your own, Priestess Cinzia Oden, will address you. Let her tell you of the dangers of heresy, and her feelings on this *rebellion*." The Holy Crucible looked back at the priestesses. One of them, also very young, stepped forward, and the Holy Crucible turned back towards the crowd, a smile on her face. "But first," she shouted, "unveil the prisoners!"

Winter was vaguely aware of a whispered conversation between Kali and Nash. She heard snippets of the words "vampire" and "heretic," and Knot's other name—Lathe—but Winter couldn't concentrate well enough to focus. She was looking at the man in drab, worn clothing at the end of the gallows line.

One of the Sons walked up behind the prisoner, lifting the burlap sack. Winter felt her knees buckle beneath her.

It was Knot.

He was bound and gagged, and stood quite calmly, facing the crowd. Some of the other prisoners struggled, muffled sounds coming from beneath their hoods as they worked futilely against their bonds. Knot stood still. His face was dirty and bruised, his hair longer than she remembered. He had grown a short beard since Winter had seen him last. Since their wedding night.

Kali turned to Winter, but Winter didn't care. Without a second thought, she reached into the pouch she carried at her waist, pulling out the frost crystal Nash had given her a few days earlier. The full dose.

"*Winter, no!*" Kali whispered.

It was too late. In a few short moments Winter felt *faltira*'s power surge through her body, fire in her veins, ice on her skin.

There *was* more power here than anything she had felt before, more than she had taken the morning of the attack on their camp, more than any power she had felt in her sessions with Nash.

Her vision darkened, but the power held her up, rapt and rigid. How pleasure and pain could be so beautifully intertwined was a mystery.

Then she screamed.

# 26

SNOWFLAKES DRIFTED DOWN, FALLING on Knot's face. The small blade Kovac had smuggled to him had nearly sliced through the bonds that held his wrists.

An eerie scream cut through the silence, and Knot felt a whoosh of air above his head. He blinked as the severed end of his own noose fell loosely around his neck.

The crowd gasped, but Knot was already moving. Someone had given him a chance, and he'd take advantage of it. The crowd wouldn't know how to react, and the Sons would be torn between keeping the crowd under control and securing the prisoners.

Knot severed the rope that bound his wrists. His final cut was too strong; he felt the sting as the blade cut through the rope and into his flesh. No matter. Knot took the noose from around his neck and swung it towards the Son closest to him. The heavy knotted rope struck the soldier in the face, giving Knot enough time to weave in and hit him hard in the throat. The man dropped to the ground. For a split second Knot considered not taking the sword the Son carried at his belt. He had caused so much death already. Why should he cause more? What right did he have?

Then a strange sense of longing took over, and the sword was in his hand. Knot's own blood was wet and warm between his palms and the sword grip. He turned in time to see two more Sons moving towards him, swords up; they stood between Knot and Olan, who was still bound. Knot advanced quickly, parrying one man's cut and stabbing the other Son in the groin.

*So easy,* Knot thought to himself, not without pleasure.

With two more strokes the second man fell, and Knot rushed to Olan, cutting the man's bonds and severing the noose around his neck.

The snow was falling more heavily now, and through it Knot saw more Sons approaching. Others were looking around wildly at the chaos. Bodies littered the gallows, most of them Sons of Canta. Out of the corner of his eye, he thought he saw one of the Goddessguard's shields flying through the air. He blinked. No one could throw a shield that fast. It reminded him of his fight with the two strangers in Cineste.

A group of City Watchmen stood below the gallows, trying to keep the crowd from panicking. In the back of his mind, Knot wondered whether the man who sent him the letter, Captain Rudak, was among them. He still might be able to find the man.

Assuming, of course, he survived whatever *this* was.

"What in Oblivion is happening?" Olan shouted.

"Don't know," Knot shouted back. "Must be someone else here who doesn't like these executions. We use it to our advantage while we can."

"The enemy of my enemy…" Olan began.

Knot shrugged. He'd never fancied old proverbs. "See to your wife," he said. "I'll get my girl."

Knot turned and rushed towards the four Sons of Canta that stood between him and Astrid.

* * *

Cinzia pushed against the Goddessguards, Kovac among them, as they shepherded her, Nayome, and the other priestesses off the gallows. Cinzia was still disoriented. One moment she had been about to address the crowd—she had been about to denounce the Cantic Arm of Inquisition in front of the entire city of Navone, for Canta's sake—and then someone had screamed, and the Circle had erupted into chaos. Now, Cinzia knew only one thing.

She had to get to Jane.

Nayome's claim that she would fake her sister's death was irrelevant. The woman could have been bluffing, and even if she had not, Cinzia did not know how much longer her sister would last. Sons swarmed around Jane, and a simple pull of the lever would open the trapdoor beneath her. Cinzia was about to turn and tell Kovac as much when she saw a flash of light out of the corner of her eye. Then someone tackled her, and they both crashed to the wooden boards of the gallows. Snow had begun to accumulate, but not enough to soften her fall. The cold wetness seeped through her robes.

Cinzia shouted, pummeling her attacker with her fists, until she realized it was her own Goddessguard. Behind Kovac, Cinzia saw both Mother Joyca and a Son who had been standing in front of her pierced together by a long, barbed spear.

"We need to get to Jane," Kovac said, but Cinzia could only stare at the matron she had known for years—now dead, killed in such a brutal manner.

Cinzia allowed Kovac to lead her away, her hands shaking.

"Yes," she whispered, unable to stop the shaking. "Jane."

Winter screamed at the power coursing through her. There seemed to be no more pain, or joy for that matter. Only *power*, boiling and raging. After what seemed an eternity of basking, clinging, suffering, enduring, she finally brought herself back to the present.

Her eyes snapped open.

Knot was on the gallows, fighting a group of Sons. She had to get to him. That was all that mattered.

She walked towards the gallows, her *tendra* working furiously around her. She smashed Sons of Canta easily beneath her power, flinging them against each other and sending their weapons in vicious arcs of death. A strong, familiar taste filled her mouth, and she realized Nash must be using his *tendra* as well. The crowd around her was panicking, screaming, cursing, gathering up children and fleeing the Circle. Watchmen tried to keep order but failed. Winter walked calmly through the crowd towards Knot. Two of the Sons who had been attacking him were down, and Knot danced beautifully between two more.

Winter reached two *tendra* out through the falling snow, picking up the Sons that stood in Knot's way. She raised them up, watching as they flew into the air higher than any building in the city. They screamed, arms flailing, and Winter almost lost sight of them in the low clouds and falling snow. Sight didn't matter, though; she could feel them struggling in her *tendra*. She smashed them together. She heard them collide with a faint crash, saw a small cloud of red, and then let them drop. The two Sons crashed onto the gallows, their dead weight breaking through the floorboards to the ground beneath.

Knot was rushing to the vampire. What business he had with such a monster, Winter didn't know, but she saw a group of Sons running towards him, weapons drawn. With one *tendron* she tore off a man's helmet, and with another she whipped a spear from another's grip and stabbed it through the helmetless man. Another *tendron* lifted one of the Sons off the ground, and yet another snatched a shield and flung it back into the group. The men screamed, unsure what was attacking them. Winter threw the spear away into a cluster of men in the distance. Goddessguards, Sons of Canta, or perhaps civilians, Winter wasn't sure.

She did it anyway. Anything to get to Knot.

Winter had no idea how many *tendra* she was using. She was slowly discovering more and more of them, acting almost of their own accord. Despite the power coursing through her, she suddenly felt very weak. Small, within the power that she held.

Someone touched her shoulder, and she nearly whipped one of her *tendra* around to defend herself before she realized it was Lian. His mouth moved. He was speaking. Winter shook her head. She couldn't hear him.

It didn't matter. She wasn't going to give up now.

"Shall I stop her?" Nash asked, blinking snow out of his eyes.

Kali's lips were pursed. "No. This may be exactly what we need. Protect her, cover her blind spots. I'm going after Lathe."

Nash nodded, but her tone worried him.

He turned to Lian as Kali slipped off through the crowd.

"Help me protect her," Nash shouted. Most of the crowd had already fled, but the fighting continued on the gallows, while Winter picked off Sons and Goddessguards one by one. She was using more *tendra* than Nash had seen anyone use in his life. He counted at least two dozen, almost certainly more.

If anyone was the Harbinger, it was this woman.

"She won't listen to me!" Lian shouted.

Winter seemed on the cusp of losing herself. All they could do was protect her and hope no one realized she was the source of the chaos. Nash dreaded what such power was doing to her. She used her power bluntly, brutally, like a child. There was no finesse, no artistry. But Winter didn't need it.

Winter flung a shield into a crowd of civilians bunched up on one of the streets that led from the Circle. Nash reached out a *tendron*, stopping the shield before it sliced into the bystanders. Just because Kali enjoyed chaos didn't mean he had to watch innocent people die.

He looked back at Winter. Her eyes were wide and dark. She walked forward slowly, her arms at her sides. Snow fell all around her, large flakes stuck in her hair and on her loose tiellan dress.

In that moment, Nash wondered exactly what manner of woman they'd found, and realized that he was frightened of her.

Knot reached Astrid, stumbling over the shattered gallows and nearly slipping on the snow and blood. He had no idea what was going on, but he was sure it was connected with the man and woman who'd attacked him in Cineste. Objects levitating, things flying impossibly through the air. Had to be connected.

But, as long as it was working to his advantage, he'd milk every second of it.

"Astrid!" he called. He approached the heavy cloth cautiously, unsure what condition the girl was in underneath. Clouds nearly covered the sky, but the sun still shone dimly in the west. He didn't think the girl could come out safely yet.

Knot heard a small, muffled moan.

"You all right?" he asked, his voice quieter. The heat of battle raged within him, kept him warm against the chill of the falling snow, but as he lifted the cloth enough to see inside, he suddenly felt very cold.

Astrid was barely clothed, gagged, her arms and legs manacled to heavy chains. Knot's left eye twitched.

Thin wooden stakes, each as long as Knot's forearm but no thicker than his little finger, pierced the girl's limbs. The bloody points protruded from her arms and legs, two in each. Four more stakes had been driven through her torso, forming a diamond around the girl's heart. Dried blood crusted the wounds, staining her arms and legs a dark crimson.

Knot pushed the horror away and knelt underneath the heavy cloth, next to Astrid. The sun was still setting, and he'd seen what direct contact with light would do to the girl. He made sure the cloth covered them both.

He removed the gag and saw tear-stained cheeks. Knot hadn't realized vampires were capable of crying.

"What can I do?" Knot asked.

Astrid looked at him, her eyes wide, devoid of the sparkle that he'd grown so used to seeing.

"Take them out," Astrid rasped. "Idiot."

Knot reached for the closest stake, which pierced her upper arm through the muscle, and pulled it out quickly. He felt the wood scrape against bone. He tossed it away. Astrid flinched, her face contorted with pain. Knot paused.

"Keep going," she said through clenched teeth. "Take them all."

Knot obliged, pulling each stake out as quickly as possible. Blood spurted with each removal. All Astrid did after the third or fourth was sob.

When it was done Astrid's eyes were closed, her body shaking. Then, Knot pulled her in and embraced her.

She curled up, the chains clinking as her hands clutched at him. Knot felt her body shake as she sobbed, her face buried in his shoulder. He heard the screams from outside, the muffled voices and sounds of fighting, but for once the itch to join the battle seemed distant, inconsequential. He sat there awkwardly for a moment, letting her cry, and felt the slightest resonance, a strange familiarity.

And then a shout.

"Get to the vampire, before the sun sets. Uncover her, quickly!"

Astrid's body stiffened. Knot released her, and for a moment could only stare at her wounds. They'd healed. Raw scars remained, but there was no bleeding. The flesh had knit itself back together.

"Go," Astrid whispered. "Tell me when the sun has set. Then we'll show these bastards exactly what sort of daemon they've captured."

Her eyes had lost all vulnerability. The green glow was fierce and bright.

Knot slipped out from under the cloth into the falling snow and the bright orange light of sunset and battle.

Cinzia finally reached Jane, still standing on the gallows. The Goddessguard behind Jane was dead, a long dagger protruding from his neck. *Did Jane do that?* Cinzia wondered fearfully. Her sister was still bound and gagged, but there was no other explanation.

Jane turned to look at her. Cinzia removed the gag and saw that Jane was smiling sadly.

"Behold," she said, "Canta's salvation." Something blurred into a group of Sons directly in front of them, and a spurt of blood shot straight up in the air.

"Jane," Cinzia said as Kovac cut her sister's bonds, "are you all right?" It was some consolation that Nayome had been telling the truth; Kovac removed the noose around Jane's neck, and

273

with it the harness that was supposed to have saved her life.

Jane didn't look at her, instead gazing out at the Circle Square. Most citizens had fled, although every street was still bottlenecked with people. Others, Cinzia wasn't sure who, struggled with a group of Sons near the gallows.

"How terrible is Her wrath," Jane quoted, wiping snow from her face, "and how sorrowful Her enemies." Cinzia recognized the line from Nazira's writings.

Then shouts from close by on the gallows forced Cinzia to tear her eyes away from her sister.

To their right, Olan was fighting off two Sons of Canta. Others ran towards him. His wife, Nara, was still bound, a noose hanging loosely around her neck.

Her Goddessguard attacked, sword swinging. Then, just as Cinzia neared Nara, she heard a faint click. She watched as the woman fell through the trapdoor.

Cinzia gasped. Behind her, Jane screamed. And, above everything, Olan howled.

Cinzia heard a faint crunch as the rope went taut.

Winter continued slowly towards the gallows, everything around her happening in slow motion.

On the dais she heard a scream and a cry of anguish near one of the ropes. She watched as a woman dropped through the wooden floor. A patch of powdery snow fell with her, floating to the ground. From Winter's perspective the woman seemed to be lowered to the ground slowly, as if angels held her arms. But angels or not, the drop would be fatal. The rope went taut. One of Winter's *tendra* flung a whirring sword at the rope, cutting the woman down, but Winter knew the gesture was too late.

On the gallows, a Goddessguard pointed in Winter's

direction. Moments later a hail of arrows came towards her, and she was vaguely aware of Nash heaving a group of shields before them with his *tendra*, swiping the shafts away. The arrows floated through the air, falling like feathers. More Goddessguards rushed Winter but she ignored them. Nash would deal with them.

She had seen Knot slip underneath the bundle of cloth only a moment before, but now he emerged, sword drawn, as two Goddessguards advanced on him. Winter was about to pick them up and smash them together when she saw several Sons approaching Knot from the other side. She lifted a nearby wagon with a few of her *tendra*. The Sons stopped advancing on Knot and watched it rise into the air. Winter threw it down at them with all her strength, and the wagon smashed to bits against the gallows, collapsing another part of the wooden structure. She saw with disappointment that many of the Sons had leapt out of the way in time. But others had not.

Winter's jaw set. She was almost there. She had almost reached him. She would not stop now.

She reached out another set of *tendra*, grasping weapon after weapon from the fallen, and sent them towards the remaining Sons. She heard the men scream.

Two Goddessguards faced Knot. One was carrying a huge longsword. Knot recognized him as the noble who'd taken Astrid. The other was Laurent, the Crucible's Goddessguard, wielding a longsword and a blackbark shield. His blond hair stuck out in tufts beneath his helmet. The Crucible stood behind them, watching over her dogs.

"I'm not sure where you enlisted the help of the Nazaniin," the Crucible said, her mouth tight, "but the High Camarilla will not be happy to know of their involvement."

Knot didn't know what the Nazaniin was, although the word did seem to echo in his mind. Then the noble rushed in on Knot's left, hefting his longsword. The massive weapon would make the man slower but gave him a huge reach, and his blows would be unblockable without a shield. Knot would have to rely on his speed and parrying to avoid losing a limb, or worse.

Knot dodged the first attack, sweeping around and cutting in at the nobleman, but Knot's blade whizzed through air as the man stepped back. That weapon's reach was definitely going to be a problem.

The sun had nearly set. If Knot could hold out a few minutes longer, Astrid might be able to help him. But she was still in chains, and he wasn't sure she could break them, even at her strongest.

Laurent deflected one of Knot's blows with his shield, the attack bouncing harmlessly off the blackbark. The Goddessguard countered, throwing Knot off balance. Knot was barely staying on the defensive; the two men would soon overwhelm him. Another sweeping arc from the great longsword narrowly missed Knot's scalp as he weaved under it. He needed a change of pace.

The Goddessguard swung at Knot again, but he made a mistake, stepping too close and slipping in the bloody snow. Knot parried the swing, catching the man off balance, and the massive sword careened away. Knot kicked the man in the chest, sending him sprawling backwards directly onto the bundle of cloth.

"An appetizer!" Knot's voice came out in more of a ragged gasp than a shout. He didn't have time to see whether Astrid got the message or not. He hoped she would understand.

He turned just in time to see Laurent's sword coming towards him. Knot parried the blow but almost tripped on a spear lying on the ground between them. He recovered and hooked his foot on the weapon, kicking the spear up at the Goddessguard, who blocked it easily with his shield. But the action gave Knot enough time to rush in. Laurent parried the first stroke, partially blocked the second with his shield, but the man exhaled sharply as the third cut into his hamstring, and the fourth went through his neck.

Knot withdrew the blade, looking for the Crucible. He didn't see her anywhere. He turned to where the noble Goddessguard was lying by the pile of cloth, his head hanging at an unnatural angle from his body. He was about to run back to Astrid, when he heard a voice behind him.

"Hello, Lathe."

Knot stopped. That name again. He turned. A woman walked towards him. Brown hair, round face, light eyes. Tall. Knot had no recollection of her.

"Astrid!" he called over his shoulder as the sun flared one last time between the clouds before sinking beneath the horizon, "The sun has set."

Knot heard rustling and dragging chains behind him.

"We've never met," the woman said, "but I've heard much about you." She wore a curiously curved sword at her hip. The weapon looked familiar, even if the woman didn't.

Snow was floating lazily down from the darkening sky. Knot shivered. Sweat stung his eyes and matted his hair, but now that he'd stopped moving, he could feel the heat leaving him. "Who are you?" he asked. He still held the longsword, the leather grip damp with sweat and blood. He was exhausted. If this woman meant to fight, he wasn't sure he had it in him.

The woman smiled, but her eyes weren't friendly. "I am many people."

Knot frowned. "You're insane."

The woman frowned back, her blue eyes cold. Before she could reply there was a scream from behind Knot, and he turned in time to see Astrid, a small blur, streak towards the woman. Knot felt a moment of panic. He could learn about Lathe—whoever that was—from this woman. Astrid couldn't kill her, not yet.

Astrid sped past him, and Knot saw the woman raise something in her hand. Astrid slid to a stop, screaming, covering her ears as she crumpled to the ground.

"What're you doing to her?" Knot shouted. He looked down at Astrid, who was bleeding from her nose. She stopped screaming, but still kept her hands over her ears. Her mouth was open wide, but no sound came out. Knot looked up at the woman, who held a small, silvery flower in her hand.

"You know what nightsbane does just as well as I do," she said. Knot watched as the woman tossed the flower carelessly onto Astrid's body. The girl had stopped moving.

"What d'you want?" Knot asked.

The woman stared at him, her face a stone-cold frown. Slowly, she drew the curved blade from her hip.

"Surely you couldn't have thought to avoid us forever? Not after what you did."

"Don't know what you're talking about," Knot said. "I don't remember anything." For the briefest moment, he wondered if he deserved to go with this woman, wherever she intended to take him. Perhaps she meant to punish him for the crimes he'd committed, whatever they were. Perhaps it was for the best.

Then he looked down at Astrid, her body motionless. He thought of Winter, back in Pranna. He could be a better man. For them, he might be.

"You're thinking of her, aren't you?" Knot looked at the

woman sharply. "Yes, I'm talking about your elf friend. She's closer than you think. If you come with me, we may allow you to see her."

Knot's jaw set. He didn't know who this woman was, or what she wanted. But she knew about Winter, and he couldn't let her live if she did.

Knot raised his sword and rushed towards the woman.

The woman's smile widened, and she raised her own.

Then, in a blur of movement and an ear-splitting crash, Knot watched a massive ball of stone smash into the woman. The huge rock tore through the gallows and through the building behind, carrying the mysterious woman with it.

Winter had almost reached the gallows when Lian cried out. She turned just in time to see another group of Sons, led by a Goddessguard, rushing them from behind.

Lian raised his sword, engaging the Goddessguard. The man dodged Lian's slash easily, slamming into him with his shield.

Winter screamed in protest, and immediately used a *tendra* to tear the shield away from the Goddessguard, carrying it back to smash the man into the slush. The Sons looked at her warily as she lifted the circular shield up with one of her *tendra*. Though the tendra was invisible, they clearly recognized the source of the danger. She snatched a spear out of the hand of one of the men.

The Sons of Canta panicked.

They ran, but didn't get far. She spun the shield and spear round and round, crushing helmets, piercing armor and mail, smashing men like rotten fruit.

Winter could feel her power draining, the *faltira* seeping out of her. Soon, she would be helpless again.

She knelt down by Lian. He was groaning but conscious. He had a gash on one of his legs, and the blow from the shield would have left a bruise, but he looked like he would be all right. He started to say something, but Winter was already standing. She ran to the gallows, reality closing in on her. She was growing cold.

Knot was there, in front of her. Facing Kali.

Winter frowned. What was the woman doing? Nash was nowhere to be seen. Something wasn't right.

Kali raised her sword. The look that passed between Knot and Kali told Winter all she needed to know.

One of them was about to die.

Winter had to stop this. She didn't have much strength left; it was seeping away by the moment. She saw the massive stone globe of the fountain, capped in snow. Winter extended all of her *tendra*, reaching around it. She pulled with all her strength, and the huge sculpture slowly ripped from its base. With one last effort, Winter flung the huge rock at Kali.

Winter fell to her knees, the exertion finally overwhelming her. Through darkening vision she watched the globe ram through the gallows and into the building behind, throwing up a cloud of debris and snow. Only rubble and splintered wood remained where Kali had been standing moments before.

Winter looked at Knot, who stared at the destruction in disbelief. Then the darkness took her.

Nash saw Kali confront Knot, and he knew it was time to go. He was frustrated at the thought of leaving Winter. She was important; he hoped he would encounter her again soon, and not on opposite sides of the battlefield. Not that she would be able to choose, of course. According to prophecy, the

Harbinger did not have the luxury of choice.

Then Nash saw the globe, and watched Kali disappear beneath it. The great twisting feeling in his gut surprised him. Even with Kali's talent, he didn't know if she would walk away from that. Unlikely.

Despite the fear gripping him, Nash turned away. He looked over his shoulder at where Kali had been. At least for now, the mission was his alone.

He made his way through the thinning crowds, pulling his hood up against the falling snow.

Cinzia could not look away. Lying limply below the gallows, was Nara. Something had cut her rope right after she had dropped, but Cinzia had heard the bones snap. The woman was dead. She was not sure how long she stood there, staring down at the body. The fighting continued around her, but she could not bring herself to move.

Cinzia slumped to her knees. People shouted, one of them Kovac. Another sounded like Jane. Cinzia could not understand what they were saying.

Could any of this be Canta's will? Could the Goddess to which Cinzia had devoted her life be a deity of anger, jealousy, and violence? As Cinzia looked down at Nara's body, a woman she had known her entire life, she began to wonder.

Then she heard a thunderous crash, and the gallows shook beneath her. Jane shouted her name.

Cinzia turned. Kovac was struggling on the ground with one of the Sons of Canta. The man was on top of her Goddessguard, pressing a dagger towards Kovac's throat. Kovac was barely keeping it away.

Cinzia felt a jolt go through her. She ran towards her

Goddessguard, looking around for anything she could use as a weapon. There, on the ground, was an abandoned spear. Cinzia picked it up, but nearly fell over as she gripped it. The thing was *heavy*. She managed to lift it, feeling a nervous energy in her limbs, and ran to Kovac. The knife blade had sunk lower, nearing Kovac's neck just above his collarbone. Cinzia lifted the spear and rammed the blade into the Son's side. The man screamed, arching his body in pain, and Kovac moved quickly. In a fraction of a moment their positions were reversed, and Kovac stood over the body of the Son, his own knife dripping blood.

Cinzia dropped the spear, her hands shaking. Kovac grabbed her arm. "Come, Priestess," he said.

"Where's Jane?"

"We can worry about her later. I need to get you to safety."

"*No*," Cinzia said firmly, wresting her arm from his grip. "I'm finding my sister."

Knot stared ahead of him. Whoever the woman had been, she was dead now.

But he feared Astrid was too.

He leapt into the rubble. Astrid had been lying near the woman, the nightsbane herb on her body, when the globe had crashed through the gallows. Now Astrid, the strange woman, and almost a third of the platform were gone, in their place shattered stone and splintered wood. Snow still fell around him, defying the chaos with its serenity.

Knot shouted Astrid's name as he dug through the snow and debris. No answer came. "Astrid!" he shouted again, louder, his voice raw and hoarse. She *had* to be alive. He hadn't come all this way to fail her.

*Again.*

To his right, the rubble shifted. He scrambled over, losing his balance on shifting stone and snow. Then he heard a cough, and a layer of debris fell away.

The girl poked her head up. "I'm all right, nomad," she said between hacking coughs. "I'm all right."

Knot reached down to help the girl out, when someone called his name. A chill went up his spine. He knew that voice.

He turned, and saw a figure limping towards him in the dusk, carrying something. Knot blinked. It couldn't be.

"Knot," the tiellan said again, and there was no doubt in Knot's mind. It was Lian.

"Help me," Lian said. He was carrying a body.

Knot suddenly felt what little hope he'd gained in the past few moments—surviving the execution, defeating the Goddessguards, finding Astrid—wilt to nothing.

*She* was there in Lian's arms. Sweat stung Knot's eyes. He heard his own rasping breath. The falling snow seemed to hover in the air around him. He moved to her, and an eternity passed between each footstep.

"How?" Knot whispered. Lian didn't respond; he stumbled and almost dropped his burden. He was wounded, Knot realized. Blood spread from a wound beneath Lian's shirt. Knot took her from him, feeling the weight of her in his arms.

The last time he'd carried her like this was their wedding night.

Her body was still. He brushed her dark hair from her face, slick with sweat and snow. His hand left a dirty smear on her forehead.

"Winter, please," Knot whispered. He touched her neck, and felt a weak pulse. She was alive.

What was she doing here? Had she followed him?

"There's a lot to explain," Lian said. "Is she…?"

Knot realized he'd been asking the questions out loud.

"Not dead," Knot said. "But we need to get her somewhere safe. Quickly."

A voice spoke, accompanied by a clanking of chains.

"Next time you're trapped in a pile of rubble, remind me not to help you." Astrid stumbled towards them, dragging her chains. "Ready to leave this city, nomad? I think it's caused us enough trouble." She cocked her head. "Ah, you've acquired some baggage. Well, the wider the company, the wider the cheer, I always say. Where are we taking this one?"

Knot was relieved to see that Astrid's scars were now nothing but smooth skin. Her hands were hanging limply at her side, and her whole body seemed to sag with weariness, which surprised Knot. He'd never seen her tired before.

Looking around, he realized that they were practically alone in the Circle Square that had been packed with people less than an hour before. But there were bodies everywhere. Mostly Cantic Sons and Goddessguards, but many wore common clothing. Navone's city center had become a field of slaughter.

Knot stood, holding Winter in his arms, Lian limping beside him. He saw Kovac, his priestess, and another woman he recognized—her sister Jane—walking towards him hesitantly. Knot couldn't see Olan anywhere.

"We must find Cinzia's family," Kovac said wearily. The Goddessguard, covered in gore, looked as exhausted as Knot felt.

Knot glanced at Astrid. "You aren't hungry, are you?"

"I can feed later. You all are lucky I feel like a building fell on me, otherwise I'd be eating one of you right now."

Kovac eyed the girl warily. Knot wasn't going to have that.

"She's with me," Knot said. "If I'm coming with you, she's coming, too." He nodded back at Lian. "So is he."

Kovac shrugged. "Safety in numbers." The man looked too exhausted to argue. "We must leave before the Crucible's forces regroup."

"Or before the Watch decides to make an appearance," Knot muttered.

"You've made quite a few friends," Astrid said. Her eyes glowed brightly, now that night had fallen. "I should leave you more often. You'd be the most popular man in Khale in no time."

Knot looked back at Kovac. "You have a place in mind?"

Astrid sighed. "You're ignoring me? I almost *died*."

Kovac nodded. "Same place we met earlier. The complex under the Oden house."

"Lead the way." Knot nodded back at Lian. "He may need a hand."

"Don't worry about me," Astrid said. "I was only tortured, stuck full of holes, and then assaulted by an entire building. Nothing serious."

"I'll be fine," Lian said, his voice hard. "Worry about yourselves."

Kovac regarded Lian for a moment, then turned to Cinzia and Jane. The two women looked shaken, but otherwise unhurt.

Someone ran towards them, and Knot tensed. "It's Olan," Kovac said.

Olan looked as weary and ragged as the rest of them, his face swollen from the beating he had taken, his shirt bloody where the crossbow bolt had pierced him. His spectacles were gone. Knot noticed clean paths running through the dirt and grime on the man's face. The only prisoner not accounted for was the man's wife. Olan just shook his head.

Knot followed Kovac out of the Circle, looking down at the burden in his arms every few moments just to reassure himself that she was real.

# 27

*Oden tunnels, Navone*

WINTER AWOKE TO THE sound of men talking and the loud, painful echoes in her own head.

She opened her eyes, but quickly shut them again. Everything was so *bright*. Light thrust spears of pain through her eyes. Winter lay there for a moment, eyelids squeezed together, breathing deeply. With an effort she tried to sit up, then gasped and fell back.

Her whole body ached. Every muscle in her body felt like a tenderized deepfish before the yearly fish fry in Pranna.

She moaned, but the sound came out more of a gasp. And, in that moment, as the pain coursed through her with all the fire of *faltira*, she remembered. Navone. Knot. Frost. The violence.

*Murderer.*

Winter did not know if the voice was her own or something else entirely, but it rocked her soul and shook her very bones.

*Murderer,* the voice whispered. And suddenly Winter was there, in the Circle Square, watching people die all around her.

*You did not watch.*

Winter gasped, trying to sit up again. She had to get up, she had to move. She couldn't stay here, alone with the voice. She had carried a dull, aching guilt from what happened in the alleyway in Cineste, but after her conversation with Kali, that guilt had faded. Now, a new, very different guilt flooded through her, smothered her. And, this time, she knew she deserved every bit of it.

*You will never be the same.*

Winter cried out as the pain from her muscles and her head paled to this new, visceral agony. A frost crystal could make the pain go away. She wished she had one more than anything on the Sfaera. If only for a moment, it would be worth it.

Knot.

*Where is he?* Winter opened her eyes again, slowly, ignoring the pain. The only light, she realized—the light that exploding across her vision—was that of a small fire near her. She was indoors, in some kind of cave. The fire burned in a crude mantle, cut roughly from the rock around it. The fire's heat kissed her body, and again she ached for frost.

Winter's mind was foggy. She craned her neck, looking away from the fire, and discerned shapes in the distance, illuminated by torchlight. She almost succeeded in sitting up, the muscles in her back, neck, and abdomen straining. She had barely raised her head when pain overwhelmed her and she fell back again. Her eyes burned with the sharp threat of tears. *I'm stronger than this. I don't need tears anymore.*

Winter squinted at the shapes. Two of them seemed to be talking to each other; she could hear their voices incoherently above the ringing in her ears.

Kali and Nash. They had found her. She strained to hear what they were saying.

"They made it through the gate this morning. I am sure of it."

"Eward was with them? He has a tendency to do what he pleases."

"I know. But he was with them, as was Father, and Mother, and the rest of the children, and Olan. Only you, Kovac, and I remain in the city."

"Why are we still here at all? We should have left with them; we need to watch over them."

"Someone else watches over them, with greater power than either of us. What of the Crucible? Did you discover anything?"

"She leaves this afternoon, back to Triah."

There was a pause.

"Just the Crucible?"

"Everyone. The remaining Goddessguard, the Sons, they are all returning to Triah."

"Goddess rising. They have given up?"

"I would not assume that. But they are leaving—between the vampire and what happened in the Circle Square yesterday, they have realized there is much more afoot here than heresy. We should take our blessings as they come."

"It is good that the family are out. We must delay our own departure; we do not want to leave at the same time as the Crucible."

There was something odd about the voices; they certainly didn't belong to Nash and Kali. It was two women who spoke, though neither sounded familiar.

Suddenly Winter's body convulsed and she coughed with pain. The two shadows in her vision turned to look at her, and one of them rushed to her side.

"It's all right," a voice said, a whisper against the sharp ringing in her head. "You're safe. Relax and lie back. You need to rest."

The woman's blond hair was tied behind her head, her

blue eyes bright. She motioned towards the other woman, who walked away.

"Where…" Winter began.

"Safe," the woman said. "I am Jane. Your friends are here. My sister went to fetch them…"

As she spoke, someone else approached. It was Lian.

"It's okay," he said. "I'm here. You're safe."

"Knot," she whispered. She wasn't sure if he understood her; she could barely understand herself.

"You need rest. We can talk later."

"Knot."

The look Lian gave her told her he understood exactly what she had said. Lian frowned.

Winter heard a new voice. New, but familiar.

"Is she awake?"

"Barely," Lian said. "You should let her rest before you see her."

And then he was there, just as she had seen him in the Circle Square, his face covered in a short beard, hair grown long and unwashed. He looked down at her, his calm eyes the color of burnished oak.

"Knot," she whispered, her voice a hollow rasp.

He gently placed the back of his hand on her forehead. "Don't need to speak right now. Lian's right. Save your strength. We won't let anything happen to you."

He bent down, and she felt his lips on her forehead. Rough and chapped against her skin.

Winter felt her thoughts slipping away as exhaustion enveloped her. Her eyes closed, but she almost smiled at the sound of his voice. Hearing it somehow made her pain less.

As she drifted off to sleep, Winter had a sudden panicked

feeling. She feared what she would find in her dreams. She feared what she would see, and, most of all, she feared what she had done.

*You will never be the same*, the voice said.

She knew the voice was right.

# 28

*Roden Gate, Navone*

KNOT RUBBED HIS FRESHLY shaven face as he looked up at the Roden Gate. The sky was clearer today, but ankle-deep snow had accumulated overnight. He pulled his cloak around him more tightly, feeling the cold air on his face. He'd shaved and cut his hair short that morning. Most of the city had been present at the massacre yesterday; being recognized as one of the people on the gallows would do him no good.

What had happened in the Circle Square yesterday seemed to play over and over in his mind. When the woman had incapacitated Astrid and confronted him, he'd assumed that she—or whoever was with her—was behind all of the destruction, the weapons and people hurtling through the air. But then the fountain globe had smashed into her. That could not have been a mistake; Knot could not believe the woman had simply been an unintentional casualty.

But if she had not been behind the massacre, who was?

The Crucible and her force were supposedly moving out of the southwest gate, abandoning the city after what had happened. And even though Knot was at the opposite corner of the city, he was still putting himself at risk. He wouldn't have left the Odens' strange cavern at all—wouldn't have left Winter—if it hadn't been important.

"What do you want?"

Knot turned to the Borderguard who had just addressed him. The soldier was young, barely eighteen, and narrowed his eyes as if Knot was going to steal everything he owned. "Looking for Captain Rudak," Knot said, ignoring the boy's rudeness. The entire city had been on edge before the inexplicable massacre in the Circle; now, everyone was downright paranoid.

"Who's asking?"

Knot frowned. The boy didn't know much about dealing with civilians. Either that, or the kid was having a particularly bad day.

"Madzin," Knot said, using the name the captain had addressed him with in the letter. "Tell him Madzin is looking for him."

"Just Madzin?"

Knot's frown deepened. "Just Madzin."

The young Borderguard turned towards the Roden Gate without another word.

Half an hour later the young man returned, his demeanor markedly different.

The boy bowed. "Come with me, sir. Captain Rudak has been expecting you."

Knot raised an eyebrow. He suspected the boy's attitude change had to do with Rudak's authority, and his opinion of this Madzin. Knot hoped he could live up to this view enough to convince Rudak to help him.

The young Borderguard led Knot through the Roden Gate and into the snowy field between the Roden Gate and the Blood Gate. Their footsteps crunched in the freshly fallen snow. No plants, trees, or crops of any kind grew in the field; it had likely been salted. Khalic soldiers wanted a clear shot at enemy troops, should the Blood Gate ever fall.

Knot looked up at the Blood Gate. The structure was truly a feat of architecture. The space between the cliffs was much narrower here than at the Roden Gate. Knot knew, in the way he knew so much that he could not explain, that the wall was nearly twenty rods high, far taller than the walls of Navone, and five rods thick. At either end of the wall stood two towers, each connecting directly with the cliffs that loomed over the Sorensan Pass.

Several Borderguards in plate armor and helmets stood in front of the large oak-and-iron gate. With them stood a captain. Knot recognized the man's rank by the red talons embroidered on his tabard. He wore only chain mail for protection—and the man was *huge*. Even without a helmet he stood at least a head above all the other Borderguards, and nearly twice as broad. The man's girth seemed a mix of muscle and fat. While the strength of such people was obvious, their dexterity could often catch enemies off guard. The man was young, too. Twenty-seven, perhaps twenty-eight. One didn't rise to the rank of a captain so quickly by winning pastry-eating contests.

The captain smiled. "Madzin, my friend. It has been too long."

Knot nodded in return, and tried to calm the feeling of excitement rising within him. Here was a man who genuinely knew him, the old him. The *real* him. "I received your letter. Thank you for meeting with me, Captain."

Captain Rudak raised an eyebrow. "Businesslike as always." Rudak motioned Knot to follow. "Let us retire to someplace more private."

The huge man walked to the corner of the Blood Gate, where the tower met the cliff. Rudak removed a key from his belt and opened a small wooden door, almost imperceptible, in the wall. He turned back to Knot, still smiling. The man's hair was curly and long, and a thick beard covered his face. He shook strands of hair from his eyes.

"The tower will suit our needs, eh? Unless, of course, you would prefer a different location…"

Knot shook his head. "The tower will do."

Rudak's grin widened. "Very well, then. Up we go." Rudak ducked through; the door barely reached his eye-level.

Knot hesitated. Despite the captain's friendliness, Knot had no reason to trust him. He was about to enter a small, enclosed space with someone who just might qualify as a giant. Even with Knot's skill, he wasn't sure he'd be able to maneuver his way out of that fight.

Chewing his cheek, Knot walked through anyway. He couldn't waste this opportunity to find out about his past.

They walked up a spiral stairway and reached a trapdoor in the ceiling that gave access to the top of the tower. Rudak opened the door and stepped out into the sunlight. Knot shivered. Rudak seemed hardly out of breath; the man was incredibly spry for his size.

Rudak relieved the Borderguard posted at the top of the tower, who saluted, and went through the trapdoor without a word.

Then, Knot and Rudak were alone.

Rudak swung his arm towards Knot, and Knot almost dodged until he realized the man was slapping him on the back. Knot stumbled forward, the weight of Rudak's arm nearly knocking him off the damn tower.

"Far too long, indeed! Canta's bones, what kept you? Heading into Roden last time I saw you, you bastard. How in Oblivion did you get back across the border without stopping for a drink?"

Knot regained his balance and stared at Rudak. The man was grinning like a madman. Rudak reached beneath his tabard, and Knot tensed. But Rudak only produced a large flask, twisting off the top. "Navone makes the best brandy north of Triah," he said, his grin widening. He offered the flask to Knot. "Take a pull."

Knot took the flask. He wondered briefly whether it was poisoned, but dismissed the idea. Rudak was not one to poison. He would meet his foes head-on. Although Knot's memory of Rudak did not tell him this, but rather his memory of men *like* Rudak.

"What d'you think, Madzy? Smell the stuff, go on."

Knot raised the flask to his nose. After a moment, he realized he was smiling. "Charred oak," he said, swirling the flask, "and cinnamon. Beneath that, a hint of fruit, and sweetness tinged with fire." He looked at Rudak. "A good year."

Rudak chuckled. "I knew you'd appreciate it. Dug up a bottle when I heard you were in Navone."

Knot brought the flask to his lips, fully aware that he had just described brandy like a noble. Apparently spirit-tasting was one more thing that came to him easily, like nautical knots, or driving a cart. Or killing. But Rudak seemed to appreciate Knot's appraisal, so once he'd swallowed a bit of the brandy, he closed his eyes, nodding.

"A good year, indeed. You chose well, Rudak."

Knot opened his eyes to see the man's smile slowly fading. Knot handed the flask back, waiting to see what Rudak would say.

"We have serious things to discuss, you and I," Rudak said. He took a swig of the brandy himself, then turned to the ramparts, facing out towards the Sorensan Pass. Towards Roden. Knot joined him, leaning on the cold, snow-covered crenel.

"Then let's discuss them," Knot said. Rudak put on a light-hearted front, but this was a serious man who knew his business. Knot wondered why he—or Madzin—would befriend such a man. Had Madzin had a similar demeanor? Was it for the mere convenience of knowing a man in the Borderguard?

"I saw you yesterday," Rudak said, "in the Circle Square. Whole bloody city saw you, you bastard."

"I know."

Rudak turned to Knot, leaning against the battlement. "I'm not sure if any of the others recognized you, but Canta rising, I sure as Oblivion did."

Knot reached for the flask and took another swallow. "Others?"

"Aye. Your other contacts in the city," Rudak said.

If Knot had other contacts here, would he have them in other cities as well? Did he have them in Cineste? Would he have them in Roden?

"Did you see any of them yesterday?" Knot asked. "In the Circle?"

"Aye. Remfeld was there, along with his thugs. The alchemist, Qan, I think I saw her, too. And at the edge of the crowd that woman, what's her name? The one that looks like a hero addict. Thin, bruised, hair practically falling out in chunks. Ugly. You know her, you bastard, what's her name?"

Knot froze. He had no idea who Rudak was talking about. None of the names rang a bell.

"Taille," Rudak said, slapping the crenel. "Taille's her name. Anyway, saw all three of them there. They didn't seem to recognize you, but how should I know?"

A thug, an alchemist, and an addict. And a captain in the Borderguard. Knot saw no common thread.

"What in Oblivion were you doing up there, Madzy? Since when do your like have problems with a Holy Crucible?"

Knot shrugged. Considering the fact that he didn't know what "like" Rudak was referring to, he couldn't exactly say. "That was more of a… personal matter," he said.

Rudak's eyes narrowed. "You don't mean that you're part of all this?" The large man waved his hand back at Navone. From the tower they could see the entire city below them.

Knot shook his head. Losing Rudak's help because the man thought he was a heretic was not an option. "Let's just say it's a bad idea to cross a Holy Crucible, in any situation."

Rudak looked at Knot for a moment longer, then burst out in laughter. "I should've known. Old Madzin tried to bed a Crucible, didn't he? Looked up the wrong skirt this time, you bastard. Every man worth his balls knows not to get involved with the Ministry. She shut you down before you even said two words, didn't she?" Knot didn't say anything—better Rudak think this than know the truth. But Rudak's suspicion, while ludicrous, couldn't help but bring a smirk to Knot's lips. Rudak stared at him. "You didn't. Madzin Moraine, you bastard, you actually did bed her, didn't you?" Rudak threw back his head, his laughter echoing off the cliffs. He clapped his meaty hand on Knot's back, once more nearly sending him toppling off the tower. Knot gripped the crenel to steady himself.

"Canta's bones, boy. A Holy Crucible. Only you would do something that stupid. I tell you, there are two types of people in this world that are just dumb enough to think they can get away with anything. Assassins and government types. Course, since you're both, you're a bad lot either way!" Rudak laughed again.

*An assassin and a government agent*, Knot thought. The former confirmed what he'd seen in many of his dreams. He hadn't considered the latter.

Knot wasn't sure how much longer he could carry on a conversation with this man without revealing that he had no idea who Madzin was. Best to wrap things up, and get what he came for.

"I do need your help," Knot said, looking Rudak in the eye. It took effort; Rudak stood more than a head taller than Knot.

"Figured you would," Rudak muttered. "I'm at your service, Madzin. You know I'm not one to deny you, or the people you work for."

Knot nodded. "I need to cross the border, discreetly. You can do this?"

Rudak snorted. "Course I can. Done it for you a dozen times over, haven't I? Safe and smooth, each time."

"Then I need you to do it again. Tonight, perhaps tomorrow at the latest."

"Very well. Just you, then? Or is there an entire *cotir* with you this time?"

Knot hesitated. That word—*cotir*—resonated. He couldn't recall it, but it sounded familiar. Just like some of the words Astrid used. Knot would have to remember to ask her about them. Which brought up another issue: Astrid, he was sure, would insist on tagging along to Roden. And he doubted he could just send Winter and Lian back to Pranna after they had come so far to find him—especially in light of some of the things Lian had told him.

Knot's jaw set at the thought of Winter. She was here, in Navone, with him. He had not been able to bring himself to share a room with her. He had avoided her, really. He wanted to help her, and he was certainly glad she was safe, but he felt incredible shame at having left her in the first place. He didn't know how to act around her. Her presence was oddly confusing.

"Not sure," Knot said. "Maybe just me. Maybe more. Can you prepare for a group, if need be?"

Rudak raised an eyebrow. "That's a new one," he said. "You're not sure how many are crossing. Shouldn't be a problem, though. Whether it's you or a group, we can get you across. Of course, by group I mean only a few people, no more than five or six. Even *I* couldn't get an entire troop through the gates."

"I know," Knot said. "That'll do." He hesitated. "Some in the group may be tiellans. Will that be a problem?"

Rudak snorted. "Won't be a problem for me. But good luck moving them around in Roden without getting noticed. I don't think I need to remind you of the penalties for that, under Rodenese law."

Knot shook his head. The best they could hope for was immediate deportation, but imprisonment without trial was more common, and, in some cases, the trespassing tiellans— and their companions—were put to death.

Rudak turned back towards the Sorensan Pass. "Tonight will be difficult, especially if it's a group. Best we plan on tomorrow night. Same time as usual?"

Knot hesitated. He couldn't agree; then he wouldn't know when in Oblivion they were meeting. But if he said a random time and it *wasn't* the "same time as usual" that Rudak referred to…

"Midnight." A shot in the dark.

Rudak nodded. "Doable. Later than usual, but we can make it work. I'll meet you near the Roden Gate."

"Good," Knot said. *This just might work after all.*

Rudak grinned. "Now let's get out of this tower. Being up so high gives me shakes."

# 29

*Oden tunnels, Navone*

"WHAT DO WE DO now?" Cinzia asked.

They had gathered old armchairs and benches from the tunnels around a small fire in the main chamber. Jane sat to her left, and Kovac to her right. Across from her stood Knot, the two tiellans, and the girl—the vampire. Winter, the tiellan woman, sat between Knot and Lian. She still looked weak, although her moving around was a good sign. Cinzia, having learned the mechanics of physicianry and healing at the seminary in Triah, had been monitoring Winter. The tiellan did not seem to have suffered any real injury, but her body was obviously recovering from... something. What it was Cinzia did not know, and Winter had refused to say. But when Cinzia looked into the girl's eyes, she saw a darkness that went beyond the color of her irises.

Cinzia noticed Jane staring at Winter, and not for the first time. Cinzia did not understand Jane's fascination with the girl; Jane had no medical training, and Cinzia had not told her sister anything she had discerned about Winter—confidentiality was paramount when it came to practicing physicianry. Besides, Cinzia was far more worried about the vampire. Astrid's eyes glowed in the darkness of the cavern. Cinzia shivered.

Knot's tiellan companions explained to some extent why he spoke the way he did. Although, strangely, Winter did not seem to speak like a tiellan at all. The group was odd, indeed.

Cinzia and Kovac had called this meeting to establish what they should do next. Part of her feared that Knot and his companions were inclined to turn her and Jane in to the Denomination. Cinzia did not trust Knot, but Kovac seemed to. Kovac said the man knew his way around in a fight, and that they might have a need for such talent. It was terrible to admit it, but Cinzia knew her Goddessguard was not wrong.

*Is he even my Goddessguard anymore?* she wondered. Her status as a priestess would not last long, given what happened yesterday. Nayome had surely seen Cinzia helping Jane. Cinzia breathed deep. She could not think of that now. There were more immediate matters.

"We have work to do," Jane said. She was looking at Cinzia. "We need somewhere to do it. Somewhere safe."

It was the first time Cinzia had heard anything about *work*. She looked at Jane in confusion.

"Our family is safe," Jane said. "It is best if they lie low for a time. Who knows what kind of retribution the horrors we saw yesterday will lead to. It is safer for everyone involved if we leave, too."

Cinzia nodded. She could still barely think about what had happened in the Circle Square. She could not believe the place where she had grown up had become the site of a massacre. And, to make matters worse, no one seemed to have any idea what had happened. Weapons had flown through the air of their own accord; she had seen Sons of Canta themselves careening over the Circle Square, smashing into one another.

And so many people had been killed.

"Perhaps we should follow them to Tinska," Jane said, suddenly. "We will be safe there." Tinska was a small town directly west of Navone, on the coast of the Wyndric Ocean.

Cinzia, however, did not think following them was a good idea. Jane was dangerous, whether she realized it or not. Cinzia was not about to expose the rest of her family to more peril.

"I am not sure Tinska is where we should go," Cinzia said.

"Our family will be there. *We* need to go there, Cinzia, to finish the work Canta has given us."

Cinzia frowned. "What work? What are you talking about, Jane?"

Jane lowered her gaze, looking into the fire. "I can't tell you," she said. "But you will understand in time."

Cinzia laughed mirthlessly. "No. I have sacrificed too much for you. We have *all* sacrificed too much for you, Jane. I am not doing anything else until you tell me what in Oblivion is going on."

"My lady," Kovac said, quietly. He was trying to stop the argument. Cinzia sighed. He was right to do so.

"Yes, Kovac?" Cinzia said.

"Perhaps we should seek to understand what *their* plans are," Kovac said, nodding towards Knot, "before we decide anything ourselves."

Cinzia nodded. "Of course." She looked at Knot, who seemed the de facto leader of the ragtag group. The man's eyes still bothered Cinzia. The eyes of a dead man. "I'm afraid our destinies are intertwined, at least for a time. Knot, have you and your…" Cinzia paused. The tiellans certainly were not his servants, but if not, what were they? "Your friends," she said, finally, "decided where you will go from here?"

When her question was met with silence, Cinzia continued.

"If you desire, you may accompany us. We do not have much, as you can see, but you can help us earn what we need

to survive. And we could use your talents should things get…
violent." Cinzia refrained from looking at the vampire. Should
Knot decide to accompany them, she could only hope that thing
would not come with him.

Knot looked down at Winter. It was the first time Cinzia had
seen him look at the woman since they had begun the meeting.
Winter just stared into the fire, her dark eyes reflecting the flames.

"I've got business needs attending, in the north. But Winter
and Lian—"

"We're going with you," Winter said quietly. "You're not
leaving me again."

Cinzia did not know what history existed between the two.
Their relationship had seemed strange to her since the moment
she first saw them together. Cinzia glanced at Lian. The tiellan
man probably did not make the equation any simpler.

"They could imprison you. Kill you," Knot said.

"Doesn't matter."

"They'll notice you eventually. I can't risk—"

"I'll wear a hood," Winter said. "I'm going with you, and
you can't argue that, *husband*. Lian can do as he wishes, but I'm
going with you."

Cinzia tried to mask her surprise. A tiellan and a human,
*married*? It was not unheard of, of course. The ritual was
technically allowed in the Cantic Denomination. But Cinzia
had never known anyone—from either race—actually willing
to *do* it.

"I go where she goes," was all Lian said.

The tiellans were willing to walk into a country whose
people, even more so than Khale, hated their entire race
so much that they had driven out or killed every last tiellan
decades ago.

304

"You're going to find out who you were, aren't you? To find out why you are the way you are?"

Knot nodded.

"Then I'm going to help you."

When Knot voiced no further objection, Cinzia took a deep breath. "Very well," she said. Their business was their own; it was not Cinzia's place to question it. And she doubted they would cause any trouble for her or her sister in Roden. Cinzia was about to turn to Jane and argue against the idea of going to Tinska when a strange feeling came over her.

She felt, oddly, as if she were meeting a close friend for the first time in many years. She no longer felt in control of her own emotions or movements; she seemed to be looking down at her body from above. Something changed, the air around her moved.

Then she saw the fire. The flames that had been glowing a bright orange shifted, first to yellow and then to green. A deep, glowing green, like the vampire's eyes. The fire flared, flames licking hungrily outward. Cinzia watched herself rise and take a step back.

Everyone else was now staring at the towering green flames. Cinzia watched both herself and the fire. Her head was angled backwards, her neck craned back, eyes closed. Then, with a snap, her head came forward, and her eyes shot open.

"*Lathe, my son, you have chosen rightly.*" It was Cinzia's own voice, she was sure of it; she could see her lips moving, could hear the words. And yet it was different, louder, more forceful than ever before. "*Make your way to Izet. Roden is important to my plan, as you will all soon learn.*" Cinzia saw that her own eyes were wide, and glowing green, like the fire. She watched those eyes turn to Jane.

*"Jane, you have been a faithful servant, and you will be blessed if you continue as such. I charge you, along with your sister and my guard, to accompany Lathe and his companions. You both have a great work to do."*

Cinzia watched herself look around at everyone at the fireside. Her face shone in the eerie green light, smiling. *"You are all important instruments in my plan. You are my children; I am your guide and keeper. I am your mother. I will look after you and keep you, until I come again to the Sfaera. So shall it be. Imass."*

"Imass," Cinzia whispered, and then she was back inside herself, looking into the dull orange glow of the fire.

She looked around, in a daze.

Knot swore, and Astrid muttered something that Cinzia did not understand. Everyone looked at Cinzia apart from Winter, who scowled into the fire.

"Cinzia," Jane said, her voice cautious, "what was that?" Her eyes were wide, her face pale in the firelight.

"I do not know," Cinzia said. Jane looked at her as if she had never seen her before. "Who is Lathe?" Cinzia asked, looking around.

The tiellans both glanced at Knot, who sighed. "Guess that's me," he said. "Might be a name I went by, before."

Cinzia tried to process what had just happened. She had been outside of herself. Some voice had come from her mouth, calling them its children, calling them instruments. The voice had a plan for them, for the entire Sfaera. And Cinzia had felt like she had just been reacquainted with a long-lost friend.

Perhaps she finally had a way to take control of things.

Cinzia looked up. "I think… I think it was a revelation."

Cinzia and Jane looked at each other for what seemed a very long time. Everyone else around the fire remained silent, as if waiting for one of them to speak.

Then Jane closed her eyes and spoke slowly. "This was different than what I am used to. It was not the way things usually work."

Cinzia frowned. Jane could have these revelations, but when one came through Cinzia, it was questionable?

"It was Her," Cinzia said, suddenly. She was not sure that was right, but she did not care. "We have all been chosen. We, here, are all Canta's servants. It is a great blessing."

"Blessings of a dead goddess don't concern me," Winter said, her voice even.

Cinzia's first instinct was anger. Cinzia was a Cantic priestess. She had just had a revelation. How could this girl not believe?

But if she doubted her own experience, how could she expect someone else to believe? What had just happened was nothing like the revelations of old. After all that had happened with her family, with Jane... in many ways, the Canta that Cinzia had always known truly did seem dead to her, now.

Cinzia shook her head. She looked at Kovac. Stalwart Kovac, solid as ever at her side. Looking at him gave her strength. It was time she took action.

"Canta has commanded us to go to Roden," Cinzia said. The idea was insane. Wandering into Roden with a pair of tiellans was true madness. But Knot and his company were going there, anyway. And, deep down, Cinzia wondered: was there a greater plan? A reason for it all, for them all meeting together in Navone, like this?

"You said we have work to do," Cinzia said to Jane. "Can we do it in Roden?"

"I suppose we can, on the road," Jane said finally. "It will not be easy, but I believe it is possible. Assuming we can cross the border."

Cinzia looked to Knot. Now the real question. "You obviously planned on getting into Roden somehow. Perhaps Canta wills us to accompany you."

Knot shook his head. "Ain't no way in Oblivion—"

"We shall go to Roden anyway, even without you," Cinzia said quickly. "Why not travel together? We can help one another. I carry the influence of the Cantic Denomination. I could get you into places that might otherwise be impossible. Would you then return the favor?"

Knot glanced down at Winter. He took a deep breath, shaking his head. This time, however, the gesture seemed one of resignation rather than refusal. "Ain't no guarantee we'll return through Navone. You may have to come back alone, either way."

The subtext was not lost on Cinzia. *You mean you are not sure you will come back at all.*

"We will find our way home," Jane said.

Cinzia's eyebrows rose; she had not expected Jane's support.

"We are about Canta's will; nothing can stop us save the Goddess Herself," Jane said, placing her hand on Cinzia's arm.

Knot looked down at Winter again, placing his hand on her shoulder. "You all right with this?"

"Of course not," the woman said, standing. "But you've all already made up your minds. Do whatever you want." She walked off towards the small side room where she had been sleeping.

Knot watched Winter go. Cinzia thought, just for a moment, that she was beginning to see what Kovac saw in this man. Despite her initial impression, he might have some good in him after all.

Knot sighed. "She has some issues with the Denomination. Daresay we all do. We won't be preached to, and you won't try to save us. We clear on that?"

Cinzia nodded. "Of course." The conversion of souls to Canta's cause was the last thing on her mind.

"Then we leave tomorrow night. Be ready shortly after dusk; we'll be crossing the border at midnight."

For a moment, no one spoke. Then the group dispersed, leaving only Cinzia and Jane. Jane was gazing towards Winter's quarters.

"What is it?" Cinzia asked.

"I... I do not know," Jane said, her voice sounding far away. "There is something about that girl. Something I do not understand."

Cinzia did not know what Jane was talking about, but she suspected Jane was trying to avoid talking about what had just happened. So be it.

At least Cinzia had a direction, a tangible task. For now, that would have to be enough.

That night, as Cinzia approached the small room she had been sharing with Jane, she hesitated. Lamplight shone from the doorway. Jane was awake. Cinzia was not ready to have that conversation. Instead, she turned around, walking back towards the large cavern, where embers from the fire still burned dully. Then Cinzia heard a voice from the darkness.

"We need to talk, darlin'."

She turned sharply, and Knot emerged from the shadows. Cinzia's first instinct was to run, to get as far away from this man as fast as she could. She wanted to scream for help.

Instead she looked the man in the eyes. "Very well," she said.

"What happened, earlier?" Knot was perhaps two rods away from her, his face only partially lit. The rest of his body was still cloaked in shadow.

Cinzia thought about repeating what she had said earlier; that it was a vision, a revelation from Canta. It was not exactly a lie.

Instead, she told him the truth.

"I do not know."

"You don't know?"

"One minute I was looking into the fire, and the next, it was as if I were... outside of myself. Observing what happened, just like all of you. I do know it was not me who spoke those words."

"You knew my name. A name you shouldn't have been able to know."

Cinzia shrugged. "That is all I can tell you."

Knot nodded. "You're telling the truth." It was not a question.

"I am," Cinzia said. Why could she tell this man, this stranger, the truth, when she could not tell her own family?

"All right then," Knot said.

Cinzia was about to say she needed to get some rest when Knot spoke again.

"I'm not takin' you because of what happened," he said. "I'm takin' you because it makes sense to travel together. Fancy fire tricks and voices of goddesses ain't particularly meaningful to me. You're coming with us because it's safer all around, and the moment necessity steps in and tells us to part ways, we will."

"I understand."

"Good."

"Why are you going?" Cinzia asked. "Why Roden? What is there for you?"

"I... lost myself. Need to get what little there is left back."

"You are not the only one," Cinzia whispered. She was not sure whether he heard her.

"Roden is a dangerous place," he said. "You may not survive."

Cinzia nodded. "I know it is. I do not want to go. And yet…"

"And yet?"

"A part of me thinks it is the right thing. I cannot explain why. There seem to be two conflicting parts of me, two factions vying for dominance. I do not know which is right."

Knot nodded. "I understand," he said.

Cinzia looked down. She did not know how, but she knew he did.

"You're honest," he said.

"So are you," she said.

"I appreciate that."

"So do I."

"All right then," Knot said again.

Another moment of silence. Then Cinzia looked back up. "I hope you find what you are looking for," she said.

But he was already gone.

# 30

WINTER LAY ON HER cot, staring at the rock ceiling above her. She shifted in her blankets, her body aching. She could move around, at least, and the sharp piercing in her head had reduced to a muted ache.

Truth be told, she didn't care about the pain. Not the physical part. The pain she feared was rooted in something deeper.

Winter shivered, despite the blankets. It seemed that night was worse than day. No people to keep her company. Even if she never spoke to them, at least they were there.

At night, she was alone. At night, her daemons came.

*Murderer.* The voice still whispered to her.

Winter shut her eyes tightly, fighting the terror that threatened to consume her. The moment it won, Winter would be back in the Circle Square. She would relive it all. But she had so little left to fight with. Her father was gone. She had found Knot, but he refused to sleep in the same room.

He had come to her, after the meeting in the cavern, but the encounter had been awkward. He'd sat at the edge of the bed, rubbing his shoulder.

"Still bother you?" She knew his shoulder flared up often, ever since they found him in the Gulf of Nahl.

"Still bothers me."

They'd sat in silence, and Winter hadn't known what to say.

*Thanks for leaving me.*

*I'm glad I found you.*

*I murdered dozens of people yesterday.*

"I don't want you to come with me," Knot had said.

"You don't have a choice." If Knot thought he could leave her twice, he was insane. "I'm coming with you, and so is Lian. And, apparently, so is that priestess and her Goddessguard, and her sister, and that vampire girl you've recruited. We'll all have a wonderful time, I'm sure."

"Didn't know this would turn into a Goddess-damned caravan," Knot had mumbled.

He'd sat there for a moment longer, his hand on her leg. Then, abruptly, he moved. To leave the room, she realized. *We're married,* she wanted to say, *just stay with me.*

She gripped his arm. "Stay," she had whispered.

He breathed slowly in and out, and shook his head. Then he was gone, and she was alone.

Winter was alone, and suddenly she was back at the gallows, piercing armor, shredding flesh. She murdered soldier and civilian alike.

Winter couldn't breathe. She threw off her blankets, despite her cold sweat. She rolled off the cot, falling to the stone floor. She had to get out. She crawled on her hands and knees to the doorway. With an effort, she lifted herself up, using the frame to steady herself. Her stomach heaved and she nearly vomited.

Winter did not know what hour of the night it was, but she knew she had to leave. She had to get out, and do *something*. She reached for her long wool cloak. One pocket concealed a dagger. Her remaining money was in the other. Winter donned the cloak, her muscles aching, and stumbled out into the hallway, towards the secret passageway that led up to the city.

There were no stars. No light that she could see. Winter remembered the old saying, suddenly coming back to her in full force. *There are daemons even daemons fear.*

Winter could almost believe such a thing. The vampire girl might even be some form of twisted proof. But that meant nothing; the girl was cursed, nothing more. Monsters were no more real than Canta, and daemons were nothing more than people. She herself was living proof.

Something strange had happened to the priestess, Cinzia, at the meeting earlier. Winter had seen the green flames reaching out of the hearth. She had heard the woman's voice, strangely deep and amplified. It hadn't been Canta. No, Winter couldn't believe that. Some crude joke, a special dust thrown on the fire. Thinking of Cinzia's strange revelation, or whatever it was, only made Winter angry. It only made her think of her wedding, and her father. This priestess had been kind to her, attending her while she recovered. But it meant little; she was still a part of the religion that had destroyed Winter's life.

Winter forced her anger from her mind, and put one foot in front of the other. At least she could move; this morning she'd barely felt capable of rising out of bed. As she walked through the night, through the city, she felt stronger. Invigorated.

Winter realized she knew exactly where she was going. She looked over her shoulder, making sure no one followed as she walked towards the market district. The streets were empty. Winter had heard the others talking about how quiet the streets had been since the event in the Circle Square. And, now— Winter guessed it was around midnight, perhaps later—there

314

wasn't a soul to be seen. The market district would be just as empty, but Winter knew that. Her course took her past the market, towards the slums. Anticipation writhed in her chest.

Most of the merchants in the market district had long since closed up their stalls for the night, but a few were still open when Winter arrived, catering to late-night customers. Produce and woodcarving shops were closed, and bars and fortune-tellers' stands were open. Street-side sellers, shouting the superiority of their wares, had retired; prostitutes, selling themselves silently, had emerged. Winter pulled her hood over her face. Her palms were slick, despite the chilly night.

Down an alley, an offshoot from the main market district, she saw hollow faces and wasted limbs. Haunted eyes stared through her and into the burn, the high, that in some cases was probably the only thing that kept these people alive.

Winter looked away. If she could find what she sought, she could make her pain go away.

Winter saw a man in a long, hooded cloak, standing half in shadow. She approached, her steps even. The man's eyes locked on her, and he shrank back with suspicion.

"I'm looking for something powerful," she said. "I can pay."

The man looked at her for a moment, his dark eyes flickering. "How powerful?" he finally asked. "I have hero and grit." He eyed her, and she stopped herself from cringing at his stare; he drank her in ravenously. "For you... a silver piece each. They'll keep you going all night."

"No," she said. "Something stronger. Something that will burn." *Time to see if Nash was telling the truth about finding it on the street.*

The man shook his head. "I don't carry any of that," he said. "Talk to Mazille. Two alleys over. A hole in the wall."

Winter walked quickly, feeling the excitement swell within her. She didn't want to be gone too long. She would prefer not to have to lie.

Winter glanced into the next alley, but it was empty except for a few huddled forms. She moved to the next, and saw a yellow glow coming from a small doorway. She moved towards the light and looked into a small room, rapping her fist lightly on the wooden frame.

"Mazille?" Winter asked. Two small lanterns hung from the ceiling illuminating a small shop. There were intricately carved pipes, vials, and other glass and wooden containers on shelves, along with stranger objects—a metal vase with tubes running from it, a strangely curved knife with grooves and weird runes carved into the blade.

"Can I help you, child?"

Winter looked up. She tried to hide her surprise at the very old, very fat tiellan woman before her. The woman's pointed ears protruded from shining silver hair, and her face was wrinkled and ancient. Most tiellans could barely find enough food to survive, let alone grow fat; this woman was outrageously large.

The old tiellan's eyes, almost hidden in folds of skin, were deep and black. Just like Winter's. Dark eyes were not common in tiellans. It was odd to see someone with the same trait.

"Someone told me to come find you," Winter said quietly. "I'm looking for something powerful."

The old woman shook her head, waving Winter away. "Sorry, child. You've come to the wrong place."

Winter shook her head. She didn't have a lot of time. "I mean something *really* powerful. Something that will make me burn."

The woman stopped, her arm in midair, folds of fat

undulating back and forth underneath. She brought her arm down and grinned.

"I thought I sensed it in you," she said, through missing teeth and thick lips. "I know how strong the pull can be. Lucky, that you were led here. I carry the purest *faltira* in the north."

Winter tasted blood. The woman was using psimancy. Winter realized, suddenly, how vulnerable she was. Nash and Kali had told her that she was the first tiellan psimancer in generations. Had they lied to her? Winter supposed it was possible that a human psimancer could be nearby; that could be what she sensed.

"You can pay?" Mazille asked.

Winter reached into the pocket of her cloak. "How much?"

A small crystal floated up and onto the wooden counter. Winter stared at the *faltira*. She tasted blood and iron strongly, now. It wasn't some nearby human using psimancy—Mazille was a telenic, she was sure.

"A gold mark for this one," the woman said, eying the small crystal. Her eyes moved to Winter expectantly.

Winter looked from the woman's wrinkled face to the frost. One wouldn't do. She needed more. "Is this all you have? I can pay for more."

The woman frowned, but then Winter saw another five crystals—five!—levitate up and onto the counter, lining up perfectly with the first. Winter eyed the *faltira* eagerly. Nash and Kali had only ever allowed her to carry one crystal at a time. Her mouth watered at the power before her. Winter felt as weightless as the crystals themselves. She could almost feel the high taking her already.

"Ten marks for all of them," Mazille said.

Winter gasped. "Ten marks? You said one crystal was one mark, how can you—"

"I set the prices how I want 'em."

Winter frowned at the crystals. She had about twenty marks left, and some silver, but that was all of her money. She didn't know how much Knot had, or how much it would take to get to Roden. She wasn't sure how she could justify spending half of everything she had all at once.

"What are their strengths?" Winter asked, mind racing.

"All full capacity," Mazille said. "Manufactured by an expert here in Navone. She knows what she's doing, this alchemist. They're almost pure; you can see they're nearly without blemish."

Winter looked closely at the crystals. Nash had taught her that she could tell frost's purity by its clarity. The purer the dose, the more powerful it was, and the longer it lasted. And the greater the high, of course. These crystals were almost clear, only the barest trace of cloudiness in each.

Winter tried to hide her eagerness. "How much for four of them?" she asked tentatively.

The old tiellan lady paused for a minute, contemplating the crystals on the counter. Then she looked up at Winter.

"One or all," she said, her voice low. "One mark or ten."

Winter swore. She looked at the crystals. She should just buy one. That's what she *should* do. One mark for a crystal didn't seem a bad price, especially for this kind of clarity. But the thought of having them all at once made her giddy. Who knew the next time she would be able to find the drug? Winter didn't know whether it even existed in Roden.

Sweat formed on Winter's brow, beneath her armpits, ran down her back. She pulled ten marks from her purse and dropped them on the counter. Mazille's eyes widened.

*She didn't expect me to pay for so many,* Winter realized. *She thought I could only pay for one.*

318

Quickly, Winter reached for the crystals. She wouldn't let the woman go back on the deal now. But, even more quickly than she reached for them, the woman's hand snapped out and latched on to hers, stopping it in midair.

"Be careful with them, girl. You are young in the power, and susceptible to its darkness. Watch yourself. Don't let it consume you."

Winter frowned. *I know* the nature of power. *I don't need you to tell me about it.* Winter put the frost into her pocket, keeping one crystal in her hand. She looked at the woman and their eyes met. She turned away. The old tiellan whispered something, but Winter didn't hear what it was. She walked into the alley and placed a frost crystal in her mouth.

In moments, she felt the power surging through her veins. Ice and fire, pain and elation. She leaned against a building. And for that moment, she was home, and she was free. Free from the horrors of what she'd done. Free from the confusion of what was happening between her and Knot. Free from the pain that had clawed at her heart since the day her father had been killed.

For just a moment, Winter floated blissfully within *faltira*'s high, feeling the flame course through her veins, shivering as the frost kissed her skin. This was peace, Winter realized. The only peace she'd ever known. This was power.

She didn't know how long it took for her to start walking again. She would make her way back to the caverns, eventually, but for now, she needed to wander.

It took a few moments for Winter to realize she was being followed. She saw him, spotting him out of the corner of her eye as she walked down an empty street. She turned a corner, trying to find a busier area, but there was no one about. She needed to get back to the cavern.

Winter looked over her shoulder. Sure enough, the figure was there. A man, she could see now. Tiellan, short and thin, wearing a long cloak that could easily hide a dagger or even a small sword. Had Mazille sent someone after her?

Winter looked around. The alley was narrow, and empty apart from a few loose cobbles. Not the ideal place to pick a fight, but Winter could imagine worse. And, right now, there was only the one man following her. Winter stopped and turned.

The man following her wasn't fazed. He continued towards her. She could make out his face, gaunt and thin, his chin long and pointed. The man opened his coat, and pulled out a long dagger. Winter tasted iron.

Another psimancer.

Winter reached out a *tendron*, picking up one of the loose cobbles, and hurled it at the man. The stone veered away and clattered harmlessly off a wall.

Winter forced down panic. She'd never faced another telenic before, but Nash had told her how to sense another's *tendra*. What had he said? Seeing with one's mind, rather than with one's eyes. Winter still wasn't sure what that meant, and she didn't think she would have time to test it.

The man was almost on her now, dagger glinting, so Winter lifted two more stones and pushed them up, keeping hold of them instead of flinging them, and smashed them together on either side of the man's head. Winter felt something assault her grip on one of the stones, but it wasn't enough to make her let go. The man in front of her collapsed to the ground as his skull crunched between the stones. Winter's mouth still tasted strongly of blood. This man was not the telenic.

Winter saw no one else. Above her was only a sliver of dark sky and the tops of the buildings on either side.

Winter didn't know how she thought to do it, other than that her body simply turned around and picked the dead man up by his clothes, shielding herself. She heard a series of thuds, and watched as four fist-sized stones fell to the ground in front of her.

Her attacker was hiding, and Winter wouldn't be able to fight him that way. There was only one option.

Winter ran.

She ran as fast as she could down the alley. For a moment, she felt herself being lifted off the ground, felt her cloak and dress pulling up against her, but she cut the *tendra* tugging on them with her own, just as Nash had taught her. Winter felt her *tendra* come in contact with something, and then she crashed to the ground and took off running once more. Another attempt to lift her up, but Winter cut the *tendra* off again, just as she felt something pelt her in the back. The space between her shoulders ached but she kept running until the blood taste disappeared from her mouth.

The next evening, as Winter gathered with the rest of the group, she fondled the remaining five crystals in a small pouch at her side. She glanced at Knot, who, as far as she knew, was still unaware of her psimancy. Lian eyed her, but she didn't care. He had promised not to say anything until she was ready, and for that Winter was grateful.

Cinzia and Jane, of course, ignored her. Winter supposed they were as yet unsure how to act around tiellans who were not servants or slaves. That didn't matter. The silly women and the goddess they worshipped were meaningless. For now, only two things mattered to Winter.

Protecting those she loved, and being sure she had enough frost to do it.

# 31

KALI'S EYES SNAPPED OPEN.

She was in a room. The lone window was closed and shuttered; through the gaps she saw only darkness.

Kali sat up, stretching. She wasn't sore, but her limbs felt neglected, as if she hadn't used them in some time. Which was true.

Kali rose from the bed. She was *thirsty*. She stood, walking towards a wooden table near the window that held a jug and a small pewter cup.

She was glad of the thirst. It made her feel alive. Grateful to have found a body.

She ignored the cup and lifted the entire jug to her lips, drinking greedily. The water was lukewarm and stale and tasted ever so slightly of dust, but was delicious nonetheless. If needing water made her feel alive, drinking it in made her feel like a goddess. Water dribbled down her chin and onto her shirt, but she didn't care. It was the most satisfying water she had ever tasted.

When she brought the jug down to take a gasping breath, her other hand instinctively moved to her chest. The note, the folded parchment, would no longer be there, of course. It had been destroyed, or might as well have been, in the Circle Square. That did not matter. She had memorized every word of it, anyway.

She would never forget.

Immediately, Kali thought of Winter. The damn girl had *killed* her. Or as good as, anyway. Murder—at least when it was committed against *her*—was not an offense that Kali took lightly. And yet Kali felt a begrudging respect for Winter. *The Harbinger*. Kali could admit it to herself now. The girl was the Harbinger. Kali had to accept what she never thought possible. To put aside the pain of her past, and actually respect the woman—tiellan or not.

The door opened behind her, but Kali didn't turn. She knew who it would be.

"Good to see you up," Nash said. "I was worried. You've never made a transfer like this one before."

Kali drank the last of the water, then turned to face Nash. "Still returned, didn't I?" She walked towards him. "You can't tell me this isn't fun for you. You get to sleep with a different woman every few months. Most men have to sneak around for that."

Nash stared at her. Kali moved towards him, feeling the sway of her hips, the grain of the wood beneath her feet, the air itself around her, between her body and the large, loose shirt she wore. The only thing she wore.

She looked in the mirror, catching the briefest glimpse of herself. Her hair was blond. She was shorter than she'd been before, and younger. Elation thrilled through her. Kali always felt most herself directly after a transition. *Thanks, Elsi*, Kali thought with a smile. Elsi had obviously taken care of the body when she had inhabited it.

When Kali had first branded her sift—her soul, essentially—onto a lacuna, she had been terrified. But the act had been necessary; her old body, her original body, was dying, and dying quickly. There had been no choice. Since that first transition, the change had gotten easier. Now, she felt herself again, or as close to it as she would ever be. She was thin, lithe, supple. Her hair long and blond. Her skin smooth, pale in the darkness.

It excited her.

"I'm back, now," she said, snaking her hand behind Nash, pulling him close. "Don't worry—I know you've been with someone else, and it's all right. I understand." She kissed his neck, letting her warm breath flow across his skin. "To be honest," she said, her hand crawling beneath his clothes, "it only makes me want you all the more."

She yearned to be with him, in her chest and between her legs. She led him to the bed, unable to keep the smile from her face. Things couldn't have worked out better if she'd planned them. They had business to take care of, of course. But, for once, business could wait. She and Nash would follow Winter, and Lathe, to Roden. There, they would end this. Her business with Lathe would conclude. And her business with Winter…

Kali smiled as Nash kissed down her neck, down and down. She had a feeling her business with Winter was just beginning.

# PART III

KILL TO FEEL

# 32

### *The Roden—Khale border*

WINTER COULDN'T HELP BUT notice that entering Roden seemed
much easier than leaving Khale.

Knot had explained that Roden's military strategy was very
different from Khale's. While Khale focused their defense on
the main accessible pass across the stone mountains, Roden
concentrated on defending their main cities and outposts, and on
maintaining their navy. Roden's tactics sounded more sensible
to Winter. The Blood and Roden Gates were intimidating, but
what was the point when they were so easily bypassed by ships?
"Products of different ages," Knot had said. Winter wondered
how he knew such information, but hadn't asked.

They had reached the top of the Sorensan Pass yesterday
afternoon, which, compared to the jutting rock peaks around
them, had not seemed like much of a feat. The road was long,
however, and they had been forced to camp alongside it that
evening. Better than camping at the peaks of the mountains,
Knot had said, or even at the top of the pass, but it was still very
cold despite their blankets and furs, and the fire they had made.

They had set up camp between two massive rows of *rihnemins*
lining either side of the road. The great stone monuments had
towered above them, reaching high into the night air. Once
again Lian had deferentially walked up to one of the stones and
placed his hand on it. No one else had seemed to know the

site's significance, although Winter had caught Knot glancing at the stones more than once. Winter had not acknowledged the *rihnemins*, despite the sense of protection they gave her. She had felt an overpowering sensation that they would be safe. But she had resented the stones for that feeling. She could protect herself. She did not need a bunch of stupid stones. She knew it was silly, getting worked up, but she didn't care. It had only been a feeling; the stones could do nothing for her, not really.

Although there had been no storm that night, and everyone seemed to agree they were fortunate in that regard.

The path down from the Sorensan Pass seemed significantly longer than the path that had led up to it, but they finally made their way into the foothills of the Sorensan Mountains. Roden's territory. The mountain trail grew less steep. Winter's body still ached as she trudged down the rocky path, but in general she felt much better. The priestess, Cinzia, tried to ask after her health, but Winter ignored the inquiries. She was sure her pain and weariness were the result of what had happened in Navone, of taking a full dose of frost. But she couldn't explain that to anyone else, least of all the priestess.

"So this is Roden," Lian said, looking around. The land was strikingly different than on the other side of the mountains. Navone was mostly surrounded by bare, snow-covered tundra, and he and Winter had grown up on the windswept winter plains around Cineste.

But Roden... Winter marveled at how green it was. Mostly the dark green of pine forests, but the snow had begun to melt in a few patches, revealing emerald, grassy hills. In Khale, everything was white. To the east she saw the blue-gray tint of the Gulf of Nahl, and from their vantage point in the foothills she could make out a river in the distance, and a few towns here and there. It was all surprisingly beautiful.

"This is Roden," Knot replied.

"I don't know why, but this isn't what I expected Roden to look like," Astrid said in a whisper. The girl's cloak hid her face.

"You've never been here before?" Winter asked.

"Nope." Astrid turned, and Winter felt the thing's weird eyes on her. "Just because I've been around for a while doesn't mean I've been everywhere under the sun."

Winter laughed nervously, hoping she'd imagined the sharpness in the vampire's voice. Astrid made Winter nervous. She felt like the thing could see into her soul, as if she knew her secrets. *You can trust her or not. It will either turn out okay in the end, or you'll wake up one night to find her teeth buried in your neck.*

All the same, Winter wasn't convinced there was much of a difference between trusting the vampire or the priestess, or Jane, or the Goddessguard, for that matter.

Winter looked at Knot, wondering what secrets he hid. She certainly hid her fair share from him. *Perhaps, in the end, trusting a daemon isn't all that different from trusting him.*

Winter and the vampire had one thing in common, at least: they both hated Canta. Winter glanced at the priestess, walking with her head held high. So *obviously* noble. Cinzia had been nothing but kind to Winter since Navone, constantly checking up on her, offering her skills as a physician, but somehow that made things worse. She was a noble human—she must hate tiellans, deep down—*and* she was a priestess. Not to mention the fact that she was stunning. The woman's wide, green eyes were far more sultry than any priestess's eyes had a right to be, and her reddish-brown hair fell thick and wavy around her shoulders. When the woman smiled, her entire stupid face seemed to light up. Jane was pretty, with long blond hair and deep blue eyes. Winter thought herself pretty, from time to time. But Cinzia was beautiful.

A noble, a priestess, *and* beautiful. Three things that Winter despised, rolled into one. Winter might have to befriend Astrid on those grounds alone.

"Makes you wonder why they're always trying to invade Khale when they have this kind of beauty surrounding them," Jane said.

"They ain't always the ones trying to invade," Knot said quietly.

"Roden is always the one to attack Khale," Cinzia said. "They think we are inferior, that we stole the seat of their empire. They hate us."

"Roden's hardly an empire anymore," Knot said. "Other than the Island Coalition and Andrinar, Roden ain't got many territories left to rule—and Andrinar's all but independent already. Calling Roden an empire is wishful thinking at best. And I wouldn't believe all you hear in histories, Priestess. Or in the Cantic seminary for that matter. Roden ain't always the one to strike first." He turned and continued down the path through the foothills. "Let's go," he barked. "Lot of ground to cover if we want to sleep in an inn tonight."

The others followed him. Cinzia, Jane, and Kovac stuck together. The three kept to themselves, for the most part. Winter wondered if she would ever get used to having them around.

The truth was, she couldn't imagine this group ever getting along. Humans and tiellans, vampire and priestess. A husband and wife that barely said one word to each other. Even Cinzia and Jane seemed to harbor some kind of resentment for one another.

Which made Winter feel a bit better about hiding her own secrets. Only Lian knew what she really was, and he avoided her at every opportunity. His concern wasn't lost on her, though. Winter had wondered, once or twice during the night, whether she wasn't relying on *faltira* too much. She didn't want to end up like those people on the street in Cineste or Navone.

But she couldn't go back to who she had been.

Almost of its own accord, her hand reached down to the pouch that held the frost. Four crystals left. She would use one tonight, she was sure of it. Not using one right now was taking every ounce of self-discipline she could muster. She was tempted to slip one in her mouth anyway, despite the lack of any real need.

As she felt the small crystals through the cloth, the feeling of unease all but vanished. She looked at Knot. She couldn't tell him, not yet; he might try to take them away from her.

She would tell him, eventually.

But it didn't have to be tonight.

Rock walls, high and thick, surrounded the city of Tir, and as they approached they realized they would have to enter through a large, well-protected gate.

Winter had said she didn't care about wandering into Roden. But now, as she approached the gates, the thin hood she drew up around her face and ears did not seem enough protection.

What in Oblivion had she been thinking?

She had shed her shabby tiellan dress, at least, which had been easier than she had expected. She now wore the outfit Kali had bought for her: padded dark leather trousers that hugged her legs, and a dark leather jerkin and shirt. Winter did not mind the clothing itself, but she had shed her *siara* as well, and that more than anything made her feel naked. The wind bit at her neck, and Winter resisted the urge to touch the bare skin. But they were in Roden, and no one could know that she and

Lian were tiellan—he wasn't wearing his *araif*, either, and they both kept their hoods drawn.

As they drew closer to the main gate, Winter realized it was actually a massive bridge that spanned the length of a wide moat. Two heavy chains ran from the far corners of the bridge to the top of the gate. The water was filthy—the stench of it assaulted her nose even from this distance.

"What kind of bridge is that?" Jane asked. The woman carried an abnormally large pack, far larger than anyone else's. *Typical noble,* Winter thought. *Probably didn't want to leave home without her entire wardrobe.* Winter was surprised Jane hadn't tried to make her or Lian carry it, or the Goddessguard for that matter. Winter had caught Jane staring at her more than once, although for what reason, Winter could not fathom. The woman was certainly odd.

"Drawbridge," Knot said. "Moves on a pivot. It can be drawn up to the entrance, blocking the gate and eliminating the bridge."

Winter looked at the contraption with interest. She had never seen anything like it in Khale.

"Why don't we have those?" Lian asked.

"We do," Knot responded. "But not in most cities. They're specific to castles and fortresses, and a few places in the south. Triah used to have one, but the city grew so large the bridge became obsolete."

"Do they actually work?" Lian asked.

Astrid snorted. Winter looked at the vampire, who rolled her eyes.

"They do their job," Knot said. "But most would say they are too expensive and elaborate to place at every entrance to the city."

"There's one of these things at every entrance?" Winter asked.

"Here, there is. They divert water from the river, sending it into the moat and around the city."

"What do we do when we get to the entrance? Will they just let us in?"

"Hopefully."

Winter raised her eyebrows. "Hopefully?"

Knot glanced at Cinzia. "Having a priestess and her Goddessguard along should ease our entry. But you and Lian need to keep your hoods up. Astrid too, for that matter."

"Is it just me or is he already trying to divide our party into social classes?" Astrid muttered. Winter shook her head; she had yet to catch on to the vampire's humor, though Knot seemed to have done so easily enough.

Hopefully Knot was right and Cinzia and Kovac would be enough. Even so, Winter couldn't help but feel nervous the closer they got to the gatehouse. Roden had slaughtered most of its tiellans decades ago, and sent the remainder on a death march through the Sorensan Pass in the middle of winter. If they hated tiellans that much, what would they do to Winter and Lian if they were discovered?

Winter reached into the pouch, fingering one of the crystals. *I should save it*, she thought. *At least until I know we're actually in danger.*

And if the danger came without warning? If she already had an arrow in her chest before she could reach into the pouch? Though she tried to deny it, she felt the pull of the frost, grasping her soul, her guts, pulling her towards it. Winter took a crystal out and swallowed it.

In moments, power filled her. Pain left and insecurities fled, although the high didn't seem to be as powerful as it once was. The freedom, the sense of wholeness that had filled her when she first took frost, or even the night she bought the crystals from Mazille, eluded her. The connection she felt with the Sfaera around her was still there, but weaker. And the time that passed in between taking *faltira* didn't seem to be getting any better, either. She felt worse. She had hoped at first that *faltira* would help her connect with her companions, but if anything Winter felt more distant from them.

She had taken a frost crystal the night before in the Sorensan Mountains. She had been trying to sleep, but memories of Pranna and Navone plagued her, so she did the only thing she knew would take those memories away. But the pain had only been dulled; Winter had not felt as free and clear as she once had.

She wondered whether the *faltira* she had purchased was flawed in some way. Perhaps she could find purer frost in Tir, that could bring back the freedom, the wholeness she sought.

Winter looked ahead as they approached the drawbridge, and saw two guards in heavy armor over light-blue tunics, both holding long, scythe-like spears.

"State your business, Priestess," one of the guards said to Cinzia. The man had a giant, ugly mole on one cheek. Winter tried not to stare. He was tall, and Cinzia had to look up to glare at him. "I am on Canta's business, and beyond your questioning. Or perhaps you'd like to explain to the local matron why you've delayed us from meeting with her on time?"

The guard immediately looked down. The shadow of his helm hid his mole, for which Winter was grateful. She couldn't stand to look at the thing any longer. "No, Priestess," the guard said. "Please, enter. May Canta bless your path."

"And yours," Cinzia said, "should the Goddess so choose."

Cinzia walked past the guards and onto the drawbridge. Winter and the others followed. *Perhaps this priestess will be more valuable than I thought.*

Another set of guards stood at the gate, but they only stared straight ahead as they walked past into the city. Winter stopped for a moment to catch her breath, her body vibrating with adrenaline and *faltira*.

"If I'd known you could be useful, I would have suggested you accompany us in the first place. Your goddess wouldn't have even had to intervene," Astrid said to Cinzia.

Cinzia raised an eyebrow. "Your mistake."

Astrid glanced at Knot. "I like her," she said with a grin. "By the way, did anyone notice the mole that took up half that guard's cheek? Disgusting. I'm just glad none of you have a mole that size. Wouldn't be able to travel with you if you did."

Winter almost smiled. Perhaps this vampire wasn't so bad, after all.

Still feeling the frost burn through her—she now regretted taking it so hastily—Winter turned her attention to the city. While the outside had looked strange, the inside was truly something foreign. The buildings were predominantly painted in bright blues and whites, but also greens, violets, and yellows. The fact that almost *every* building was painted made her jaw drop. In Khale that much paint would cost a fortune. Every so often she glimpsed a larger building, rising three or four stories above the rest. These taller structures appeared to be a series of tiered squares, one rising above the other, ornately decorated roofs or balconies wrapping around the buildings at each new level.

"We're definitely not in Khale anymore," Astrid whispered. Winter nodded in amazement. She had always thought Roden would be drab and violent.

"Sure ain't," Knot muttered. "I don't want to be caught out in the streets. Finding an inn is our first priority. Best stick together."

In the distance, Winter caught a glimpse of the familiar peaked rooftop of a Cantic chapel, a stark contrast to the other buildings in the city. Winter felt drawn to the building, despite the animosity she felt towards it.

*There's nothing for you there,* she told herself.

"We should keep away from the chapel," Cinzia said quietly. "Their questions would not be… constructive."

They turned down the next street. Winter took one last look at the chapel, then followed. Partway down the street Knot stopped, suddenly. He was looking at an open unmarked door.

"I know this place," he murmured. Then, before Winter or anyone else could say anything, he walked inside.

Winter followed him into a hallway with four doors leading off it, three closed and one open at the far end, through which Knot passed. Winter followed and saw a small common room of sorts. Odd that there had been no sign outside to indicate there was an inn here. Knot approached the innkeeper. He was old and withered, his skin in folds and his long mustache gray, but his eyes were alert.

Winter motioned for the rest of the group to stay in the hallway as she walked slowly towards Knot.

"By the Goddess, Madzin, it has been far too long," the old man was saying. He looked up at Knot with a frown, although Winter had a sense that this frown was the man's way of smiling. Her father had been that way.

"Ain't that the truth," Knot said. "Got rooms to spare tonight? My friends and I arrived later than we'd hoped, and we're looking for a place to rest our heads."

The old man raised his gray, bushy eyebrows. "I'd be offended if you stayed anywhere else." Watching the man, Winter had the impression he wasn't joking. The man glanced at Winter.

Knot followed the man's gaze. "She's with me," he said.

The old man nodded, eying Winter suspiciously. "Not the company I'd expect you to keep, but I guess you never know. How 'with you' is she?" he asked.

"She knows everything," Knot said. Winter couldn't help but see the irony in the statement.

"Very well, then. How many others are with you?"

"Need three rooms. Your prices changed?"

The man looked at Knot strangely. Winter immediately felt uneasy.

"For you, Madzin, they're free. Just as they've always been," the man said, though his voice had taken a different tone. The man leaned toward Knot, and Winter tensed. The frost was fading from her system, but she still had a dagger at her waist, should it come to that. *And*, she thought, *I could always take another crystal.* A part of her almost hoped for trouble, just so she could have the excuse.

"And your safebox is secure. I've seen to it myself."

"Can't be too sure of anything these days, can you?" Knot chuckled, and Winter was surprised at the naturalness of it. She was almost sure that Knot didn't know—or perhaps even recognize—the man, but he was playing along well enough. The man joined in with Knot's laughter, and Winter relaxed.

The old innkeeper handed Knot something and Knot motioned for Winter to follow him back into the hallway where the others were waiting. He opened one of the closed doors and led them into a small room.

"Who was that man?" Winter asked.

"Don't know," Knot said. "He recognized me, called me by a name I've heard before. Same name the Borderguard in Navone used. Face wasn't familiar, though."

"How many names is that?" Lian asked. "Three, now?"

"Yes," Knot said, his tone even. "Knot, Lathe, and Madzin."

"So which one *are* you?" Cinzia asked.

Knot shrugged. "I've got something I need to take care of. Cinzia, Jane, and Kovac, the room next door has two beds—you can take that one.

"Winter and Astrid, you'll be in this one. Lian and I will take the third."

Winter rolled her eyes. It would have been too much to expect her husband to share a room with her.

"I'll be gone for a while," Knot continued, "so everyone get comfortable." His gaze rested on Winter. "I'd like to speak with you when I return, Winter. If that's all right."

Winter shrugged and said nothing, although a faint nervousness crept through her gut. She wasn't ready to tell him, yet. She couldn't.

"Wait," Lian said, as Knot headed for the door. "How do we know this place is safe?"

"We don't," Knot said. "So stay on guard."

Then he was gone.

The others slowly dispersed. Astrid claimed she wanted to explore the city. Jane's gaze lingered on Winter as she left, a gesture Winter promptly ignored.

*Don't know why I'm getting so much attention,* she thought to herself. *I'm by far the least interesting person around.*

Then she was alone with Lian.

She looked at him uneasily. It was the first time they had been alone since Cineste. The room was small; from where

Winter sat on the bed, she could almost reach out and touch him as he leaned against the opposite wall. Winter realized that her hand was already in the small leather pouch at her belt, fingering another crystal.

She drew her hand out quickly; she hadn't even noticed it snake its way down there.

"Why haven't you told him?" Lian asked.

Winter had dreaded this conversation, from the moment she chose not to tell Knot about *faltira*.

"Why haven't *you*?" Winter probably would have told someone already, if their positions were reversed.

"Ain't my place. You know that. He's your husband, he needs to hear it from you."

Winter looked down at her lap. "Why does he need to hear it? I can do a few things now that I couldn't do before; I don't see why I need to make a scene of it."

"It's more than that," Lian said. "You've changed. I told you this frost stuff could mess you up. You didn't listen to me, and that was your choice. But… Canta rising, Winter, think of *Navone*. You can't ignore what happened there."

Winter felt her face flush. "Don't pretend you understand what happened in Navone. What happened there wasn't my *fault*, Lian. It wasn't me."

*You don't need to be angry at him*, she told herself. *He's only trying to help you*. But she couldn't contain the anger. She couldn't stop it.

"You don't know what it's like," Winter said.

"I don't need to understand it to see that you need help," Lian said. He sat next to her on the bed. Winter felt uncomfortable, his arm against her own, his thigh touching hers.

"Why don't you just leave," Winter muttered. "Go start

your stupid revolution. Save the tiellans."

Lian snorted. "That can wait."

"Return the tiellans to their former glory, or whatever. Make us what we were during the Age of Marvels. Do something that's worth your time, Lian."

"I know what's worth my time and what ain't."

"I'm not," Winter whispered.

Lian sighed. "I just feel like you're… like you're drowning, again. But there's no way for me to jump in after you, this time."

"I don't need you to save me."

Lian threw up his hands. "Someone has to! That's all you seem to need from anybody. I saved you from drowning. Your father tried to save you from the life in Pranna. Knot was going to save you from the same thing. And now, someone needs to save you again."

"I don't need *saving*." Winter tried to remain calm. Losing her temper would do no good.

Then Lian grabbed her shoulders. Winter was surprised at how roughly he did it; he squeezed her so tightly her arms hurt, forcing her to look at him.

"You killed people, Winter," he said, looking right into her eyes. "I watched you do it. I saw you take the frost. I know it wasn't Nash; I helped him protect you. What you did… that ain't something you just *come back from*. D'you realize that? D'you even realize what you did?"

His grip on her was tightening, his fingers digging into her skin. Winter wrenched herself away and slapped him, hard. She stood. She had to get away from him. How dare he bring up what happened in Navone?

"You're envious," she said. *That's not true*. She didn't even know why she was saying it. "You're envious because frost affects me and not you." He wasn't. He loathed *faltira*, and he loathed her. She could see it in his eyes.

Lian just looked up at her sadly. The fight, whatever had made him shake her, seemed to have drained from him.

"You hear yourself?" he asked. "D'you even hear what you're saying?"

Winter knew exactly what she was saying; it horrified her.

Lian shook his head. "I used to love you. You used to amaze me. The way you made those flower crowns when we were children, or the way you could steer your father's boat when you were a little girl, so confident. The way you brushed your hair behind your ears drove me crazy. I used to look at you and marvel. But I don't know you anymore. You even dress differently."

"We *have* to dress differently, Lian. We're in Roden, for Canta's sake."

Lian shrugged. "There's more to it than that. There is for you, anyway. You're a stranger now."

"I've always been a stranger to you," Winter whispered. "But I never had the strength to say so." With the exception of her father, she had been a stranger to everyone, no matter how hard she tried.

Either Lian didn't hear what she'd said, or he didn't care. "What's worse," Lian said, "I see that look in your eyes. The look I once had, I see in you. It just ain't for me."

"I don't love him," Winter said. Knot was her husband, but that didn't mean she loved him. She had known, ever since they were first engaged, that she didn't love this man. She admired him, she was intrigued by him. But love?

"If that's what you tell yourself, then I'm sorry for you," Lian said.

Winter remained quiet. What could she say?

They remained there, in silence, for a moment.

"Knot might be a psimancer," Lian said.

Winter looked up sharply.

"On the boat, that night when we first found him... your father made us promise not to say anything. But something happened. Objects moved of their own accord. I thought it was a daemon, but... Bahc explained things differently. I wanted to tell you earlier, but you wouldn't let me. Now you know."

Winter wasn't sure what to think. Knot was a *psimancer*? A telenic, by the sound of it, if things had been moving of their own accord. Did *Knot* know? Was that one of the things he was keeping from her?

Lian stood. "If you don't tell him soon, I will. You're endangering everyone. Someone has to take responsibility for that, even if you won't." He walked towards the door, then stopped. "I hope you tell him yourself."

Lian left her alone. Winter wanted to cry, to feel tears stream down her face. Or she wanted the anger. She wanted anything but this.

Silently, she reached into the pouch and pulled out a crystal, pressing it to her lips. She swallowed it, and in minutes she and all her pain were swallowed up, and Winter just sat there, floating on the verges of sensation.

# 33

"WHAT DO YOU MEAN you can't read Old Khalic?" Jane asked incredulously. They were in the small room Knot had assigned them in the inn. Kovac stood guard at the door. Cinzia told him he needn't be so formal, but he had insisted. She sat on one of the beds, staring up at Jane, who paced in front of her.

"I mean I *cannot read it*. Why does it even matter, Jane?"

Jane stared at her, frowning. "I just do not know how I am expected to *translate* if I do not have someone who speaks Old Khalic. I thought you did, that's why Canta told me that you were the one who needed to help translate it in the first place."

"Translate? What are we supposed to be translating?"

"We are going to translate the Nine Scriptures."

Cinzia blinked. In all the chaos of the Holy Crucible and the massacre in Navone, helping her family escape and deciding to go to Roden, Cinzia had completely forgotten.

Jane claimed to have found the Nine Scriptures.

"You... you brought it here?" Cinzia asked.

"Of course I did. I was not about to leave it in Navone."

Cinzia's curiosity was piqued. Jane could not have the real Nine Scriptures; such a thing was impossible. But whatever Jane *had* found...

Cinzia sighed. "Why would you think I could read Old Khalic?" she asked. "It's not even an *option* at the seminary."

343

Jane frowned at her. "There is no way for me to know that, is there? Why do they *not* teach Old Khalic at the seminary? The language is the heart of Canticism. Canta Herself spoke it. How can people hope to understand anything without at least attempting to learn it?" Jane mumbled something further under her breath.

"What was that?" Cinzia asked.

"The fact that they do *not* teach it seems more evidence that the Denomination itself is failing."

Kovac shifted by the door. The conversation would be making him severely uncomfortable. Cinzia's face flushed. The Denomination had its flaws, she was the first to admit it. Given what had happened in Navone, Cinzia was not sure she could ever go back to it. But the fact that her sister was so *blatantly* against it made her furious.

"Sorry," Jane said, her voice softer. "That was unkind. I should not criticize something you have spent so much of your life working for."

Cinzia rolled her eyes, but she appreciated the apology.

"I'm just having a hard time finding direction," Jane said. "I've felt less connected since leaving Navone. I have not heard anything from Canta since I turned myself in to the Crucible. I know I—we—are supposed to translate the scriptures, but if you cannot read Old Khalic, I've no idea how to do it."

Despite Cinzia's confusion, she felt for Jane. Cinzia had been through it herself, in a way.

"I am sorry, too," Cinzia said. "Things have been difficult for all of us."

Jane sighed, and stopped pacing. Finally. It was driving Cinzia mad.

"You are right," Jane said. "I am being selfish. All I can

think about is what this means for me, how I can overcome my problems, when you have problems of your own."

Not exactly what Cinzia had meant, but she couldn't disagree; Jane *had* been selfish.

"I cannot imagine what it would be like to have lived your whole life as a priestess, only to come home to a family who seems to have abandoned everything you stood for. I am so sorry, Cinzia."

"It is all right," Cinzia found herself saying. Right now, Cinzia wanted to be at peace.

"Thank you for putting yourself in my shoes. I shall try to do the same." *Although how I will ever be able to see the world through your eyes, I do not know.*

Jane nodded. "All right," she said. "Well, what do we do now, Cinzi?"

Cinzia sighed, leaning back on the bed and staring at the ceiling. "I do not know." She certainly could not read Old Khalic. But she would not mind seeing the scriptures. If only to decide for herself whether they were what Jane said. "Where are they? Can I see them?"

Jane glanced at Kovac. "I was expressly forbidden to show them to anyone except those who were to help translate."

Cinzia frowned. She did not think it was a good idea to send Kovac away, but… "Kovac, we need to eat at some point, anyway. Would you mind going down to the common room and ordering us dinner?"

Kovac frowned. "Mistress, I do not think——"

Cinzia walked over to her Goddessguard and placed her hand on his arm. "We will be safe on our own for a few moments."

Kovac nodded, glancing at Jane. Then he left the room, closing the door behind him.

Cinzia turned to her sister. "Now can I see them?"

Jane sighed. "You are the only one who has been shown to me as a translator. I suppose it cannot hurt."

Jane walked to her pack and reached inside, pulling out odds and ends. Clothing, a coat, an extra pair of traveling boots. Then she pulled out a large cloth bundle and set it on the bed, which creaked under the weight.

Jane smoothed her skirts fussily, and Cinzia was of half a mind to tear open the bundle immediately. Could Jane not sense her anticipation?

"You will have to help me," Jane said. "Hold it up while I unwrap."

Cinzia did as she was told, and almost fell over as she tried to lift the thing.

Jane laughed. "Heavier than one would think, is it not?"

Cinzia nodded. The bundle felt as if it were made of lead. She repositioned herself and lifted again, this time ready for the weight. Jane reached underneath and unwrapped the thick cloth.

"Okay, set them down," Jane said. Cinzia did so with relief, her arms already burning. How had Jane carried these all the way from Navone? No wonder her pack was so outrageously huge, and she refused to let anyone else shoulder it. She had not wanted to risk anyone else coming in contact with the Nine Scriptures.

Cinzia found herself looking directly at the Nine Scriptures. *Or what Jane* claims *to be the Nine Scriptures,* Cinzia corrected herself.

They did not look very *old*. Cinzia had expected them to be tattered, soiled, and generally... well, very old-looking. The book before her did not look that way at all. It was very large, more than half a rod in height and nearly as wide, and more than two spans thick. The cover was of worn, creased leather.

Cinzia reached towards the book. She glanced at Jane, who nodded. Cinzia touched the cover, felt the softness of the thick leather; it seemed to overlay a hard metal of some kind.

Cinzia lifted the cover, and gasped. She looked at her sister.

Jane smiled. "Not what I thought, either. But it makes sense. Paper would fade, rot, tear. This—whatever this is—has done nothing of the sort."

Cinzia ran her fingers over the pages, if they could be called pages. They were not made of paper, or vellum, or any material Cinzia had ever seen, but rather an extremely thin—although durable, as Cinzia ran her fingers along their edges—metal. The metal had a matte finish, hardly reflecting anything in its dark-gray surface. On occasion the pages *did* reflect, or perhaps shone with a reddish tint that rippled across the metal. Hundreds of tiny characters were etched into the first page. Cinzia's fingers brushed against the imprints, feeling their contours. It *felt* like metal, smooth and cool. The sheets were not bound, she saw, but connected by three large rings embedded in the thick covering, each ring running through the inside edge of each page.

"They were very well crafted, as you can see."

"Yes," Cinzia whispered, her voice hoarse. As one who had grown up with a woodworker for a father, she knew good craftsmanship when she saw it. This was exquisite.

"They are made of metal," Cinzia said, catching another scarlet ripple across the front page.

"I think so," Jane replied. "That's one of the reasons it is so heavy I assume. Although I have a feeling that if the pages were made of any metal *we* know of, it would be much heavier still."

"Their reflection is red." Cinzia knew how simple she sounded, but she could not help it. She still could not accept that these were the Nine Scriptures, but she had to admit, the book certainly *looked* the part.

"They do. Not always, and only at certain angles. I have not quite understood in what conditions the red tint occurs."

Cinzia stared at the first page, taking it all in. She looked closely at the characters, reading the title out loud.

"'The Codex of Elwene,'" Cinzia read. "'A compendium of Canta's Life and Her Great Miracles, and Her Prophecies, and Her Teachings. Copied from the Scriptures of the Nine Disciples that Canta chose during Her time on the Sfaera, and abridged by the hand of Elwene.'

"Title is a bit long," Cinzia murmured. "It does sound interesting, though. The Codex of Elwene. I thought you said these were the Nine Scriptures? Although I suppose it mentions them. This Elwene person put them together, apparently? Seems a bit arrogant to name a book after oneself."

Cinzia realized she was rambling, and when Jane did not respond, she looked up. Jane was staring at her, mouth slack, eyes wide.

"What?" Cinzia asked. Then she understood.

She had just read the title page.

Cinzia looked down. Sure enough, she could read every word. This first page contained the title, and below that a description of the purpose of the book and what it would mean for the people of the Sfaera.

"You told me it was written in Old Khalic," Cinzia said.

"It *is* written in Old Khalic. Which you expressly told me you *could not* read."

"This is not Old Khalic, Jane. This is Rodenese. You could read it just as well as I."

Jane's eyebrows shot up. "*Rodenese?* Cinzia, this," she said, pointing at the characters on the page, "is *not* Rodenese. There is not a single Rodenese character in this entire book. I have checked, time and again."

Cinzia looked down at the page, about to point out the contrary, when she realized something odd. She did not see any Rodenese characters on the page. She could read it, just as well as she could read anything, but no single mark made sense to her; it just looked like a strange mess of scratches and circles. When she looked at the page as a whole, at entire words and sentences, she could read it easily.

"I do not believe it," she said. She heard a thump beside her, and looked at Jane slumped into one of the chairs by the desk, her hands at her temples.

"This is why She wanted you to help translate. This is why She wanted *you*."

"What are you talking about?"

Jane looked up at her. Cinzia was surprised to see tears on her sister's cheeks. Was not this what Jane wanted?

"Don't you see?" Jane asked. "You are a seer, Cinzia. Not a seer as you know, in the Denomination today, but a *true* seer. You can translate this, with Canta's power."

Cinzia put a hand on Jane's shoulder. "This is a good thing, is it not? We can translate this together. Bring the Nine Scriptures— the Codex of Elwene—to the people, bring them the truth about Canta and Her works." Cinzia could hardly believe what she was saying. Cinzia was already struggling with her faith in Canta, and had no faith at all in what her sister was teaching.

But this book, these scriptures, and the fact that she could, somehow, read these characters... *that* was tangible. That was something Cinzia *could* believe.

"You are right, of course," Jane said softly. "This is probably for the best. I need to be humble and accept Canta's will."

Cinzia was about to ask what Jane meant by that when she stood, a new smile on her face.

"Let's get started, then," she said. "We have a lot of work to do."

Reluctantly, but with the first feelings of excitement and anticipation in her chest, Cinzia obliged.

# 34

KNOT KNOCKED QUIETLY ON the door, rubbing his temples. Another headache had just begun, and it worried him. Since they'd left Navone, he'd had several. They came at different times, for a half-hour or so, then faded. Knot did the only thing he knew to do about them. He ignored them.

There was no answer. He knocked again, louder.

"Come in." Knot heard muffled movement beyond the door.

He slung the leather pack he'd just obtained over his shoulder and opened the door. Winter jumped as he entered.

"Canta rising," she gasped, "you didn't have to bloody scare me like that."

"You said 'come in'—what'd you expect, darlin'?"

She just shook her head, so Knot turned to close the door behind him. When he turned back, he felt a wave of emotions. Her long hair was frizzed and sticking to her face, and he could make out the tracks of tears down her cheeks. Her clothing, mostly form-fitting leather—very different from the traditional tiellan garb she'd worn in Pranna—clung to her at odd angles.

Knot felt a powerful stab of regret at all that had happened to her. He hadn't wanted her to get hurt, but he'd hurt her anyway. He should never have left her. Least he could do was tell her the truth.

"You all right?" he asked, heaving the pack off his shoulder and setting it down on the bed. He looked at her, not sure what to do.

"I'm fine." Winter sniffed, wiping her nose. "You wanted to talk?"

Knot felt awkward. He didn't know whether to embrace her, try to act natural, or something else altogether.

She stood at an angle from him, near the side of the bed furthest from the door. Her arms were wrapped around her stomach, and she looked at him through stray strands of long black hair.

"Well?"

Knot frowned, rubbing his head. The ache was fading, but it was still there. He could tell she wasn't in the greatest of moods. Best to get to the point.

"Right," he said. "You heard what I said to the innkeeper?"

"Most of it," she said.

She wasn't going to make this easy for him, that was certain.

"Yes… he mentioned a safebox to me. Do you know what a safebox is?"

Winter rolled her eyes. "What about your safebox?"

"I told him I'd lost my key, and he said that wasn't a problem. Since he knew me, he could give me the spare."

Knot waited for a reaction. Winter stared at him but didn't say anything, her arms crossed. He wished they would sit down.

"I took the key, and opened the safebox." He nodded to the leather pack. "That was inside. Thought I'd show it to you first." He hesitated. "Wanted to tell you… about myself. Tonight. Figured this might help." He wasn't sure what else to say.

He thought he saw her eyebrows rise slightly. It was encouragement enough. He reached down to empty the pack onto the bed.

Winter joined him, looking down at the assortment of items that tumbled out.

The most eye-catching of them was a sword. The blade was roughly the length of a simple longsword, about a rod long, but slightly curved. It looked very similar to the sword the strange woman had drawn on him in Navone, before the Sfaera globe had crushed her. It was lighter, thinner, more balanced than most longswords he'd used. The blade, encased in a sheath of white leather, was of a simple, dark metal. The handguard was thin and wrapped around the entire circumference of the blade. The white leather of the handle matched the sheath, and below that the pommel was a simple, intricately carved piece of metal—a daemonic face of some kind that Knot didn't recognize.

A pouch, containing enough coin for them to all travel to Triah and back without a problem, also fell onto the bed. A small crossbow the length of Knot's forearm, jet-black in color and accompanied by a dozen small black bolts. Half a dozen stones of varying colors, all roughly the size of Knot's thumb. A set of thin throwing knives, also jet-black. A necklace of a bright, silvery metal, the pendant a pearl-white stone. A stack of papers listing every possible official assignment Knot could think of—he could get in and out of Roden a dozen times and never be questioned. And, last of all, another leather pouch, this one full of small shards of some kind of crystal. The pouch contained a dozen of the strange objects. Knot emptied them onto the bed as well.

In the time it'd taken Knot to sort through the items, Winter had become much more animated. Her dark eyes glinted as she stared down at the bed. Her cheeks were no longer pale, but flushed and red.

"The weapons and the money are obvious," Knot said.

"The papers are orders, exemptions, and official declarations. Probably forgeries. But these other items," Knot separated the stones, crystals, and necklace, "could be for anything. The necklace is probably decorative, but why I would keep it in the safebox, I don't know. The stones could be just as meaningless. Might've been a rock collector, of all things, before I washed up in Pranna." Knot had meant the comment to be funny. Winter didn't laugh, and he didn't feel much like it, either.

"These crystals?" Winter said, one hand reaching slowly towards them. "Do you know what they're for?"

"No idea," Knot said.

Winter picked up one of the crystals, cradling it in her hand. She seemed mesmerized by it. Knot looked at her, his eyes narrowing. Her forehead was sleek with perspiration. Had she been sweating when he walked in? He wasn't sure. The weather in Roden was milder than in northern Khale, but Knot was still chilly in his furs and cloak; Winter wore only padded leather and a cloak. Her hands were trembling.

"Feeling all right?" he asked.

She looked up sharply, setting the small crystal carefully back on the bed. "Fine," she said. "Just been feeling a bit ill, lately."

Knot nodded. He wondered why he hadn't noticed it before. He suddenly felt guilty for forcing her to listen to him.

"If you'd rather we spoke about this later, when you're feeling better—"

"No," she said. "It's not that bad. Please," she looked at him, finally glancing away from the crystals, "tell me what all this means."

Knot sighed, looking back down at the assortment of objects. *That's the question, ain't it?* There was a lot he still didn't know. But it was time to tell Winter what he did.

"Can't remember anything about my past," he said. "You know that. You've known it since we first met."

Winter gave him a *get-to-the-point* look, and Knot didn't want to lose momentum. Not when he'd finally worked up the courage to tell her.

"That's not entirely true," he continued. "I've had dreams about places I never remember visiting, people I've never seen. They're real. Least, I think they are. They usually don't make much sense, may not even be accurate. But considering what I've seen, I can make some pretty good guesses about my life."

"From dreams?" she asked.

Knot nodded. "Dreams, but also… there're times, in the middle of the day, when I'm doing something mundane, and then I'm somewhere else entirely. In Pranna I'd be hammering a nail, and then my mind would go somewhere else, even if my body just kept hammering. Glimpses into my past. Things I've done."

"Why didn't you tell me?"

Knot looked away; his gaze settled on the sword. He'd gone back and forth between a number of ways to express it, but now, looking at the sword, he figured bluntness was best.

"I killed people," he said. "That's what I do in my dreams. I kill people."

Winter began to say something, but Knot spoke over her. He had to get this out.

"Not the way a soldier kills people. Not the way of a thug or executioner, either." He glanced back at her. She seemed to have cooled down, both physically and emotionally, but the black eyes staring back at him were blank, unrevealing.

"I was an assassin. I *think* I was, anyway. I killed people for money, but it's more than that. In my dreams, I'm *enjoying* it. The hunt, the chase, the secrecy, the kill. I thrived off it.

I killed soldiers, generals, nobles, whole families, rich, poor. I've killed them all, in my dreams. The Borderguard in Navone all but confirmed it, told me I'm an assassin, and some kind of government agent."

Knot had skirted the issue with Astrid once or twice, but this was the first time he'd said it out loud. The detachment in his voice surprised him. He felt as if he were stone underneath his skin, and nothing else. Neither cold nor warm, just hard and unyielding.

"If, as they claim, I worked for those people you traveled with," he said, "the Nazaniin, then they are powerful. The papers from the safebox—and what happened in Navone, of course—prove that, if nothing else. The Borderguard captain recognized me, the owner of this inn knows me… Whoever I was, whoever I worked for had a long reach.

"I still don't know why I was in the Gulf of Nahl, but it had to be because of something I was doing in Roden. A job, maybe, and something went wrong, something to make Rodenese fighters come after me." Knot took a deep breath. "And because they're after me, you're tangled up in it, too. I don't think the Rodenese who sent the men to our wedding or the Nazaniin will leave us alone, not until I figure this out. That's what I need to do here."

Winter hadn't moved—or reacted at all—since he'd begun speaking. She only looked at him, her large, dark eyes shining.

"That's it," he said, feeling incredibly anticlimactic. "I'm an assassin. Or, at least, I was."

They stood there for what seemed a very long time. When Winter spoke, her words were quiet and even. Knot would have much preferred shouting, crying, sarcasm, *anything*, really, to the quiet reason of her voice.

"That's what you've kept from me?" she asked. "That's the reason you left? That's the best you can do?"

Knot was unsure of what to say, or whether to say anything at all. He saw it clearly, now. He'd told himself he'd left her to protect her, and that'd been true, in a way. But, deep down, he knew there were other factors, too. Race. His past. He'd left because he was selfish.

"I shouldn't have," Knot whispered. He felt shame like a weight around his neck. He wanted to reach out to her and touch her, but knew he couldn't. Didn't deserve it. "I was scared and selfish," he said. "I didn't know what else to do."

"You think I *wasn't* scared? That I wasn't worried about what would happen to us? About who you were?"

Winter slapped him. Knot felt the sting of it on his cheek as she continued, her voice louder. "How dare you think that you were the only one, Knot! That you were the only one who had doubts. Who was afraid." She hit him again, her fists pounding against his chest. She pushed him back against the wall and hit him again and again.

Knot absorbed the blows easily. He reached out, wrapping his arms around her. He just wanted to make everything all right again. He tried to embrace her, but she fought him, punching and kicking. She stumbled back, but almost as quickly returned, burying her face in his chest. He stood quietly, his arms slowly rising around her, one around her back, one to her head, barely touching her hair. Winter was motionless in his embrace, trembling, but Knot couldn't hear her crying.

"I'm sorry," he whispered.

*I'm so sorry*.

She shifted in his arms. He looked down to see her looking up at him. They remained that way for a fraction of a second, and then he felt her body rise up to meet him. He didn't kiss her back, at first. He didn't want to let himself. But soon his lips moved with hers, and all questions fled. They didn't return until sometime later, among rumpled sheets and discarded clothing, objects from the safebox strewn across the floor as they'd been hastily swept from the bed.

# 35

*Navone*

NASH WATCHED KALI SLIDE down the rope on Navone's wall like a spider slipping down a strand of web. In the distance, moonlight illuminated the Blood Gate's outline against the large black mountains. Getting over the city wall had been easy enough, but he was still worried about the gate; the telenic power flowing through him wouldn't amount to much if things went badly there. Not even Winter could have made a difference if the guards got it in their minds to kill them. Nash shivered. He had never seen anything like the destruction Winter had wrought in Navone.

He looked down at Kali, almost at the end of the rope. Kali was invaluable in a battle, but she was also their best hope of preventing one. But Nash feared she wasn't focusing enough on prevention.

Nash was still unused to her new form. Their lacuna, Elsi, had barely seen twenty summers. But she was Elsi no longer; Kali now inhabited Elsi's body, as surely as Nash had always been—and always would be—stuck in his. Kali's ability to brand other lacunas with her sift had only recently been discovered, and was the subject of some debate. Only one other acumen was capable of such a feat; Kosarin had only done it once. Kali had transferred her sift at least four times, now. Nash didn't mind the changes in some ways, but he had grown used to Kali's maturity, her authority. Her most recent body, brown-haired and tall, had personified those qualities. Now, it was difficult to take her seriously.

It was difficult to trust her. Each previous time Kali branded her sift onto a new body, Nash had found her, the real Kali, easily. He couldn't explain how. It was a feeling, a sense he got that the person he interacted with was the same woman he had known for years. This time, that task was proving more difficult.

When Kali touched down, Nash slipped down the rope after her, half-sliding and half-climbing. Lowering himself with his *tendra* wasn't an option; he simply wasn't strong enough—few telenics were. But Nash didn't mind; sometimes he liked to do things the slow way. After he landed, he reached a *tendron* upwards to unhook the grapple and pull the rope down. He coiled the rope around his body as they moved quickly across the snow on the edge of the field. Soon they neared the gate, its two massive towers looming above them in the darkness like ancient giants.

Kali motioned for Nash to wait. He normally took point, but Kali had taken the lead before he could talk her out of it, and he had followed, knowing it was better to let her have her way.

The Blood Gate was closed and no Borderguards stood on the Navone side, but there would certainly be at least a pair on the other, facing Roden. Nash didn't see any guards patrolling the wall, but he knew they were there. He had studied city defenses and guard patrol routes extensively. Roden and Khale weren't at war at the moment, but that didn't mean suspicions weren't stoked like glowing coals, waiting to ignite. Likely the Borderguards' attention was on Roden. Even so, Nash eyed the walls and arrow slits warily. "Likely" had never been a word he bet on.

Kali motioned him to advance. Nash did so, broadening his focus to stay aware of any changes in their surroundings.

They made it to the base of the gate without incident. Nash looked at Kali, who nodded. Going over was their only option. He unraveled the grappling rope and swung the cloth-covered hook into the air and over the battlements, guiding the grapple with a *tendron*. He tugged on the rope, making sure it was secure, then began climbing full-speed up the wall.

He strained past the rush of breath and blood in his ears to hear any voices or movement of guards. Nash was about to reach over the battlements when he froze.

A whisper.

The rope trembled slightly, and Nash grabbed for the battlement with both hands. Just as the rope slipped down, Nash heaved himself up and over, onto the wall, rolling into a crouch.

Two Borderguards stood by the severed grapple, one holding a sword, the other a crossbow. Out of the corner of his eye Nash noticed another guard at the other end of the rampart, also raising a crossbow.

Nash drew two long, thin daggers from his belt. He threw one to his right and it slid into the throat of the guard further down the rampart. The man who had severed the rope went down next, a puncture blooming red as Nash withdrew the other dagger from his neck. He lashed out at the other man, dodging a sword swing. Nash danced around the guard, pulling the man's head back with one hand, and slitting his throat with the other.

Nash pulled his thrown dagger back to him with a *tendron*. He looked down at Kali. She held one end of the rope in her hands. Nash reached a *tendron* and pulled it up. He looked around, listening intently, hoping no one else had heard his scuffle with the guards. Nothing. He retied the rope to the grapple and secured it, glancing down at Kali to signal it was safe for her to climb. Nash crept to the other side of the rampart, looking furtively down at the other side of the gate, facing the Sorensan Pass.

Two Borderguards stood watch, holding long spears. They apparently hadn't heard the commotion on the wall. Nash breathed a quiet sigh. It was fortunate that the guard's scream had been cut off so quickly. He sent a quick prayer to Canta in thanks.

Behind him, Nash heard a quiet scraping sound and turned to see Kali climb over the battlements. Suddenly, her voice spoke in Nash's head.

*Permission?* It was her way of knocking. They agreed long ago that she would never intrude on his thoughts; she would ask, and if he accepted, she would proceed.

*Go ahead.* The method was simple: Kali projected words into Nash's head, and Nash only had to think his response. It made Nash monitor his thoughts, of course—an acumen as powerful as Kali could hear almost everything if she concentrated. But the communication was useful—especially for a pair of assassins.

*Guards?*

*Two, on the ground, unaware.*

Kali nodded. Then she smiled. *Lower me. I'll take them; you climb down after.*

Nash frowned. Kali could handle two guards, but he worried what she would do to them. A quick, honorable death was one thing. What Kali had a tendency to do was quite different. She didn't view it as such, of course. Taking a lacuna, wiping the mind of another human being, was all business to her.

*Nothing to worry about, darling. I'm all business, as you say.*

Nash frowned. He had not intended for her to hear that last thought.

*If you're that worried, you can go on your own.*

Nash shook his head. *It's all yours.*

Nash pulled the rope to him with a *tendron*, catching the grapple in his hand. Then he walked with Kali to the edge of the battlement. They were directly over the gate and between the two Borderguards. Kali drew a dagger in one hand, similar to the two Nash carried at his belt, and in her other her vex, a long, thin, needle-like weapon. She nodded at him, and with two *tendra* Nash gripped her leather jerkin by the straps—specially designed for the purpose—that ran from her waist to her shoulders. He lifted her slowly, up and over the battlements, and lowered her down past the gate. He watched her descend, again reminded of a spider on a strand of web. Nash blinked. The strain of so much telenic power was taking its toll. He needed to be careful, or he would start losing senses.

When Kali was barely above the guards' heads, Nash let go and watched her fall the rest of the way to the ground. Both men jumped in surprise. The Borderguard to Kali's right was lucky. She moved fast, faster than Nash ever could, and stabbed the man through the eye with her vex. Kali visibly relaxed as she turned to meet the other guard, hands lowering to her sides and shoulders drooping slightly. The guard, who had at first made a move towards Kali, now stood perfectly still.

They faced one another for a moment, and Nash turned away, fixing the grapple to the battlement. He didn't care to see this part. When he touched down, Kali was waiting for him.

*She keeps getting better at this,* Nash thought. He told himself, not for the first time, that he would have to speak with Kosarin when they returned to Triah. Kali was an amazing woman, an incredible psimancer, but lately had shown signs of… erratic behavior. The only person who could obliterate a person so quickly was Kosarin himself.

Perhaps Nash was just getting old. Kali's use of her acumency had never bothered him before. But, then again, she never used to make lacunas unless absolutely necessary. He wished he could go back five years, and be that man who was with that woman.

*You worry too much, Nash. I'm fine.*

*Is it done?* he asked, already knowing the answer.

*Done and done. Nash, meet Dahlin.*

Nash looked at the Borderguard, standing straight and stiff, staring at him blankly. Nash shivered. The blank look of a lacuna was one of the most disturbing things Nash knew of. It was the look of a dead man, with only brief hints of tortured life in its depths. To look at a lacuna was to look into Oblivion itself.

Nash hated that look.

Nash and Kali walked up the Sorensan Pass and the lacuna followed, his footsteps unsure, behind them.

# 36

*Tir*

"IN THE BEGINNING, THERE was the Praeclara, and all the souls who dwelled in it, which numbered three and three and three again."

Cinzia stared at the page for a moment before continuing, not quite believing that she was reading what she was reading. The fact that she could make sense of the strange markings seemed otherworldly. Most of the markings, anyway. While most of the characters formed into words she could read, there were still a few symbols that did not shift into anything Cinzia recognized. They seemed to serve a different purpose than the normal alphabetical characters, but what that purpose was, she did not know. Her sister seemed unconcerned. If there were a few oddities, what did it matter?

How could she see these words when no one else could? What did it say about Jane, about the Cantic Denomination, or her? There had been a time when Cinzia felt a constant, easy connection with the Goddess, but that connection was all but gone now, the memory far away. And yet, here she was, reading a language she did not speak. *Something* was behind that. And then there was the vision, or revelation, or whatever it had been. Jane never referred to it, and Cinzia preferred it that way until she could get a handle on her own feelings.

For now, translating was enough. Implications could be dealt with later.

Cinzia sat on the bed, her legs folded beneath her, the wide book propped up on them. Jane sat at the desk, a large quill pen in her hand and a stack of blank pages beneath her chair. Jane had brought everything in that ridiculous pack of hers.

Despite Cinzia's attempts to convince her otherwise, Jane had insisted that, at least for now, Kovac not see the Codex. Kovac, in turn, had insisted that he be present in order to protect them. They had compromised by taking one of the sheets from the bed and hanging it from the bedposts nearest the door, blocking Kovac's view of Cinzia. Kovac himself sat in a large, stuffed chair on the other side, near the door. Cinzia knew Kovac was not sleeping, though she had insisted he try. It was well past midnight now, and they all should have retired hours ago. But Cinzia's curiosity propelled her forward.

Cinzia wondered if Jane planned on translating the entire book. It must be hundreds of pages long, perhaps thousands. The strangely thin, metallic sheets made it difficult to tell, and there were no page numbers. They had already translated the title page, an introduction, and some kind of preface—all seemingly written by this Elwene woman, of whom neither Cinzia nor Jane had ever heard—but had barely made a dent in the massive tome.

"Are you going to continue, sister, or just keep staring at the page?" Jane asked.

Cinzia looked up. "Yes, sorry. I'll keep going." She looked down at the page, searching for where she left off. She would read a few phrases or a sentence or two, and then pause briefly, allowing Jane to catch up. It was a tedious process, but at least they were getting into the real meat of the document now. The book of Elessa was the name of the first section they were translating. Elessa, of course, was one of the original Nine

Disciples that Canta chose while she walked the Sfaera. Elessa, Ocrestia, and Cinzia—after whom Cinzia herself was named— were known as the First Three. That was all traditional doctrine within the Denomination. Elessa, however, seemed to speak of a different first three.

*"The first of the first three,"* Cinzia continued,

> was Andara, the God of Gods. She was in the beginning, and She was the Beginning; She was in the end, and She was the End. With her was Ellendre, High God of Life and Death and Before and After. He was with Andara in the beginning, and He was with Andara in the end. And with them also was Canta, the Daughter-God, with power beyond measure, and wisdom beyond measure, and love beyond measure. These three were the first three, in the beginning, and so it was.
>
> The second three were thus: the Brother-Gods Emidor, Irit being the first, Orit being the second, and Erit being the third. And thus the brother-gods served the First Three, in thought and in deed, in the beginning, and so it was.
>
> The final three were thus: the Sister-Gods Adimor, Irali being the first, Orali being the second, and Arali being the third. And thus the sister-gods served the First Three, in thought and in deed, in the beginning, and so it was.

"What is it, Cinzi?"

Cinzia had stopped reading, and now stared down at the page before her.

"I've seen *four* of those unchanging symbols in this section,"

Cinzia said quietly. "They have to be there for a reason."

Jane sighed. "I can make note of them if you like, but I do not think there is much we can do until we know what significance they carry, if they are significant at all. Perhaps later they are explained?"

"Perhaps," Cinzia said quietly, staring at the symbols. The first two came after the names of Canta's parents, respectively. The third came after the phrase "the Brother-Gods Emidor," and the fourth after "the Sister-Gods Adimor." That did not seem coincidental. "Can you at least make a mark of where the symbols are?" she asked, looking up at Jane. "If they *are* important, if we do discover their meaning later, it might be helpful to know where they occurred."

"That sounds simple enough."

Cinzia could tell Jane did not think the symbols were important, but better to be safe.

"Now what about the passage you just read?" Jane asked.

Cinzia rubbed her chin absently. "We are taught this in seminary," she said. "The names are slightly different, changed over time, perhaps, and I've never heard of those names referred to in threes... but otherwise the story is the same. Why are we translating something that is already known, Jane?"

Jane looked up from her writing. "We are bound to come across things we already know. Canta's true religion is not *completely* different from the Cantic Denomination. I trust we will come to understand more as we translate more."

Cinzia frowned. She still chafed at the thought of the Cantic Denomination being wrong at all. But, then again, how could a religion led by the Goddess that Cinzia knew—a goddess of immeasurable wisdom and love—be responsible for what the Holy Crucible had caused in Navone? Cinzia still did not know what power had caused that chaos. But she suspected it had something to do with Nayome. There was no other explanation.

And, if that was the case, perhaps Jane's claims were not so outrageous.

*Do you realize what you are implying?* Cinzia asked herself. She did not pursue the question further. It scared her far too much.

"Cinzia, are you listening to me?" Jane stretched. "Goddess rising," she said, through a yawn, "one would think you would concentrate on such an important task a bit more."

Cinzia pursed her lips. "I have much on my mind, sister."

"Of course. Sorry. But as I was saying, even the name differences between the Codex and what you were taught can be significant. The distance traveled by a door at its hinge is short, but the distance at its very edge is far greater. So it could be with these differences. Ripples create waves. Small things, in the end, can go a long way."

Cinzia raised her eyebrows. Then she laughed. Jane frowned, but Cinzia could not help it.

"Listen to you," Cinzia said, getting control of herself but still smiling. "You sound just like one of the old matrons. Or worse, like Priestess Joyca, when we were little girls!"

Jane's frown deepened, but Cinzia knew it covered a smile.

"You should have listened to your matrons more closely," Jane said. "And Joyca was a good woman. Not the most engaging, perhaps, but she meant well."

"Not *engaging*? She could put the entire city to sleep with her sermons. We used to say that only someone with her goodness could wield such power. Anyone else would have used it for evil!"

Now Jane didn't even try to hide her smile. From behind

the makeshift curtain, Cinzia heard Kovac's voice. "I wish someone would use it on you two right now. It's bloody late, if you'll forgive my saying."

Cinzia and Jane stared at each other for a moment, wide-eyed. Then they burst into laughter.

Two hours later, Cinzia rubbed her eyes, tired from reading. They had continued translating through the night despite Kovac's comment, and managed to get through almost fifty pages. They were nearing the end of the book of Elessa, although it had said nothing about the Disciple Elessa in it yet, and remained very similar to what Cinzia knew from the seminary.

Andara and Ellendre created the Sfaera for all the souls to live on, with Canta's assistance. Then came Erit and Arali's Betrayal and the Ruin, and the Imprisonment of Gods and the Day of Daemons.

Questions resurfaced in Cinzia's mind as they translated—things she had always wondered about during her time in the seminary, but to which she had never found answers. Why did Ellendre and Andara not see the Betrayal beforehand? They were all-powerful and omniscient, but they did nothing in anticipation of the Betrayal, which they either must not have foreseen, or *had* foreseen and still did nothing. Cinzia was not sure which scenario disturbed her more.

And the organization of the Praeclaran existence still confused her. She knew the Gods resided in Praeclara, but what did they *do* there? Just sit around? There had to be a purpose. Otherwise it seemed far closer to Oblivion.

Cinzia turned a page. More on the Day of Daemons, and something about the Nine Daemons themselves. Cinzia sat up. She remembered brief mentions of the Nine Daemons at seminary, but little detail had been given. Cinzia had been terribly curious about them.

Cinzia was ravenous for more. Her curiosity commanded her, and she craved the knowledge almost like a drug. But there was another reason, one that was beginning to frighten her.

She loved the sense of power.

Ever since her vision in Navone, she had felt more in control. The feeling had grown stronger as she translated. But she still wondered why Jane had not brought up the vision. Perhaps because, up to that point, Jane had been the only conduit. There was more than a little pride involved, if Jane was anything like the girl Cinzia remembered.

She glanced at Jane, who had abandoned her seat at the desk to lie back against the bed at Cinzia's feet, staring up at the ceiling. Jane looked tired. And her hand must be hurting from hours of writing. Cinzia remembered similar pain after the seemingly endless essays she wrote at the seminary.

"Shall we call it a night?" Cinzia asked. She wanted to keep going, but she did not want to press Jane too hard. Her sister had the more difficult part, as far as Cinzia was concerned.

Jane breathed deeply. "No," she said, stretching her hand. "I brought candles for a reason. We might as well use some more of them."

"You should not work yourself too hard."

Jane smiled as she sat back at the desk. "I'll be fine. I can never work too hard in Canta's service."

"You will not be sore in the morning?"

"I'm sore now. Might as well keep going, yes?"

Just like the Jane that Cinzia remembered. "We might as well," she said. She stood and peeked around the sheet. Kovac had finally fallen asleep in the chair, breathing softly. Cinzia smiled. "Why did you not tell me he was asleep?" she whispered. She reached for an extra blanket. "He might be cold." Cinzia gently laid the blanket on her Goddessguard. One of them should sleep at least.

*My Goddessguard*, Cinzia thought fondly, though the thought was marred by another.

*If I can even still call him that.*

"Where did we leave off?" Jane asked.

Cinzia returned to the bed and opened the book. "I remember exactly," she said.

"'And in the eleventh year of the Day of Daemons,'" Cinzia read, "'the Nine Daemons arose in the Sfaera...'"

They did not stop until early morning.

# 37

WHEN WINTER AWOKE, HER first thought was not of the man sleeping next to her, but of the frost she had seen the night before.

She pulled the blankets more tightly around her and turned to look at Knot. In the darkness she could just barely see the outline of his body. His chest rose and fell.

She sat up and leaned her head against the wall behind them. What had she done? Last night had been a mess; first the conversation with Lian, then taking frost—for the second time that day, and for no reason at all—and then Knot, and what he had found in the safebox, and who he was...

An assassin. Winter had never seen him hurt anyone until the wedding. She knew of a confrontation with some men in Pranna, once, but she hadn't been there. She had only heard stories, and even then hardly believed them. The Knot she knew was kind, quiet, gentle. The Knot she had known since their wedding night was the same, she realized. He just had a side to him that... wasn't. A side that killed people, and was really, *really* good at it.

*That's one thing we have in common.*

Winter hadn't intended to sleep with him; she hadn't thought he would accept her advances, even in the moment. Part of her didn't regret it, was glad they had finally consummated their marriage; it was about time, he was her *husband*, for Canta's sake. Tiellans were nothing if not dutiful.

But another part of her felt dead. She had hoped their first time would be special. Now it was something she hardly remembered among the knot of complicated, confusing emotions, and the physical pain. Eranda had told Winter her first time might hurt. Maybe the first few times. Winter touched her stomach, pressing gently as her fingers moved down. Dull pain pulsed between her legs.

There had been a moment during the night, as Knot laid her gently on the bed and moved on top of her, that Winter's mind suddenly returned to that night, in Cineste, in the alleyway. She almost panicked, then. But she forced herself to breathe, to fight through the horror and pain, and she focused on the discomfort of the moment. There had been pleasure last night, too, but it was difficult to find amidst everything else.

Beside her, Knot stirred. Winter watched him, but his breathing continued, steady and even. She looked at the window. The shutters were drawn, only darkness through the slats. Not sunrise yet. Her eyes returned to Knot.

She had thought that all she wanted was to find him, to start their lives together for better or for worse. Now she had found him she felt nothing.

Her eyes focused on the crystals Knot had shown her the night before, scattered across the floor. She was sure they were frost. Lian had said Knot was a psimancer. These crystals supported that, although Knot claimed to not know what they were. Winter would have sensed him, if he was using psimancy. She would have tasted blood, but she hadn't.

The crystals from Knot's pack were right there, within reach. Had he counted them? Would he know if one was missing? Or two, or three? A few of the floorboards had cracks between them. They could have slipped through. Winter could tell him that, if he even asked.

The crystals were so close, so easy to take, and Knot wouldn't even know. She shouldn't take one now, there was no reason for it. It would be a waste.

Except for the fact that she *wanted* one.

Slowly, Winter pushed the covers away, trying not to disturb the blankets on Knot's side. The bedframe creaked and Winter froze, her hair falling in front of her eyes. She brushed it back, listening for Knot stirring. When she was sure he hadn't woken, she continued her slow, laborious movement off the bed. Soon she was standing in the middle of the room, the air cold against her skin. She reached down and picked up one of the crystals. She stared at it, turning it over in her hands. The dim light of early dawn was beginning to leak around the shutters, bathing the room in a soft blue-gray hue. Then, before she had registered what she was doing, Winter put the frost in her mouth and swallowed.

She was reaching for the other crystals when Knot's voice startled her.

"Good morning."

Winter nearly jumped out of her skin. She turned to see Knot sitting up in bed, staring at her. He yawned. "It *is* morning, ain't it?"

*When did he wake up?* Winter wondered. *Why didn't I hear him?*

She was suddenly very aware of how naked she was. She reached for the nearest thing to cover herself—Knot's cloak. She was grateful the room was still mostly dark so Knot couldn't see her flushed cheeks.

Then the effects of the frost hit her, and Winter nearly dropped the cloak. She breathed deeply, letting the pleasure burn. Excitement filled her—now she had three more crystals.

And not just any crystals. Nash claimed the Nazaniin had the best alchemists in the world. Their frost was the purest in the Sfaera, and the most powerful. Winter could feel that power coursing through her.

"I was just… starting to pack," she said. "We kind of made a mess of things."

*In so many ways.*

"Guess we did," Knot said.

Even with the euphoria of the frost, Winter still didn't want to drop the cloak. Shame burned within her as hot as the drug. And something was wrong. This dose *was* powerful, there was no denying that. But the elation that had once accompanied frost seemed to have lessened; the pleasure was not as sharp.

Winter watched Knot, not sure what to do. She wished she could see his face more clearly, could know what he was thinking.

"We'd better get going," Knot said. "Should be on the road when the sun rises."

Winter nodded, standing there awkwardly, the cloak pressed against her body. Knot rose, heedless of his own nakedness. He stretched, and began rummaging through his things. His body was lean; muscle and sinew stood out as he moved. She had always thought the way he moved was odd, like a cat. Watching him move now, without any clothing, made her even more curious. She knew what he could do with that body, in more ways than one.

*Why doesn't he feel self-conscious?* Winter wondered. She wanted to feel careless around him, the way he seemed to feel. But it seemed impossible.

In no time at all Knot was dressed. Winter wrapped the cloak around herself more tightly.

"I'll make sure the others are awake," he said. She looked at him through long strands of her hair. He looked as if he were about to say something more, but instead he sighed, and kissed her on the forehead. Then he turned, and left.

Winter stood, staring at the door.

They left the city shortly after the sun rose over the gulf. The weather was not as cold as it had been in Khale, but the clear sky made for a chilly day. The padded leather that Winter wore kept her warm enough, although she wished she could wear her *siara*, if only to provide further protection against the chill. Instead, she pulled her cloak more tightly around her body, and walked on.

"Here on out, we follow the river," Knot told them, his staff thudding against the path as they walked. "It'll lead us to Izet. The capital. Hopefully, the place where all this'll end."

The wide river he spoke of flowed to Winter's right, the water gray and swift—her father's fishing boat could fit end-to-end at least twice across. It seemed to have sliced its way through the hills; to the right of the path was a sheer drop down to the water of at least two rods. Knot had called it the River Arden. He had said it was glacier-fed, flowing down from the Stone Glacier in the Sorensan Mountains. A thick pine forest rose to the left of the path.

Winter found herself caressing the crystals in her pouch. She had five left, including the three she had taken from Knot's stash that morning. The voidstone that Nash and Kali had given her was still there as well, though they had never taught her how to use it. Winter wondered whether she would ever learn, now, though the thought was fleeting—she had frost, after all. What use was a silly little stone? But she had to make the crystals last. She couldn't take them whenever she wanted, let alone two in one day as she had yesterday. She had to control herself. Who knew when she would be able to find more?

She wondered what she was becoming. She could see the addicts in Cineste clearly in her mind's eye. Winter shivered. She did not want to become like those people. And she wouldn't. She could stop. Would she be able to concentrate better without frost on her mind all the time? Perhaps. She would definitely be able to contribute her remaining money to the group funds if she didn't have to reserve them for frost, though the money Knot had found last night seemed more than enough to get them to Izet. Thinking about life without frost, Winter wondered whether her relationship with Knot wouldn't be easier, too. Things with Lian certainly would be. But whether she liked it or not, she could not live without it.

And wasn't frost just an excuse? She could make amends with Lian, she could come clean with Knot. Frost wasn't what stopped her, just her own stubbornness.

Nevertheless, gaunt faces stared back at her in her mind. The stained clothing. Black, frostbitten limbs from living out in the cold with no shelter or warmth.

*I should just not take it for a few days.* If she could go a few days, she would know she was fine. If she couldn't… then, perhaps, it would be time to admit she had a problem.

*A few days. I can do that.*

Even so, Winter found her gaze straying to Knot's pack. He hadn't said anything about the missing crystals. She hoped he never would, so she wouldn't have to lie to him.

Winter glanced at the vampire, walking softly beside her.

For some reason the girl seemed to stay close to her. It had bothered Winter at first, but given that both Lian and Knot seemed to be avoiding her, she appreciated the company. Cinzia, Jane, and Kovac walked behind. Lian hung back with them, although what he saw in the humans Winter didn't know. That Lian the revolutionary, who had hated humans since they were children, preferred their company to hers...

This was stupid. Lian could do what he wanted.

There was a sudden sound and Winter looked back to see Kovac steadying Cinzia, who had stumbled on a patch of loose rock.

"Behold Canta's grace," Astrid muttered. Winter smirked.

Knot looked back. "You all right?"

"Fine," Cinzia said. "We had a long night."

Astrid raised an eyebrow. "And here I thought priestesses weren't allowed to do that sort of thing."

"Stop," Jane said, with enough authority that Winter found herself halting without even thinking about it. "You will not speak of my sister that way." Jane's gaze rested firmly on Astrid.

The vampire stepped towards Jane. There was a smile on the girl's face, but her cloak concealed her eyes. Winter was glad of it; she had seen Astrid's eyes and their eerie glow. The priestess apparently felt the same way, and took a step back. Even the Goddessguard seemed to flinch.

Jane, however, stood her ground. "You do not have to be this way, you know."

Astrid snorted. "I am what I am. There's nothing me or you or anyone else can do about it."

Jane shook her head. "You think you are beyond saving, but you are not."

"Might want to check your doctrine on that one. I'm a

daemon, according to your stupid Denomination. That goddess you're talking about, the one that you claim loves us all? She's the one that cursed me to begin with. Pretty sure there's no love lost between us."

"The Denomination is wrong."

For once, Astrid seemed speechless.

"Whatever," the vampire finally said. "I don't need the Denomination, I don't need whatever it is *you* think you believe, and I sure as Oblivion don't need your pity." Astrid turned and continued along the river.

"Wait," Knot said. Winter looked at him. Something in his voice was odd, strained somehow.

"If you think I'm going to apologize, you have another thing—" Astrid stopped in mid-sentence just as a man, clad in a long, dark-green robe, stepped out of the forest to their left and pointed a longsword at Knot's neck.

Winter grasped one of the *faltira* crystals—her fingers had already been wrapped around one of them—and placed it in her mouth. *So much for going a few days without*. Power filled her almost immediately. The high was still more tempered than it had once been, her pain and pleasure dulled. The high was less, but the need was more. Perhaps taking two crystals would help.

But now wasn't the time to test that theory. More men appeared from the forest, clad in dark green. Robed men, at least a dozen of them. The same green robes worn by her father's killers and by the ambushing party on the road to Navone. Winter and her companions were surrounded.

Yet, Winter smiled. She was not helpless anymore. Revealing herself as a psimancer would be risky, of course. Knot would have questions, questions that would lead him to what happened in Navone. But that didn't matter. If she could not protect her friends with telesis, what use was it? Reaching out a *tendron* towards the man threatening to kill Knot, she pulled at his sword.

Nothing happened.

She frowned. She reached again, trying to grasp at anything, feel anything. It was as if she hadn't taken the drug at all. Winter felt the high inside of her, but outside, where she normally felt the crackle of raw energy and leashed power, she felt nothing. She reached again and again, trying to use multiple *tendra*, railing against whatever force stifled her, but nothing happened.

Winter was completely powerless.

Knot froze when the sword touched his neck. How had he not seen these men? They belonged to the same group that'd attacked during the wedding, that much was certain. The green robes and the way they carried themselves were enough to know that.

The others around Knot seemed to have frozen in place as well. Even Astrid was still. The sun still shone brightly, and one wrong move on her part would be disastrous.

The man who held a sword at Knot's neck spoke with a Rodenese accent, his words harsh and clipped. "Our creation has finally returned to us," he said from beneath his hood. "Took you long enough."

Knot thought quickly. His own sword was sheathed on his back; it'd be impossible to reach without getting one in the belly. His pack would be a burden as well; he'd need to slip out of it when the fighting started.

"You do not recognize me?" the man asked, drawing back his hood. The man smiled broadly, his light eyes wide. His long blond hair was tied back, loose strands falling in front of his face and down his shoulders. "We spent so much time together, you and I," he said, almost fondly. "You truly have no recollection?"

"What're you talking about?" Knot asked. The man's face meant nothing to him, but he'd come to Roden to confront his past. Perhaps it was happening sooner than he'd anticipated.

The man laughed. "Call me Tokal, please," he said. He lowered the sword. "Tiring, holding a sword out so long. I admit, I'm not sure what name you use these days. Who exactly do you think you are?"

Knot frowned. The man handled the sword casually, but Knot knew an act when he saw one. The man knew how to use the weapon.

"Knot," Knot said. "Call me Knot. Already know who I was, before. Lathe. An agent of the Nazaniin. But I don't remember anyone named Tokal."

"*The* Tokal, my good man. It's a title, not a name." The man's eyebrows rose. "And Lathe… yes, very good. Very good indeed. Do you know who else you were, ah, before?"

The only other name Knot knew was Madzin, but he'd assumed it was just an alias Lathe had used in Navone. He wouldn't reveal it. Best to see what this man was up to.

"Oh, delightful," the Tokal said. Knot almost expected him to clap his hands. "You've no idea what you are, you beautiful fool. You are correct about this Lathe. And yet, you are not. Lathe died more than a year ago, I'm afraid. You may contain parts of him, but you are not him. He is a piece of the puzzle. You are something far more… manufactured. An experiment. A conglomeration of souls crammed together. A creation of science and magic is what you are, my dear Knot."

It didn't make sense. A creation of science and magic? What in Oblivion was he talking about?

"What do you want from me?" Knot asked.

"Same thing we've wanted since we first discovered you in that town. We want *you*." The Tokal glanced at Winter. "Of course, priorities change. The tiellan is far more important than you are at this point." He glanced over his shoulder. "Take them."

And there was Knot's opening. It was just a glance, but it was enough for Knot to whip his staff up towards the Tokal's face.

The man parried easily with his sword.

"You are used to fighting men," the Tokal said with a smile. "I am something altogether different."

Then everything erupted into chaos.

Winter watched Knot's pack fall to the earth as he slithered out of the straps and around the man's blade, his staff a blur. Everything was eerily silent, just for a fraction of a second. Then there was shouting and clanging weapons and guttural grunts.

Winter looked around wildly, unsure of what to do. She reached out with her *tendra* once more, but still nothing happened. She gripped her dagger so tightly her hand began to hurt. She heard a loud crack to her left and turned just in time to see Lian fall to the ground, a green-cloaked man standing over him, staff in hand. Winter rushed the man with a shout, but the man parried her clumsy attack and knocked her to the ground. The snow was cold on her bare face and hands, biting into her flesh.

Winter looked around in horror. Whatever green-robed men had been after them before, these ones seemed twice as dangerous. They wore no armor underneath their robes, they moved too quickly for that. Even Knot seemed to be struggling to defend himself against the Tokal and another man who was wielding a long, flexible staff. The three danced around each other, weapons blurred. Winter rose to her hands and knees. She wanted to help Knot with the dagger still gripped tightly in her fist, but she didn't know what to do. She felt frozen, half-afraid she would strike Knot by accident. She tried again, in vain, to reach a *tendron* out to something, anything. Nothing.

She could *feel* the power within her, knew it was there, but she couldn't access it. Perhaps the frost she'd bought from the old woman in Navone was off, somehow. Some of the crystals might be duds. Maybe she'd taken one of Knot's, and they weren't what she thought at all. Or, perhaps, her powers had left her.

Whatever the reason, Winter was helpless once again.

There was a shout to her left, and she saw Kovac beside her, fending off one of the attackers who wielded a thin, club-like weapon. Cinzia snuck up behind the man, carrying what looked like Jane's massive pack. With a heave the priestess swung the pack down on the robed man's head, and he fell to his knees. Kovac's sword took the attacker through the chest.

*What in the Sfaera is in that pack?* Winter wondered, with just a glimmer of respect for the priestess.

Winter stood in time to see Astrid sprint past, heading straight for two more robed men. Lian was still on the ground, not moving. One of the robed men stood over him, reaching into his robe. Winter raised her dagger and rushed forward.

Behind her someone shouted, and the man standing over Lian turned at the sound. He turned right into Winter's dagger. She pushed forward with all her weight, pushing the blade into the man's belly. He fell to the ground.

Before she could react, before she could even pull her dagger away, someone grabbed her from behind. She screamed, slammed her elbow back into the man's ribs, felt a grunt of hot breath in her ear. She elbowed him again with all her strength, but this time the man must have leaned away. She slammed her heel down on where she thought the man's foot would be, but only connected with churned snow and mud. A sweaty hand clamped over her mouth, stifling her scream.

Winter's eyes darted for anything she could do or use against her captor. She couldn't see Astrid. Knot still fought the two men, his staff whirling. She attempted another muffled scream, all the while trying to reach out with all of her *tendra*, but each failed attempt drained her of what little hope remained. She tripped as the man dragged her backwards, her feet trailing, making ridges in the slush. Winter kicked, screaming into the hand clamped over her mouth, but breathing was increasingly difficult, let alone shouting.

She heard a cry in the distance, as she was dragged away, followed by a splash, something heavy falling into the river. She felt a wave of panic. Had Knot fallen? The river was fast and freezing. If he couldn't get out quickly, he would not survive.

With the splash, something seemed to change in the air. Like a flock of birds that suddenly change course at a sign of danger, the robed men stopped fighting and retreated into the forest, taking Winter with them.

The initial shock of the freezing river chilled Knot's body. He swallowed a mouthful of gritty water and came up again, spluttering.

He had to get to land.

He thrashed as he was swept along, the riverbanks a blur of green, white, and gray. His muscles strained as he tried to swim east—the west bank was steep, it was unlikely he'd be able to climb it. But the current disoriented him. At this point, any bank would do. He couldn't stay in this water long. He had only a few moments before his muscles cramped up and his body shut down.

His left calf tightened, the muscle forming a painful knot beneath his skin. The cold, once shocking, was now more of a dull ache.

Then, Knot remembered.

A ship at night, the air cold, the waters black and violent. Knot was there, in his own mind, just like one of his dreams. He was there, but only to observe.

A room, darkly lit by a single candle in the corner. No windows, no furniture except a table in the center of the room. His stomach twisted as he looked at the table, remembering what'd happened there. Dried blood encrusted the table and floor. Blood on his hands, too. Not his own. He glimpsed several dark shapes in the corner before leaving the room.

Outside, the ship's boards quaked beneath his feet, snow and salt water stung his eyes. Shouts behind him, but he didn't look back. He ran the other way, bare feet padding down the wet boards of the deck. He could smell the salt on the air.

Someone stepped out in front of him. A green robe. He dodged the man's grasp, reaching for the man's head with both hands and twisting. The man fell to the deck, limp.

More shouts behind him, and he felt a sudden pain in the back of his leg. A crossbow bolt protruded from his calf.

He looked back up just in time to see two more green-robed men rushing him. He lashed out at one, but the other—they were *fast*—grabbed his arm, holding him against the railing.

The ship bucked, cresting over a wave. He tried to yank his arm out of the man's grip but failed, just as the other rammed into him from behind. Then everything was tumbling, end over end, snow and sea and ship, and he was falling.

The water was so cold, like ice, and he couldn't breathe. He tried swimming, but felt another sharp pain, this time in his shoulder. He swallowed seawater, gagged, swam, stopped, and then it was done. The sound of waves, the men shouting, the ringing in his head was gone. There was nothing left but a distant chill.

Cinzia watched the men run off down the path, trying to understand what had just happened. One moment their leader had been talking to Knot, the next, everyone was fighting. Cinzia had been swinging Jane's pack at anything that moved, and then, just as quickly, the green-robed men took off, faster than Cinzia thought possible. Unnatural.

Cinzia, Kovac, and Jane were left standing. Lian was on the ground, unconscious.

"We have to get Knot," Kovac said beside her. "He'll freeze if we don't get him out." Cinzia nodded. Knot had been defending himself against two attackers by the riverbank, but they had finally overcome him and pushed him into the freezing water.

"Where's Astrid?" Cinzia asked. The girl was nowhere to be seen. Had the men taken her too? Had she run away?

"Doesn't matter, Priestess." Kovac sheathed his sword and started jogging downstream. "She'll find us or she won't."

"Of course," Cinzia whispered. She looked back at Jane. "Will you be all right, with him?"

"He's coming round," Jane said, kneeling on the ground beside Lian. "We will be fine. Go."

Cinzia grabbed her pack. She had flint, steel, and tinder. They would need to warm Knot once they got him out of the river.

"Follow us as soon as you are able!" she shouted over her shoulder.

Cinzia did not wait to hear Jane's response, and rushed after Kovac.

# 38

*Along the River Arden, Roden*

DARKNESS FELL, BUT WINTER'S captors showed no sign of slowing. They sprinted along the riverbank, a pace they'd kept up since that morning when they'd taken her. Their endurance seemed inhuman, but it wasn't the only thing about them that bothered her. None of the robed men had said a word, not since the man who had called himself "the Tokal" had spoken to Knot. And while she had seen them take food out of their robes to eat as they ran, and a few take sips from waterskins, otherwise they had all kept running, switching her from shoulder to shoulder throughout the journey. Each man accepted her without complaint, tossing her onto his back, holding her legs over one shoulder and her torso over the other.

The Tokal, obviously the leader, ran at the head of the pack. Occasionally one of his companions would run ahead, perhaps to scout. No words were ever exchanged that Winter could hear.

They wore the same robes as the men who had attacked at her wedding and on the road to Navone. But these men seemed different, somehow. More disciplined. More coordinated. Faster. The Tokal had told Knot that he was different than a normal man.

Winter's bound feet and hands had grown numb hours ago. A long strip of thankfully clean cloth gagged her mouth. She must have lost her dagger back where they had been attacked.

She did not have her pack, her supplies, nothing but the clothes she wore and her mother's necklace of black stones around her neck. And her pouch, of course. Her pouch of *faltira*, still on her belt, underneath her shirt. She had tried getting to it, but the man carrying her shook her roughly when she squirmed. Not that it would matter if she could reach the pouch; she wasn't even sure *faltira* worked, now.

The men's shoulders dug into her as they ran, and Winter's neck ached from trying to keep her head still. She would have tried to convince them to let her run on her own if she thought keeping up with them was a remote possibility. Her body hurt so much that she wondered whether it might be more comfortable for them to drag her.

Winter didn't know what value she could possibly have to anyone, except for her psimancy, and she wasn't even sure she had that anymore. She would have thought Knot would attract the most attention, or Astrid. Winter was nothing. A poor tiellan girl from a small fishing town in northern Khale. She had nothing to offer anyone.

Except, perhaps, Knot.

Knot's fate—or that of Lian, or Astrid, or even the priestess and her sister—was a mystery. She wondered if they were dead. If they'd survived, there was no way they could catch up to this pack of tireless, silent men.

And Winter wasn't sure they would want to. She hadn't exactly been pleasant company. That was painful to think about. She needed to focus on something more constructive. Why hadn't the frost worked when the men attacked? The first possibility was that the crystal had been a dud. She didn't know whether it was one of the crystals from Mazille or one she had stolen from Knot. Neither were reliable sources.

Or the frost *had* worked, but Winter was somehow being blocked from using the power. Kali had never mentioned such a possibility, but neither Kali nor Nash had told her everything they knew about psimancy. Perhaps they had even *possessed* something with this power, and hadn't told Winter about it in case she ever decided to use her abilities against them.

But, in the end, Winter *had* used psimancy against them. She had killed Kali. They would have used that kind of blocking power then, in Navone, if they had it.

Of course, there was another option. Winter might have burned herself out. That frightened her more than anything. And she deserved it. She knew what she had done in Navone. She knew what she was capable of. She knew what the dark voice whispered to her when she was alone.

*Murderer.*

Either way, the craving still raged. Had the bonds not stopped her, Winter would have reached into her pouch long ago, not caring whether a crystal gave her power or not, not caring whether it would help her escape. She would have taken one because she *needed* to take one; it was all she thought about. The craving to feel just one more burn.

*What is wrong with me?*

She had been captured by a group of unknown, powerful men. She had no idea what these men would do to her when they arrived wherever they were going. Her companions catching up to her was all but impossible, assuming they even cared to do so. Assuming they were even still alive.

And yet all she could think about was putting another crystal in her mouth.

She was, Winter admitted to herself, pitiful. And perhaps slightly insane.

*You decided to go a few days without frost,* she thought to herself. *Now is as good a time as any.*

Perhaps it was stupid to deny herself of the one power she truly had, when she might need it most, just to prove a point. But if she could get out of this on her own somehow, without frost, she could finally stop worrying. She could live her life knowing that frost wasn't necessary. Helpful, but not necessary.

The man carrying her slowed. Winter thought he would pass her off to another; they seemed to have some unspoken system of when to slow and who would take her next. But, this time, the man actually stopped. Perhaps they were finally taking a rest.

Winter craned her neck, trying to get her bearings. It was dark, but she saw the deep pine forest to her left. To her right was the river. She couldn't see it—it was more of a black empty space—so much as hear it, rushing in the night.

Her captors stood in silence. She wondered what they were doing. There were ten of them. She had counted more than once while they carried her. But no one spoke or moved. They all just *stood* there, looking at one another. Winter's skin crawled.

One of them—Winter thought it was the Tokal, though she could not be sure in the darkness—moved away, and the others followed. Up ahead, Winter saw lights. Lanterns, bright orbs of glowing yellow.

As they approached, Winter realized they were walking towards some sort of dock, stretching out onto the blackness of the river.

At the end of the dock was a boat.

Smaller than her father's fishing boat, but sturdy and well-crafted, built for river-running. A single sail was lowered on the mast. The river current would be enough to carry the boat downstream, she realized, if that was their bearing.

The men approached the dock. Up ahead, another man waited, carrying a lantern. He was older and stooped over, with a large black beard. The man spoke as the group approached him, with the clipped accent of Roden.

"I hope you are who I was sent to meet," he said, eying them warily. Winter didn't blame him. The men looked strange enough in their large robes, even without the bound and gagged woman one of them carried over his shoulder. Winter found herself hoping that this strange boatman would notice her and contact the authorities, ask her if she was all right, tell them to put her down, anything. The boatman's gaze lingered on Winter, just for a moment—a moment bright with hope—but then he looked away.

The Tokal spoke. "We are."

"Very well, come aboard," the stooped man said.

The Tokal turned to look at Winter. His face was inches from hers, and she twitched as he reached a hand to caress her cheek.

"I'm afraid we must part ways for a brief moment, my dear. But fear not. We shall see one another again, in Izet. We have great plans. You will play an important role in what is to come."

Winter jerked away from the man's touch. She would have loved to tell him to go stick his prick in an angry wasps' nest. But the Tokal had already sprinted off towards the forest with three other robed men.

"The river's swift tonight," the boatman said, "and my bones bespeak a tailwind. If that be the case, we may arrive in Izet early as dawn."

No one responded as the seven remaining robed men walked onto the boat, silent as stones. The boatman's gaze lingered on Winter once more, briefly, and then he turned away.

"I can tell you all are a silent bunch so I won't question you. We'll be off. Raise the plank there, if you would," he said, nodding to one of the green-robed men. The man did as he was bidden, and Winter heard the sound of an anchor being drawn up.

She was alone. Knot could not save her. If she wanted to escape, it was up to her. There were only six robed men left. Six was better than ten, to be sure. Winter looked at the boatman once more. His lingering glance… perhaps there was something there she could exploit. If she could just get him alone.

Slowly, the beginnings of a plan—without frost—began to form in Winter's head.

# 39

ASTRID RAN THROUGH THE undergrowth, feeling the caress of the leaves, the night breeze through her hair.

Running was maybe an understatement. She moved faster now than any man could sprint. She hadn't been quite as fast during the day, and the green-robes had developed a freakish lead. But now the sun had set, and she quickly gained on them.

Astrid loved running at night. She was faster, her skin tougher and more durable. She could see further, hear more, feel the cool air and the mist of the river on her skin better than she ever could during the day.

There were less-fun changes, too. Her fangs pressed against her lips, pricked her tongue. She'd never really gotten used to them. She developed claws, long, retractable, hardened razors that extended half again her fingers' normal length. Which, of course, wasn't all that long to begin with, considering she had nine-year-old-girl fingers. But the visual effect was disturbing. Even to her. Even after all these years.

As a general rule, Astrid avoided looking at them. She avoided looking at herself at all.

The green-robes slowed up ahead, close to the river. Astrid reined in her pace to match, finally coming to a halt. She had followed them at a distance, stealthy as could be. If they'd harmed Winter during daylight, Astrid wasn't sure she could have stopped them. She hadn't been able to do much against them that morning. Whoever the green-robes were, they were fast, and they fought with uncanny coordination. That, combined with the threat of the sun, had forced Astrid to be cautious.

She hated being cautious.

But she'd come all this way. Might as well do it right.

Astrid liked Winter, for the most part. Stubborn girl, but strong. And Knot liked Winter, which was enough for Astrid. Bringing Winter back to him would hopefully solidify his trust in Astrid again. Trust she didn't deserve, but trust that it was necessary to re-establish.

With her enhanced vision, Astrid saw that there were dark stains on the men's robes. A good sign; sweat was a mortal weakness. Hopefully it meant these men would not be too difficult to take down, if she could catch them by surprise. Their silence was strange. She should be able to hear a good part of what they said to one another, but she heard nothing.

Astrid narrowed her eyes. She didn't like this silence one bit.

The men walked down a small dock protruding into the river. Someone stood on the dock, waiting for them.

"I hope you are who I was sent to meet," the man said.

"We are," one of the green-robes—the one with the stupid name—responded. He approached Winter. Astrid tensed, preparing to move in, but then the Tokal and three other robes sprinted off into the forest.

Astrid grinned. All the better.

The remaining robes followed the man down the dock, one of them still carrying Winter over his shoulder. Astrid smiled. The boat was an enclosed space. She was fond of enclosed spaces. Slim chance of getting surrounded. She licked her lips at the familiar pang of hunger—real, *true* hunger. She needed to feed. She had tasted blood in Navone, but the last time she had truly fed had been weeks earlier. This might be her chance to skewer a few fish with one spear-thrust, but she'd have to time everything right.

Astrid moved slowly towards the shore. When the last of the green-robes had boarded the vessel, the stooped man unfastened the lines and followed them. In seconds, the boat moved away with the current of the river, slow at first, but picking up speed.

Astrid moved faster, closing in on the shore and running along the bank. Timing would be key; she didn't want to end up in the river. She hated swimming.

With a burst of speed, she rushed ahead of the boat and jumped.

She soared through the air, over the water, in front of the boat. The boat caught up below her, and she slammed into the back of the vessel, barely grasping the boat's rail in time to stop herself from tumbling into the river. Her feet splashed into the water beneath her. It was cold, probably freezing, but it didn't bother her as much as it once would have. Astrid was a creature of the cold. She'd long since grown used to it. She pulled herself up and over the railing, her feet landing softly on the deck.

One of the green-robes stood before her, surprise etched on his face. The man didn't scream, which Astrid found odd— she certainly gave him enough time to do so, though at this point, it didn't much matter whether he did or not.

Astrid lunged. Her claws cut through him easily, and his head spun around almost full circle.

Whatever else they were, these men definitely were mortal.

She looked around but there was no one else in sight. The

man hadn't given her away. Astrid looked down at the corpse, the lifeless, lacerated face staring blankly into nothing. Blood still ebbed slowly from his wounds; she could smell it, on the air and on his skin and in his veins.

And then Astrid was on top of the man, burying her fangs in his neck. The blood was bitter and sweet all at once. The most delicious—and the most horrible—taste Astrid could imagine.

Footsteps on the wooden deck. Soft and measured, but Astrid heard them. She raised her head. These men were different. She wouldn't be surprised if one could just sneak up on her and—

Astrid heard the blow before she felt it, the staff shattering against the back of her head. It stung, might even bruise, but obviously the green-robes hadn't realized what they were up against, yet. A blow like that would have knocked anyone else unconscious, maybe killed them.

To Astrid, it was a tap on the shoulder.

She whirled on her attacker, a low growl beginning deep in her chest. The green-robe stared at her, eyes wide. Three more appeared.

She could only wonder how she appeared to them. Her claws and fangs, her glowing eyes, her entire face covered in blood, a stream of it running from her mouth, down her neck, onto her clothes. They would dismiss her childlike form quickly.

Astrid felt a moment of uncertainty. Had all four of them found her together? Armed, and grouped? Unlikely, and yet here they were. Had the green-robe she'd killed and fed from managed to send some kind of signal? Perhaps someone had been watching.

Unlikely, but it was the only answer Astrid could think of as she charged. She hadn't finished feeding; she still wasn't satisfied.

That only made her bloodlust stronger.

The green-robes were well trained, Astrid gave them that. Surely they knew what she was by now. She couldn't imagine the Rodenese viewed vampires differently from any other part of the Sfaera. Cursed of the cursed, damned of the damned. Daemons.

Astrid went for the one who'd struck her first, her clawed hand entering his chest and exploding out the other side. She dodged attacks from the others quickly and easily, springing up against the railing, from the railing to the wall, and from the wall into the air directly behind the three remaining men before they could turn around.

Astrid shattered one man's spine with a blow to his back, and screamed in pleasure. She dodged another swinging staff and rammed the attacker into the wall of a cabin. Astrid heard him gasp quietly, that small expulsion of air, and between that and his crunching bones she knew he was gone.

More footsteps, too many for the remaining green-robe to make on his own. She turned and saw two more arriving, one wielding another staff, the other a longsword.

*Already?* Their response time seemed inhuman.

She spun, her claws lashing in an arc. One halted just within her reach. A small red line appeared at his throat, growing slowly wider. Blood jetted into the night. The other rushed at her, staff swinging, but Astrid knocked it aside and slid her claws into his ribs, heaving him over the railing and into the freezing water.

Astrid turned, grinning, just as the sword swung down on her. Her hand shot up and she caught the blade with a clang, the sound of metal on stone, inches from her face. Before the green-robe could react, Astrid whipped his weapon from his hands. She turned it on its owner, leaping up to his eye-level, and swung. The man's head fell with a thud to the deck, his body close behind.

Astrid looked down at the bodies around her. Seven. Now to find Winter. After that, they needed to wait for Knot and the others.

*Assuming Knot survived.* She knew he'd been thrown into the river. She had wanted to go in after him, but she knew what he would have wanted her to do instead. Or, at least, that's what she told herself. Other things had driven her away. She needed to be sure Knot wasn't around when she made contact this time. After she found Winter, Astrid would have to try to communicate again. She couldn't risk her mistress's wrath.

*But first,* she thought, looking at the carnage around her, feeling the grinding pain in her belly, *I need to finish what I started.*

Astrid found Winter in the cabin with the boatman, already free of her bonds and gag. The old man was steering the boat, his face covered in sweat, eyes darting around wildly. He mumbled incoherently as Astrid walked in. She had cleaned herself up as best she could, and tried to keep her eyes away from him.

"I was doing fine on my own. Would've been out of here in no time." Winter nodded to the boatman, smiling. "He was about to help me escape."

Astrid raised an eyebrow. "Not shy with the sarcasm, are you?"

"You're one to talk."

Astrid smirked. "Not sure how far you'd have gotten if I hadn't provided a nice distraction and killed all your captors. You're welcome, by the way."

Winter's smile faded, and she lowered her head. "It is good to see you alive."

"Depends on your definition," Astrid mumbled. "Are you all right?"

"I'll be fine. What about Knot and the others?"

"Knot was thrown into the river, and Lian knocked unconscious." Astrid hesitated. Best not to worry the woman, not until they knew for sure. "Should be fine, though. Seems you were the one the green-robes were after." She wondered if Winter knew why.

If she did, she didn't show it. "Where are they? Will they be able to find us?"

Astrid sighed. This girl had issues. Astrid gave her credit for attempting to escape, but Winter was obviously reckless, and Astrid could guess why. The girl needed to come clean, although it would have to be her own choice.

"They'll catch up soon enough," was all Astrid said.

The boatman was gibbering now, looking back and forth from Winter to Astrid. Astrid cocked her head in the man's direction.

"What's with this one?"

"Not sure," Winter said. "When he heard the fighting he just started mumbling."

The man's muttering grew more frantic. Astrid made out the words "Izet," "traveling," and what sounded like "religion," but she couldn't be sure. The man's accent was thick, and he spoke faster than she could keep up with.

"Tell him to get us to shore," Astrid said. "The western shore. We'll wait for the others."

Winter nodded and turned to the boatman. Astrid stepped out onto the deck. Hopefully the man would calm down if she was out of the picture. She watched the dark water flowing past. She and the river had some things in common, both flowing down preordained paths to a preordained destination.

She heard Winter's footsteps behind her, and turned.

"Thank you," Winter said. "I'd gotten that man to help me out of my bonds, but I don't know what I would have done from there."

The girl appeared to bloody mean it.

"Welcome," Astrid muttered.

The boat rocked against the shore with a soft bump. It was not an ideal spot—they would have to jump over the railing and land in the bushes below—but it would do. In his state the boatman could hardly do better than this.

"Let's go," Astrid said.

"We could take the boat," Winter said, her hand on the rail. "We could wait for the others, and take the boat the rest of the way to Izet."

Astrid shook her head. "A riverboat is too confining. There might be other robed men waiting for their companions along the way—we're better off leaving the river altogether, once the others catch up to us."

Winter nodded, patting the rail. "You're right. How do we get off?" Winter asked.

"Do you have any gear?"

Winter held up a pack.

"Like this," Astrid said, and lifted Winter gently and tossed her over the side. The girl hit the bank and tumbled. She'd be fine. She was tough.

Astrid ran back to the cabin. The man looked at her in horror, his mouth working, but no sound escaped.

"I'm sorry," she said. "I don't think you deserve this, but I can't have you talking. Canta save you."

She slit the man's throat, and he fell gurgling to the deck.

She walked back onto the deck and leaped over the side, landing softly in the undergrowth.

"Winter?" she whispered.

"I'm here."

"Let's go," Astrid said. "We need to find better ground to make camp."

"And then what?"

"We wait."

# 40

WINTER RELEASED THE MAKESHIFT sling as it passed its zenith, and the small rock flew into the bark of a distant tree, just wide of a chattering squirrel. The animal leapt away in a shower of bark.

"You missed," Astrid said.

Winter frowned. "I didn't." She walked towards where the squirrel had flown into the undergrowth.

"Yes you did."

Winter had awoken that morning to two things: Astrid standing over her, and her own rumbling stomach. She hadn't eaten since breakfast the day before. The whole day of travel on the shoulders of the robed men had left her sore and hungry.

Astrid had offered to catch something for them to eat, but Winter had declined, namely because she didn't relish eating anything that had been caught by Astrid. But she also wanted to do something with her own hands. And, if she could get away from Astrid long enough to take *faltira*, that was only a plus.

Winter had been well on her way to escaping before Astrid showed up; if she could have jumped in the river, the men wouldn't have gone in after her. She wasn't sure what she would have done once she was *in* the river... but it would have worked. That's all there was to it. And she had taken a crystal last night to make sure her power still worked. She had moved only small things, rocks and dead twigs—she didn't want to make Astrid any more suspicious than she already was. But Winter had slept easily that night, content in the fact that, while her powers hadn't worked the previous morning, they *were* working now.

That didn't stop her, of course, from wanting to make sure they *still* worked. She wanted to be sure.

*You only have three left,* she told herself. *You should ration them.* She would have to find more when they reached the next city. Either way, Winter was confident. She could handle herself without frost, that much was obvious. She just needed to keep her supply well padded, and everything would be fine.

Winter poked around in the foliage, finally finding what she was looking for. She raised the squirrel up triumphantly.

"Aiming for a spot near them on the tree stuns them, and doesn't damage what little meat they have. Then you find them," Winter twisted sharply, breaking the squirrel's neck, "and kill them. Now, we have breakfast."

Astrid rolled her eyes. "Nothing like starting my day with burnt squirrel."

Winter didn't bother responding. Honestly, she didn't care what Astrid preferred to start her day with.

Gray clouds blanketed the sky, but Astrid wore her cloak nonetheless. The large gray hood dwarfed her. *She's so small,* Winter thought. Last night, the girl had been terrifying. But now, looking at her, Winter could almost believe she wasn't. Winter just saw a little girl. A little girl who spoke more than she should, but a little girl all the same.

Winter wondered whether Astrid felt guilty for killing the men last night. What she had done in Navone still harrowed her. Did Astrid feel the same remorse?

*Astrid killed to save you. You killed for no reason at all.*

*I killed to save Knot,* Winter thought. But she knew it wasn't entirely true. She had killed innocent people along with Goddessguards and Sons of Canta.

"You need to get out of that head of yours," Astrid said.

"What do you mean?"

"Talk it out with someone, whatever it is. Get it into the light. Light kills daemons; I know that better than anyone. But if you keep them in darkness… they thrive."

Winter's breathing grew heavy. Did Astrid know about *faltira*? Did the girl know about her abilities? What else could the girl be referring to?

"Some things are best left hidden."

"Until they're revealed, and they always are. You think you're better off keeping secrets; you think you're better off not hurting those around you. You're wrong. Secrets come out one way or another."

They walked back to their camp in silence.

"Hope you didn't let the fire die," Winter said, changing the subject. "Otherwise you can find your own breakfast."

Astrid snorted. "The fire's fine. And don't worry, you can eat all the breakfast you want. I don't have much of an appetite this morning."

Winter wasn't fond of the way the girl said "breakfast." She shrugged. "If that's what you want."

Their camp was little more than a fire and some impressions in the pine needles. Gear was sparse, other than what Astrid had taken with her on her pursuit and the pack that Winter had salvaged. They had decided not to light a fire until this morning. No point in attracting unwanted attention.

Winter took out one of her small knives and began gutting the squirrel.

"I'll be back," Astrid said, walking off into the foliage. "Enjoy your breakfast."

"Where are you going?"

Astrid looked back at Winter, meeting her eyes. "Everyone has secrets," the girl said.

Then Astrid was gone.

For a brief moment, Winter wanted to follow her. What secrets could the girl have? But the compulsion faded at the realization that if she discovered whatever it was Astrid was hiding, she might have to reveal some truths of her own.

Winter sighed, looking down at the squirrel. She *was* hungry. It had been a long time since she had hunted an animal. She used to do it all the time with her father, hunting harts and hares and even snowbears on occasion. But in the couple years before they found Knot, they had needed to spend more and more time on the water to reach their fish target, which had meant less time in the forest, where Winter loved being even more than the sea.

Bahc had said it was her mother's fault, her love of the forest. Her father came from one of the sea-faring tiellan tribes, while her mother's ancestors were from the deep eastern woods. People had always said her parents had been the perfect match. Winter wished she could have seen them together. Her father had spoken of her mother often, but never of what they were like as a couple.

She missed them. But, in a small way, in a way that made her feel filled with poison, she was glad they were dead. At least they didn't know what she had become.

The squirrel was nearly cooked when Astrid reappeared with a smile on her face.

"Hope that thing serves six," she said. "They're almost here, and they look tired. Probably been traveling all night."

Winter couldn't stop her own smile from spreading across her face. The squirrel would make a meager meal for six but she could find some herbs and roots to supplement it. Meager or not, she would gladly share it.

"I'm glad he's back, too," Astrid said. She grinned at Winter, who raised her eyebrows. Astrid snorted. "I just like him, is all. He's not my type, anyway. Not to mention the age difference."

Winter's cheeks grew hot. Who actually spoke that way? The girl was insane.

"Fine, I know when I'm not wanted," Astrid said, but she was grinning. "I'll be close. If they return before I do, call for me." Then she hesitated. The levity was gone from her face, and if Winter didn't know any better, she would've said the vampire looked earnest.

"You don't need him, you know," Astrid said.

"What?"

"I mean… don't take this the wrong way—I'm glad that you two found each other. Hope that you can heal whatever rifts separate you. But don't mistake your own strength for his. You're strong, Winter. Not because of Knot, or Lian or anyone. *You* are strong, and… you can do a lot. Knot can help you, and if you can, I think you should accept his help. Canta knows, you need help of some kind. But you don't need his love to be worth something. Just like you don't need what's in there," she nodded at the pouch at Winter's waist, "to be truly powerful."

Then Astrid turned, and disappeared into the forest.

# 41

EVERYONE SAT AROUND THE fading fire as Astrid and Winter told their story. Knot's hands trembled; so much had happened in the past day. Astrid had run off, he'd been thrown into a freezing river, and Winter had been taken.

But then the priestess and her Goddessguard—perhaps they were worth having along after all—had saved him, had warmed him by a fire. The group had walked all day and all night to find Winter, who'd been cooking breakfast as if nothing had happened, and Astrid, who hadn't run off after all.

And now here they all were, safe. An ugly bump on the back of Lian's head and blisters from walking all day and all night were their only injuries. Knot had expected opposition when he insisted they walk through the night, but everyone had agreed.

But the previous day was distressing for other reasons. Why did the robed men take Winter of all people? Winter and Astrid said the men had been taking Winter to Izet, the capital of Roden. Knot's final destination. Would he encounter the robed men there, again? That they rarely spoke, that they had kept such an unnatural pace for so long, made it clear that they were not normal soldiers.

And Knot could tell that both Winter and Astrid were holding things back. There were gaps in their story. Though those gaps occurred *after* Astrid and Winter had escaped the robed men. Knot needed to speak to them both alone, though he wasn't sure how.

An opportunity presented itself when Astrid stood and gathered a few waterskins to fill. They'd taken their time that morning, allowing everyone to rest after a long night of traveling, but they needed to move soon. Daylight was too valuable a resource.

Knot stood to follow Astrid. Winter and Cinzia were laughing at something Jane had just said. Lian and Kovac sat talking quietly. It was good they were all getting along. Winter seemed to have a difficult time getting along with anyone, lately, let alone humans.

Astrid noticed him following her and stopped. "Not interested in the fireside chat, nomad?" she asked.

Knot shrugged. "Need some fresh air."

Astrid laughed, continuing towards the riverbank as he caught up with her. "You need fresh air like I need a tan. What do you want to talk about?"

Knot was unsure where to start. "Thought you'd left us," he said as they reached the water.

"I did." Astrid bent down, waterskin in hand. "I just decided to come back."

The girl could be so damn frustrating.

"Thanks for noticing, by the way," Astrid said. "Good to know I was missed."

Knot grabbed her arm and turned her to face him. "I need to know I can trust you," he said.

Astrid stared back at him, her eyes afire. "You can trust me."

"Wish that was good enough," he said, "but it ain't."

"It has to be. That's all you're getting. That, and the fact that I saved your wife."

"That's why you did it? To prove your trustworthiness?"

Astrid rolled her eyes, shrugging away from his grip. "I did it because she was in danger, Knot. You're twisting this around. Don't get all twisty on me."

Knot took a breath. Astrid was right. He didn't need to make this about himself.

But it *was* about Astrid.

"You saved me in Navone," Astrid said. She tossed all but one of the waterskins to the ground and knelt, dipping the last into the river. "That's not something I just betray."

"What I heard in Brynne—"

"I don't *know* what you heard in Brynne," Astrid said, shaking her head. "It wasn't real. It didn't happen. I wish I could help you believe that. I *wish* you could trust me. I don't know how to make you see, other than to keep doing what I'm doing." She grabbed another waterskin.

Knot wasn't sure how to respond. Was she right? What else *did* he expect of her? He remembered how vulnerable she'd been in Navone. The horrific need of her embrace. He hadn't known what to do with her then, and still didn't now. He sat down on the bank next to her. The ground was cold beneath him, damp with melted snow.

"I want to do the right thing here. Just don't know what that is," he said.

They sat silently while Astrid filled the rest of the waterskins.

"You remind me of someone," she said. A slight breeze stirred the hair around her face.

*Goddess, she's so young,* he thought.

"Someone I knew a long time ago," Astrid continued. "Someone I'm not even sure... I have memories of him, but I don't remember much. I don't know his name, I don't know

411

who he was to me. But he made me feel safe."

She looked at him, strands of hair blowing across her bright green eyes. "I feel that around you," she said. "I haven't felt that way around anyone else, and... and I want to hold on to that as long as I can."

Knot nodded slowly. There were few people he'd felt safe around since waking in Pranna. Bahc had been one. Winter, at one time, had been another. Now, Knot wasn't so sure that was the case.

And Astrid. Knot wanted to trust this girl, curse of the Ventus be damned. But how could he?

They sat watching the gray water flow past. Trees covered the bank opposite them, and beyond that was only leaden, cloud-covered sky.

"How do you do it?" Astrid asked. Knot looked at her, not sure what she meant. "I mean... how do you kill people? I've seen you do it. We're both pretty sure you had a lot of experience with it, at one point. How do you do it and... and not feel anything?"

Knot shrugged. Why would Astrid care about such a thing?

"Shouldn't I ask *you* that?" he said. "Seems you might have a bit more experience."

Astrid shook her head. "I've killed hundreds of people. Sometimes I relished it, craved it. Especially in the beginning. But, lately... I feel it. Every time." She looked at him. "Why do we do what we do?"

"To survive," he said. "We make choices. Same with the people we fight. We can't control what they do, we're left with one option."

"You really believe that?"

Knot hesitated, watching the river flow. "No," he said. "No, I don't."

"I don't, either," she said. "But we end people's lives, anyway. We leave children parentless, take husbands and wives from one another. We do it because if we didn't the same would be done to us. What gives us that right?"

*Because we're better at it*, Knot wanted to say.

"Some people do not have the capacity to kill," he said instead. He didn't know where the words came from, but he'd heard them before. No, it was more than that. He'd *said* them before. "Those people, even in defense of their own lives, can not take the life of another. And society could not survive without them; they are the ones who build it. We protect them so they can build, so they don't have to fear. Others can take a life, if the situation calls for it, during war, for their Goddess, or in self-defense or the defense of those they love. They do so reluctantly, but they do it. These people become great warriors, but they carry what they do with them; the lives they take haunt them. And then there are those few who take life and feel nothing. They kill for any reason, from small and petty to great in scope and with honor. These people become villains or true heroes. They will become one or the other, there is never any middle ground."

Knot looked at Astrid. "It's not that I feel *nothing*," he said. "I don't know what I felt before, but since Pranna, I feel it, too. I crave the kill beforehand, and I regret it afterwards. I detest myself but I do it anyway."

"I know the feeling," Astrid whispered.

"Don't let go of that feeling," Knot said fervently. "If you've kept it, after all of these years, you've managed something... something incredible. Never let it go."

"Wouldn't it be best to not kill at all?" Astrid asked.

Knot shrugged. "That's a luxury I can't afford." *And a choice*

*I don't think I can make on my own anymore.*

"We'd better get back," he said. "Cover some ground while it's still daylight."

Astrid nodded. Knot helped her up, then took some of the waterskins to carry.

"One more thing," he said, as they were walking back to the camp.

"Don't ask me about your wife," Astrid said.

Knot raised his eyebrows. He *had* been about to ask about Winter. How had she known?

"It's not my place," Astrid said. "If you want to know about her, ask her yourself. I think she'll tell you. I think she needs to."

Astrid was right. He should talk to Winter himself, not go behind her back.

# 42

*Roden*

CINZIA DROPPED HER PACK to the ground with a sigh. Other than a short nap that morning, she had walked for nearly two days straight. She tried not to complain. Everyone else had done the same thing, with the exception of Winter and Astrid.

And, the night before that, Jane and Cinzia had stayed up the entire night translating. All in all, Cinzia could hardly believe she was still on her feet. She was exhausted, and yet she felt an odd sense of energy about her. If needed, Cinzia almost thought she could go another mile or two. Or stay up a few hours to translate. Or both. It might be delirium from sheer exhaustion, but she was clear-headed. And she *did* feel tired, but her strength seemed to come from something outside of herself.

Jane cleared snow from a rock and sat on it. She took off one of her boots and began rubbing a foot with both hands.

"Here," Cinzia offered, sitting in front of her sister and holding out her hand. Jane looked at her in surprise. Cinzia could not blame her; their relationship had not been cordial since they left Navone. Translating brought them together, but otherwise, the tension between them only seemed to grow.

"Thank you," Jane said, as Cinzia took her foot and began massaging it through the heavy stocking.

Cinzia smiled. "What are sisters for?"

Knot had divvied tasks among them before they stopped for the evening. Kovac and Lian were already gathering wood for a fire. The tiellan had been reluctant to be around Cinzia's Goddessguard at first, but now the two seemed to get along. Lian muttered something as they walked off into the forest, and Kovac chuckled. Cinzia smiled.

Hunting fell to Winter and Astrid; between Winter's skill with the bow and sling and the vampire's... well, the vampire did not seem to have trouble bringing in hares, squirrels, and other small game, and Cinzia was not sure she wanted to know any more than that.

Knot, Cinzia, and Jane set up the sleeping area and cleared a space for the fire. Knot carried a large canvas sheet in his pack that he sometimes strung up between trees, above their heads, if snow threatened on the horizon.

Cinzia, still massaging Jane's foot, felt her sister flinch.

"Sorry." She must have hit a tender spot. Jane's face briefly twisted in pain, but then she nodded at Cinzia.

"It's all right," Jane said. "Thank you."

"I suppose you'll want me to do the other one too?" Cinzia smiled, more genuinely this time. When they were girls, Jane could never get massaged on just one side of her body. She needed symmetry.

"You remember that?" Jane asked, lifting her other foot.

Cinzia removed Jane's boot. "Just because I was gone for seven years does not mean I've forgotten who you are."

Jane smiled, but before she could respond, Knot approached them.

"How are you both?" Knot asked. He asked them often, which impressed her despite the deadness in his eyes.

"A bit sore, but we could be worse," Cinzia said.

"Past few days have been hard. Can't promise the next few'll be any easier."

Cinzia shrugged. "We chose to accompany you." She glanced at Jane, who nodded. "We shall stay with you for a while, yet. At least until we reach the capital."

Knot's lips pursed. He looked tired. *I should feel that exhausted*, Cinzia thought to herself, looking at Knot's slumped shoulders, the circles beneath his eyes. Of course, Knot had fallen into a freezing river the day before, and that was bound to have some effect.

"Very well." Knot glanced at Jane. "As far as what we talked about earlier…?"

Jane nodded. "Yes, if you are still willing to accommodate us. Yes."

Cinzia raised an eyebrow. She had no idea what the two were talking about.

"I'll set up the canvas, then. You won't have complete privacy, but it should give you some security while still allowing warmth from the fire."

"Thank you," Jane said, smiling up at him. Knot walked away.

"What was that about?" Cinzia whispered. She finished massaging Jane's other foot, and Jane put on her boots.

"Translation," Jane said. "Just because we are in the wilderness does not mean we can take a break. We are already one night behind."

"That's why you asked Knot to set up the cover," Cinzia said.

Jane nodded. "He said he would tell the others to respect our privacy. I think they will, Cinzia. These are good people."

Cinzia frowned. She actually agreed on that point, with one exception.

"And the vampire?" she whispered.

Jane shook her head. "She is just a child."

"She is a *daemon*, Jane. What greater threat could there be?" A part of Cinzia wanted to believe Jane. Astrid seemed to have good intentions, but that did not change the girl's nature. At some point, the daemon would emerge.

"I am not sure the Sfaera is as black and white as you think. Evil and good are not one-time choices. We must choose them every day, every minute, and we all make choices that fall on both sides of the spectrum."

Jane's words had merit. The Cantic Denomination taught a strict dichotomy between good and evil, but the world Cinzia knew was not so exact. Her father had rarely attended chapel, but he was still a good man. On the contrary, many of the people who frequented Cinzia's services in Triah were some of the most despicable she knew. They attended the services, but learned nothing.

Jane was right. The world *was* full of contradictions. But Cinzia could not concede; any give on her end might make Jane think she believed in Jane's visions.

"Let's get to work, then," Cinzia said, "so we can get some translation in before we sleep."

"Wait—what was that last part?"

Cinzia looked down at the Codex. "'And it shall come to pass in those days that a great nation shall rise, greater than any that hath heretofore been seen.'" She looked at Jane. "That part?"

"Yes. Were there any symbols in that section?"

Cinzia nodded, looking back. They had kept track of the untranslatable characters, but she was beginning to suspect Jane was right. They were never mentioned in the text, and

Cinzia had not discerned any meaning from them.

She described them to her sister, anyway. There was no reason not to. If they turned out to mean nothing, then they meant nothing.

"Go on," Jane said, once she had finished recording the symbols. They sat in the makeshift tent Knot had made for them, Cinzia cross-legged by the entrance farthest from the fire, a blanket wrapped around her. The Nine Scriptures lay in front of her. Jane sat on a large rock, her back to the fire, a candle lit at her side, manuscript paper and a pen and ink on her lap.

"'And that great nation,'" Cinzia read,

shall be named after the constant star, whose light shines the brightest during all seasons, during all years, during all lifetimes. Her government shall rest upon the shoulders of many, and her religion upon the shoulders of few. At her heart shall be the learned, and their secret unions, and combinations, and societies. From the learned shall issue forth many murders, even unto the whole Sfaera.

There shall be great suffering, though they know it not.

There shall be great strife, though they see it not.

There shall be discord, and prejudice, and violence against all of Canta's children, yet her children will not suspect.

And there shall be secret wars, and whispers of wars, until that day when the small nation shall rise up against the great.

Beware that day, when the serpent rises up against the eagle.

Beware that day, when other denominations rise up against the mother.

Beware that day, when murders abound, and the slaves fear for their lives, and the Queen of Chaos rises up against the Sfaera.

For in that day shall the Daemons rise again. In that day shall the Nine return, seeking their vengeance. In that day shall the Goddess die, and her children shall weep and mourn her passing. And there shall be no comfort.

Cinzia wrapped the blanket more tightly around her shoulders. The letters shifted and blurred beneath her eyes.

"That last part…" Jane whispered. "You must have it wrong."

Cinzia willed her eyes to focus. She had read it correctly. She had yet to miss a phrase or a word. But she read it again anyway.

"'In that day shall the Goddess die, and her children shall weep and mourn her passing.'" Her voice was hoarse from reading. "'And there shall be no comfort.'"

"Are you sure?" Jane whispered.

Cinzia nodded. The words only now had begun to sink in.

"Canta's Fane," Jane repeated. "Canta's Holy Fane. It can't be true. It must mean something else, the prophecy must be twisted, a code of some sort. Where are the symbols in this passage?"

Cinzia shook her head. "There are none."

Cinzia stared at the page, the strange letters shifting and merging. Certainly no symbols. But a code…

*Perhaps…*

She flipped back a few pages. The strange metallic sheets were not flimsy, but they did not quite seem solid, either.

Concentrating on the dizzying letters, she realized it might be easier to look through the dictation instead.

They had translated two of the Disciples' books—Elessa and Baetrissa—so far, and were now working on the book of Arcana, which was easily the most confusing. The Codex seemed to follow a fairly straightforward structure. Ten "books" in all, the first nine written by each of Canta's Nine Disciples: Elessa, Baetrissa, Arcana, Cinzia, Danica, Lucia, Ocrestia, Sirana, and Valeria. The last book seemed to have been written by the mysterious Elwene who had put the book together.

Elessa and Baetrissa reviewed histories and stories Cinzia already knew, from the Creation of the Sfaera down to Soren's Folly and the Khalic Novennium. The book of Arcana, however, was baffling. Neither Cinzia nor Jane recognized a single story.

And now they'd come upon this passage.

Cinzia set the Codex aside. "Look back at your dictation," she told Jane. "Go over the part we just read, about the great nation." They needed to get to the bottom of this whole Goddess-dying business.

Jane shuffled through her notes. "'And it shall come to pass in those days, that a great nation shall rise, greater than hath heretofore been seen.'"

"That has got to be Khale," Cinzia said. "No greater nation on the Sfaera, at least not now. What did it say about the government?"

"'Her government upon the shoulders of many, her religion on the shoulders of few.'"

"Definitely sounds like Khale." Cinzia felt a thrill.

"Yes," Jane said, "this is the very definition of our republic. And the religion ruled by the few... there are nine seats on the High Camarilla?"

Cinzia nodded. "And the Camarilla is overseen by the Triunity, which has only three."

It seemed obvious that the book was referring to Khale. And not just Khale in general, but as the nation was *now*—quite specifically.

"Go on," Cinzia urged.

"At her heart shall be the learned, and their secret unions and combinations, and societies. From the learned shall issue forth many murders, even unto the whole Sfaera."

Jane looked up. "Murders?" she said. "Who are the learned?"

Cinzia nodded, tapping her index finger to her lips. "The learned must be the Citadel—they are famous for educating those in power, even in other countries, and for their scholarship. They are at the very heart of Triah, too. The murders, though… I do not know. All this about secret unions and societies makes even less sense. The Citadel is not secret."

"The Citadel isn't, but the Nazaniin are."

Cinzia paused. Winter's voice had come from outside the tent. Had she been listening the entire time?

Cinzia and Jane exchanged shrugs. The more information available, the better. Jane only cared about who *saw* the Nine Scriptures, not who heard them.

"The Nazaniin are real?" Cinzia asked loudly through the canvas. Cinzia had thought the Nazaniin were a cautionary tale told to children, until she'd met Winter and Knot. She had heard them mention the word a few times, but had not felt she could ask about it.

She leaned out of the tent. Winter sat by the fire right next to the tent—no wonder she had overheard.

"The Nazaniin *are* secret," Winter said, "and they specialize in killing people. That's about all I know, but I suppose it's more than most." Winter glanced at Knot, who was sitting nearby. What was really going on with those two?

"That fits with the text," Jane said from within the tent. Cinzia crawled back inside as Jane reread another passage.

There shall be great suffering, though they know it not.
There shall be great strife, though they see it not.
There shall be discord, and prejudice, and violence against all of Canta's children, yet her children will not suspect.

"Right," Cinzia muttered. "If what Winter says about the Nazaniin is true... it makes sense. Unseen violence."

"A dragon sleeps beneath the most peaceful time Khale has ever known," Jane said.

Cinzia raised an eyebrow. "Did I translate that? What part is that from?"

"Just an image that came to mind," Jane muttered. "I thought at first the violence referred to the tiellan rebellions, but—"

"Doesn't make sense," Astrid interrupted. Cinzia rolled her eyes. Was *everyone* listening in?

"Everyone knows about the rebellions," Astrid said. "Whatever you're reciting said 'they know it not,' 'they see it not.'"

"Do you people not have anything better to do?" Cinzia asked through the canvas. Jane was suppressing a smile.

"We don't, actually." That was Lian. "We've set up camp, found dinner, made dinner, eaten dinner, and now we're all ready for a night's rest. You two are keeping us up."

"If you actually told us what you two were doing in there,

we might be more helpful," Astrid said. Cinzia wasn't opposed to the idea. They needed help.

"All in due time," Jane said. "You each have parts to play in what comes. Each of you will realize what part that is when the time is right. Some sooner than others."

"Well if that isn't just cryptic as all Oblivion," Astrid muttered. Outside, the others laughed.

Cinzia could not help but smile. Her sister could be maddeningly enigmatic at times. She was glad to see Jane smiling, too.

Perhaps there was hope for this ragtag group, after all.

# 43

*Tir*

"WHERE ARE THE DAMN STONES?" Kali asked, rummaging through her pack.

"I already told you, I don't know," Nash said.

Kali continued digging, pulling pouches and weapons and other odds and ends out one by one. They were in Roden, finally, at an inn in Tir. They made it through the Sorensan Pass easily enough. There were rumors of a party headed by a Cantic priestess and her Goddessguard, so it seemed the group had only recently left.

She was close.

Kali knew it, could feel it. That was why she wanted to check in with Kosarin; she wanted clear orders for when she encountered Lathe again. She couldn't afford to fail this time.

Kali found the voidstones inside one of the leather pouches in her pack. Through a voidstone, any psimancer could communicate, no matter where they were on the Sfaera. Acumens, like Kali, could even see through another lacuna's eyes if the lacuna held a personalized voidstone. These forms of communication were new and highly experimental, but the Nazaniin had reaped vast benefits. Kali suspected the Cantic Denomination's psimancers had discovered communication through the Void as well; many of the Denomination's recent movements had been too organized to have been planned without instantaneous communication.

"Dahlin, approach," Kali said, reaching out to the lacuna with her mind. The man walked up to her, face blank.

*It's a shame*, she thought as she looked at the man. *He would have made a much more pleasing companion if I had more time to brand him.* Dahlin was handsome: tall, with dark hair and a sculpted face. He looked like a statue. An ancient, deific work of art.

*And I destroyed him,* Kali thought, not without pleasure. *I snuffed his life away, and now he is mine.* It was business, of course, but Kali couldn't help but feel the rush. She had never felt so powerful, so in control, as she did when making another being her own.

"You're contacting him now?" Nash said.

"Of course. Now's as good a time as any. I don't want any misunderstandings."

"You've adjusted the formula for the new lacuna? There weren't any problems?"

"Yes I have, and no, there weren't. Relax."

Nash nodded reluctantly. He wouldn't press the issue. There was too much at stake. As much as Kali enjoyed Nash's company—as much as she respected him as a psimancer—she sometimes wondered about his commitment.

She turned back to the lacuna, pulling out one of the voidstones from the pouch. It was pale white in color, with a black-painted design on one side, a series of slash marks forming a rough-edged rune.

Kali placed the stone in the lacuna's hand, and then backed away. Reaching into the bag once more, she pulled out a complimentary stone, this one charcoal black and its marks chalky white. She tossed the pouch on the bed behind her, holding the small stone in her hand.

Kali did not know why voidstones possessed such power. They had first been discovered, decades ago, in the catacombs of the Citadel in Triah. After that, Nazaniin agents began discovering voidstones throughout the Sfaera, bringing them back to the capital to be studied. Their origin and method of creation was unknown. Some speculated the stones dated as far back as the Starless Era. Others posited that they had always existed. Some thought the stones gifts from Canta and her angels—a ridiculous theory, in Kali's opinion, but popular nonetheless. Kali wasn't sure where they came from. But she did suspect they were only just scratching the surface of the stones' potential.

As she clutched the voidstone, Kali found her other hand moving to her chest. But the parchment was gone. She needed to get used to that.

Kali opened her mind, and immediately she was in the Void. An aptly named place, metaphysical or not, for all around Kali was blackness. Some claimed it was darkness, but it was more than that. The Void was more tangible than shadow, less malleable. This darkness did not retreat; it devoured light.

Kali's presence swept through the Void. Small lights appeared, pinpoints in the distance, like stars in the night sky. The holes in the Void passed beside her, above her, below her, around her, quickly and silently. Most were white. More rarely there were blue pinpricks, purple spaces, red holes and green glows in the sea of black. Kali concentrated on the stone in her hand, or rather the stone in her body's hand back in Roden. Then, directly in front of her, another pinpoint of light appeared, approaching her rapidly. She was traveling through a tunnel, spiraling down it faster than light itself, until—

Kali was in Triah. Beneath the Citadel, in the headquarters

of the Nazaniin, in the room psimancers had recently deemed the Heart of the Void.

This chamber was the central meeting place for the Nazaniin. Even at night, candles, torches, and lamps shone brightly. The floor was made of alternating white, black, and red tiles, and it was equipped with long tables and chairs painted in the same colors. Cabinets and bookcases lined the walls.

"Rune said you would contact us," a familiar voice said. "I had hoped he was wrong, for once."

Kali turned—or, rather, the body she now possessed turned—to see Sirana standing directly behind her.

Kali frowned. She brought her forearm diagonally across her chest in the salute of the Nazaniin, although her movement was casual. Sirana was a powerful psimancer, and that Kali could respect. But she was too emotional. Too willing to let her feelings get in the way of the mission. How Kosarin had overlooked those flaws, Kali did not understand.

"Where's Kosarin?" Kali asked, hearing her voice meld with the familiar low baritone of Kosarin's personal lacuna. Only a few people had direct access to it; she was one. Sirana was another.

"He's busy," Sirana said. "What is it you need, Kali?"

Sirana looked older than the last time Kali had seen her. Pale, almost withered. Her short red hair wasn't as neat as Kali remembered; stray strands fell from a messy bun into the woman's eyes. Her clothing was disheveled, and there were dark circles under her eyes. But the eyes themselves were the same penetrating green as always.

Sirana was one of the most powerful of the Nazaniin, but she was getting old. Kali's mouth twitched. A pity Sirana wasn't the acumen in the Triad; otherwise Kali could think of a perfect replacement. As a telenic, Sirana would only be able to see Kali's vague image imprinted over the lacuna in Triah—she would be unable to see through Dahlin's eyes, here, in Tir.

*Everything in due time,* Kali told herself.

"We've crossed into Roden in pursuit of Lathe and his companions. I want to update Kosarin on our situation and confirm our orders."

Sirana stared at her for a moment. The woman was sizing Kali up, deliberating. Kali could feel it, along with something else, something Sirana was hiding.

"It's fortunate you've contacted us," Sirana finally said. "Your orders have changed."

Kali kept her face expressionless.

"In light of the events in Navone, we have concluded that, whatever Lathe's intentions are, he cannot be allowed to continue on his current path. Your orders are to execute him and bring his body back to us."

A surge of anticipation burst through Kali. She had known, from the moment she had been assigned this mission, that it would end this way. She would confront the most powerful Nazaniin agent in history.

She would confront him, and kill him.

"And the Harbinger?" Kali asked. The girl was special. Kali had accepted that. She had even come to respect Winter, despite her tiellan blood.

"Kill them all," Sirana said, her voice hard. "The girl is not the Harbinger. We've come to a consensus about that, at least. Kill her, kill Lathe, kill anyone with them, and come home. Those are your orders, Nazaniin."

Kali blinked. Kill Winter? Surely that was folly. The girl was the Harbinger. She had to be. A knot of worry twisted in Kali's chest. She and Winter had much in common. Killing her would be... difficult.

Something about the way Sirana gave the order bothered Kali; she had not met Kali's eyes. Strange. Sirana, while she let her emotions rule her sometimes, was not soft. She never balked, neither in giving nor in taking orders. Of course, Kali could understand why. Sirana was ordering Lathe's execution. But business was business. Emotion had no place in it.

"Are you sure, *Triada?*"

Sirana looked away from the lacuna.

"They're of no use to us," she said evenly. "Kill Lathe, kill his companions. Those are your orders. Do you have a problem, Nazaniin?"

"No, *Triada,*" Kali said. "I must obey." As always, Kali would do as she was commanded. If Kali could not rely on obedience, what else was there?

Just as Kali was about to return to the Void and her own body, the large double-doors to Sirana's right opened and Kosarin walked into the chamber.

"Good evening, *Triadin.*" Sirana saluted him.

"*Triadin,*" Kali said, also offering the Nazaniin salute—her movement crisp and clear as she snapped her forearm across her chest.

Kosarin Lothgarde, the Venerato of the Citadel, was one of the most powerful men in the Sfaera, and only part of that power came from being the director of the Citadel. His real power emanated from his post as leader of the Nazaniin, and one of the most powerful acumens in recorded history.

"Kali," Kosarin said, his deep, drawling voice echoing through the chamber, "good you checked in. We were hoping you would. Your new body is young, I see." He looked Kali—

or, rather, the image of Kali projected through the lacuna—up and down. Kosarin himself wasn't young, though he still had a surprisingly powerful build. He kept his head shaven, but grew a short circle beard around his mouth.

"Yes, *Triadin*," Kali said.

Kosarin looked at her, blue eyes glinting behind silver spectacles. "There were no problems with the transformation?"

Kali smiled inwardly, noting the eagerness in his voice. She had hoped to make her report to him if only to tell him about her most recent transformation.

"It all went smoothly, *Triadin*," she said. "The previous body was destroyed, but I still managed to return without a prolonged hiatus."

Kosarin's gray eyebrows rose as he lowered his head to look at Kali above his spectacles. "The body was destroyed *while you were in it?*"

"Yes, *Triadin*," Kali said, unable to stop the pride in her voice. "I was fortunate to sense what was happening before I lost consciousness, and it took me a while to regain myself in this body, but it worked." What she said wasn't entirely true; she hadn't sensed the massive globe coming towards her at all, but she had somehow woken up in Elsi's body, anyway. She figured that was an aspect she would keep to herself, for now, until she figured out exactly what had happened. She wasn't comfortable with everyone knowing how close she had truly come to death.

"How long?" Kosarin asked.

"Two days."

Kosarin nodded slowly. "Very good. You've accomplished something unprecedented; I'd like a full report as soon as you return to Triah."

Kali nodded, excitement building within her. It was finally happening. She was receiving the recognition she deserved. The sight of Sirana rolling her eyes made Kali want to grin.

"I will, *Triadin*. Nash and I should catch up to Lathe and his company within the next few days. After eliminating them, we will return to Triah as quickly as possible."

"Ah," Kosarin said, glancing at Sirana with a half-smile. "I see you didn't hold back. Very good. I admit I was worried that you wouldn't be able to deliver the orders given your history with one of the targets. I'm pleased you overcame your sensibilities."

Sirana said nothing, and Kali's sense of elation burned all the brighter.

"If you will excuse me, I have matters requiring my attention." Sirana walked quickly out, via a side door of red lacquered paint.

"I'm afraid I upset her," Kosarin said, sighing. "It wasn't my intention."

If Kosarin ever accomplished anything without first intending to do so, then Kali was a puff-tailed goat. "Permission to speak candidly, *Triadin*."

"Granted," Kosarin said, moving to a central table, stacked with papers, books, and a large map. There were no boundaries on the map, Kali noticed. Not between Khale and Maven Kol or Alizia, and certainly not between Khale and Roden.

*Odd.*

She had to be careful with what she would say next. Being too bold could mark her as a potential target, but to not make herself clear would be useless at best, and would earn Kosarin's wrath at worst. But, if Sirana would not answer her questions, perhaps Kosarin would.

"*Triadin*, my orders are to eliminate Lathe and his

companions, including the tiellan woman we once presumed to be the Harbinger."

"And?"

Kali hesitated—questioning an order was bad form, but in this case she felt she had to make an exception. "*Triadin*, if you don't mind me asking, what has led us to believe that the girl is *not* the Harbinger? I have seen her power, sensed her potential, and it is beyond anything I have ever seen before. And she is tiellan, sir."

"The prophecies are changing, Kali. You know it. I know it. We have known it for some time, now. This girl… she is powerful, yes. Rune has seen it, and he has shown me. But she is not the Harbinger. Other tests must be passed, other paths taken, before the true Harbinger reveals itself."

"Very well, sir." The bitter disappointment Kali felt was surprising.

*She's just a tiellan,* Kali told herself. *Remember that.* Kali touched the place where the parchment had once rested in the pocket near her breast. She would remember. She would remember, and obey. Orders were orders.

"Is that all, Kali?"

"No, sir," Kali said. "I have one more concern."

"Go ahead."

Kali took a deep breath. This was it. This could be her moment. "As competent as Sirana is, *Triadin*, she has a personal investment in this mission. Is her involvement wise?"

Kosarin looked at her with his crystal-blue eyes, and Kali suddenly panicked. Was he excavating her? Excavation should be impossible over such a distance, but she had heard things about the *Triadin*, impossible things… The image Kali projected onto the lacuna was only that, an image—her body and mind were still far away in Roden. And yet the way he looked at her…

Then Kosarin chuckled, a short bark of a laugh, his large shoulders shaking up and down.

"The ambition of youth," he said. "Inconsistencies? Of course I've noticed them. Sirana was never perfect. Neither am I. But we should oblige her, should we not? She has been through a great deal, if you haven't forgotten."

Kali frowned. Of course she knew what Sirana had been through. That was why she was unfit to lead. Nevertheless… "I'm sorry, sir. I didn't mean any disrespect."

"I'm sure you did not," Kosarin said, in a such a way that made Kali think the man was sure of the exact opposite. "Your ambition is good, Kali. Don't lose that. You're one of the most gifted psimancers I've seen in decades. But you still need to respect the offices of the Triad. Do not lose sight of our structure."

Kali nodded, looking at the tiled floor.

"And don't forget," Kosarin continued, the humor gone, "that Sirana could still best you in a psimantic duel."

Kali resisted the urge to raise her eyebrows. Any Nazaniin knew that a trained acumen could take on a trained telenic in just about any scenario. If there was another acumen more powerful than her within the Nazaniin, besides Kosarin himself, she would be surprised.

"You don't believe me, and that's all right," Kosarin said. "But just remember that Sirana has had years of experience fighting acumens, telenics, even voyants. And she has had *me* as a teacher. So, as powerful as you are, my dear, I'm afraid she still outranks you. In every way."

Kali stood her ground, face reddening. She wasn't sure how much of her blush the *Triadin* would see in her projected image, but she was sure he would sense her emotion, whether he saw it or not.

"Don't despair. You are right, to an extent—Sirana hasn't been at her best, lately. You still have much to learn, but believe me—if you *do* take the time to learn it, you will go far. But remember your most important rival will not be Sirana. There can only be one acumen in the Triad at a time, Kali. I don't plan on stepping down anytime soon."

Kali nodded. Her cheeks and ears still burned from embarrassment, but she looked up to meet his eyes. He was right; her rivalry with Sirana was petty. And, while she felt some of her pride returning at Kosarin's praise, she felt humbled, as well. She was a powerful acumen, but was she powerful enough to challenge *him*?

Her assignment was a test of sorts. If any telenic could rival Sirana's power, it was Lathe. And it was Kali's duty to kill him. Kali would not fail.

"Don't worry, sir," Kali said. "I'll get the job done."

"That's all we ask," Kosarin said, smiling. Then he waved her away, already turning his attention from her to the papers on the table in front of him.

Kali began the process of extracting her projection from the lacuna, but then heard Kosarin's voice.

"Kali," he said, not even looking up, "when I give you an order to kill Lathe and his companions, I mean to *kill* them. Quickly and simply. This is business and business only; I know how your mind works. Do I make myself clear?"

"Yes, *Triadin*," Kali said, her throat dry.

"Very good," Kosarin said. "Now go. I have work to do."

Kali nodded, and within seconds she was back in the Void.

# 44

*Roden*

Cinzia lay awake, tossing and turning. She should be exhausted, and yet all she felt was a strange sense of invigoration. The blisters on her feet, the soreness of her legs, none of it mattered.

"Cinzia?" Jane whispered in the dark. The fire beside them had faded to glowing embers long ago.

"Yes?" Cinzia could barely see Jane's outline against the glowing coals.

"I cannot stop thinking about what we translated today," Jane whispered. "All of those 'bewares'..."

Cinzia nodded. The same lines echoed in her mind as well. "'When the serpent rises up against the eagle,'" Cinzia said quietly. They could both remember lines from the Codex surprisingly well. "That must mean Roden and Khale."

"Why? Khale's sigil is the gryphon."

"It was the eagle first. King Artis VI changed it to the gryphon. Ironically, we did not have the gryphon on our sigil until the animal itself became extinct."

Jane made a small *hmph* sound.

"What?" Cinzia whispered. "We learned *some* useful stuff at the seminary."

"But if she—Arcana—saw *our* day, why reference the sigil we had a thousand years ago instead of the one now?"

Cinzia shrugged. It was a good question. "But the serpent

makes sense, too. Roden's sigil is the dragon."

"Khale and Roden have fought for centuries. She could be referring to any of those conflicts."

"Or to a war yet to come," Cinzia whispered. "She referred to a secret war earlier in the book."

Cinzia's eyes had adjusted to the darkness now, and she realized she was looking directly into Jane's eyes.

"Did we walk into the middle of a war?" Jane asked.

"We are here by Canta's will, are we not? The revelation I received in Navone... Canta commanded us to come."

It was more of a question than Cinzia intended it to be. And, she realized, it was the first time either of them had brought up the strange event since it had happened.

"I do not know, Cinzia."

And, just like that, the seed of doubt that Cinzia had carried around in her chest since Navone blossomed like a midwinter rose.

What had she done?

"We should discuss that another time," Jane whispered. "The passage we read today bothers me far more."

For a moment Cinzia wanted to scream. How could Jane do this? How could Jane let Cinzia lead them into Roden—into *Roden*, of all places—when she was not even sure it was the right thing to do?

Slowly, Cinzia calmed herself. Deep breaths. She had no right to criticize Jane. They had needed to get away from Navone, away from the Denomination, and Cinzia took the only path open to them. She had done what she needed to do.

"Arcana warned of other religions," Jane whispered, oblivious to Cinzia's inner turmoil, "who rise up against the mother."

Cinzia sighed. It all came down to this. Somewhere inside her she knew, this was her moment. This was her time to call Jane out, to accuse her of rebelling against the Denomination. The Nine Scriptures themselves said so.

But Cinzia hesitated. She had experienced her own vision. She was translating the Nine Scriptures, for Canta's sake. What did that mean? How did that fit into this puzzle? She looked at Jane, knowing this was her chance, her opportunity to express how she felt. She was watching it pass her by.

They both remained silent for a moment. Finally, Jane spoke. "It seems we both have something we want to refrain from discussing," she whispered.

Cinzia smiled up at her sister sadly. "Some pair we make."

Silence. Cinzia almost thought that Jane had fallen asleep, when her sister spoke again.

"The last part, Cinzia… about the Queen of Chaos, about servants fearing for their lives, what is that about?"

Cinzia sighed, trying to calm herself.

"It probably refers to tiellans," Cinzia said. "Although why they would fear for their lives, I do not know."

"Do not be naive, sister," Jane said. "Despite the Emancipation, they are still not treated as equals. Winter and Lian both said attitudes towards tiellans are becoming more cruel. They are moving to the cities, now, where they can at least band together."

Jane was right. Cinzia did not like to think about it, but tiellans were *not* treated as equals. Cinzia had conditioned herself to ignore such things, but there it was when she looked for it. "Perhaps the persecution of tiellans will escalate even further," she whispered.

A cold lump formed in Cinzia's stomach. She had never thought tiellans deserved their lot; she had certainly never considered them evil, as many had. The hatred towards tiellans was rooted in fear, as hatred often was. During the Age of Marvels tiellans had been powerful, wielding magics and great enchanted weapons. Humans had yet to develop such wonders. If tiellans ever discovered the truth behind the legends, they could dramatically upset the status quo. Cinzia could understand fearing such a thing; that did not mean she approved of the hate.

"What about the Queen of Chaos?" Cinzia asked, shaking her head. "Do you know anything about that?" Her sister did not respond. "Jane? Do you know what the Queen of Chaos is? Or who?"

Jane's face was pale. Finally she shook her head. She would not meet Cinzia's eyes, instead looking off into darkness. "I don't think so."

Cinzia frowned, not convinced, but then Jane changed the subject.

"The last section," Jane said. She sighed. "About the daemons, and about Canta…"

"The daemons shall rise again?" A chill ran down Cinzia's spine. "What kind of daemons?" Daemons were only tangential to Cantic doctrine; there were vampires and other creatures of the night, considered part-daemon. But true daemons, the stuff of legends and bedtime stories, had not existed for millennia.

Jane shook her head. "It says the Nine shall rise again. The Nine Disciples? Why would they seek vengeance on Canta's children?"

Cinzia frowned. "Perhaps for what they did to their Goddess." Canta's life on the Sfaera had ended when she was tortured and murdered by her own children.

"Or… it could be referring to the Nine Daemons," Jane whispered. "The Daemons from the beginning."

"There are daemons even daemons fear; always at night they gather near."

Cinzia had not said the words; nor had Jane. Fear was suddenly a desperate man drowning in Cinzia's chest, flailing and struggling. Then, a green glow illuminated the sisters.

Astrid sat beside them, her eyes like dull green fires. Like the fire of Cinzia's revelation in Navone.

"Where in Oblivion did you come from?" Cinzia gasped, breathing for the first time, she realized, since the girl had said the words.

"You two really have a privacy problem. You can't expect people not to eavesdrop when you're chatting like two grandmothers at a baby's nameday party."

Cinzia shivered. She was familiar with the adage, of course. *Daemons even daemons fear.* And now, with a vampire sitting next to her and thoughts of the Nine Daemons on her mind, Cinzia realized what the children's rhyme might actually mean. Stories were often based in truth. Perhaps the truth here was far more literal than she had thought.

"Do you know what daemons the passage refers to?" Cinzia asked.

"I know that I have nightmares of my own," Astrid said quietly, "that are far more terrifying than anything I've seen in the waking world."

"There are daemons even daemons fear," Cinzia repeated.

Astrid shrugged. "Or I'm just crazy. Who knows. Anyway, you two should get some sleep. Only a few hours 'til dawn."

Then the girl was gone. Whether she had gone to her own bedroll, or out into the forest, Cinzia did not know.

"Astrid is right," Jane whispered. "We need rest."

Cinzia nodded, but fear still crawled beneath her skin. Did

Jane feel the same thing? How could she not?

"Very well. See you in the morning, sister." Cinzia lay back. She needed sleep, but finding it after such a scare was unlikely.

Then Jane's hand grasped her own beneath their blankets.

"I love you, Cinzi," Jane said.

With her sister's touch came a wave of comfort. Not enough to quell Cinzia's fears completely, but enough. Enough to get her through the night.

"I love you, Jane."

Cinzia closed her eyes, waiting for dawn to break.

# PART IV

## DAEMONS EVEN
## DAEMONS FEAR

# 45

*Outskirts of Izet, Roden*

As Knot approached Izet, he half-expected the ethereal blackness of his dreams to loom in the distance, with sparks and bursts of strange color, or to see the blue light shine brightly, high above all. But there was just the blue sky and the sun, snowcapped rolling fields around them, mountains in the distance, gray and white and sharp as daggers. And, at the joining of two rivers at the Gulf of Nahl, a city.

Hundreds of flat, squat huts with snow capped roofs spread out before Knot. The city spilled outside its main protective wall and into the surrounding countryside. Within the wall were more squat buildings, rarely any taller than two stories except for the massive dome of the imperial palace rising above the city near the sea.

Knot had seen Triah, or at least remembered the city from his dreams, and in almost every way that city put this one to shame. Izet's imperial dome, however, was breathtaking.

They had barely reached the outskirts of the city; huts and houses were dotted sporadically on patches of land, animal pens and fences sprawling around them. The closer the houses were to the city wall, the more packed together they were.

Knot had asked Cinzia and Kovac to shed their Cantic livery before entering the city. He worried the clothing would draw attention. It had been useful in crossing the border, but a Cantic priestess and her entourage would turn heads. They still had the clothing, should they need it, but Knot had a feeling they would not. His gut told him so. And, if he'd learned one thing in the past year, it was to trust his gut.

Winter and Lian wore large hoods, covering their ears, but Knot knew their group looked suspicious. Three people with their hoods up in the middle of a sunny day—Astrid wore hers too, of course—wasn't normal. But it was cold, and Knot hoped that would be enough of an excuse.

Knot rubbed his temples. Another headache was forming. He could almost sense when they were coming, now. The odd tingling, directly behind his eyes, eventually progressed to a full-blown pounding throughout his skull. The worst ones felt as if his forehead were on a chopping block being repeatedly split by a blunt axe.

Winter's arm brushed against his own, and Knot flexed his hand, feeling a tingle work its way up to his shoulder. Winter's spirits seemed to have lifted since her kidnapping; she was more talkative, more open. Knot had actually seen her speak to everyone in the group, including the other humans, without scowling or snapping at them, which seemed a step in the right direction.

Fortunately, Knot was no exception. She almost treated him like she had when they were courting, before their marriage. Knot was grateful, but he also wondered where the new attitude was coming from. Winter was different in so many ways. Knot still had trouble getting used to her tight leather clothing. There'd been a few times when he had to consciously stop himself staring. The only thing that seemed to remain of the girl he had known was the dark stone necklace around her neck. The same necklace she'd worn the day they were married.

Knot reached back and lightly touched the bundle of cloth wrapped around his sword. He had yet to use it, but he was strangely comforted by the fact that it was there. *Just do what you always do,* he told himself. *Keep going forward. Everything else'll fall into place.*

Hopefully.

At first, as they approached the city wall, they barely noticed the sound: a low hum, almost a vibration. As they drew closer, the hum escalated. The hum of a crowd.

"Canta's breath," Lian said beside him. "Hope this ain't another execution. Why do we always arrive in cities during a party?"

Knot glanced at Winter, whose face was tense and pale.

"What's wrong with her?" Astrid said. "Looks like she's just seen one of the Nine Daemons."

Both Cinzia and Jane looked up sharply. Knot frowned. He knew that whatever the two had been translating—he had heard them discuss the Nine Scriptures, but was slow to believe it—talked about daemons, and monsters, and prophecies. Knot didn't care for whatever in Oblivion it was. He had more immediate concerns. But the two women did seem jumpy.

Knot looked back at Winter. Thinking back on the destruction she'd witnessed in Navone must be painful. Tentatively he reached out. She flinched as he placed his hand on her shoulder, but she didn't shrug him off. She didn't look back at him, either, but at least she didn't push him away.

The streets grew crowded as they approached the imperial palace. They walked along a wide street, in the wake of a mass of people.

The Rodenese were tall. Most of the women were almost as tall as Knot, some taller, and most of the men dwarfed him by more than a head. They were fair, too, light of hair and eye.

They arrived at a massive avenue leading directly to the huge domed palace. The road was paved, wide enough for three or four wagons to pass each other easily. People crowded the sides of the street, overflowing into connecting roads, waiting impatiently.

Winter stepped up beside him. "Should we ask what is going on?" She seemed nervous; these crowds were definitely reminding her of Navone.

Knot looked around. It seemed the people watching from the road were commoners, for the most part, bundled in dull wool coats and jackets. As Knot looked up, he saw many others watching from the balconies of the buildings that lined the street. These people were obviously of a higher class, wearing colorful tunics and long, form-fitting coats. Curiously, the men who watched from the balconies seemed to all have clean-shaven faces. A strange habit for the upper class, and impractical for such a climate. But, then again, the nobility that Knot had known—or that Lathe had known, he supposed—never cared much for practicality.

After shaving in Navone, Knot had regrown his beard. Fortunately the common men around him seemed to care less about shaving their whiskers than the nobles, many of them wearing full beards. Knot didn't want to showcase the fact that they were foreigners. The robed men had planned on bringing Winter here, after all. Attracting attention was a bad idea on all fronts. But Winter was right. They needed to understand what was going on.

To Knot's surprise, Astrid took the initiative.

"Excuse me," the girl said. Knot turned to see Astrid tugging at the hem of a woman's skirt, looking up at the tall, straw-haired woman expectantly.

"Oh my," the woman said, looking around. "Are you all right? Lost your family?"

"No, they're close by," Astrid said. Knot was surprised by her accent; she spoke with the clipped rhythm of the Rodenese perfectly. "Why are all these people here?"

"Your parents haven't told you? Poor child." The woman's eyes settled on Knot. He felt more than a little disdain boring into him.

"This is the parade of glory," the woman said with a smile, looking back down at Astrid. "The emperor and all of the finest lords are here, and the high priestess and every matron in Roden. Even the Ceno are here," the woman said, almost muttering to herself, now. "Although the emperor isn't too happy about that."

"What's a Ceno?" Astrid asked.

Knot received another disapproving glare. "A Ceno," the woman said, "is a monk of our new religion. Some of us are tired of belonging to the religion of our enemies. We've returned to our old gods, seeking their protection."

"Oh," Astrid said.

Suddenly trumpets blared from the direction of the massive domed palace in the distance. People began talking more loudly, voices rising in excitement.

Astrid scurried away from the woman and resumed her place at Knot's side. He made sure everyone else was close—Winter and Lian were on his other side, Jane, Cinzia, and Kovac behind him—and moved with the rest of the crowd to the edge of the road.

"Should we even stay for this?" Winter whispered beside him. "I thought we wanted to avoid attention."

"We do," Knot said. "Sometimes the best place to hide is out in the open. And might be we could learn something from this."

A low, steady drumbeat sounded in the distance. Murmurs of excitement flowed around them like water, from person to person and parent to child. Every eye looked to the palace, at the opening gates.

A large, colorful wagon pulled by a team of horses rolled out of the gateway. Four soldiers marched in front of the horses, dressed in the sky-blue of Roden.

The wagon was huge. Even from this distance Knot could see that it towered above the soldiers, at least three or four times their height. It was oddly shaped too, elongated. A section jutted over the horses, a fabricated animal head of some kind.

"Holy Oblivion," Winter said.

"What *is* that?" Astrid asked.

"It's a dragon," Jane whispered behind him.

Before Knot could say anything, a deep roar sounded from the wagon and Knot looked back just in time to see a jet of bright orange flame burst outwards from the head of the giant beast. The crowd burst into a chorus of oohs and ahs.

The wagon moved slowly down the road behind the four soldiers. It really did look like a dragon, fierce and horned, with wild painted eyes and a gaping, fanged mouth. The head trailed forward over the horses on a long neck, swinging slowly back and forth. Wings of cloth and wood framing spread out from the body of the wagon, casting large shadows over the crowd on either side. It was, for the most part, ice-blue, similar to the uniforms worn by the soldiers. The entire thing was constructed of wood and metal, hinges and interlocking plates.

The dragon spouted another cone of flame, this time blue in color, and the crowd cheered even louder.

"Canta rising," Cinzia whispered beside him. Something in her voice made Knot turn. She stared at the dragon, her face pale, lips slightly parted. Jane whispered something in her sister's ear, and Cinzia nodded slowly.

As the soldiers and the dragon drew closer, Knot observed shiny steel plate armor, glinting in the sunlight, beneath sky-blue tabards. The soldiers carried long spears and large, diamond-shaped shields painted the same sky-blue.

The dragon towered above the soldiers, blocking the sun with one of its dark-blue wings. Knot felt the heat of another blast of blue flame, and wondered what sort of pyromancy produced the effect. When he looked closely, he saw creaking wheels behind the beast's large, cumbersome legs. The crowd cheered and applauded as the dragon lumbered past.

*An oversized puppet*, Knot thought, *that breathes fire*. The huge tail, nearly the entire length again of the rest of the body, swung listlessly behind the construction.

Behind the tail marched ranks of drummers and trumpeters. Knot counted thirty in all, as their instruments, of many varying sizes, filled the air with sound. Each player wore tight white trousers, a light-blue tunic, and a strange white cap that covered only the top of their head. They looked straight ahead, blowing through brass horns and banging large drums in perfect time. Behind them a troupe of dancers, jesters, and acrobats moved in time with the deep drumbeats.

"They've got to be freezing their asses off," Lian said behind him.

It was true; Knot could see his breath in front of his face, but the dancers, male and female, twirling and leaping past, wore little more than transparent silks and mesh. Probably working hard enough to stay warm, at least, though Knot doubted they were given a choice.

"One of the costs of living in an empire," Knot said. "A lot less opportunity to say 'no.'"

Behind the array of performers and acrobats marched more soldiers. Knot knew these on sight. Reapers. Instead of the sky-blue of most Rodenese soldiers and banners, they wore midnight-blue and dark-gray lacquered armor. Each man carried a round shield and a melee weapon: heavy axes with curved blades and spikes, morningstars, maces with heavy iron heads, and warhammers. At their waists, each carried a longsword and a dagger.

The Reapers were Roden's elite soldiers. Each man was trained from birth to fight and kill, alone and in formation, in the name of the emperor. They marched in perfect ranks behind the performers. The strange chaos and movement of the dancers contrasted starkly to the order of the Reapers' march.

Behind the Reapers came another wagon, one that Knot would have called massive had it not been for the huge dragon that came before. This one was also shaped as a dragon, albeit more subtly than its predecessor; six white horses, draped in blue, preceded it, their shoulders almost as tall as Knot stood.

At the top of the wagon stood someone Knot *did* recognize. Knot had seen the man's strong jaw, cold eyes, and shining bald head in his dreams.

Emperor Grysole.

A Reaper guarded each corner of the wagon, while the emperor stood at the peak of a small pyramid in the middle of the rolling dais. He wore a long, fur-lined cloak of sky-blue, underneath which gilded plate glinted in the sunlight, forcing Knot to squint. Emperor Grysole waved lazily at the crowd.

"Who is that?" Winter asked.

"The emperor," Knot said. "I... I know him."

Winter looked sharply at Knot. "You know him? You mean you remember him?"

Knot shook his head. "Not exactly. Seen him in my dreams, but never recognized him or put a name to his face. Now that I'm seeing him here, in person... I *do* remember him."

"What are we supposed to do about that?" she whispered. "How do you know the emperor of Roden?"

"Don't know," Knot said, hesitating. "But I don't think we're friends."

Behind the emperor came another formation of Reapers, marching perfectly in time. Then, on another large wagon, stood a woman in a crimson dress.

"The high priestess of Roden," Cinzia whispered. "Highest ranking clergywoman in the empire." The Trinacrya embroidered on the high priestess's dress was the only contrast to the flowing scarlet fabric. If the emperor had been lazy when waving at the masses, the high priestess was downright disdainful. A formation of Goddessguards and priestesses marched around her wagon, dressed in Canta's red-and-white.

"Below her stand the matrons," Cinzia said. "Dressed in white."

Knot saw the women Cinzia indicated on the wagon a few pedestals lower than the high priestess. The Cantic Denomination's hierarchy was strict: priestesses reported to matrons, who in turn reported to a high priestess, who reported to the High Camarilla itself—and that was only the priesthood. The Arm of Inquisition and the Mind of Revelation had their own separate structures.

The crowd quieted significantly as the Cantic procession

passed. Many still shouted their adoration, but others remained quiet, glaring at the wagon and the red-and-white-clad women.

As the tail end of the procession approached, the crowd burst into the loudest applause and shouting yet.

No wagons rolled with this last section; only a small wooden chariot drawn by two healthy but plain-looking geldings. A cluster of seemingly normal citizens preceded the chariot. Worn and dirtied farmers, blacksmiths and butchers still wearing their aprons, merchants in fine-fitting suits. Two figures stood in the chariot, one hooded and one not. Both wore familiar dark-green robes. Knot recognized the unhooded man immediately by his long blond hair.

It was the Tokal.

"Knot—" Winter whispered.

"Ease back into the crowd," he said. "Hide your faces best you can." It was unlikely that anyone could pick out their faces in such a mass of people; there had to be thousands lining the avenue. But Knot had never been keen on taking chances.

Behind the chariot walked another cluster of figures, all robed in dark green. Knot's chest tightened. His heart pumped through his chest. If the men noticed them, if they recognized Knot or Winter, the game was up.

"Who are they?" Cinzia whispered as they watched the group pass.

"Must be the Ceno," Knot said under his breath. By the sound of the crowd's cheers, this had to be the group the woman had spoken of to Astrid. "Roden's new religion."

"*Old* religion," Astrid corrected him. "They sure seem popular." The crowd cheered even more loudly for this group than for the emperor.

"If they're a new—er, newly reformed—religion," Jane

asked, "why hasn't the High Camarilla sent a Holy Crucible here?"

"Roden's laws are different," Cinzia said. "The Denomination can regulate religion in Khale because our government gave them that power. In Roden, other religions are allowed. Canticism only became the major religion by default, when the Azure Empire was formed."

The robed men passed by, and slowly Knot relaxed. They hadn't been noticed—or, if they had, no one had done anything about it.

Another group of trumpeters and drummers marched by, followed by another group of sky-blue-clad soldiers in formation, and then the parade moved down the street, out of sight. The gates of the imperial palace had been closed, and the crowd in front of it was already dispersing. The crowd around Knot were chattering excitedly. Knot watched them and for a brief moment his eyes met those of a young boy on his father's shoulders. The boy looked at Knot openly, eyes wide, pale hair blowing in the wind.

Within Knot, something stirred. He felt an odd sense of protectiveness. The boy's father lifted him easily from his shoulders, tossed him into the air and caught the child in his arms. The boy giggled, and then Knot lost sight of them in the crowd.

Knot wasn't sure how to explain what he felt, but... he *wanted* that. He wanted to toss his own children up into the air and—

No. He didn't *want* it. He *missed* it.

Knot shook his head, uncertain where the feelings came from. What the Tokal had told him along the River Arden still echoed in his mind. *A creation of science and magic...*

Behind him, Lian and Winter were whispering quietly. Winter looked at Knot.

"That was close," she said. "Do you think they noticed us?"

Knot chewed his cheek. "No way to be certain. If they did, they didn't do anything about it."

"We need to get out of the main street, nomad," Astrid said. "We're not safe out in the open."

Knot turned away from the procession. "Let's go find a place to stay."

They found their way onto a small side street, leading away from the massive avenue.

"You recognized the emperor," Winter said as they walked.

Knot nodded. He knew what he had to do, now. Green-robed men or no, he at least had an idea of where to begin.

"I need to speak with him," Knot said.

Winter's eyes widened. "With the *emperor*? Are you out of your mind?"

Knot laughed and it felt empty. *Of course I'm out of my mind,* he thought. *I'm not sure I ever remember being sane.*

"This is the closest thing to a lead I've had since arriving in Roden. Need to see where it takes me."

"What's this?" Lian asked from beside Winter. "You want to see who?"

Knot knew the idea was madness. He also knew that it was exactly what he needed to do.

"What?" Lian asked. "If we're seeing someone, I'd like to know who. Just for, you know, security purposes."

"He wants to see the emperor," Winter said quietly, looking around. Knot had already made sure they weren't being followed, but he felt good knowing Winter worried about it as well.

"The who? You mean that man riding the ridiculous dragon, with the hundreds of guards around him? *That* emperor?"

Astrid slipped between them, somehow glaring at Winter, Lian, and Knot all at the same time. "If any of you could *think*, you would agree that here and now is not the time to discuss it."

Knot noticed an older couple walking past them, looking curiously at their group. Knot pressed his lips together. Adults taking orders from a child wasn't the most ideal image to project, even if Astrid was right.

Cinzia was quick enough to cover, however weak the attempt. She smiled at the couple as they passed. "Thinks she owns the whole Sfaera sometimes, you know?"

The couple looked at her blankly, and continued on their way. Knot sighed.

"Astrid's right," he said quietly, when the couple was out of earshot. "We need a plan."

"Damn right we need a plan," Lian muttered. "If we're going to be chatting with the emperor of Roden, we'll need a whole lot more than that."

# 46

NASH WATCHED THE LAST of the procession pass by, deep in thought. The Triad's recent orders still bothered him. Nash had no problem carrying out orders; he had done so his entire life. But Winter was different. She was the Harbinger, for Canta's sake. The Triad were too removed from the situation to understand, but Nash wasn't sure what he would—or could—do about it.

He turned his thoughts back to the parade. He needed a distraction.

The mechanical dragon had piqued his interest. The frame was nothing complicated, but the blue fire and the control of the flames surpassed what Nash had seen from even the most advanced pyromancers at the Citadel.

The spectacle had further implications. Nash knew of only one reason for the Rodenese people to hold a parade of glory. It was once a time-honored tradition almost as old as the empire itself, but about two hundred years ago the tradition had ceased. While studying at the Citadel, Nash had learned the origins of the parades of glory. They were public displays of power, when Roden was about to go to war.

Not many were aware of that, likely including most commoners in the crowd. But the emperor and his counselors would know. The parade and the re-emergence of the Ceno were worrisome.

"Nash," Kali said beside him, "get the horses ready. We need to find this *cotir*."

He nodded, but his frown remained as he moved to the four horses they had bought in Tir. The longer Nash participated in this wild chase, the more he knew it was going to end badly. It was inevitable. Their quarry included Winter, for one, who had strength beyond anything Nash had seen. If without his guidance Winter had become addicted to frost so that she couldn't function, they might stand a chance, but Nash wouldn't wish that on anyone. Winter had shown signs of dependency, but such signs were typical of all psimantic variants, especially in the beginning. Nash didn't want to risk his life on that assumption. And if Lathe ever came around to using his talents, he could best Nash or Kali, maybe even both of them at once. That wasn't even counting the vampire.

Nash did not like the odds.

When the horses were ready, he led them over to Kali. She waited, observing the dispersing crowd. She had to be thinking the same thing that he was about the parade, but they wouldn't talk about it in so public a space. They would go to a local inn, a front run by Nazaniin operatives, where they would be free to talk. Perhaps they would also be able to make use of the local *cotir*. There was a local group on record, and there was always a chance they weren't all variants. If there was at least one actual in the *cotir*, they might stand a chance against Lathe, Winter, and that vampire.

Nash was surprised that Kali could find her way so easily through the city when, as far as he knew, she had never been here before. Of course, that had never stopped an acumen. Kali had likely memorized Izet's layout before they even left Triah, just in case.

"This is it," Kali said, approaching a small, metal door in one of the larger huts.

Kali knocked twice on the door with the pommel of her stiletto dagger. After a moment, she knocked once more, sharply. It was a common code for Nazaniin establishments, and the door cracked open immediately after the last knock. It was dark inside, and Nash couldn't see who had opened the door.

"Send someone to tend our horses," Kali commanded. Then she walked inside. The new lacuna, Dahlin, followed her, Nash bringing up the rear. He brushed past a small round man who then slipped outside to follow Kali's orders.

Inside, Nash passed through a thick black curtain—the source of the darkness inside the doorway, he realized—and into a brightly lit corridor.

The craftsmanship of the inside of the hut contrasted starkly to the dilapidated outward appearance. The floor was polished wood, and tapestries and paintings hung on the paneled walls. Ahead, the hallway split into two staircases. "This way," Kali said, taking the stairs leading up on the left.

Nash hated dealing with other *cotiri*. Especially foreign ones. He never knew where their allegiance truly lay. Of course, the information flow to low-tier *cotiri*—especially those in countries outside of Khale—was tightly controlled. But it was impossible to completely stop it. There was always a leak.

They moved up the stairs in single file, emerging into another short hallway. Kali walked towards an open door at one end. The room beyond was a mess. There were two desks on opposite sides of the room, each covered with a layer of papers, writing paraphernalia, boxes and tools. A single bed stood against one wall, but it too was covered, with a huge pile of clothing, blankets, and more papers.

A man, tall and thin, hunched over one of the desks.

"I'm here in service of the *Triadin*," Kali said. "I require assistance."

The wiry man jumped out of his chair at the sound of Kali's voice. Not a good sign; this *cotiri* hadn't seen much fieldwork. He peered at them from behind a pair of misshapen spectacles. His hair was graying, although his face—smooth, pale, and elongated—didn't look aged enough to justify it. In many ways, he reminded Nash of an old horse. Past its prime.

"Mistress!" the man squeaked. "I apologize for my obliviousness! I was researching," he said, glancing at the papers on his desk.

"Who are you?" Kali asked.

The man's tall body folded at the waist in an awkward bow. "Erenjin, mistress. The voyant of this *cotir*."

*Interesting,* Nash thought to himself. *A rare thing to see a voyant this far from Triah.*

"If I may be so bold, mistress," Erenjin said, "who do I have the honor of billeting in our humble outpost?"

"Kali," she said. She didn't need to tell the man anything further; both she and Nash had made enough of a name for themselves. "My associate, Nash," Kali said, nodding towards him. "And our lacuna, Dahlin. Do you keep a full *cotir* here, voyant?"

The man nodded. "We do, mistress. Vera and Ohme are out, but I'm expecting their return any time. Yes, any time indeed." He continued nodding as Kali stared him down. "Vera is our acumen," he blurted out, "and Ohme our telenic. They are both very skilled, and both Ohme and I are actuals. I'm sure we will do anything within our power to help you. Anything at all."

Nash eyed Erenjin, looking the man up and down. Two actuals was good, although he wondered at their abilities.

Any voyant with real talent would have been recalled to Triah years ago.

"How skilled are you?" Kali asked. "We are searching for a group of travelers, they just arrived in the city. Can you scry their position?"

Erenjin cowered, looking at the floor. "Mistress, I apologize. Although I am indeed an actual, my skills as a voyant are woefully limited. I have very little control over my sight."

Nash frowned. Powerful voyants were a rarity indeed. Clairvoyance was often more a novelty than an asset. Nash had only met a few voyants, other than Rune, who actually served the Nazaniin's purposes in any useful way.

Nash could sense Kali's frustration bubbling beneath her calm exterior. Kali was all business, but when she grew overly anxious or frustrated, she could lose her calm at any moment.

"I will try, of course," Erenjin said quickly, "but I caution you not to expect much. And, should I fail, we have an intricate network of spies and informants in the city. It will be a simple matter to find the travelers you seek."

Nash nodded, looking at Erenjin. He was speaking with a bit more confidence now. At least he had initiative. The most important role of a voyant in any *cotir* was to provide information, and this Erenjin, despite his limitations, seemed to fulfill that duty one way or another.

"Very well," Kali said. By the tone of her voice, she wasn't impressed, but at least she was placated for the moment. "Get in contact with this network of yours." She stepped close to Erenjin, looking into his eyes. She only came up to his chest, but she still seemed the largest in the room. "Don't fail me, Erenjin. Here, *I* am the *Triadin*."

Erenjin nodded, although Nash was impressed at the

confidence in his eyes, now. He had misjudged the man. Erenjin was absent-minded, but also intelligent.

Should he fail, Nash would still pity him.

Nash shook his head. "This is folly. How can we expect to win against the Harbinger? How does that serve any purpose?"

They were settling into the room Erenjin had shown them to. Kali stood by the window. What had begun as a clear, sunny day had quickly become overcast. Now snow fell, covering the street and rooftops.

"Kosarin said she is not the Harbinger. He gave us orders, Nash. That's all there is to it."

Nash sighed. "She *is* the Harbinger. Can't you feel it?"

Kali remained silent, staring out the window at the falling snow.

"If her innate ability and the fact that she's a tiellan psimancer aren't enough, there's the massacre in Navone. She bested you, Kali."

"She didn't best me," Kali said sharply.

"Maybe," Nash said softly. "But there's the feeling I get in my gut, the draw I feel to her. I've only heard of such power in one place, Kali."

Kali turned to face him, and suddenly Nash knew. He knew the minute he saw her beautiful, clear gray eyes. Eyes that had been blue only weeks before, but somehow kept the same piercing clarity no matter what color they took on. He had seen that hardness, that stubbornness in her eyes before. He loved that about her. And, now, it would drive them apart.

"None of that matters," Kali whispered. "It does not matter what I've seen or sensed. It does not matter what I feel. I've been given orders, Nash. I *will* carry them out. You can help me obey, as you have always done. Or you can choose a different path. But mine is set."

Kali stood on tiptoes, and Nash felt her smooth lips against his cheek.

"Whatever you choose, know that I... I am grateful for your company. I am grateful to have traveled with you, Nash."

Nash bowed his head. "Love you too, Kali." What Kali had said was as close to it as Nash had ever heard from her.

"You can choose differently," Nash said, in one last attempt.

"This is the only peace I have in my life. Without orders, I go back to that scared little girl on the streets of Mavenil."

Nash sighed. "What are our plans, then?"

"We wait for Erenjin's intelligence. Then, we follow our orders."

Kali met Nash's eyes. He knew what Kali would do to him if he betrayed her. Nash clenched his jaw. How could he make such a decision?

Without another word, Kali turned and walked out into the corridor. Nash sat back on the bed, mulling over his options. Either was a risk. Either was a betrayal.

# 47

"I WANT TO EXPLORE the city," Winter said, "I don't see what you're so upset about." That was the thing, though. She knew exactly why they were upset.

Winter had taken her last *faltira* crystal that morning, despite taking one last night. And another yesterday evening. And another yesterday morning.

She needed another.

Other than finding Knot's stash and borrowing another few crystals from him, the only other way she could think to find more was to go out into the city and get it.

"She's crazy," Astrid said, looking at Knot. "Anybody else see this? She's completely insane."

Winter met Knot's eyes. They were in Winter's room at the inn. The other humans were downstairs, eating a meal. And Lian... Winter was not sure where Lian was. That worried her—or, at least, it should have worried her a lot more than it did.

*He's probably just in the other room,* she told herself. Once she found more frost, she'd make sure he was safe. Winter had wanted to catch Knot alone before they went down, but Astrid had wedged herself into their conversation.

"She's right, Winter," Knot said. "You're tiellan. You're not going out alone."

Winter clenched her jaw. Her eyes strayed to Knot's pack.

She had no argument against what they were saying. None that they would understand, anyway.

"Remember the Ceno monks?" Astrid said. "The men I saved you from a couple of days ago, who we just saw wandering the streets of the city in a bloody parade?"

"I just… I need to get out," Winter said. "I can't stay inside, it's driving me crazy." She looked at Knot, hoping her face was pleading. Convincing.

Innocent.

"Too dangerous," he said. "Can't believe you're even trying to argue, darlin'. No room for discussion."

"Monks?" Astrid said, looking back and forth between Winter and Knot. "Crazy psychos who want to kidnap you and kill the rest of us?"

Winter glared at the vampire. "Fine," she said. "Whatever. I'll meet you down there in a few minutes."

Winter stormed out, hoping she was being dramatic enough that they would at least feel bad for not letting her go.

*What's wrong with me?* Did she really want them to feel bad for her, for wanting something so ridiculous?

A part of her was glad they had stopped her. What she asked was beyond dangerous. Astrid was right—it was insane.

Which was why what Winter did next surprised even her.

Back in her room, she closed the door behind her. Her room was on the second floor, the window overlooking a narrow alley. Winter wrapped her cloak around her tightly, pulling the hood up over her face. The drop was long, but Winter had jumped from higher places. Probably.

Winter swung her legs over the ledge, watching them dangle below her. She took a deep breath.

Then she let herself drop.

* * *

It took Winter longer than she would have liked to find the grit district, especially with a sprained ankle from the fall. She followed the telltale signs as she limped through the dreary streets. Emaciated faces, huddled forms cowering in corners and alleyways. Shifting eyes.

Winter felt outside of herself, as if she were watching someone else limp along, pulling the cloak tightly around her shoulders, hood down over her face. She should be terrified out of her mind. She was out, alone, in a human-dominated city, in a foreign land pursued by a group of deadly monks.

Yet such emotions were fleeting. Just as Winter watched someone else walk through the streets of Izet, her feelings belonged to another girl, too. They remained on the edge of her consciousness, unable to permeate. She kept walking.

Many of the people Winter passed disgusted her. Most were grit and hero addicts. These people had lost all they had for the sake of a simple powder or vial of liquid. She couldn't imagine losing herself like that; at least she gained something when she got high. These people gained nothing, and lost everything.

She approached a pale, thin woman, eyes sunk so far into her head she looked like a skull with hair. Winter asked the woman where she could find *faltira*, using the key words and roundabout phrases she had come to know. The woman looked at her blankly, and Winter suddenly wondered whether the woman was even alive, or whether she was speaking to a corpse. But eventually the woman raised her skeletal arm, pointing down the alley.

The dealer was easy to spot. They were always healthier than the addicts, always cleaner. Better dressed. Less desperate, more dangerous.

Winter approached the man without inhibition, fingering the dagger at her belt. She didn't have frost to help her, but she could handle herself. She needed this, and nothing would stop her.

The man was tall and lean, and young. No older than Winter herself. He wore dark trousers, and a long dark shirt beneath a long, threadbare overcoat. He saw Winter approaching, and smiled.

"What's your pleasure?" he asked. His eyes were a striking blue, the color of midday sky, but his smile was crooked and marred by an assortment of missing teeth.

Winter told him what she needed.

The man's grin widened. "You're lucky," he said. "I'm one of the few that carries it round here. But it's rare, even more so since the Ceno have re-emerged, and it'll cost you a gold piece for a crystal." Winter watched the man's eyes look her up and down. "But I'd consider other payment, if you don't have the gold."

"I have the gold," Winter said. "Let me see them first."

The man frowned, his eyes darting. "Not here," he said. "Follow me." He turned into a small alleyway, looking over his shoulder.

Winter hesitated. Something tugged at her, begged her not to follow the man.

"You coming?" he asked.

Frost's pull was too strong. Winter had to have it. She nodded, and followed. The shadows had grown tall and long as dusk approached, and the alleyway was darker than the street. *Best to get this over with as quickly as possible.*

The man reached into his long overcoat. Winter was vaguely aware of her body tensing, but she relaxed when the man's hand emerged holding a small pouch. He reached in and pulled out a crystal.

Winter stared at it, fighting herself. Her whole body hungered after the thing, as if a piece of her were missing and only that small crystal would replace it.

The man yanked the crystal away, putting it back in the pouch before Winter even realized she had been reaching for it.

"Payment," he said.

Winter nodded, reaching for her purse beneath her cloak. Her hands found nothing.

It wasn't there.

Panic flashed in her. Someone must have stolen it from her, picked her pocket as she…

No. It had not been stolen. She had forgotten to take it with her when she jumped out of the window. It was still at the inn, on a table in her room. She could see it clearly in her mind.

Winter stood silently, not sure what to do next. She needed frost. She needed it now.

"Well?" the man said. "Where's the gold?"

Winter stammered a response, but she knew it wouldn't make sense. She sounded like a witless idiot.

The man's face grew hard, his stupid grin long gone. "No payment, no business," he said. Then, his hand reached towards her. Winter saw more than felt his fingers brush her face, trailing down her neck.

"Unless you make a payment of a different kind."

Before Winter could even think about what the man implied, she saw herself reach for her dagger. Hand to hilt, blade from sheath.

Winter plunged the dagger into the man's heart.

He looked at her, eyes large and round. His face contorted,

mouth opening wide in a soundless scream, wider than seemed right or possible. Winter saw the gaps in his teeth, the cracks in his lips, the tendons and muscles straining in his neck. Then he fell to the ground.

Winter withdrew the dagger, wiping it on the man's overcoat. She reached into the coat, grasping the pouch. She opened it. Three crystals. Three would be enough. She put the pouch in a pocket in her cloak, and turned to leave the alleyway.

Winter didn't make it three steps before she came back to herself. She felt as if she were waking from a dream. She looked down at her hands, covered in blood. She looked back at the man, lying dead.

She fell to her knees, stomach clenched, and vomited into the slush. When she was done, she collapsed on the ground. She felt the wetness of melted snow and her own vomit beneath her. She rolled over on her back, looked at the sky, and saw snow falling. She wondered when it had begun snowing. Why couldn't she remember?

She didn't know how long she stayed there, but slowly she realized she had to stand. She couldn't stay like this. She stood and looked back at the man's corpse.

Winter's eyes widened in horror. The man was standing, looking at her. He clutched the dagger in his chest with one hand, and reached out to her with the other. Winter screamed. She turned to run but slipped and fell. She looked back at the man, but he was lying on the ground. Dead.

*Murderer.*

Winter was suddenly back in Navone. She was screaming, she was picking up men and crushing their bodies together, flailing shields and spears in wide arcs and not caring how many Sons of Canta, Goddessguards, or innocents she killed. She was back in Navone, and she was a murderer.

And someone was shaking her.

Winter gasped, opened her eyes, and realized the piercing shriek she heard was her own.

"What in *Oblivion* are you doing?"

Astrid held her by the throat, shaking her, and Winter's whole body convulsed under the vampire's strength.

"What's *wrong* with you? You've put us all in danger. You've risked all of our lives for your damn addiction. You realize that? Do you even know what you're doing?"

Winter gurgled a response, but even she didn't know what she said. What was there to say? Maybe the vampire would strangle her. Winter's eyes flicked towards the dealer's corpse. She did not deserve better.

"Canta rising," Astrid whispered. "You really are insane."

And, for the first time, Winter saw herself as she was. The person she was on the inside and the person she had been watching as if from afar came together. She saw herself, lying in an alley, in a pool of blood and her own vomit, screaming. She watched herself jump out a second-story window. She watched herself shun, sneak around, and lie to those she loved. She watched herself put her own life at risk, just as she took the lives of others. Winter watched herself with horror that only the self-aware understand. She remembered the hollow faces, the black limbs of the addicts in Cineste. She remembered what her father had told her. Those people had lost everything they cared about because they had come to care for one thing only.

And then, Winter understood. She *had* lost everything. Her husband did not know her—she would be surprised if he even cared. She had shunned her best friend. She had lost her identity; what she wanted eclipsed what and who she was. And her purpose, Winter's desire to protect those she loved... she was doing anything but that. She had put them at risk.

Her entire life, she'd been looking for a home. Perhaps the only place in the Sfaera for her was in the slums, among dying addicts.

Astrid released her grip on Winter's throat. Winter gasped, able to breathe once again.

"Come with me," Astrid said. "Quickly. Quietly. There's something you need to tell Knot. And if you don't do it, I'll bloody well do it for you."

Winter knew she would.

She had to.

Winter stood in Knot's room alone. Apparently Astrid, Knot, and Lian had all ventured out to look for her, while Cinzia, Jane, and Kovac had remained in case Winter returned. Neither Lian nor Knot had come back yet.

Winter fingered the pouch at her belt, the one she had taken from the dealer. Winter shivered. There seemed to be only pain left inside her, from the man she had killed, from what she had done in Navone, at the distance she felt from Knot and Lian, from losing her father.

She could escape that pain, though. Winter reached into the pouch, put the frost to her lips, and swallowed. She waited impatiently, hoping the high would take her away. She waited. And waited.

And waited.

After a few moments, Winter took another crystal. Still, it had no effect. Panicking, she reached into the pouch and took the last one.

Nothing happened.

The man had given her fakes, and she'd killed him for it.

Winter sat on the bed, face buried in her hands. Her cloak smelled of vomit and blood. She felt exhausted, yet her mind raged. She saw herself plunging the dagger into the man's heart. She saw it as clearly as she saw all the death she had caused in Navone.

She *was* a murderer. She had tried to deny it before, but now...

There was another option. The dagger rested at her hip. Simple to slide it through her own heart, as easily as she had slid it through the dealer's. She wouldn't have to feel this way.

She looked up, and her eyes locked on the pack in the corner of the room. Knot's pack.

Winter almost leapt towards it, emptying its contents onto the floor. The pouch of crystals wasn't difficult to find. She held it close to her heart, felt the satisfying weight of it in her fingers. Nine or ten crystals left. Enough to keep her going for a few more days. Enough to numb her.

She raised one *faltira* crystal to her lips just as the door opened behind her.

Winter's head swung around, and her hand dropped to her side. *Canta's death,* she thought. *Of course this would happen.*

"Hello, princess."

It was Lian.

Immediately Winter moved away, sitting down on the bed and wrapping her arms around herself. She was conscious of the frost in her fist, could feel its lightness.

"Where's Knot?" Winter asked.

Lian closed the door behind him. "Not back yet."

"If you're going to give me some lecture about putting everyone in danger, spare me. I know what I've done. Last thing

I need is you to rub it in my face."

Lian only stood there, watching her.

"What do you want, Lian?"

"I want you to listen," Lian said quietly. He sat next to her on the bed. "Look at me, Winter."

Instinctively, Winter looked away. How could she face him after what she had done?

"Please," he said. "I need you to see me."

Winter realized she was shivering. She turned to look at Lian. His cheeks were wet.

"I'm so sorry," Lian whispered, looking right into her eyes. He was leaving her; that much was obvious. Beneath the fear and the guilt, Winter was relieved. At least now he would be free of her.

Winter laughed mirthlessly. "Now you wish you hadn't left Pranna with me in the first place. I tried to warn you, dummy." She nodded. "It's good you're leaving. You need to get home."

"What in Oblivion are you talking about? I ain't going nowhere. Would you just let me apologize?"

Winter stared at Lian in shock. What could he possibly have to apologize for?

"I abandoned you when you needed me most. I was envious, I'll admit it. The power you developed, I wanted it for myself. But that ain't all of it. I was scared, and I was selfish, and I just… I was wrong, Winter."

Winter could hardly understand what Lian was saying. She was the one who had abandoned him, she was the one who had turned him away, but *he* was apologizing to *her*? The weight of it all, the secrecy, the lies, all came crashing down on her.

Winter wrapped her arms around Lian and hugged him tightly, just as her tears began to fall.

"I've killed people," Winter said, sobbing into his shoulder. "In Navone, that was me. I killed all those people. I've killed others, just to get more *faltira*. I don't know what's happening to me. I don't know how I got here, I don't know, I just..."

Lian held her as she sobbed. "I know," he whispered. "I know what you've done. I don't care. I still love you."

Winter pulled away. "How can you say that? I lied to you, to Knot and everyone else. In Navone, I *slaughtered innocent people*. How can you love me after all that?"

Lian shrugged. "Never said you were perfect, princess. Just said I love you."

Winter laughed despite herself. She wiped the tears from her cheeks.

Lian smiled. "Don't get any ideas, though. You're a married woman. I'm talking about love in the friendly, non-touchy sense. But you need to know I care for you, and I'm here to help."

"Thank you," Winter whispered, hugging him again.

"This don't mean we ain't got work to do. You've got issues. Just wanted to tell you that you don't have to face them alone."

Winter's pain was still there, but it was less somehow. Not the way it dulled when she took frost—this was different. This felt more like relief. This felt more like healing.

Lian left the room, and Winter waited. There was one person she still needed to talk to.

Knot arrived shortly after Lian left. He looked at Winter for a moment, then closed the door quietly behind him. The room was a disaster. Winter had tossed Knot's belongings out of his pack and all over the floor looking for his *faltira*, before Lian had arrived.

"Sorry about the mess," Winter said, looking up at him.

"What're you doing, darlin'?"

*This is your chance. You can tell him everything, right now. Let it go. If Lian can still love you, after all you've done, perhaps he can, too.*

So Winter told him, starting with her first conversation with Kali and Nash, about actuals and variants and *faltira*. She watched Knot's eyes widen as she told him about the first time she took frost. She told him about the crystals Kali and Nash had given her, about the powers she had discovered and the pull frost began to have on her, how strong it was and how strong she felt when she took it.

He watched her intently through it all. She ached for him to come to her, to put his arms around her, to tell her that everything would be all right and that he would help her get through this, but he remained by the door, his arms at his sides.

She almost didn't tell him about the events in Navone, but she somehow found the courage. The massacre had been her fault. Knot needed to know that. Then she told him the rest: how she had decided to keep it a secret, how she had resolved to stop using frost at first but the pull had been too strong, how she had snuck away to gather more. Winter told him about all the times she had *wanted* to tell him.

And then she stopped. Her voice had long ago become hoarse.

Knot was still staring at her, she knew, but Winter didn't want to meet his eyes. She looked at the floor, her face burning.

But her burden had eased somewhat. The pain was still there, but she felt better. Better than she ever had with frost, she realized. A great weight she hadn't even known she had been carrying had been lifted.

The floorboards creaked. Winter saw Knot's boots out of the corner of her eye. He knelt down in front of her. She didn't feel his touch; instead, he began gathering up his things, folding the clothing and placing it neatly on the bed.

Winter remained where she was, unsure of what was happening. She had just told him everything, she had bared her soul, and his reaction was to tidy up?

"Are you going to say anything?" she whispered.

He continued as if he hadn't heard her.

Winter felt a sob rising from deep within her chest, but willed it down. She had cried enough. There was no point in more tears.

Then Knot sighed. "Won't say it ain't your fault," he said. "Won't say you haven't hurt me and others. You lied to us all, put us in danger. You're more of a liability than any of us could have suspected, that's the truth."

He looked into her eyes, kneeling before her.

"But I love you," he said.

Winter fought the lump rising in her throat. Was it too much to hope for? She could hardly believe this was real.

"I love you, too," Winter said. And, perhaps for the first time, she meant it.

Knot helped her stand. She felt his arms around her, holding her tightly.

"I'd say I forgive you, but for two things." Knot pulled away and looked at her. "First, I'd already forgiven you, the moment you said anything. And second, I'm pretty sure I need forgiveness just as much as you. So that's something we can both work on, darlin'."

Winter smiled, and reached up to kiss him. "I like that idea," she said. Deep inside, she still wondered. It couldn't be this easy. No one was this forgiving. She knew they were not out of the woods, yet. But they might make it.

# 48

KNOT STARED AT THE cloaks Lian had just thrown at his feet. Two of them, both dark green in color.

"You need to get into the palace, right? Figured these might help," Lian said.

They all stood in the room Knot and Winter had shared the night before. Lian had called them together that morning to discuss a plan for infiltrating the palace. They were all here—Cinzia, Jane, Kovac, Lian, Astrid, Knot, and Winter—standing in a circle.

Knot's thoughts strayed to all that had happened with Winter. If he blamed anyone, it was himself. If Knot hadn't arrived in Pranna, none of this would have happened. That didn't change the betrayal he felt. He'd said last night that he'd forgiven her, and he wanted that to be the case. But Knot was beginning to wonder whether it might take more time than he'd hoped.

Astrid nudged him. "You there, nomad?"

Knot chewed his cheek. "Where'd you get these?"

"The attack by the river. Before me and Jane caught up to you, I grabbed the robes from two of bodies. Figured they might come in handy."

Knot rubbed his chin. "How will these help us get into the palace?" Knot had an idea brewing, but he wanted to hear from Lian first.

"I've been watching the palace gates," Lian said.

Astrid snorted. "When have you had time to watch the gates?"

"I snuck out yesterday, while you all were eating."

Kovac frowned. "You should not be going out alone." The Goddessguard glared at him. "Sending even one tiellan into the city is too great a risk."

Lian shrugged. "Desperate times. But I noticed something. The only people who get in and out of the palace are nobles and these Ceno monks. The green-robes just walk right in. The guards send everyone else away, unless they're accompanied by the ones wearing robes. Just like those ones." He looked at Knot. "Winter and I need to wear hoods anyway. All we'd have to do is escort you through the gate. Then you're free to find the emperor."

"What about Astrid?" Knot asked. He hadn't asked the girl, but he assumed she was coming with them.

Astrid smiled up at him. For a moment, Knot felt the same sensation he'd felt in the crowd the day before, when he had locked eyes with the boy on his father's shoulders; he felt that twinge of attachment and concern in the back of his mind.

"I can handle myself," Astrid said. "You all make your way in and I'll meet you inside. Getting over the wall won't be any trouble."

Knot raised an eyebrow. "Don't kill anyone."

Astrid's smile broadened, like a child about to eat a sweet roll. "Won't unless I have to."

"What happens once we're inside?" Knot asked.

Lian smiled. "The noble district is north of here, between us and the palace. I stopped by this morning—the nobles just walk about their district without a care in the Sfaera. It'd be an easy thing to stop one of them, find a discreet place, and ask some questions about the palace."

"Why would a noble answer your questions?"

Knot glanced at Jane, who obviously hadn't understood Lian's meaning.

"Because he'll have a rabid vampire threatening to eat him if he doesn't," Astrid said.

"You mean you're going to… to…"

"We'll kidnap a nobleman," Knot said. "We'll scare him a little. Just enough for him to tell us what he knows."

For a moment Knot thought Jane would protest, but she surprised him.

"You will do what you must," was all Jane said.

"What if the particular noble you capture has not been to the palace? What if he has no information to give?" Cinzia asked.

Knot looked at Lian. It was his plan, after all.

Lian shrugged. "We capture another? I don't know. Never said my plan was perfect."

Knot nodded. It was crude, but the plan had merit. The green robes were a valuable contribution. If Knot had more time to think, he could probably come up with something better. But for now, this would have to do.

Astrid raised her hand. "I know I'm probably the only one who cares, but I'd just like to point out, for the record, that this plan isn't that great."

"It's fine," Winter said quietly. "Not perfect, but we're all ears if you have a better idea."

Astrid shrugged. "Not my department. I criticize strategies, I don't make them."

"We'll follow Lian's plan," Knot said. "Lian, Winter, Astrid, and I will go to the noble district this afternoon and see what information we can gather. After that, we go to the palace."

Winter squeezed his hand.

"What about you lot?" Lian asked Cinzia.

"I believe we shall sit this one out," Jane said. She glanced at Knot.

Knot shrugged. "Fine with me. You're the ones who wanted to get into Roden. What you do here is your business. Best to stay at the inn, though." The fact that Knot wasn't sure he would return didn't seem worth mentioning.

"And if it is too dangerous to meet here?" Jane asked. "If you cannot get here, or we have to leave… where shall we meet, in that case?"

Knot nodded. It was a good point. Honestly, he hadn't thought much about what would happen after he confronted the emperor.

"What about our last camp site?" Astrid suggested. "Outside the city."

Jane nodded. "I think we can get there. Very well." She looked back to Knot. "Canta willing, we can get a large chunk of work done before we see one another again."

"Your mysterious translation?" Astrid asked.

Jane nodded. "We have fallen behind. Catching up is important, for all of our sakes."

Knot expected Astrid to respond with disdain, or at least sarcasm. Instead, the girl surprised him. "Canta guide your path," she said.

Both Jane and Cinzia bowed their heads in response.

Knot cleared his throat. "Well, that's our plan, then. We'll regroup just after noon to prepare and run over any final details. Until then… rest up."

Astrid snorted. "Rest up? That's the best you can do? No

rallying remarks, no encouraging words? *Rest up?*"

Knot frowned. Of course the girl couldn't stay serious for long. Then he realized everyone else was laughing.

Before they left for the noble district, Winter confronted him. She wore one of the robes Lian had pilfered. It was a bit large on her, but for all Knot could tell, she looked like a Ceno monk.

"I still don't know why I can't have *one crystal*," Winter said, glaring at him.

Knot shook his head. "Don't know why you're fighting me on this. Wasn't that part of our agreement? Keeping one crystal with you wasn't part of the bargain."

"I can help in a fight," she said. "If things get bad, if we're ambushed, I can be *useful*. I can protect us."

"You can help us most as you are. You're too much of a risk otherwise."

Knot couldn't help but notice Winter's tight grip on the dagger at her waist. Her knuckles were white. She took a deep breath.

"I'm sorry," she said. "It's just… it's hard, knowing I can't take it. But you're right."

"As soon as we're through here, we're going to those shamans Astrid mentioned. We'll do whatever it takes. Hold out until then. If you can't do it for yourself, then do it for us."

"You think she meant what she said?" Winter asked.

Earlier that morning, Astrid had told them about a group of shamans in western Khale who had supposedly found a cure for addictions to hero, devil's dust, and grit. Knot hoped the girl was right. If she wasn't, he didn't know what they'd do after Roden. They certainly couldn't continue like this.

"I think she did." Best to not reveal his concerns just yet. He didn't even know whether they would survive the night.

"At least keep a crystal ready?" Winter asked, looking back at him. Her grip on her dagger had relaxed slightly. "That way, if I need to—if *you* think I need to—then you can give me one, and I can help. At least give me that hope. Otherwise, I think I'll go crazy." She laughed, but the sound was hollow.

Knot believed her about going crazy. What he had seen in the past few days certainly qualified. He patted the pouch at his belt. "I'll keep them ready," he said. "But I decide if you need it. Don't ask me; you already know the answer."

Winter nodded.

"All right," Knot said. He'd worried she wouldn't back down.

"One more thing," Winter said.

She took a step towards him. Knot tensed; he imagined her trying to take the *faltira* from him. She would not be able to do it, but he did not want to see her try.

Instead, she reached around her neck and unclasped the necklace of dark stones she wore. Her mother's necklace.

"I want you to have this."

"I... I can't take that."

Winter rolled her eyes. "Look, it's no big deal, all right? I just want to... I need a symbol. Something to work towards. This can be it: I give you this necklace now, and when I'm better, when we're better, you can give it back to me. That's all."

Knot reached hesitantly for the necklace. "It's just a symbol," he repeated.

Winter nodded. "That's it. Temporary."

Knot took the necklace, surprised at its heaviness. He was about to put it in the pouch where he kept the *faltira*, but instead he clasped it around his own neck. The weight felt unnatural. But at the same time it felt right.

Winter smiled at him. It was genuine, and Knot could not help but smile back.

"We ready, then?" he asked.

"Yes."

"Then let's go meet the emperor."

# 49

Winter watched for Knot as she stood in her designated position outside the noble district, wishing she'd made more of a case to keep a frost crystal herself. Why was she here, otherwise? She couldn't fight. She didn't have her bow; carrying such a weapon was too much of a risk, especially in the Ceno robe she wore. Beneath the cloak she concealed one of the small crossbows Knot had given her from his pack, but the weapon felt unnatural in her hands. They shook so violently she could barely hold the thing steady. She wished for the smooth curved simplicity of her bow. The crossbow was all hard angles and levers and cranks, and although it didn't take nearly as much skill as a bow, Winter knew she would never be as useful with this as she was with her own weapon.

And she would never be as useful with her bow as she could be with frost.

Winter pushed all thoughts of *faltira* away. She had promised Knot.

Winter pulled her cloak more tightly around her. *I never thought I'd miss the cold of Pranna.* She wore the clothing Kali had given her beneath the cloak; she had grown used to it now, and the garments were certainly practical. But, beneath the cloak, she had also stashed her *siara.* Winter could not say why. She had seen it in her pack that morning, and suddenly felt an overwhelming desire to wear it. It was hidden of course, and no one would recognize her as a tiellan unless they looked directly underneath her hood. But she was glad to have her *siara* with her. It felt right, especially now that she had given Knot her necklace.

She looked up at the sky, gray with dusk.

Winter sent up a bitter prayer. *If you're up there, wench, you'll stop the snow. We've been through enough. You should know that by now.*

Lian nudged her, standing at her side. She looked at him, and he nodded at the road ahead.

Knot walked along the side of the street, moving slowly with the rest of the pedestrians as carriages and horses passed quickly through the middle of the cobbled road.

Winter and Lian remained where they were, observing the small gate to the nobles' quarter from a block or so down the street. Everyone seemed to give them a wide berth. She wondered if it was because of their Ceno robes. Winter glanced furtively in Astrid's direction, where she knew the girl was hiding in an alley.

Hopefully, only Knot and Astrid would have to take action. Winter and Lian were only there in case things "went south," as Knot said.

She watched a snowflake float down through the air, falling slowly until it landed at her feet. She swore as she saw another snowflake fall from the sky, and another, and another. Lian frowned at her, but she ignored him, tugging the thick green robe around her once more and stomping her feet on the ground. Canta's bloody bones, it was *cold*.

Knot walked by. Winter tried to keep her eyes from him, but couldn't help glancing every few seconds. He walked steadily down the edge of the road, dressed in his usual brown and green wools and thick wool cloak, although the cowl was down, revealing his face.

After a few moments, Winter nudged Lian. It was time for them to follow.

Ahead, Winter saw an opening in the narrow street. It was a small, decorative square, perhaps only three or four times the width of the street itself, with a circular fountain at its center. At each corner of the square stood four other fountains shaped as dragons, wings outstretched and maws open wide, facing the center. No water flowed from any of them; it had likely been cut off for the winter.

The square was not particularly impressive, and from what Winter understood there were a number of other similar squares in the noble quarter, marking the intersections of the major streets. This was only one of many. A few nobles stood around the square, chatting, while others walked through it, perhaps a dozen in total. With luck, Knot would find an unsuspecting nobleman, drag him into the alley, and get the information they needed.

This was it, then. Their destination. This was where it would all—

Winter stopped suddenly, staring ahead at a small group of nobles who had just walked up to the central fountain. They'd entered the square not long after Knot.

One of them in particular caught Winter's attention. At first she thought it was a passing resemblance. But, as she and Lian came closer, she realized it was much more. The short blond hair, striking gray eyes, slim figure. The woman looked right at Winter, and smiled. Elsi had hardly spoken a word, hardly showed any emotion at all while they had traveled together. And now she was looking at Winter with a smile so familiar she could have been...

Next to Elsi, Winter saw Nash.

Winter didn't need to see anything more. She reached beneath her robes for the crossbow.

*So much for Lian's plan.* She had been proud of him; it could have worked. Winter raised the crossbow and aimed it at Nash's heart.

Winter fired, feeling the weapon snap lightly in her hands. At the same time she felt someone grab her, rough hands wrapping around her body and neck. She screamed, her voice piercing the night air as the bolt she had just fired sailed directly at Nash, then suddenly veered off course as if swatted by an invisible hand.

Knot recognized the trap as he approached the square. The familiar twang of an assassin's crossbow and Winter's scream from the street confirmed that their plan was compromised.

Knot had already spotted the three by the central fountain, two women and a man, as threats. Two other men near the street also looked suspicious. The remaining nobles screamed and fled in panic.

Knot needed to deal with the closest threats first. He reached into his sleeve, grasping a throwing knife from a brace he'd attached to each forearm. He spun and threw one at the man who'd grabbed Winter, only to see that Lian had already shot him in the back with a crossbow. Knot's knife sank deep into the man's eye with a spurt of blood, but the weapon was wasted. He had already loosened his grip on Winter. She pushed him away from her and looked at Knot, wide-eyed, angry, and pleading.

He knew what she wanted, but he would not give it to her.

Knot faced the three in the square. The older of the two women, brown-haired and bony, advanced on Lian and Winter wielding a sword. Lian had drawn his own longsword and taken a defensive stance. Knot could only hope Lian could hold his own against her.

Before him, the blond woman drew a familiar sword, slightly curved, just like the one he wore on his back. Knot held his staff tightly. The woman attacked before he could reach his sword.

Winter reloaded her crossbow as quickly as she could, distantly aware of the chaos unfolding around her. Her fingers still trembled, although she wasn't sure whether the effect was from the battle or the lack of frost in her system. She felt far away, as if anything she did would not be in time.

Winter loaded another bolt into the brass groove, but her fingers fumbled over the crank. Because the crossbow was so small, there was no stirrup for her foot to steady the weapon. In front of her, a tall, brown-haired woman was quickly backing Lian into a corner. Winter couldn't see Astrid anywhere, or Nash, for that matter. Knot and Elsi fought near the fountain, their weapons blurring. Winter blinked. Had Elsi faked her simple demeanor? The woman Winter watched now did not seem like the Elsi she remembered. If Winter didn't know any better, she'd say this woman was far more similar to…

Winter shivered, just as she heard movement behind her.

She spun, swinging the crossbow with all her weight. It was compact, but still made of wood and metal, and connected with an audible crack that made the bones in Winter's hands throb.

The attacker took the blow much better than Winter hoped. He faced her, snarling, a stream of blood flowing from his forehead, over his nose and twisted mouth.

Winter swung the crossbow at him again, but he dodged it easily this time, and swatted it out of her hands. The weapon clattered to the cobbled street, and then he rushed at her, swinging a heavy mace. Winter put her hands up, knowing immediately the futility of such a defense, and suddenly her world turned upside down.

She found herself lying in the street, in a daze, the cobblestones cold against her cheek. Her arm and head ached. She tasted blood in her mouth. For a moment she panicked that Nash was about to impale her with one of his *tendra*, until she remembered. She wasn't on frost. The blood was her own.

Winter rose to her knees and almost vomited. She wiped her cheek and her hand came away crimson. She saw a shadow. The man stood over her.

Winter dropped and rolled, just as the mace crashed into the cobbles. In the same motion she drew her dagger, and sliced the back of the man's ankle. He screamed in pain, dropping the mace, and fell to the ground clutching his leg.

Winter dived on top of the man, plunging her dagger into his chest. She felt a thrill of elation. She wasn't helpless, after all. She could fight. She could still protect those she loved.

Then she felt a sharp blow to her skull, and collapsed.

For the first time in his life, Nash did not know what his next move should be.

He'd sighted the vampire and pursued her down a side street, only to lose her. Kali had ordered him to keep the vampire busy, but Nash didn't like being drawn away from the square. He'd incapacitated Winter with a blow to her skull after she killed Erenjin; he hoped the blow had been light enough not to cause too much damage. Better she stay unconscious than get her hands on frost. Or, worse, get herself killed.

Nash was aware of Lian fighting the acumen Vera, but he

couldn't bring himself to interfere. He had accepted Kali's orders to distract the vampire for a reason.

The vampire was the only one Nash did not mind killing.

Out of the corner of his eye, Nash saw a blur of movement. Instinctively, Nash rolled to the side, landing in a crouch.

The vampire stood before him, smiling.

Nash reached into his waistcoat pocket, pulling out four small stiletto daggers. He tossed them into the air, simultaneously reaching out with multiple *tendra*. The projectiles shot towards the vampire, who somehow dodged all but one, which ripped along the girl's arm. That was not nearly enough. Vampires weren't easy to kill.

Nash drew his sword, circling the girl. In his other hand he carried a large satchel. He allowed himself a glance in Winter's direction. The girl was still on the ground, not moving. If she could stay that way for the rest of the fight, Nash might be able to save her. He didn't know whether he could save anyone else. But the girl he would save. He had to.

First the vampire. Nash dropped the satchel to the ground. He reached inside with nine *tendra*—the maximum he could confidently control—and extracted a variety of weapons. Swords, short spears, daggers, and his two circular blades danced in the air before him.

The vampire looked at the weapons, still smiling.

Nash attacked, swinging weapon after weapon. He advanced as if he wielded nine weapons with nine different arms, lashing out with tentacles of fury. But the girl was *fast*. She leapt up, dodging his first barrage, slamming against a stone wall behind her. He attacked again, but she dodged weapon after weapon, sliding, leaping, and flipping from wall to ground and then up in the air again.

*Nash,* Kali's voice pierced his thoughts, unbidden and unwelcome, *what in Hade's name are you doing? Kill that girl. Do it now.*

*Please.*

Nash clenched his jaw. The vampire was fast and strong, but he had fought worse. Once he pierced her with wood, she'd be crippled, and killing her would be quick work from there.

Thing was, Nash had already decided what he was going to do in this fight. It was insubordinate, and it was betrayal, but the more Nash thought about it, the more he knew. It was the right thing to do. He knew the risks. To upset an acumen, especially one of Kali's power, was a death wish. But he could live with that. He couldn't live with what the *Triadin* had asked of him. He felt sorry for Kali. He knew that she believed they'd found the Harbinger. And yet she was so focused on following orders, on pleasing Kosarin, that she could not admit the truth.

Then he knew he wouldn't kill any of these people—not even this girl, this vampire. Especially not the Harbinger.

He was tired of killing his own.

Kali must have heard his thoughts. *This is it, then?* she asked in his head.

*I'm sorry.* He was surprised that Kali could summon the concentration to speak so clearly in his head given the blindingly fast duel she was engaged in with Lathe, but she would hear him.

*We each do what we must. Best of luck to you, Nazaniin.* Then her presence in his head was gone.

Astrid leapt from the building, sending up rubble and mud and snow as she landed on the cobbled street. She weaved to the left, then leapt up again, flipping backwards and landing against a wall, claws digging into stone.

The man was toying with her. She knew that much. He probably could have killed her by now, or at least injured her, but he was only keeping her on the defensive. Astrid's mind raced, looking for a trap, but nothing stood out. All she could do was avoid the man's blur of psimantic attacks, dodging and leaping.

Knot and the blond woman still dueled by the fountain. Astrid couldn't see Lian or Winter, but she *did* see the brown-haired woman who had been fighting Lian stalking closer to Knot.

Astrid rolled to the side, only to leap into the air once more. She latched onto a building with her claws, leveraging herself up to the roof. Brown Hair was sneaking behind Knot, now. Astrid ran along the rooftop, weapons crashing into the stone behind her. Then she leapt into the air, sailing over the blond woman and Knot. She landed directly on Brown Hair, tackling her to the ground. They rolled, the woman ending up on top. Just as Astrid intended.

Brown Hair's eyes widened as one of the psimantically wielded swords pierced her lower back.

It pierced Astrid as well, but for her it was only pain. For the woman on top of her, it was deadly.

Astrid pushed the woman away, wincing as the blade slid from her own belly. She staggered to her feet, only to see the blond woman disarm Knot.

Astrid cursed. She must have distracted Knot when she landed behind him. Knot stared at the woman, her sword at his throat. Astrid looked behind her. The weapons that had been swarming around Astrid had clattered to the ground. The other man, Nash, stood calmly, his arms folded.

Astrid turned back to Knot, tensing her legs to pounce. The woman still held her sword to Knot's throat.

"I'll save you for last," the woman whispered. Then, she turned to face Astrid. "Slaying a vampire and a Nazaniin assassin in one night will make me famous." She walked towards Astrid. Behind her, Knot stood still, his arms at his side, eyes wide.

*Why aren't you moving, idiot?* Astrid wondered.

The woman's eyes flickered past Astrid towards Nash. "I do not have to slay two Nazaniin tonight," the woman said. "Come back to me, Nash. You can still be on the winning side."

"I'll settle for the right one," the man said.

Then, quite suddenly, Astrid couldn't move.

Pain scoured her body, her bones, neither burning nor piercing but a pain of essence, of all the power and fury of existence. She stood rigid, mouth wide open, saliva dripping from her fangs. A small, extended croaking sound reverberated in her throat.

The woman had *nightsbane*.

Kali frowned, holding the herb-laced blade before her, watching the daemon suffer. She did not like to watch suffering. But if it weren't for the antics of this little bitch they would have apprehended Lathe long ago. It was almost a pleasure to see the girl burn with pain. Almost. At least it distracted Kali from the pain she felt herself.

Behind her, Lathe struggled against the mindtrap she had woven around him. Kali would have liked to kill the psimancer at his best. Killing the man would have to do.

She sent a small psionic burst into Lathe's mind, just to deter him from even thinking about breaking the trap.

The burst failed. Kali looked back at Lathe in surprise. Her mindtrap was still in place, but her burst had sailed straight through him, as if…

As if there were nothing there at all.

Kali narrowed her eyes. This was unexpected.

"Lathe, use your abilities!" Nash shouted. "It's your only chance against her!"

Kali frowned at Nash, tightening the mindtrap she had already woven around him.

"I'm sorry it has come to this," Kali said, and she meant it.

"Winter is the Harbinger," Nash said. "You know it, Kali. Accept it. Do what you know is right."

Kali swallowed. She had her orders. Her orders were what was right.

"I'm sorry, Nash. You've lost your purpose."

"I haven't," Nash said, his voice tired. "I've just found a better one."

Out of the corner of her eye, Kali saw a flash of movement. The staff Lathe had wielded suddenly spun into the air, speeding towards her.

Kali concentrated a massive psionic burst directly into Nash's mind. His head snapped violently backwards, his eyes rolling up into his skull. Her former lover's body collapsed into the streaks of red in the muddy snow. His mind had exploded in his skull; nothing was left of him.

Kali looked back at the vampire, painfully rigid, upright. The nightsbane that soaked her sword would immobilize the beast as long as Kali stayed within a certain radius. Kali frowned, thrusting the blade into the vampire's tiny chest. The girl released one choked, cut-off scream, and then fell to the ground twitching.

Kali turned to face Lathe. Her mind searched for others, and found Lian, and then Winter, both unconscious. Kali reached into her own mental reserves, preparing another psionic burst.

She had planned on making it quick for them.

But that was before they had forced her to kill Nash. Now, Kali felt a growing rage. She would make their pain last.

Knot watched in horror as Astrid squirmed and twitched on the ground, strange gagging sounds escaping her mouth. The girl vomited a stream of blood, reddening the churned slush around her. Knot was still trapped, as if his limbs were cut off from his mind. He couldn't move. But there was something else there, the faintest remnant of a memory, almost tangible, like the smallest tear in fabric.

Knot heard a scream. First Lian, then Winter, their voices rising together in pained unison. Both had been unconscious; Knot had watched them fall. This woman was doing something to them. Knot felt a pressure inside his own skull, but whatever it was it didn't seem to penetrate. The woman frowned at him.

Whatever she was doing, he needed to stop her.

Knot concentrated on the tear in his mind, prying at it. Nothing happened. He tore at the hole, throwing his whole existence at the thing.

"Who are you?" Knot asked. He needed to buy time. If he could only break through…

The woman laughed, with a sadness that reminded Knot of a lonely, listless song. "Of course. After all this time, you do not know. My name is Kali."

Then Knot stopped. He had been going about it all wrong. In the past year, everything he had found talent in had come to him instinctively. Tying knots, fishing, fighting. It had all just happened. Perhaps the same was true with this. If he could relax, perhaps his mind would remember.

In that moment, something changed. Whatever the woman

had been doing to hold him back was gone.

Reaching into the bundle strapped to his back, Knot drew out the sword, the grip both familiar and strange in his hand. His shoulder flared as he reached back, but the pain lessened as he rushed towards the woman. Kali.

She reacted quickly, drawing a dagger from her belt, but her sword was still embedded in Astrid's chest. Knot didn't wait for her to retrieve the weapon.

He rushed in, parrying Kali's first blow, slamming his elbow into her nose, and then burying his sword up to its hilt in her chest. Warm blood leaked slowly onto his hand.

Kali looked up at him in surprise. Her eyes were wide, her mouth wider, opening and closing like a fish. She wheezed blood and bile. Her gaze darted around frantically.

Faster than Knot could have expected, the woman's dagger whipped up towards his throat. Faster still, Knot ducked, slipping his sword out of the woman's chest. He backed away as Kali fell to her knees.

"Lathe," Kali rasped, "I'm s-sorry... I was only... following..."

"My name," Knot said, raising his sword, "is Knot."

Then he lunged forward, thrusting his blade through Kali's neck. Her eyes died, and she slumped backwards. Knot withdrew the sword as she slipped into the bloody snow.

His blade hanging limply at his side, Knot turned to his friends.

Their screams had stopped, but none of them stood up. Knot didn't know whether they were dead or unconscious, and before he could find out, the distant sound of hoof beats and footsteps grew closer. A full contingent of Reapers, accompanied by robed Ceno, entered the square.

"Take him alive," someone ordered, "and anyone else still breathing."

Knot's sword fell from nerveless fingers. Their plan had failed.

His last thoughts were of Winter before he felt a sharp pain on the back of his head, and then blackness.

# 50

Cinzia peeked around the partition they had set up in their room. Kovac stood by the door, arms folded behind his back. He wore full plate armor, though he still looked bare without his Goddessguard tabard and insignia. His longsword and dagger were sheathed on either side of his waist.

"Kovac, please sit. You need to rest, I feel as if you have been standing around all day."

"I'll stand a little longer yet, my lady."

They had just returned from supper in the common room. Cinzia had eaten stew—again. She wondered if these places ever served anything else. She had splurged tonight, though, and taken some mulled wine as well. The drink had tasted of cinnamon, and left a warm, pleasant feeling in her stomach.

"I do not believe we have anything to fear," Jane said. "You should rest, Kovac. You need it." Cinzia looked at her sister gratefully, glad she was pitching in.

"I'll rest when you do. Until then, I'll do my duty."

Cinzia shook her head. She had known there would be no arguing with him.

"Do you think they made it into the palace?" Cinzia said to no one in particular. Knot and the others had been on her mind since they left. The distraction had made translation difficult; the words and symbols seemed more blurry than usual.

Jane pursed her lips. "They are in Canta's hands, now. How they will fare tonight, I do not know. But our paths will cross again. At least with some of them."

Cinzia shook her head. "You cannot know that, Jane. Why say such things?"

Jane smiled sadly at Cinzia. "Believe me or not, but I know what I know."

Cinzia looked under the bed, where they had hidden the Codex of Elwene behind their packs. "A little help?"

They pulled out the book together and placed it on the bed. Then, Jane turned to Cinzia. "Tell me about your revelation," she blurted. "What happened in Navone?"

Cinzia rolled her eyes. "You want to talk about it *now*?"

"I... I haven't known what to say. But I have realized that does not matter." Jane's blond hair was unkempt, her blue eyes reflecting the candlelight.

Cinzia shook her head. She was not happy that Jane was bringing it up now, after so long, but at the same time she felt relief. She *needed* to talk about it.

"I do not know what happened," Cinzia said. "It was not me that spoke, that much I am sure of. It felt as if... as if I were outside of myself, watching the whole thing." She was conscious of Kovac listening on the other side of the partition. Apparently Jane trusted him as much as Cinzia did. That was good. Kovac was a man worthy of their trust. "I know it sounds strange. It may seem that I believe my own revelation while doubting yours, which is... unfair, to say the least. But the truth is, I have no idea what happened in Navone."

Jane sighed in relief. "There is something I need to tell you, Cinzia. About what happened." She grasped Cinzia's hand. "Perhaps we should sit," she said, leading Cinzia to the edge of the bed. "I had a dream last night. Canta appeared to me."

Cinzia sat up straight. "What?"

"I had a dream in which Canta appeared to me. Which is strange for a few reasons," Jane said, cocking her head to the side. "She has never appeared to me in a dream. It has always been face to face."

Cinzia raised an eyebrow. She might have argued such an insane stipulation if she had not been used to such things from Jane by now.

"And there is something else." Jane's eyes were determined. "I have not spoken with the Goddess since Navone. Since the day I turned myself in to the Holy Crucible."

"What does that mean? What are you saying?"

"In my dream, She explained why She had not contacted me. Someone—some*thing*—has been blocking Her. Since that night in Navone. Something has been deflecting Her contact with the Sfaera."

Cinzia shook her head. "Impossible. Canta is all-powerful. Nothing could stop Her from connecting to the Sfaera if She willed it."

"That is what we have been taught. But think about what we are *translating*. Think about the prophecies. The night is coming. Dusk is already upon us. Things are changing, and I do not think even Canta has the power to stop them."

"Even if what you say is true," Cinzia said, "what does that mean? That my vision, whatever that was, was not from Canta? That makes no sense. If not from Canta, then whom?"

"I do not know," Jane whispered. Her hand tightened on Cinzia's. "But it was *not* Canta. She told me that much. It was not Her, Cinzia."

Cinzia's mind raced. She had certainly experienced

*something* in Navone, and her ability to translate a language she didn't know was inexplicable. But, if she believed Jane…

*No.*

"You are wrong," Cinzia heard herself say. She stood up. "What you are saying… Jane, it is all wrong. Your visions are not real. Your dream is not *real*. None of this is real, it *cannot* be."

Cinzia walked around the partition, storming past Kovac.

"Cinzia!" Jane called after her. "Where are you going?"

"Priestess—" Kovac said, but Cinzia did not stay to hear him protest. She opened the door, and walked out into the hallway, her sister's words weighing in her stomach like stone.

Instead of going down to the common room, Cinzia found herself going up. The inn was three stories tall, one of the taller buildings in that part of the city, and Cinzia remembered that it did not have the domed roof so popular in Izet. She needed space to breathe. She needed fresh air.

*What am I doing in Roden?* She had dragged Knot and Winter, Lian and Astrid into this mess. Goddess, Cinzia had made Kovac come all this way, and for what? She had thought at first that she had been leading, taking control. Now, she realized, they had all been puppets.

The way she saw things, there were three options. If Canta had sent her the vision, then perhaps everything would be all right. But in her heart, Cinzia knew that was not true. Whatever had happened to her at the fireside had not been due to the Goddess. The revelation was hollow, and Jane's words only reinforced her certainty.

Perhaps there was no Goddess at all. Perhaps her vision was a freakish accident, some combination of fumes in the air and humors out of balance. It was no more a stretch than the existence of an immortal, all-powerful woman in the skies who dictated events on the Sfaera. Her family separated, her hometown the scene of a massacre, her position in the Denomination compromised. The Goddess Cinzia worshipped would never allow these things to happen, or so Cinzia had always believed. Only her ability to translate had forced her to reconsider. That strange power came from somewhere.

The last option frightened Cinzia the most. If it was not Canta who gave her the vision, and it was not an accident of nature, it was something else. If what they were translating in the Nine Scriptures was any indication, it was something very dark indeed.

She reached a small door at the top of the stairs, but saw that it was padlocked. Cinzia kicked the door in anger, then remembered the dagger at her waist. Both she and Jane had armed themselves since the attack by the river. Cinzia slammed the dagger's pommel down as hard as she could onto the padlock. The lock held. She slammed the pommel down again, and again, and again, until finally the lock broke. Cinzia almost tumbled into the snow as she crashed through the door onto the roof, into the cold night.

She had not brought a cloak, and the air was cool against her skin. Snow fell, points of white stretching into the infinite dark above. She walked to the edge of the roof and looked out at the city below, clutching the dagger tightly in her fist.

Quite suddenly, the vastness of the city, the snow falling all around her, the expanse of dark sky overhead made her feel tiny. Insignificant. The guilt and confusion of the past few months roiled inside of her. She felt undeserving of life. Cinzia raised the dagger, looking at the blade. She ran a finger along the edge, drawing a line of blood. She barely felt it.

If Cinzia were to plunge the dagger into her chest, what

difference would it make? Her family would survive. Her guilt for bringing Jane and Kovac to Roden would be gone. Let the darkness take her. Cinzia was one speck in the vastness of the Sfaera; the loss of one speck meant nothing.

Cinzia raised the dagger. She longed for peace.

And, suddenly, she had it.

In a rush, the darkness left her, and Cinzia felt serenity. It was as if she had been in a dark room, and someone had suddenly thrown open the shutters, allowing sunlight to fill her heart. She felt all this, and something more.

She felt love.

"Canta?" Cinzia whispered.

There was no response.

"Is it that simple?" she whispered, marveling.

Again no response, but Cinzia knew. She felt the cool air around her, heard footsteps and low voices in the city below. Perhaps Cinzia *chose* to know, but that did not matter. The feeling was real enough. She was only a speck in the Sfaera, to be sure. But there was a power out there that loved her.

Cinzia dropped the dagger and took a step back, gazing out at the snow. What had been overpowering before, was now a beautiful vastness. A vastness in which Cinzia had a part.

Her decisions were her own. Her actions could not be undone. But, now, Cinzia would do what she could, with the time that was given her.

Cinzia turned away from the edge of the roof in time to see Jane rushing towards her.

"Cinzia! What are you doing? We looked all over for you, we thought you had gone downstairs!"

"I'm all right," Cinzia said, and meant it. She started walking back towards the door.

"Where are you going?" Jane called out behind her.

"We have work to do." Perhaps they were not supposed to be in Roden. But they could apply themselves to the translation. Perhaps they could be of some help.

Perhaps they could do something good.

"Priestess, I insist you do not go off on your own. It is too dangerous."

Without thinking, Cinzia wrapped her arms around Kovac. "I'm sorry. I know I scared you. But I am all right, now." Kovac was rigid in her arms at first, then he slowly relaxed. "You needn't worry," Cinzia said. "I will not do that again."

Kovac's voice, however, remained stiff. Her Goddessguard, ever solemn. "My lady, I do not think this is appropriate."

Cinzia smiled, resting her head on his armored chest. "I know," she said.

When she pulled away, Kovac was frowning at her. "The least you can do is get some rest, my lady. You've hardly slept. You cannot continue like this."

Cinzia smiled once more, then stepped behind the partition. "I can rest when my work is done," she called, over her shoulder. She sat on the bed, the Codex at her side. She realized that Jane was staring at her.

"What?"

"Something has gotten into you, sister. Are you sure you are all right?"

Cinzia took a deep breath. She did not know how to begin to describe her feelings. "I am, Jane. I promise. Let's get to work."

Jane was still staring.

Cinzia sighed. "I hope you are not tired? I think I could translate all night, if you feel able."

Finally Jane seemed to relax, settling back into her chair at the desk. "I am tired, but I'm not. I feel the exhaustion, but at the same time I feel something else, something pushing me on."

"I feel the same," Cinzia said. It was curious; they had stayed up translating for too many nights, but Cinzia truly did not feel tired. In fact, ever since beginning the translation she had more energy than she had any right to have on so little sleep.

"Canta strengthens us," Jane said. "The translation is that important. There is something we need to find, I think. Something She is pushing us to learn." Jane paused. "I fear we are not learning it fast enough."

"Then let's stop wasting time," Cinzia said. But, when she opened the book, she could not find her place. She had grown used to opening the Codex of Elwene to the exact place she left off; it was a small miracle she attributed to whatever power allowed her to translate in the first place. But, this time it did not work. Cinzia peered at the words, trying to figure out what she had last read. They were nearing the end of the book of Arcana, she knew. Tonight, with any luck, they would finish the book of Cinzia as well.

But they could not finish until Cinzia found her place. Cinzia frowned, flipping through unfamiliar pages. Usually the words took only a moment to coalesce, to come together. Something was wrong.

She could not read the words of the Nine Scriptures. The symbols were meaningless.

"Cinzia... do you feel that?"

Cinzia shook her head, turning pages rapidly. She had to be mistaken. But the symbols were nothing but gibberish.

"Cinzia, something is *wrong*."

Why would Canta do this to her, now, of all moments? Just

when she had felt such connection with the Goddess, Cinzia's power to translate was taken away.

"*Cinzia!*"

Cinzia looked up at Jane, eyes wide. Then, she heard the voice.

It was low, and deeper than any voice she had ever heard. The sound vibrated, shaking her very bones. The voice was wreathed in a fiery resonance, like the sound of a heavy log thrown onto a bonfire.

The voice emanated from behind the partition. With it, came fear.

"*You are too late,*" the voice rasped. "*The Rising begins.*"

"Kovac?" Cinzia whispered. The voice was not his, that much she was certain. And yet he was the only one behind the partition. "Are you all right?"

"*Kovac is gone. I could not get to you on the roof; I cannot reach your sister; but this man now belongs to me.*"

Cinzia looked at Jane. Jane's eyes were wide with fear; tears streamed down her face.

"*You are both too late. Your efforts are all in vain. You have been under my power since I touched your soul in Navone. And now, tonight, the Rising begins. Tonight, we reclaim the Sfaera. Tonight marks the end of your Goddess.*"

"Who are you?" Cinzia asked, her voice trembling. She dared not look beyond the partition.

"*We are the Nine. And I... am... fear.*"

Then something rushed at Cinzia and she screamed. A hand wrapped around her throat, slamming her against the wall. She blinked through watery eyes. Kovac stood in front of her, one hand at her neck. His other hand held Jane, also by the neck, pressing her against the wall. Cinzia clawed at the hand that held her; she punched it, hit it with all her might, but Kovac's arm was like stone. She kicked and flailed but Kovac did not move.

The voice rumbled from Kovac's throat.

*"Fear me."*

Through tear-filled eyes, Cinzia saw Kovac's face. His mouth was twisted in a grotesque sneer, his eyes burned with green fire. Tendrils of iridescent smoke rose lazily from them. Cinzia felt her strength drain away.

*"Fear me, and tremble."*

Still kicking, Cinzia's thigh brushed up against something at Kovac's waist.

His dagger.

Cinzia reached down, stretching as far as she could, and her fingertip brushed the dagger's pommel. She strained against the hand that held her with all her might. She couldn't breathe. Darkness closed around the edges of her vision.

*Canta, help me!*

*"Fear me, and die."*

Cinzia's hand wrapped around the dagger's pommel. She pulled it free from Kovac's belt, and thrust the blade into her Goddessguard's eye. She felt the metal scrape violently against bone.

Kovac screamed, and the sound was a terrible hybrid of the deep, fiery voice and Kovac's own. Cinzia fell to the floor as he released her, Jane beside her.

Kovac's scream faded, and the large man toppled back, crashing to the floor.

The green light in his eyes was gone. The iridescent smoke was gone. The remaining eye was Kovac's, one that Cinzia had known for years, the pale-blue eye of her Goddessguard.

Cinzia rose to her hands and knees, gasping. She felt as if she would never get enough air. She looked at Jane. Her sister lay on the floor, eyes wide, chest moving in short wheezing breaths.

"Jane," Cinzia rasped, helping her sister up. "Jane," she said again. Her breath allowed no more.

Jane, eyes still wide, nodded slowly. She waved Cinzia away, indicating something behind her.

Cinzia turned in horror, afraid Kovac was alive—afraid whatever daemon had possessed him was still there. But Kovac was dead, blood leaking from around the dagger. The other eye, wide open, seemed to look right at Cinzia.

"I am sorry," Cinzia tried to whisper, but the words would not form.

"The Codex," Jane whispered, clutching her throat. "Translation. We need to finish it."

Cinzia nodded. She crawled past Kovac's body to the bed. Strangely, she felt no sense of horror. But she knew it was close.

The pages of the book fell open to where she had last left off.

Face pale, throat burning, Cinzia read the final words on the last page of the book of Arcana.

And then shall it come to pass, that the Harbinger shall journey into the heart of the dragon, along with he whose mind is lost, and the ancient youth, and the pure in heart. Yet all shall desire that they never had departed their home, that they never had left the lands of their people. What was lost shall be found; what was found shall be lost. The innocent shall pass away; the cursed shall live on. And all shall learn fear as the dragon is slain, the Queen of Chaos is born from the Harbinger's ashes, and Daemons rise once again in the Sfaera.

# 51

ASTRID DREAMED.

She dreamed of herself, not as she was now, but as she was before, innocent and weak. She sat on a chair in a one-room cabin. The walls were wood, the floor was dirt, there was a window in each wall that showed only darkness outside. The only door, directly in front of her, was closed.

In her dream, Astrid waited.

Astrid waited for years it seemed, perhaps centuries. She waited patiently at first, but then Astrid began to wonder when *she* would arrive. Astrid grew anxious, feeling tightness in her chest, the fluttering of her heart. Anxiety turned to fear. She gripped the chair with both hands, knuckles turning white.

*She* was coming. *She* would be here. Astrid couldn't know when, but it had to be soon. Her eyes darted from window to window. A knock at the door, any minute now. The horror consumed everything and left only terror. Sweat dripped from her brow, and she shivered.

There would be a knock, any second, a knock, any second now, a knock, a knock, a knock, a knock, a knock, a knock…

"Wake up, little one."

Astrid's eyes snapped open. *She* would be here. Any second, now. A knock, a knock, a…

She looked into the eyes of an old woman in Cantic livery, smiling down at her. A priestess. "It's all right, my dear," the woman said, her voice kind. "You were having a dream. An evil dream."

Astrid glanced around, squinting. She was in a bright white room, with candles and torches everywhere. A Cantic chapel. Astrid tried to raise an arm to shield her eyes, and felt a sharp, searing pain. Her arm wouldn't move.

She looked down. She was nailed to a table; long white wooden spikes protruded from her arms and legs. The wood seared her flesh like fire.

"Where am I?" Astrid asked, struggling but knowing it was futile. "What are you doing?" She tried to keep the panic from her voice.

"I'm helping you heal, child," the woman said, smiling down at her. "You're lucky we found you. The Black Matron said you would be here; she told us your mission. The guards thought you were dead. We found you, and we knew otherwise."

"Why keep me here?" Astrid asked.

"The Black Matron instructed us on how to cleanse you," the priestess said. "We will let you go, you mustn't worry. Your suffering will not be eternal. Your pain will not last."

Astrid forced herself to breathe calmly. "You're going to let me go?"

The priestess would not stop smiling. "Of course, child. The Black Matron orders you to continue in the company of this Knot fellow. Great things are happening. Great things that will change the Sfaera, and they're beginning here, in Roden. As soon as we let you go, you must find Knot and his companions in the imperial palace."

Astrid's mind raced. She liked Knot. She liked Winter. She had hoped to escape the Denomination, the Black Matron's influence, hoped that all three of them could live normal lives. She hadn't wanted to betray them.

She saw how wrong she had been.

They were going to let her go. But this priestess seemed to have more in store for her first.

The priestess reached below the table, standing up with a bucket in her hands.

"The Black Matron insists you contact her more often. The last she heard from you was in the wilderness, along the River Arden. And before that, Brynne. If she didn't know better, she would think you were trying to escape your duty."

The priestess dipped her hand in the bucket. It emerged dripping with water. She flicked her hand at Astrid.

Astrid closed her eyes instinctively, flinching as the droplets hit her. Why flick her with water? What did the woman expect—

Suddenly Astrid's face *burned*. She whimpered, shaking her head.

"What is that?" Astrid asked, through clenched teeth.

"That, child, is water. Water that has had nightsbane soaking in it for the last few hours, to be specific."

There was a knock at the door.

"Enter," the priestess said. Astrid strained, but couldn't see who it was. "The water is perfect," the priestess said. "I'll need another dozen buckets or so. Fetch them immediately."

The door closed, and the priestess looked back at Astrid.

"Have you ever wondered why you breathe, child?" The priestess smiled and reached below the table. Astrid heard a cranking sound, and the table started to shift. She had been lying flat, but now she was moving to an angle, her feet rising in the air as her head dipped lower.

"Considering you're immortal, one would think it wouldn't be necessary. But, for some reason, you do it anyway. We've studied your kind extensively to understand why you breathe, why the sun ignites your skin, why your eyes glow, but no physical explanation exists that we can find.

"Most of us have simply decided that it is part of your curse. You must live through everything we live through, and live through everything that would kill us, as well."

Astrid was paralyzed with fear.

"We both have parts to play, my dear." The priestess unrolled a thick cloth, dipping it in the bucket. "Mine involves cleansing you. You need to know that, wherever you are, we will find you. You are bound to us. We are your only hope."

The priestess placed the wet cloth over Astrid's face, smothering her in fire. The pain cut so deeply she could hardly breathe.

And then came the water.

# 52

WINTER WONDERED WHETHER SHE was dead.

She had a fierce headache, worse than any *faltira* hangover. She was someplace dark. And damp. And cold. She lay on a stone floor that sucked the heat from her body, but she was too sore to move. Even lifting her head was painful.

*Is this Oblivion?* Many people thought of Oblivion as a place of burning and torture, but the descriptions that had always frightened Winter the most were of impenetrable darkness and lasting pain, the coldness of both body and mind.

Complete and utter isolation.

She could remember fighting in the square. She remembered a man with a mace. Beyond that, everything was blurry. Nash had been there, and Elsi. No, not Elsi. Kali. Winter was sure of it.

She attempted a few croaks of sound. She called out to Knot, Lian, and Astrid—even to Cinzia and Jane, but there was no response. She was alone. How long had she been here? Surely not more than a day. She remembered someone trying to give her water, but she had choked violently. Now her throat was parched. She called out again, her voice echoing eerily in the blackness. She planted her hands on the ground, pushing herself up with great effort. Her arms burned and her muscles strained, and despite the darkness, her mind spun dizzyingly fast. She collapsed back, spasming with pain.

So much for sitting, let alone standing.

She heard a clanking, the first sound she had heard in ages, it seemed.

"Hello?"

A shaft of light blinded her. Winter shut her eyes, but the light burned through her eyelids.

"She's awake," a deep voice declared. Winter wasn't sure whether the echo was in her own mind or the dungeon. For that was clearly where she was.

"So she is," another voice responded. "The princess rises from her beauty sleep." A chuckle, dry and gravelly.

*Princess.* The word echoed in Winter's mind.

"That's enough," the first voice said. "We've got orders."

Winter squinted, eyes slowly adjusting. Two men stood above her, clad in mail and long, pointed helmets.

"She's a lucky one," one of them said. Winter recognized the high, reedy voice as the second who had spoken. "Meeting the emperor and the Tokal-Ceno in one day. A blessed one, even."

"I said that's enough," the first man said. "Or didn't you hear me the first time?"

"I heard you, I heard you," the second man mumbled.

Rough hands gripped Winter beneath her arms, hauling her to her feet. It took her a moment, but she finally managed a shuffling gait, with both guards supporting most of her weight. She thought about praying, until she remembered the goddess she would pray to. The one who had abandoned her long ago. What would she say, anyway?

*Bless my friends, that they can live through this, that they will be better off than me.*

*But if not, bless them with a quick death. Receive them quickly into your embrace.*

# 53

THE GUARDS PUSHED KNOT into the throne hall of the imperial palace, but Knot could only think of the dream he'd had in the dungeon. It had been a new dream. He had not killed anyone. He had not fought at all.

Knot had been a grain farmer, with a small plot of land and a family. Knot remembered kissing his wife in the morning, a plump woman who laughed warmly, and his two children, a boy and a girl. Both younger than ten summers. The boy woke early with Knot to milk their cow, and they had walked together in the dawn, and he had put his hand on the boy's shoulder.

Knot stumbled and fell on his face, landing hard on the cool marble floor. There was a chorus of laughter from the Reapers around him. Hands grabbed him roughly, pulling him back to his feet. Knot looked around the spacious hall. His eyes focused on one person.

Winter lay prostrate on the ground before a large throne. Lian was beside her. They both looked bruised and filthy. Dried blood trailed from their ears and noses.

At least they'd survived.

Astrid's screams as she writhed in the snow still echoed in Knot's skull. The sword, laced with nightsbane, must have killed the girl. Even if it hadn't, the Reapers would have and figured out what she was. They would not have let her live.

Knot found his grief for the vampire hard to understand. But it would do him no good to dwell on it.

Winter and Lian turned their heads, and Knot's eyes met Winter's, but before he could acknowledge her a Reaper standing hit her sharply with the butt of his spear, forcing her face to the ground again.

"Madzin Moraine. I never thought I would see you again. Not after what we did to you."

Knot lifted his gaze to the throne, a large sky-blue lacquered seat on a platform of golden stairs. Sitting in it was Emperor Grysole.

He was tall, taller than Knot. The man's head and cheeks were smooth and freshly shaven. He wore simple white trousers, a white undercoat, and a tight-fitting sky-blue overcoat that wrapped around his body. He wore no crown or jewelry other than a large gold ring on the little finger of his left hand.

Glancing up, Knot took in the expanse of the chamber. The throne hall was circular, with white-and-blue marbled floors, and massive pillars—as big around as Knot was tall—lined the circumference. Above Knot loomed the largest dome he'd ever seen. An elaborate mural covered the curved expanse, depicting the Age of Marvels, showing epic battles and mystical creatures. Large stained-glass windows let in starlight.

"Not Madzin," Knot rasped, glaring at the emperor. Whoever Knot really was, this man could tell him. But that didn't matter if they couldn't get out of here alive. Knot took stock of his surroundings. Two Reapers guarded the door through which he had entered, and two more stood at the base of the throne platform. The three Reapers who had brought Knot stood guard over him, and two more stood by Winter and Lian. A servant of some kind stood near a smaller door to the left of the throne. Eleven enemies. Knot wasn't bound, but he feared eleven would be too many. And, even if he caught them by surprise, surely one would escape to warn others.

*Where's that damn vampire when I need her?* The thought only brought sadness.

The emperor smiled, his thin lips curling upwards. "I should have guessed. Who are you, then? Darcen? Elenar? Hoc? Someone else entirely? Have you reverted all the way back to Lathe?"

Knot frowned. "Lathe" was familiar to him, as was "Madzin." The other names meant nothing.

*A conglomeration of souls crammed together.* That was what the Tokal had said. *A creation of science and magic.*

"My name is Knot," he said.

The emperor's eyebrows rose. "Knot? A *new* name? Unexpected, albeit lacking in creativity."

Behind Knot, the doors to the throne hall burst open, angry shouts sounding outside. Knot turned.

At the head of the group walked the Tokal, his long blond hair waving. Behind him strode a dozen Ceno monks, green cowls over their heads, hands hidden in wide sleeves.

*Add thirteen more,* Knot thought to himself. His odds were plummeting. As the Ceno entered, Knot felt a heavy weight upon him. The feeling was too tangible, too real to be despair. It was as if a veil had been placed over him, blocking him. From what, he did not know.

"Ah, Tokal-Ceno," the emperor said, "welcome to our little hearing. Glad you could make it."

The man scowled at the emperor. "Had I actually been informed of it, Your Grace, I'm sure we would have been here much earlier."

"You're here now," the emperor said, waving his hand, "and

that's what matters. Count the marbles in the bag, not the ones on the floor." He nodded towards Knot. "You remember our good friend Madzin? Or Knot, as he prefers now."

The Tokal looked at Knot and smiled. "Of course. We saw one another quite recently."

"Knot wasn't a sift we gave him, Tokal. Why does he call himself that?"

The Tokal raised an eyebrow, and turned back to the emperor. "I honestly don't know, Your Grace. I was hoping to find out, assuming you're planning on releasing him back into my custody?"

"What's a sift?" Knot grunted.

The emperor and the Tokal both looked at him, surprise etched on their faces.

"You've forgotten psimantic terminology?" the Tokal asked.

Knot narrowed his eyes. He knew what Winter had told him of it, but they had only spoken briefly. "Sift" was not a word she had used; Knot didn't see what it had to do with him.

"I should have known," the Tokal muttered. "I'll make it simple, so you and your elvish friends can understand. According to the art of acumency, a sift is a soul extracted from its body, capable of branding onto something else. A voidstone, another body, or a number of other repositories. Normally, only one sift can brand a repository." The Tokal glanced at the Ceno monks behind him. "But we have been experimenting. You, my dear Knot, were our first successful branding of multiple sifts into one body."

"An amalgamation of souls," Knot whispered.

The Tokal smiled. "Precisely. Psimancers make the best repositories, after all. Far better than a normal body. But we were loath to kill off one of our own."

"So when the Nazaniin sent you to assassinate me," the emperor said, his voice booming throughout the hall, "we were able to skewer two fish with one spear."

"Yes, of course," the Tokal said. "Thank you, Your Grace." He looked back at Knot. "We had to obliterate you first—extract your mind from your body—which explains your memory loss. Of course, when we branded you with the other sifts, we assumed you would take on *their* memories… but something was lost in the process."

"How many sifts in total, Tokal?" the emperor asked. "How many did we brand him with?"

The Tokal frowned. There was definitely tension in their relationship, Knot noted. Something to exploit later.

"We began with nine, Your Grace," the Tokal said. "Not including Lathe's original sift."

Knot looked back at the emperor, unsure what to believe. He was not just Lathe. He was Lathe and nine other people, crammed into the same body? The idea seemed insane, and yet it explained how so many tasks were easy to him.

"Of course, you did not wake for some time after the procedures," the Tokal said. "The sifts remained dormant. We kept you on our research vessel in the Gulf of Nahl, waited for months, almost losing hope that your mind had survived the process. But then you awoke. And you escaped!" The Tokal laughed. "Our own ambition had defeated us, I'm afraid. The talents you inherited from your sifts were too much for us to control. At first, we thought the water had claimed you. But imagine our surprise when, over a year later, we heard of a human man getting married to a tiellan in a small town in northern Khale. A man who had shown up about one year earlier, with no memory of who he was or where he came from."

"It pays to have an extensive network of little birds," the emperor said.

The Tokal ignored him. "We sent a group to retrieve you and your tiellan bride. We needed both of you for what was to come. Unfortunately you led us on a merry pursuit. We had hoped, of course, that the return protocol would work, and that you would come back to us on your own. But a year didn't seem a very good response time, so we assumed the protocol was corrupted. Yet here you are, at our doorstep. The return protocol worked— you remember the blue light, no? And what luck—you defeated another Nazaniin *cotir* on the way. Skewering two fish with one spear, as the emperor said. It is rather satisfying."

Knot looked at Winter. He couldn't see her face. What would she think of him, now? He'd all but caused the death of her father, been the catalyst for this entire journey. She must hate him.

"Why do you need us both?" Knot asked. "You said you wanted to take both of us in Pranna. But when you attacked us by the river, you only took Winter. Why?"

The Tokal raised an eyebrow. "I assume Winter is your wife? Of course she is. We need her, that's all. You'll find out why soon enough, old friend."

The emperor frowned. "What is this, Tokal? You said nothing about needing the elf girl."

"Did I not?" The Tokal chuckled. "My apologies. We need her for a small ritual we shall be performing. It actually concerns you, Your Grace. We were hoping to begin now, in fact, if you would care to be present."

The emperor frowned. "Concerns me? What sort of ritual of yours *concerns* me, Tokal? I thought I'd seen enough of your grisly artifice."

"Just this last one, if it pleases Your Grace. I must insist, for the good of Roden."

The emperor's lips contorted. "Very well, Tokal. But afterwards," he said, indicating the servant near the side door, "I'll have a bath. And a flask of 152 Cordonat. *Immediately* afterwards."

The servant nodded vigorously, scurrying out.

"Very well, Tokal, get on with it," the emperor said.

Knot's jaw tightened. He didn't know anything about rituals, but he was sure he didn't want Winter to be a part of this one. He looked around. Impossible odds. Even if Astrid were here, their chances would be slim. But Knot had to do something.

"I'm afraid we'll need the throne," the Tokal said, placing a foot on the first gilded step of the platform. "Rituals of power should be performed in places of power, after all."

The emperor frowned. "You can perform the ritual well enough down there, Tokal. Forgive my superstition, but I won't abdicate the throne freely, metaphorically or otherwise."

The Tokal smiled. Knot's gut churned. Something was going on here.

"I hoped you would say that," the Tokal said. "It will make this much more fun." He nodded his head towards the emperor, and suddenly Knot knew.

This was a coup.

"Take him," the Tokal said. The two Reapers at the base of the throne turned and made their way up the stairs.

"What is this, Tokal? What are you doing?" the emperor demanded.

"What I've waited to do for years, Your Grace."

The emperor stood, red-faced, glaring down at the Tokal. "You're a fool. Don't set yourself up for failure."

"I never do," the Tokal said. "Kill the servant," he shouted, "and lock the doors. We're about to witness a terrible tragedy. The assassination of our emperor at the hands of Khale."

*Of course*, Knot thought. The Ceno wanted power, and Knot and his companions had given them the perfect excuse to take it.

Grysole's once red face paled as he looked at the Reapers approaching him. "Henrik. Foval. You have both served me for years. Defend me now!"

The two Reapers did not respond. They took the emperor roughly between them, and looked at the Tokal.

*They've been bought.* The two Reapers at the door behind Knot must have been bought as well; they were closing and barring the door. The Reapers who'd brought Knot into the chamber, however, and the Reapers who stood by Lian and Winter, seemed loyal to the emperor. Weapons drawn, they glared at the Ceno monks, who brandished swords of their own. Two Ceno had sprinted after the servant through the side door as soon as the Tokal made his move.

"Hold him," the Tokal said, walking up the gilded steps.

"You cannot do this," the emperor said. All majesty had fled him.

"I can." The Tokal drew a long dagger from his robe. "Quite easily, actually." Then, he gripped the emperor's bald head with one hand, pushing it back. He chanted in a strange language as he raised the dagger.

Then he slit the emperor's throat.

As the emperor's blood gushed onto the gilded steps, the Reapers around Knot—the men still loyal to the emperor—shuffled nervously.

Now that the Tokal was making his move, it was best Knot make his. Siding with the empire seemed pointless, given what he had just witnessed. But the Tokal wanted to kill Winter, and that made things clear. Part of him was desperate to ask the man questions; who were the nine people sharing his head with Lathe? But getting Winter to safety was all that mattered. Finding out who he was could wait. If these green-robed men were anything like those who had ambushed them by the river, he would probably die, but he had no choice but to fight.

Knot lunged towards the nearest Ceno, punching him in the throat and reaching for the man's sword.

*"Bring her to me!"* the Tokal screamed.

Winter cringed. A group of monks attacked the Reapers who were guarding her and Lian. It was four against two; the Reapers fought well, killing two Ceno, but were soon dispatched. One of the monks grabbed Winter and began hauling her towards the throne. The other moved towards Lian, sword drawn. Like the men from the river, these men did not seem to communicate in any visible way.

She struggled, but she had no weapon. She wished, above all things, that she had Knot's frost. If she could only take one *faltira* crystal, she would bring death to all these men who meant harm to her and hers. Although the last time she had taken frost in the presence of the Ceno, she hadn't been able to use her powers. Were the two things connected?

Winter tried to wrench free of the Ceno's grip, but he was too strong. She tried stamping on his foot, but only succeeded in tripping herself up, and was dragged bodily up the steps towards the waiting Tokal. The Reapers who had betrayed the emperor ran down past her. Winter looked over her shoulder. Lian was still struggling against the Ceno monk. Somehow, he had gotten a sword but he was barely holding off the monk's attacks. *He won't last long.* Knot, along with two remaining Reapers loyal to the emperor, fought off four Ceno not fifteen rods from the throne. The two Reapers who had stood guard at the door rushed towards the melee. Winter could not tell which side they would join.

"Knot!" Winter shouted. "Two from the throne, two from the door!" He probably already knew the four men were closing in, but she had to warn him. He wielded his sword as a part of him, weaving and spinning in a delicate dance, only to turn and smash his fist into a Ceno's skull, or stab one through the gut. She remembered him fighting the monks at their wedding. A dragon-eel among deepfish. Lightning across dark water.

Two more monks went down at Knot's hand, though they took one of the remaining loyal Reapers with them. The four other Reapers converged on him.

And then Winter was at the throne, her arms held by the Ceno, the Tokal before her.

The Tokal was chanting in a language Winter had never heard, the syllables soft and flowing; Winter might have thought it beautiful if the man didn't have a dagger to her throat. The hilt was chipped. *A strange thing to notice when I'm about to die.*

Below, Knot screamed her name. Winter looked down; the last Reaper who had stood for the late emperor had fallen. The three Reapers who had attacked Knot now held him between them; all the monks had fallen, it seemed, save the one who held Winter.

If Knot couldn't help her, all hope was lost.

The Tokal stopped chanting and smiled at her. "Your sacrifice will not be in vain, my dear. Yours will be greatness and glory; dusk is upon us, and you shall usher in the fall of night."

Winter looked on in horror as the Tokal raised the blade. She thought of her father, of his strong hands and weathered face, of the way he embraced her the day of her wedding. She thought of Lian's apology, and Knot's tentative forgiveness.

Was it really all for nothing?

Then, several things happened at once.

Everyone looked up at the sound of shattering glass, falling like rain, followed by a soft thud. A small form landed on the marble floor between the Reapers holding Knot and the doorway. The figure stood, no larger than a child.

At the same time, two monks—the men who had gone after the emperor's servant—burst in from the side door, and ran towards the throne.

And Winter suddenly saw Lian, shouting, barreling up the gilded steps, sword in hand.

The monk who held Winter must have been distracted by the breaking glass, and his grip on Winter loosened as he barely managed to dodge a thrust from Lian's sword. He did not manage to dodge Winter's fist as she swung it at his face. Lian's second thrust went through the man's chest, and he collapsed, falling down the stairs.

Lian pushed Winter down the steps as the Ceno fell, away from the Tokal. "You always did need saving, princess. You always did—"

The Tokal reached out, quick and soft as a whisper. A growing line of red spread across Lian's neck and he fell to his knees, blood bubbling from his mouth. Winter felt the hot spray of it on her face.

"Fool," the Tokal said. "Tiellan blood was all I needed. Yours or hers, it didn't matter. The girl's death would have had a certain poetry, but yours... yours will do."

Lian fell down face first, his blood spattering the gold steps.

"No," Winter whispered. She looked from Lian's body up to the Tokal, who stood tall, triumphant. He lifted his hands high in the air, one still holding the dagger, as he continued his ethereal chanting.

Winter ran up the steps, slipping on blood as she bent to take up Lian's sword. Then she rammed the blade through the Tokal's heart.

The Tokal did not flinch, but remained standing, chanting, his eyes staring skywards.

Winter withdrew the sword and stabbed him again through the belly. Once again, the man didn't move.

With a sob, Winter withdrew the sword and swung once more, the blade biting into the Tokal's neck. The wretched chanting stopped, and the man rolled down the steps to the marble below.

Winter looked down at herself, covered in blood. She slumped into the throne, looking at the bodies below her. The emperor, the Tokal, the monk, and Lian. So much death.

She realized that everyone was staring up at her. Knot, the Reapers, the remaining Ceno. Even the girl. Astrid, Winter realized numbly. What did it matter? Her mother. Her father. Lian. Chaos and death followed her. She would never escape it.

Knot called Winter's name. The Reapers had released him the moment she killed the Tokal. Knot almost felt sympathy for them. They had lost two leaders in one day. But it didn't stop him from killing them. Their shock made the task simple.

"Winter, please," Knot said. Two Ceno remained, but they did not matter. He looked back at Astrid. He had felt such hope when she crashed through the sky-window. Knot did not know how she was alive, but he didn't care. With her help, they *would* make it out of here.

And then Knot had watched Lian die, and had been unable to do anything to stop it.

Astrid blurred across the room towards the remaining Ceno. She dispatched both easily. In the same moment, Knot felt the strange veil, the shroud he had felt ever since the Tokal had entered the chamber with his Ceno, lift from him. He felt an odd, but somehow familiar, power.

"I'm sorry," Astrid whispered. "I was too late."

Knot shook his head, unsure what to say. He looked back at Winter, still slumped on the throne.

"Winter," he pleaded, "we need to get out of here."

Winter met his eyes. She stood, wordlessly.

"Don't know if we *can* get out of here," Astrid said. Knot blinked. The vampire was standing beside him, looking up.

In midair, directly above the throne, a strange gaping shadow twisted.

"Winter, come down from there!" Whatever the shadow was, Knot did not want to face it. And he definitely didn't want Winter directly below it.

Winter finally walked down the steps. Knot embraced her tightly. "I'm so sorry," he said.

She said nothing in return, but at least she seemed to be coming back to herself. Her daze frightened him. Above them the shadow contorted, growing larger, a black gaping tear that shimmered and shifted like moonlight on water but completely dark. As if it drew light into itself.

Then, slowly, a dark mist began to pour from the shadow. The mist tumbled and cascaded over the throne, unfurling and eddying as it reached across the marble floor, shrouding everything in black. The lacquered throne, the golden steps, the blood, the white-and-blue marble were no longer visible. In their place Knot saw only darkness.

"Um. Guys?" Astrid took a step back. The mist rushed towards them.

Knot released Winter from his embrace and took her hand. Then, he heard the voice. Deep, low, and wreathed in flame.

*"You cannot escape. We will consume you."*

"What...?" Knot stepped back again, pulling Winter with him. She stared at the mist, her expression blank. The billowing black cloud was three or four paces away now.

And it was moving faster.

"That," Astrid said, "is what *I* have nightmares about."

Knot peered at the girl. Her eyes were wide. She was... trembling.

"Run," Astrid said. Then she took off in a streak, and Knot pulled Winter along with him. A crack of thunder shook the room.

The mist suddenly spread a hundredfold, enveloping the entire throne hall. Knot gripped Winter's hand more tightly as the black mist enfolded them both. Knot only had time to see Winter's eyes widen in horror as she was torn away from him, her mouth opening in a scream.

Then Knot was alone in the blackness.

# 54

THE MIST SWALLOWED WINTER'S scream as it pulled Knot from her. One moment she was holding his hand, the next he was sinking back into the dark, and then Winter was alone.

All around her was nothing but blackness. She looked down, but could not see her own body. She could feel it; she placed her hands on her face, her arms, her belly, but she saw nothing. The dark was tangible, overwhelming, and Winter felt as if she would drown in it.

*Perhaps this is Oblivion. Perhaps I am dead.*

Then, the Voice. A deep, booming growl, every syllable rolled in flame. The same one that had spoken as the mist poured from the shadow above the throne.

*"Not death. Death is the easier path; I bring something else."*

Winter looked up. She shook her fist at the Voice in anger.

"I'm not afraid! You've already taken everything I love. You have no power over me!"

The Voice laughed, deep and booming. *"All things fear, daughter. And so, I have power over all things."*

Screams in the distance. Winter thought they were her own, at first. It was difficult to tell in the black. But, as she listened, the voices grew more distinct. One was a woman. There were two others... two men, Winter thought. They sounded familiar, but she could not place them.

"If you think a few screams will scare me, you're—"

Winter stopped. One of the people was screaming her name. And finally she recognized the voice. A deep pit of horror opened up within her.

"Papa!"

The screaming stopped. Before her were three figures. Her father, in furs and wool, and Lian. Between them was a short woman that Winter did not recognize. Her hair and eyes were raven-black, just like Winter's. She wore a red dress, simple but elegant. She smelled, faintly, of cinnamon.

"Mother?"

Winter's father shook his head. "Do not speak to her, Winter. You have no right. You stole her from me, you made my life miserable by taking away the only person I loved. I hated you for that." Her father's soft brown eyes grew hard. "Every moment, I've hated you."

Winter stepped back in shock. Her father had never spoken this way.

"And how do you repay my kindness? How do you repay my sacrifice? By destroying yourself. Losing yourself in this *faltira*, in this ridiculous world of psimancy and magic."

"Murderer," her mother whispered.

Winter's heart crumbled. "I'm so sorry, Papa, I didn't mean to let it go so far. I didn't mean for any of this to happen, you have to believe me!"

Her father shook his head. "What is done is done, Winter. Don't waste my time with excuses."

Winter stared at her father, unable to speak. How could he say such things? He had loved her, her entire life he had loved her.

Hadn't he?

"Murderer," her mother said.

"I never forgave you," Lian said, shaking his head. "What I told you was a lie. I knew we would die here because of you. I lied to you, but I see now I should have told you the truth. I should not have given you the benefit of the lie. I'm disappointed in you, Winter. You are not the woman I thought you were. You are much less."

"Murderer!" Winter's mother stepped forward, a frown creasing her beautiful face. "You killed those people in Navone. All those innocent people. You killed the dealer in Izet, and others besides. You are a murderer. Like the season for which you are named, you leave everything cold and barren in your wake. You are a murderer. That is all you will ever be."

"Mother, I—"

"You murdered *me*, daughter. Do you think there is forgiveness for that? Do you think I could ever care for you when you took my life away?"

Winter hung her head. She had nothing to say.

They were right.

One moment Astrid had been sprinting away, hearing Knot and Winter's footsteps behind her. The next, she was devoured by the black, completely alone.

"Shit," Astrid whispered. She knew the Voice; she had heard it before, in her nightmares. All daemons knew Him, and all feared Him.

*"Astrid, my child. You could be such an elegant, horrific fiend. Why choose the path of misery?"*

"How are you here?" Astrid asked. "How are you doing this? I'm awake, I know I am."

*"I could not then, my child. Now, things are different. The door is*

*open. Our path is set. The Rising begins."*

Astrid shook her head. "No," she whispered. "You cannot reach me when I am awake!"

*"Things have changed, daughter."*

Astrid closed her eyes, despite the impenetrable darkness, and rocked back and forth. When had she fallen to the floor? She didn't know.

*"No, Astrid. Open your eyes. Your nightmare wakes."*

Astrid's eyes snapped open. She was sitting, alone, in a cabin. There was a single door in front of her. Closed. Astrid gripped her chair with both hands, tightly, her knuckles turning white. She breathed quickly, shallowly. Her heart pounded in her ears, in her head. *She* was coming. *She* would be here. Astrid didn't know when, but it had to be soon.

A knock.

Knot fumbled about, shouting Winter's name. The blackness reflected his shouts back at him; he was trapped, alone, defeated.

"Winter!" he shouted again. He could see nothing, not even his own body. "Astrid!"

No response. No response, except for the Voice.

*"You are alone, my son. You are alone, and you are mine."*

"Who are you?"

There was no answer.

*"Who are you?"* Knot asked again. Still, no response.

Then, the Voice rumbled through the void. *"You know my name."*

"Don't know anything about you," Knot said. "What d'you want from us?"

*"You know my name, as I know yours. Your heart spoke it at your wedding. Your body whispered it in Navone, when you found her, and*

*every day afterward. Your soul cries it out every time you kill. I have many names. I am the First. I am the Fear. Speak my name, and tremble."*

Knot did not know how, but the name came to his lips. He said it, he feared it, and the Voice was right. He did tremble.

"Azael."

The Voice rumbled, a rolling fire in the void. A laugh.

*"As for what I want from you… there is one thing, and one thing only."*

Suddenly a little girl rushed towards him from the darkness. At first Knot thought it was Astrid, and ran towards her. But as he ran, Knot saw it was not the vampire. This girl was too young, her hair too dark. The way this girl looked at him was not the way Astrid looked at him. This girl looked at him as if…

"Papa!"

It was the girl from his dream, the dream from the dungeon. When Knot dreamed of owning a farm, being part of a family, this had been his daughter. As Knot recognized her, love formed in a colossal blossom. It spread through him, warm and powerful. The girl leapt into his arms, embracing him tightly.

"Papa, I'm so glad you're home." She buried her head in his shoulder. He felt her soft skin on his neck, her fine hair against his face.

"Ava," Knot said, recalling her name, recalling everything; recalling the way she would pat his cheeks as he carried her to bed, the way she would laugh when he let her pinch his nose, the way she kissed his ears after a winter day's work because she liked the feel of the cold on her lips.

"I've missed you," Knot said.

"Your cheeks are wet, Papa," Ava said, patting Knot's cheeks, smiling, her brown eyes wide.

Then she coughed. Her tiny body convulsed. When Ava

looked up at him again, she was different. Her face pale and thin, lips cracked, eyes empty.

"I'm sick, Papa," she said, and coughed again. Blood seeped from her mouth and nose.

"Oh, Goddess," Knot whispered. He laid Ava down on the bed, the bed that was right next to him. Knot remembered, vaguely, that there had once been blackness where the bed now stood, that he had once been somewhere else and not where he was now, but none of that mattered anymore.

His daughter was dying.

"Goddess," Knot begged. "Please." He felt Ava's forehead, hot as flame.

Ava coughed again, and began to cry. The sound of it was the sound of Knot's heart tearing in two.

"It hurts," his daughter managed between sobs. "It hurts, Papa."

"I know it does," Knot said, looking down at his daughter and knowing with certainty that there was nothing he could do. "I know it does."

Then, Ava's eyes widened. "Light, Papa. I see light."

Knot trembled. "Let the light in, Ava. Let it in."

When Ava spoke again, her voice was sad. "The light goes away, Papa, there is only… only dark." His little girl's eyes widened even further. "They want to take me! Save me from the dark! Save me from the monsters, Papa!" Ava gripped his hand tightly in hers; Knot felt her fear through her skin, ugly and crawling. Ava stopped screaming only to cough, wetly, violently, and then scream again.

"Save me, Papa! Save me!"

Cough.

"The monsters…"

Cough. More blood.

"They want to take…"

Ava coughed again, then looked up. She choked. Her eyes froze in horror.

Silence.

Then, Ava was gone, and Knot was left alone, once more, in the black. He looked up.

"Why?"

The pain of what he'd just seen, the pain of realizing that it was an actual memory, was as wide as a gaping chasm. Above all, the fear that he might see it again consumed him, crawled beneath his skin.

"Why?" he screamed.

*"Because we all experience pain, my son. My pleasure is to remind you of it."*

Then, suddenly, the black mist receded. The darkness that shrouded Knot's mind and the chamber drew back, and Knot found himself once again in Roden's throne hall. He was kneeling on the marble floor, head in his hands. He looked up. The golden steps up to the throne, still covered in blood, were directly in front of him across the room. The great doors to the chamber were behind him, so close he could touch them. To the left Astrid sat on the floor, clutching her knees, rocking back and forth. In the distance, to his right, Winter lay on the ground, not moving.

Knot was about to run to her when he noticed the figure standing by the throne. A tall, dark figure, cloaked in black. The hood was drawn up, creating deep shadow where the man's face was hidden. The robe hung loosely, falling in folds to the floor. The folds, Knot realized, reached outward, blending with the black mist that still crept along the marble. Knot blinked. He could not tell where the cloak ended and where the mist began. One was an extension of the other, but he could not tell which.

Above the figure, the shadow in the air still twisted, shimmering.

*"It has been ten thousand years since I could have such direct influence on the people of the Sfaera."*

The figure was the one who had spoken in the darkness, Knot was sure of it. He knew by the mindless terror he felt, the way his judgment clouded as the figure spoke. He knew because he was paralyzed with fear; he could not move, could not call out to Winter or Astrid. And yet, as the figure spoke, the voice focused. When it had once echoed in Knot's ears and around his head, it now seemed closer to the voice of a man; still deep and rumbling, but changed.

"I'm happy to see my talents are still honed. You three were wonderful test subjects. But I'm afraid I must take my leave. My colleagues arrive."

Slowly, the black mist gathered closer to the figure.

"I shall leave you in the company of some old friends of mine. They have been starved for friendship, one might say. Ten thousand years elicits some dreadful cravings. Something you understand, my dear Astrid."

Above the dark figure, the shimmering shadow grew larger.

"Farewell, my children," the figure said. "Until we meet again."

The black mist converged on itself, and the figure was gone.

As the strange figure disappeared, the growing shadow above the throne coalesced, and a large, dark shape dropped from the portal. In the same moment Knot realized his transfixion, his paralyzing fear, had ended.

"Astrid!" Knot shouted, "we need to leave. *Now.*"

"I said that ages ago, remember? Why in Oblivion didn't you listen to me the first time?"

Knot ran towards Winter. She was slowly rising to her feet. A flood of relief rushed through him. *Not dead,* he thought. *I still have her. Let Oblivion take me, but at least I still have her.*

Before Knot had gotten three steps, a deafening screech echoed around the domed chamber.

Knot looked up. There, towering over the throne, at least twice the height of a man, was a monster unlike anything Knot had ever seen.

Winter stood shakily, her legs trembling. When the monster shrieked, they nearly buckled beneath her once more. She covered her ears with both hands and looked up in horror at the beast that now stood before the throne. Its thin, snakelike body twisted with sinew and muscle, but it stood tall on hind legs. Two thin arms, ending in claws each as long as swords, extended far from the creature's body. The thing's head was massive, a gaping maw as long as a man, nearly half the length of the rest of the creature's body, displaying hundreds of long, slender fangs. The jaw seemed to weigh the rest of the creature down, giving it a hunched appearance. A spiked tail trailed behind the beast, waving lazily.

Never could Winter have imagined such a horror, not even in all the stories of the Age of Marvels.

"Astrid," Winter heard Knot say, "what in Oblivion is that?"

Astrid had only one word. "Outsider."

The monster screeched again, opening its long maw even wider. The thing's head turned, and suddenly Winter realized the monster was staring right at her with deep, dark pits of eyes.

Knot shouted her name; he was running towards her. He

would not get to her in time, Winter knew. If the creature chose to pounce, it could be on her instantly.

Then Winter heard a different screech. A blur sped across the room and time seemed to slow as Astrid collided with the creature, knocking it off balance. The Outsider stumbled, then looked down at Astrid. The vampire barely stood as tall as the thing's knee.

Winter heard the beginnings of a rumble in the monster's chest as it swiped at Astrid, faster than Winter could blink, and the girl careened across the room into one of the huge marble pillars. It burst, crumbling into hundreds of pieces.

Astrid stood, shakily, but if the monster could do such a thing to her, what hope did any of them have?

"In the name of the emperor, we command you to cease!"

Winter looked behind her. The doors to the chamber opened, and almost two dozen Reapers marched in. As they saw the creature by the throne, the soldiers froze.

"What in Oblivion...?" Winter heard one of them mutter. But, to their credit, they moved quickly into formation. They drew their bows.

For a brief moment, the only sound was Knot's footsteps as he ran towards Winter. The Reapers kept their bows drawn, aimed at the Outsider. The creature slowly shifted its gaze from Winter to the Reapers, black eyes gleaming. Then the Outsider's maw opened wide and it screamed, loud enough for Winter to cover her ears and cringe.

"Fire!" one of the Reapers shouted.

Knot reached Winter just as the first volley struck the beast. "Are you all right?" he asked.

Winter stared at him hollowly. Of course she wasn't all right. Lian had just died. She had just experienced... she couldn't even think about what had happened in the dark. And now a monster she could not have imagined in her wildest nightmares was looking at them like a hungry child looked at freshly baked cherry tarts.

"I'm fine," Winter said.

The Outsider screeched as the Reapers' arrows struck. It stamped its feet in anger.

"Liar," Knot said.

"Complaining never helped anyone," Winter said. Despite her promise, she couldn't stop herself from glancing at the pouch at Knot's waist. Still there. Still full of *faltira*. If she could just have one crystal, she might be able to help…

"No, Winter. We can get through this without that."

Then Knot smiled. He turned to face the Outsider. "Besides," he said. "I think I've learned a few things about myself in the last few days." He nodded at the Reapers. "Hopefully we can use them to get out of here."

"Sounds like a good plan to me."

Winter turned to see Astrid limping towards them. She looked tired, but other than her limp mostly uninjured.

In the distance, the Outsider leaped from where it stood by the throne, traveling nearly two-thirds the length of the chamber to land amidst the Reaper formation.

Winter swore. The creature had leapt at least fifty rods. The thing crashed into the Reapers with a screech, scattering them, but the soldiers recovered quickly and attacked, hacking away with their weapons while a few of them hung back, firing arrows. With each swipe of its long claws, with each whip of its tail, the Outsider incapacitated more and more soldiers. The Reapers screamed, at first in bloodlust, but soon the screams turned to panic, and soon, too soon, they were silent. Crushed armor, broken weapons, and bloodied bodies were all that remained.

"So much for our distraction," Astrid muttered.

The Outsider picked up one of the bodies at its feet with a massive claw and lifted the Reaper, stuffing the man into its maw. Metal and bone crunched and screeched, and in seconds the Outsider swallowed what remained of the man. Winter watched as a bulge sank down the thing's snakelike body. Then, the Outsider's head swiveled along its neck, and, once again, it looked directly at Winter. Winter saw the blood on the thing's claws, on its teeth. She saw the way its huge mouth turned up. She could have sworn it was smiling.

"I can handle this," Knot said.

"You'd better do it quick," Astrid said. "I think another one's coming."

Winter's eyes widened as she turned back to the strange portal. Astrid was right. Another form dropped to the floor, and as the shadows coalesced they formed another Outsider, similar in form and size.

Knot stepped forward. "Astrid, hold off the new one. I think I can kill the first, but I need time." As Winter looked at him, she realized that he was suddenly... different. More in control. Despite his bruises, his filthy clothing, he looked calm.

"I'll do what I can," Astrid said. Then, she sprinted off towards the new Outsider.

Winter was about to ask what she could do when she saw, in the distance, the Reaper's discarded weapons rising around the Outsider. She blinked. For a moment she feared that it was some sort of magic that the creature was using, but as a sword slashed through its thigh and a spear embedded itself in the thing's shoulder, Winter knew.

*Canta rising. He did it.*

Knot had remembered how to use psimancy.

The Outsider screamed as a mace smashed into its jaw. Then its gaze shifted from Winter to Knot.

*It knows,* Winter realized. It could sense psimancy, somehow. It knew what Knot was doing. But it was too late. The Outsider had already been wounded heavily by the Reapers; blood dripped from dozens of wounds. Knot sent weapon after weapon into the creature, slicing through the thing's hide, crushing bone and muscle.

Winter sensed, almost immediately, that her own psimantic power was greater than what Knot was using at the moment. She couldn't help but sense it, just as she couldn't help but feel the compulsion to suddenly reach for Knot's pouch and take the frost. She resisted.

While Knot did not appear as powerful as Winter, the *subtlety* with which he used telesis, the intricacy of the patterns, the continuous motion of each of the objects he controlled, was incredible. A weapon that Knot held in one *tendron* suddenly flew forward, slicing straight through the Outsider, and was caught on the other side of the creature's body with another *tendron* only to be flung back through the Outsider again. At the same time, almost a dozen other *tendra* hacked and slashed and stabbed as the Outsider screamed, fighting a dozen invisible foes. Winter could not see the *tendra*, of course, she could barely sense them, but as she watched she could imagine their patterns.

It was beautiful.

With one final moan, the Outsider fell to the ground. The floor shook.

Astrid screamed. Winter turned. The girl was darting around the second Outsider, avoiding blow after blow, leaping over the thing's tail, sliding underneath its heavy footsteps.

"There's more!" Astrid shouted.

Winter looked at the twisting shadow-portal above the throne, where two more dark forms emerged, taking form as they fell. One of them had two sets of horns on either side of its head.

Winter's jaw set.

"Get me one of the bows and a quiver," Winter said. "I can help."

Knot hesitated, then nodded. A bow and quiver veered through the air towards her, and Winter caught them.

"Stay back," Knot said.

Winter nocked an arrow to the bow. She watched as Knot gripped his sword, a dozen bloodied weapons seemingly flying through the air around him as he sprinted towards the monsters.

At first the power had been invigorating, cleansing in its pure burn. It had come easily, as if by instinct. Knot suspected that when he had broken whatever barrier Kali had woven around him the night before, in the fountain square, he had somehow opened a gate for his telesis. He had sensed his power easily since that night, except in the presence of the Ceno monks. And he, or at least his instincts, remembered.

Knot rushed towards the Outsiders, pushing his *tendra* ahead of him, watching as the weapons plunged through the second Outsider that Astrid faced. All fifteen of the weapons carved straight through the creature, bursting through in a bloody mess on the other side. The beast wavered on its thin, sinewy legs, then crashed to the ground.

*Two down. Two to go.*

"More coming through!" Winter shouted behind him. "We have to close the portal!"

Knot glanced at the shifting blackness. Four more shapes—*four!*—fell to the floor. Knot took a ragged breath. He could sense something there, around the portal. Something familiar, but he was not sure what.

Knot dodged, rolling to the ground, narrowly avoiding the swipe of a large claw. Immediately Knot gathered his *tendra* and sent them at the creature, a bloodied weapon held in each. The Outsiders shrieked and howled all around him. They were all similar in appearance, with small variations—one had long, curved horns, another's claws were far larger than the others', another seemed to have some kind of bone armor growing from its hide. The marble floor shook at their footsteps. Knot slashed at the arms of one of the Outsiders with his sword, severing the thing's claw at the wrist. The monster screamed, but only for a second. Astrid leapt into the air, landing on its hunched back, and plunged her fist—and the length of her entire arm—into the back of the thing's head. The monster went limp as Astrid leapt again, only to be swatted in midair by an oversized claw and sent flying across the throne hall into another pillar.

And then, something changed; a shift, a slight change in the air. Knot wielded fifteen different *tendra* at once, advancing on the four Outsiders that had just dropped from the blackness.

He needed to close the portal. Something nagged at him, something familiar, but he had no time to think. It was something about his *tendra*, something he should remember. Something about a connection.

Before any memory could emerge, the whole world went silent.

One minute he could hear the screeching of the monsters, the whispers of his weapons slicing skin and scraping bone, the sound of his own breath popping in his ears. Knot had just begun to hear another sound, a great, deep roar, far louder and far deeper than the screeches of the Outsiders, as another shape—larger than all the others—formed in the portal. In one moment, Knot heard all these sounds. The next, there was nothing. No sound at all.

The change caught him off guard and he hesitated. And Knot knew, the moment he hesitated, there would be a consequence.

A massive claw struck him, and then Knot was flying through the air. The blow must have been glancing—he fell to the marble quickly and slid to a stop. Shakily, Knot rose to his feet, trying to retain control of his *tendra*. His weapons had been carried with him, as if he had been holding them in his hands. He advanced on the Outsiders once more.

He needed to close the portal, but the new shape, far larger than any of its predecessors, was already tumbling to the marble floor with a great crash. Cracks spread from the point of impact. Still, he kept fighting, using the power that surrounded him, enveloped him, burned through him. His chest and bones vibrated, and despite not being able to hear, Knot knew the huge creature coalescing beneath the portal, growing larger and larger, had roared once more.

Another shift, this time to his entire body. He had no control over his limbs. Knot went limp, falling to his knees, head lolling. He felt so empty, so hollow. There was nothing inside of him.

But he could still see, so he still fought. His physical limbs were nerveless, but his *tendra* obeyed. He attacked the Outsiders instinctively with his *tendra*, but there was nothing he could do against this many. Out of the corner of his eye Knot saw Astrid rushing towards the Outsiders again only to see one vault across the room and land on top of her. Another Outsider leapt against a pillar, propelling itself downward, crushing into the Outsider that was already on top of Astrid.

Knot wanted to shout, to scream and warn her, he wanted to help her, but his *tendra* were already occupied fighting off three more of the creatures.

There was nothing he could do.

In a burst of bright blood, Knot saw a shape dart straight up, through the abdomen of one of the Outsiders and through the thigh of the other. Astrid sailed through the air and landed in the distance, covered in gore.

Suddenly Knot's body shook, convulsing, and he thought he was dying for a moment until his head lolled to the side and he saw that Winter was shaking him. Tears streamed down her cheeks, her mouth moved, she was shouting, but Knot heard nothing. Behind Winter, a dark form towered above them both, taller by far than any of the Outsiders that had yet emerged.

And then, blackness.

Winter had sobbed when she saw Knot fall. One moment, he had been fighting, winning, it had seemed, and the next one of the monsters had thrown him across the throne hall.

"We've lost," Winter whispered, crouching over him. "We are lost."

At least three of the Outsiders still remained, closing in on Astrid. The portal was still open, and the huge shadow that had fallen from it moments ago now rose up, rumbling a low, sustained growl. Winter looked up. The monster towered as tall as the pillars that held up the massive dome. Huge legs, thicker than the pillars themselves, loomed to either side of Winter. Four more limbs, legs or arms, Winter was not sure, planted themselves around her, and the ground shook. The massive monster's jaw gaped, as large as the first Outsiders that had emerged. The creature's slow-forming, deafening roar pulsed in her chest. More Reapers rushed into the room, but Winter knew they were running to their deaths. If two dozen of the soldiers could not handle one of these creatures, it would take an army to even injure the massive monster that towered above them.

Winter looked down. She could not believe it. She couldn't believe it would end this way, that it—

There, at her feet, was the pouch of *faltira*.

Winter had made her choice, she and Knot had made it together, and she had chosen not to take it. She had *promised* not to take it. And, looking down at the pouch, Winter truly didn't want to. She remembered seeing in a way that was completely outside of herself what she had become. The woman lying in blood and vomit in the alley. The woman jumping out a window. The woman who had betrayed those she loved, forgotten all but the *need*. Winter knew what it had done to her, what it had done to her friends. She hated the drug. As much as she loved it, as much as she craved it, she hated it even more.

Then Winter looked at Astrid in the distance, covered in blood. Astrid snarled at the encroaching monsters, but all Winter saw was the little girl, who cared though she tried to hide it.

Winter's gaze shifted to Lian, dead on the golden steps. Whatever Lian had told her in the blackness did not matter. Winter chose not to believe it. This was her friend, who had remained with her. Her friend who had saved her, after all.

Winter looked down at Knot. She knelt and touched his face. She bent, kissing his cheek.

"I love you," she whispered, and she had never meant anything more.

Everything inside of her screamed not to do what she did next. She knew it would destroy her. It would destroy her when she had only just found hope.

And then she realized a difference. Every time she took *faltira*, every time she slunk through alleyways and slipped frost while no one watched, she did it for herself. She did it because she wanted to feel the burning ice.

This was different. In this moment, Winter knew. She belonged with these people. *They* were her home. And, to protect her home, she had to give it up. Looking at the people she loved, Winter knew this was not for herself. This was for something greater.

This was for them.

Reaching into the pouch, she took a *faltira* crystal and placed it in her mouth.

Then she took another.

And another.

And another.

Winter swallowed every last *faltira* crystal. The power came more quickly than ever, surging through her, familiar and strong. Then it multiplied, searing her veins, burning her marrow. Then it multiplied again, and she gasped, her eyes rolling back into her skull. Again it multiplied, and again and again, until Winter threw her head back and screamed.

Sealing off the portal was easy. It was similar to a *tendron*, Winter realized. *Go for the link.* She did as Nash taught her, attacking the source rather than what the *tendron*-like thing held, the strange connection to their world. Just like that, the shimmering shadow blinked out of existence.

Winter reached out her *tendra* and ripped four massive pillars from either side of her away from the wall. The dome shook. The great monster, the last monster that had emerged, looked down at her hungrily. It knew.

Winter smiled. The power no longer flowed through her. It no longer burned her, no longer caused her pain nor pleasure. All of that was gone, insignificant.

Now, she *was* the power.

W‌HEN THE WORLD WAS quiet once more, Astrid looked up and saw the stars. They were no longer visible only through the sky-windows in the throne hall's massive domed ceiling; now, she could see them everywhere.

The dome was gone. Winter had shattered it, sending half of it flying out into the night. The other half she'd somehow collapsed into the chamber, killing the remaining Outsiders. Of course, that was after Winter had beaten the giant monster to death with four of the massive pillars, crushing the beast into the marble floor again and again. She had consumed the daemons in a great whirlwind of rock. Astrid had never seen anything like it in the long years she'd walked the Sfaera.

Now Astrid made her way through the rubble and bodies as quickly as she could, carrying one limp form over her shoulder. She could only save one, and she had known all along who it would be. She didn't have much of a choice. Winter must be dead; no one could survive taking in that much power. Lian was already gone. Hardly a choice at all, really.

Astrid clenched and unclenched her jaw as she climbed the massive mountain of debris, trying to get up and over the palace wall. She cursed herself every step of the way.

If only she had gotten there sooner, things might have been different. If that bitch of a priestess had let her go earlier, had allowed her more time to heal from the torture. Even thinking about the previous night filled Astrid with horror. Astrid had wasted all of the daylight hours waiting for the nightsbane to leave her body and regaining her strength.

If only she had gotten to Lian before he died.

Instead, Astrid had failed. Now she was picking up the pieces.

Knot stirred over her shoulder.

Astrid stopped immediately. She set him down, looking into his eyes.

"You there, nomad?" she whispered. He coughed, his eyes clouded. She let out a long breath.

Knot's eyes flickered. His mouth opened, but no sound came out. Astrid felt a tremor in her chest. She had to be honest with him. If she wasn't, he would never forgive her. Perhaps he never would, anyway, but she had to try.

"She's gone," Astrid said. "I'm sorry, Knot. She's gone."

Knot shook his head, unintelligible rasps escaping his throat.

"I am sorry," Astrid said, wishing she knew how to comfort him. He pushed her away, trying to rise to his feet. "Wait," Astrid said. "You're not strong enough."

Then, at the base of the huge mountain of rubble, Astrid heard voices. She put her finger to her lips. She didn't know if Knot could hear the soldiers below, but he had to be silent for both their sakes.

Knot had enough sense to stop struggling, and lay still.

Astrid poked her head up over the rubble. At least a score of soldiers rummaged below, and Astrid thought she could see other shapes moving towards them in the distance.

"Canta rising," one of them said. "The entire dome..."

"You said there were others," another said. "Where are they?"

"Saw them going up that way."

A few of the soldiers moved towards the rubble.

"We need to leave," Astrid whispered. "They're going to find us."

Knot looked at her for a moment. Then, he shook his head. "Winter," he mouthed.

"No," Astrid said. "She's gone, Knot. We need to go. It's what she would have wanted."

His face hardened, and he shook his head again.

Knot's cold eyes and set jaw left her no choice. She punched him hard in the head, and he collapsed back into the rubble.

"Let's go," she whispered to him, lifting him back up on her shoulder. "We don't have much time."

By the time she reached the crest of the massive pile of debris, the soldiers below had spotted her. They shouted, and a crossbow bolt whizzed by her ear. Astrid swore.

Below her was the palace wall, flush with a low cliff that jutted over the sea.

Astrid squinted. A small fishing boat, out either very early or very late, was not far from the cliff. Perhaps half a mile. The water would be cold. She did not know whether Knot would survive.

But if she did not jump, neither of them would.

Astrid cursed. She hated swimming.

Another bolt whipped past her. Then she leapt.

The voice that spoke was deep, like a rush of fire wreathed in darkness.

*"Awake, Daval."*

Daval Amok, one of the High Lords of Izet, sat up in bed. He had never heard the voice before, but the Tokal-Ceno had described it to him. Daval had dreamt of it, hoped for it, all the long days of his life.

Daval's bones creaked as he twisted, placing his feet on the warm hardwood floor. Servants kept him warm throughout the night; they knew how irritable Daval became when he had to walk around in the morning on cold floors. There was no warming his feet if they weren't warm in the morning. And if there was one thing that Daval despised, it was cold feet.

Daval hesitated. He had heard a voice, had he not? Perhaps he had only dreamt it.

*"I am real, Daval. As real as the stars. I require your assistance."*

A wave of mindless fear swept through Daval. Just as the Tokal had described it, the fear was insanity and death rolled together. Daval trembled from excitement as much as terror.

"My life for you, my Lord," Daval whispered. His chamber was dark; too dark to see anything.

Was the Master here with him? Was Azael in Daval's own bedchamber?

*"The Tokal is dead. He accomplished the work I set for him, and his sacrifice will not be forgotten. But I require a new mouthpiece, Daval. You were the Tokal's second. Now, you shall be mine."*

Daval blinked. "My Lord, I... I am honored." Daval hesitated. Could it be? "The Tokal was successful, my Lord? Do you mean..." Daval fumbled for the candle and tinderbox next to his bed. His hands found the box, the flint and steel, and he struck the two together. Daval felt the grind of them in his hands, felt the heat of the sparks as they leapt from the flint.

He felt it, but he saw nothing. There was only darkness.

*"Yes, Daval. After thousands of years, the Ritual has been completed. The Tokal-Ceno ushered in a new Age. The Rising has begun."*

Daval tried the flint and steel once more, heart racing.

Again, there was only darkness, but that did not matter. A chuckle escaped his lips. Daval was living through the Rising. He would be on the Sfaera when the Nine took mortal form. He would stand witness.

"That is… that is wonderful news, my Lord," Daval said, setting down the flint and steel. He did not need such things. Azael would provide. Instead he put his hand on the dark green robe he kept near his bed at all times. Daval smiled, despite the fear.

*"Indeed it is. Are you ready to begin, Daval?"*

"Begin what, my Lord?"

*"Your transformation."*

Daval nodded slowly. "If you seek to create, let yourself first know destruction," he quoted.

And then, in the darkness, Daval Amok, High Lord of Izet, screamed.

Cinzia and Jane stood on the rooftop of the inn, looking at the palace as the sun rose over the imperial dome.

Or, at least, what remained of it.

The massive dome was gone; during the night, Cinzia and Jane had awoken to a thunderous crash, and ran up to the roof. They did not know what had happened, but they both suspected that Knot, Winter, and Astrid had been a part of it.

And, of course, the Voice from the night before.

"The sun rises, but dusk falls," Jane said. "The Rising has begun."

"It is not the Rising we were hoping for," Cinzia said.

"No. Nine Daemons are no substitute for the Goddess. But we must do what we can. There is still hope."

Cinzia nodded. She was only sure of two things, now. The

first was that Canta was real, that the Goddess loved her and had a plan. That much was well and good. But the second was that something else was out there, too. The Nine Daemons. Other things. Cinzia still did not know whether she believed in Jane's visions. But she did believe they had work to do. Someone had to protect the Sfaera from what was coming.

It might as well be them.

Cinzia hefted her pack. They had gathered all their belongings last night, and rested as much as they could. They had placed Kovac... Kovac's body... covered, underneath the bed. Hopefully they would be long gone before he was found.

Cinzia held back tears. That horror still seemed distant. She could not believe her Goddessguard was dead. But the time for mourning would come.

"It feels as if nothing will ever be the same," Cinzia said.

"Nothing ever will be," Jane said. "The world will be different now. We will watch it change, for better or for worse."

Cinzia was not sure what that meant, but she had no energy left to ask.

"Are you ready?" Jane asked. Cinzia felt her sister's hand on her arm.

Cinzia took a deep breath. "I am ready," she said.

Deep in the dungeons of the imperial palace in Izet, Enri Crawn slipped a bowl of water through a slot at the bottom of a large, iron-enforced door.

He didn't know why this new prisoner had been brought down to him, but he didn't much care. It wasn't his job to ask questions.

There were more interesting things going on, anyway. Supposedly, the imperial dome of the throne hall had been completely destroyed. Enri didn't know what kind of force could cause a disaster of that kind. Some people said it was faulty building work, in which case Enri didn't envy those involved. Anyone who had renovated, painted, or even cleaned the throne hall in the past decade would probably be dead, soon enough. Or down here, keeping him company. Perhaps that was why the girl was here, although he doubted a tiellan could have had anything to do with the destruction. Why the girl hadn't been killed on sight was beyond him.

Word had spread that the emperor and the Tokal-Ceno were in the throne hall when the dome collapsed. Some said they were both dead, others that they were in hiding; and others still said the collapse was the work of Khalic assassins. Enri didn't know the truth of that, but he did know that the Ceno seemed to have taken charge.

Standing on tiptoes, Enri peered into the cell. The occupant was still there, unmoving. As far from any occupied cell as possible. Enri didn't ask questions, of course, but he did find that order odd.

Enri peeked through the bars at the young tiellan girl inside. She didn't seem conscious. For all Enri knew, she was dead.

Suddenly, the girl's eyes snapped open. She stared at Enri, and Enri gasped, backing away.

He stood there for a moment, breathing heavily. What in the Nine Daemons was wrong with this girl? She'd scared him half to death.

Slowly, Enri rose on his tiptoes once more, peeking into the cell. The girl seemed to be sleeping again, her eyes closed.

Enri shivered. A strange girl, that one. No wonder they'd driven the tiellans out ages ago. They were an odd lot, and just unnatural-looking. Enri marveled at the girl's peculiar features—elongated ears, black hair, black eyes, dark as midnight. Enri was of half a mind to ask his wife if she had heard of such a thing; he had never seen black eyes before.

But he knew he wouldn't. He would go home, eat the burnt dinner she'd made for him, put his feet up, and smoke a pipe. That's what he always did.

After all, Enri never asked questions.

## ACKNOWLEDGMENTS

FIRST OFF, THANKS TO my agent, Sam Morgan, for not laughing at me when I completely botched my first pitch to him. Somehow he saw through my uncannily awkward social skills and a bumbling, all-but-incoherent description of *Duskfall*, and decided to take a chance. He hasn't stopped fighting for me since, and his storytelling acumen (see what I did there?) has helped me make this a much better novel. Thanks as well to Joshua Bilmes, Krystyna Lopez, and the whole JABberwocky team for their input, praise, criticism, and of course top-notch representation. You folks do incredible things.

Just when I thought I couldn't make the novel any better, my editor, Miranda Jewess, entered the picture and put *Duskfall* through the editorial fire. The polish and clarity of the book you hold in your hands are in large part due to her meticulous critical eye.

Scott Morris, Marc Cameron, Rachel Husberg, Chris Welton, and Christopher English were phenomenal beta readers. Their feedback was invaluable, and I'm truly grateful they lent me their brains for a while. Steve Diamond also deserves a shout out. He's one of the most intelligent readers I know, and on more than one occasion he's spoken up for me and my writing when I've been too shy to do it myself. He's a great writer and a great friend.

I've had a lot of fantastic teachers in my life, and they've played a part in shaping me as a person and as a writer. I'm especially grateful for Martin Lang, Sally Cook, Kelly Kirk, Kathy Steele, Madison Sowell, and Steve Tuttle. Speaking of educators, Brandon Sanderson taught me a lot about the craft of writing science fiction and fantasy, but he taught me even more about the business, and there's no way I'd be where I am now without his advice. His encouraging and enthusiastic critique of the first draft of Duskfall in his class eight years ago was a huge motivator for me to keep writing and keep revising. I'm privileged to have learned so much from such a phenomenal author.

Mom and Dad: thank you for reading to me and helping me tell stories when I was young. You told me I could dream, and you believed in me when I did. I can never thank you enough for that.

My parents-in-law deserve a special thanks as well. It's one thing to support an aspiring author—it's quite another to support one who wants to marry your daughter. That takes a special kind of courage, and I'm grateful for it.

So many other family members deserve my thanks—they've all been an incredible support to me through the process of writing this book. Their enthusiasm and excitement mean the world to me, and I'm so grateful to have each of them in my life.

This book was my baby until my actual baby Buffy came along, and even though she's only been around for the tail-end of the process, I somehow can't help but thank her and be grateful for every moment I spend with her. She makes my life better.

If you combined all of the love, support, patience, and investment of each of the people I've listed above into one person, that person would still be a poor facsimile of my wife, Rachel. Her steadfast confidence in me is what makes this book—and my writing—possible.

# ABOUT THE AUTHOR

CHRISTOPHER HUSBERG GREW UP in Eagle River, Alaska. He now lives in Utah, and spends his time writing, reading, hiking, and playing video games, but mostly hanging out with his wife, Rachel, and daughter, Buffy. He received an MFA in creative writing from Brigham Young University, and an honorary PhD in *Buffy the Vampire Slayer* from himself. *Duskfall* is his first novel. The next installment in the Chaos Queen Quintet, *Dark Immolation*, will be published by Titan Books in June 2017.

www.christopherhusberg.blogspot.com
@usbergo